about:blank

a novel

Edward Gooderham

ABOUT BLANK

ISBN: 9798870060293 (Paperback)

Cover design by Raúl Lázaro.

First printing edition 2023.

For my parents

And for a long time yet, led by some wondrous power, I am fated to journey hand in hand with my strange heroes and to survey the surging immensity of life, to survey it through the laughter that all can see and through the tears unseen and unknown by anyone.

—Nikolai Gogol, *Dead Souls*

chapter:one

For reasons of hygiene, absolutely no standing inside the trolleys. Dog dirt, the notice illustrates, goes from shoes onto packaging then onto produce and ultimately into mouths. Luke recalls childhood trips to the supermarket, charioted around while his mother gathered the necessaries. The chicken dippers, the fish fingers, the spaghetti hoops. Those little potato letters that later, plated, he would collate to spell his name. How frightening to think that all that time he was literally eating shit.

How far the world has come since then. What strides have been made in the intervening decades. Today, by scanning a barcode, Luke can check the ethical and environmental ramifications of muesli. Payments are made simply by wafting a card at a screen. Extraordinary progress, everywhere and in all domains, yet freeing a trolley still requires a one pound bloody doubloon.

Ripe for disruption, the whole system. Supermarkets should be operating contactless release, linking in loyalty card schemes and extracting valuable consumer data in the process. Somebody should be explaining this to them. Luke would do so himself, were he not busy launching his own app. On which front, yet another setback:

An email from a potential investor has stipulated more users, despite Luke clearly explaining that to get more users, he needs more money.

He swoops on the avocados, groping freely with left and right. Too hard, too hard, too soft. He wipes his palm on his jeans, vowing never again to set foot in a supermarket. As if Steve Jobs ever went grocery shopping. So many productivity hours, wasted gathering fuel. Perhaps the most efficient approach would be to blitz the lot and give everyone their own flask. No need to cook, no need to chew, no need to wash up. Zero risk of ingesting dog merde.

Luke retrieves his phone and consults his list, picking up a knob of ginger. Cradled in his hand it looks like a tiny leprous foot. He would love – no, he cannot let slide this avocado farce. Nearby, a supermarket worker is unloading celery with most of his arse visible. He wears an apron, two hats and fingerless gloves.

'Sorry,' says Luke. 'Sorry mate.'

Two Hats looks up.

'Yeah, uhm, I was wondering if you had any ripe avocados.'

No reaction. To ask had been a mistake.

'No, fine, these though actually,' says Luke, pointing to a box of loose potatoes. 'Do you know what variety these are?'

Luke means as in are they for mashing or roasting or salads, or baking then stuffing with tuna or beans, cheese, whatever.

'Yes,' says Two Hats. 'Potatoes.'

Ugh. Luke can never remember whether they count as part of his seven a day, potatoes. Not that it matters, because his morning smoothie is making a mockery of that target. Right now, in his freezer, there must be more blueberries than his grandparents managed to consume in over two centuries of combined living. At three for two it makes sense to buy in bulk, to stockpile for when the global berry season one day comes to an end.

Luke rounds the aisle, spotting a box of peanut butter balls; how he adores these little twats. Pure protein too. He bundles nine into the trolley before pushing on to beverages. Teas, tisanes and infusions. Three fruits, two fruits and red fruits. Blackcurrant and cherry, cinnamon and fennel. Nettle, turmeric, liquorice. Echinacea, whatever that is. Luke tries different ways of pronouncing the word, letting it ricochet around his headvoice.

Dried goods next, then confectionery, then dairy and the freezer aisle. before finally approaching the tills. He surveys his haul, wondering how many thousands of miles it has travelled to get here. So much packaging too. That documentary – the one his mum keeps banging on about, with the puffins and the plastic – is going to leave him chastened.

Look at them all, these mugs, waiting patiently while the automatic checkouts are free. Luke snorts. To still be putting faith in humans is an example of just how stupid humans are, and precisely why nobody should be putting any faith in them. He strides past these ones, towards the machines. The first and second are out of order. The third is demanding three hundred and six pounds, eleven pence. The fourth appears to be working.

Luke opens his rucksack and places it in the bagging zone. He positions the trolley at his hip and begins to scan. The first few products come through clumsily as he gets a feel for the barcodes, but soon he finds his rhythm, settling into an easy rockabye motion, thinking how even this technology will soon become outdated, as more and more stores adopt –

PLEASE PLACE ITEM IN THE BAGGING ZONE.

The chamomile tea. But it is in the bagging zone? Luke takes the box out of his rucksack, puts it back in again.

PLEASE PLACE ITEM IN THE BAGGING ZONE.

It is in the cunting bagging zone. Luke makes a disgruntled face in the direction of the cashiers. Two Hats eventually sees him.

'Machine not working?'

'Yeah no it's not working mate.'

Two Hats hurries out from behind his till, but before even reaching Luke he has understood the issue.

'Not in the backpack,' he says, retreating. 'Into the bagging zone, then into the backpack.'

Luke raises his eyebrows, mistakenly assuming he is rolling his eyes. He yearns for the day when this imbecile is finally rendered obsolete. He tips out, back into the bagging zone, the items that have already been bagged. The tea is acknowledged and he continues scanning. The peanut butter balls are slung through rapid fire, then he comes across the first of his veg. He finds the red onion icon, taps it, nothing. Taps it again, nothing. He turns to Two Hats:

'Yeah sorry, the onions won't weigh. Can't get the onions to weigh.'

'Scales out of order on that machine. Sorry, for fruits and vegetables you must come to me.'

Luke often wishes he was American, as in the Silicon Valley kind: moneyed but unimpeachably progressive. Right now, however, he would choose to be a bruising Alabama Republican. He would have come shopping with a loaded assault rifle, and therefore be properly equipped to commit the atrocity he wants to. Everyone would die, Two Hats last and most painfully.

He retrolleys his booty, seething. Naturally he now has to queue with all the other simpletons, and he passes the time by willing a showdown with Two Hats, a showdown that will never come, but would have entailed Luke being polite and saying nothing. Really he wants Two Hats not for a confrontation, but because the other cashier is a woman and Luke is buying condoms. The words *For Her Maximum Pleasure* are splashed across the box.

Now a girl around his age appears. She opens another lane, calls next please, and that means Luke. Aisha is her name, and she smiles sweetly until Luke remembers that he needs to unload his items if she is to ring them through. By the time he has finished, already so much is waiting to be bagged. Luke starts stuffing his rucksack, but soon the beeping has stopped, he can sense that Aisha has reclined, meanwhile he still has to try and...

'Can I get two plastic bags please?'

Beep beep and the bags are with Luke, who begins trying to prize them apart.

'That's going to be £94.66 please.'

'Pardon?'

'Ninety four, sixty six.'

The display confirms it. An absurd amount, surely erroneous, but there is a queue and Aisha is attractive so there can be no querying.

'Contactless?'

'Only under twenty pound,' says Aisha.

Luke knows that, obviously, but his question has bought time. The bag handles refuse to be separated though, and Aisha ends up doing it for him, smiling the smile people smile when they help the elderly or disabled. He thanks her and reaches for his wallet. In goes the card, followed by a furious bit of bagging. Then the pin, then more bagging.

'Declined,' says Aisha.

'Yeah, uhm, could you try it again please?'

This at least gives him time to get everything stowed, notably the condoms. Aisha will have seen the box. Probably she suspects Luke of wanting to hurry home so he can wank into one or all of them.

'No,' says Aisha.

'Ah,' says Luke. 'Cash then.'

He counts five, ten, twenty pounds, before hopefully tipping out some shrapnel. Seventy pence.

'Sorry, I'm going to have to remove a few items.'

The news is greeted with frustration in the queue. Of zero comfort to Luke is his knowledge that soon the world will be cashless, or that even before then, billionaire status will afford him a valet to settle transactions.

'If I could just... '

Aisha tilts the screen towards Luke. To his astonishment, he sees that his vitamin powder, *Ultramax Boostability,* costs nineteen pounds.

'Yeah we can get rid of that, and the oil, the chocolate too please, all the balls, those two teas, yeah. However many of the berries, say seven no six with the three for – great, thanks. The pineapple, the papaya. Flax, yep, pecans cashews almonds clear all those out. Lentils. Okay, how much does that come to now?'

Luke jettisons and jettisons.

'£51.10.'

'Shit, fuck, right,' he says.

The next woman in line, a sophisticated brunette who smacks more of the Milans or Miamis of this world, but who Luke now encounters here, at Tesco, on Morning Lane, in Hackney – this woman is tapping angrily at her thigh.

At moments like this, Luke worries that he will forever be English. He will go through his whole life apologising, not for anything he has actually done, but for the few centuries of untrammeled power that preceded his birth. He will never be proud, he will always be meek, and however many times he kneels at the altars of science and progress and reason, he will forever remain that cowering little Anglican, shivering through a midnight mass in the Home Counties. He will never be Californian.

'Yeah okay so the rocket and the tomatoes can come off. Sweet potatoes, regular potatoes. In fact the packaging of these mushrooms appears to have been breached, so maybe – no, get rid of those. Flageolets too. The black and the brown rice, okay where are we?'

Aisha makes him wait. Down to the very barest of essentials.

'£40.06.'

Now what? Condoms are pricey, but not for ten times his coveted billion, not for all the billions would he extract them in this manner, with this audience.

'Okay, the pearl barley. Sumac, the muesli, the granola, the milk one, chickpeas, two of the sweetcorn. Sweetcorns. The bags, can we refund those?'

'£21.70.'

'Right, perfect, because I have my trolley pound, so what I'm going to do is give you this, which is twenty pounds seventy, plus the pomegranate to mind as like a kind of security while I return the trolley. Then I'll run back with the pound, at which point you'll hand over the pomegranate. Awesome, great, cheers Aisha.'

Luke cedes the necessary, zips up his rucksack and races to rehouse the trolley. He returns with the magic pound to reclaim his pomegranate, which he pops in the pocket of his hoody before leaving the supermarket forever. Walking home in the drizzle, he contemplates his startup conundrum: he must find users if he wants investment, but only with investment will he be able to target those users.

When he explains this to Julie, the girl he has agreed to meet later, she will no doubt call it a Catch 22. Supposedly she is a writer. According to Ram and Lucy she is clever, very cultured, which Luke understands to mean frigid and boring. She does at least look smashable though; worth some research on the greatest novels of all time.

But if his card is being declined, Luke must have exceeded his overdraft. Yet again he will have to remember to forget his wallet (without forgetting to remember his condoms). Right now his poverty feels crueler, more oppressive, than that of the most destitute Bengali orphan. He turns into his street in Hackney, one of the trendiest neighbourhoods on planet earth, and approaches the door of the flat his parents have bought for him. Nice, but still far from Palo Alto. Nor is it any clearer how Luke is going to make it to that promised land. Success depends on money - that much he knows. But to get the money it appears he needs users, and to get the users he very obviously needs money.

chapter:two

Julie was used to men rejecting her. Not in their capacity as males, but as agents and publishers and journal or magazine editors. Most recently, Shane from *Vice* had snubbed her article about *Coolschooling,* calling her theory anecdotal and reductive. Which was bollocks, because it was empirically sound, and it went as follows: guys were forever measuring girls against a cultural canon that they decreed themselves and was always the same.

First there was the mob film, involving an American actor with an Italian surname, who would curl his mouth downwards and say something hostile before shooting a rival in the face. Iconic, was always the adjective. Then there was the casually misogynistic buddy comedy. Then there was *The Big Lebowski*, then there was Radiohead. And when there was a writer – if there was a writer – his work was described as raw, which meant it revolved around either whole pharmacies of drugs, or a voiceless woman being fucked and cast aside.

By way of illustration, you might be talked at about *Goodfellas*, *Wedding Crashers*, Jack Kerouac, *The Big Lebowski* and Radiohead. Alternatively it could be *Scarface*, *Anchorman*, Charles Bukowski, *The Big Lebowski* and Radiohead. And so on and so forth. The order changed and there were of course deviations: science fiction novels she had never heard of, perhaps *Fight Club*. But importantly the books were written by men, the films and series starred men, and any female characters had to be whores or sluts or strung out on cocaine.

Woe betide the girl who dared disagree with any of these selections. If you tried to argue that *Goodfellas* lacked any real depth, that *Anchorman* was puerile, that Kerouac was a freewheeling hack, you would be met with the most condescending of all condescending looks. It was a universal look, understood everywhere and seen nightly across the globe, iconic in its own way. It was a look that said: bless your little cotton socks. Bless your *Jane Eyre* and your *Pride and Prejudice*. Bless your *Pretty Woman,* your *Bridget Jones*. Bless all the films Matthew McConaughey made after we stopped considering him cool, before we started considering him cool again. Bless most blessedly *Sex and the City*. Bless you not choosing the craft lager. Bless you wanting your meat well done. Bless you ordering a milky coffee, and at this blessed hour.

Luke at least started well. He was on time but not early. When he kissed Julie on the cheek he smelled of soap, rather than cheap deodorant or expensive aftershave. He did not insist on ordering her a negroni or a tankard of stout. Then there was everything she already knew about him, everything Lucy and her boyfriend Ram had told her in their attempts to make this happen, most of it probably lies. He was funny, he was charming. He would one day be worth millions.

Yet just like every other guy, he felt compelled to start telling Julie what was cool. When an opinion was at last aired, it stirred another, and another, until a bona fide tornado of cultural righteousness came tearing across the table towards her. *Go Your Own Way* started playing in the background and suddenly he was talking about that scene in *Casino*, the one where Joe Pesci curls his mouth downwards, says something hostile and then boom: *Casino* was iconic. What had happened to De Niro though? In old age he had made one or two good comedies but that was it. What had happened to comedy though? There had not been an objectively good comedy, a genuinely funny film since – all of this in unbroken monologue – *American Pie*. Did she remember Tara Reid? What had happened to Tara Reid though? She made that and *The Big Lebowski* then literally nothing else. Now *that* was a film. That opening scene, in the bowling alley, with the Dylan track. He was a genius though, Bob Dylan, a deserving Nobel and a proper, proper poet. Surely there was no finer living musician, except maybe the lead singer of Radiohead, the ginger guy. What a band they were, a truly gigantic band.

Video games, next. He said that the roleplay universe had assumed the place of the nineteenth century novel in society. It required persistence from the player, and the kind of sustained curiosity that accompanied the great serialised work of Dickens and Balzac. True literary quality, he continued, was nowadays to be found there, in video game writing. Julie had already heard half the population of London claim that this famous mantle had been taken up by the television series, which as opinions went was one of the most trite, but this was something new. She asked Luke what his favourite nineteenth century novel was, and braced herself for some idiotic yet somehow predictable segue into the genius of Hunter S. Thompson.

'Probably *Anna Karenina,*' said Luke.

Pardon? The plot hinged on a woman getting fucked and cast aside, true, but there were very few drugs and it could hardly be described as raw. Julie was caught off guard; she allowed herself to believe that Luke might legitimately like literature. Then he referenced one of her favourite passages, Koznyshev and Varenka picking mushrooms, and she began wondering whether the night might end with his toadstool in her mouth. Only when he waded into the theme of moral struggle did he start sounding less and less sure of himself, at which point she began suspecting him of swotting up online. When he referred to the author as Leo Trotsky, she understood that he had never read the book, perhaps never read any book.

But already Julie had convinced herself that Luke was worth sleeping with. Plenty of guys, after learning she liked books, might simply have ignored the subject altogether, or talked about their favourite sports biographies and business manuals, because in any event they all had words and pages and a title, so what was the difference? Luke had at least had the decency to do some research. He had at least had the decency to lie. Unlike her ex.

For Chris, books were like the vintage ashtrays Julie had bought while in Paris for their sixth and final anniversary. They might once have served a purpose, and putting them on display distinguished you as a person of refinement, but to actually pay money for them – to actually still be using them in 2019 – was anachronistic in the extreme. Nobody smoked, nobody read, not anymore. Not unless they were actively trying to be pretentious.

He had begun to say as much out loud. He confessed that his dream did not entail coming home late on a Friday, getting into bed and watching Julie read some pointless saga about two slags in Naples. What it apparently did entail was nine pints, three minutes of missionary and a marathon of televised sport.

When she finally ended it, Chris refused to accept the decision. It was totally out of the blue, he said. She was a bitch. He would change, but she was a bitch. After she moved out he entered psychopath mode, sending threats followed by flowers and even a midnight dick pic. His pleading helped ease Julie through the separation and to where she was now, which was desperate to shag anyone, absolutely anyone, as long as he was not Chris.

Enter Luke. They had been set up by Lucy, presumably because she wanted to avoid having a morose spinster on her hands. She had briefed Julie that he talked a lot, and he did. Mostly about his job, mostly shit. He was a freelance brand consultant, whatever that meant. Listening to him go on, Julie was embarrassed on behalf of anybody who had paid him actual money to prepare a Powerpoint presentation. In a matter of minutes he mentioned millennials maybe twenty times. Other regularly repeated words included innovative, aspirational and Apple.

'The thing about internet startups,' said Luke, 'Is that each successful one is unique, but bad ones all fail for the same reason.'

'The opposite of families then,' said Julie. '*Pace* Tolstoy,'

'Err, yeah.'

Luke had his own app, a social media platform named Blank, which he pitched as a cross between Tinder and Facebook. The objective was to harness geolocation technology and inbound data, allowing users to find other users with similar interests. Rather than operating via a fed interface, on which you listed and invariably lied about your likes and dislikes, Blank would run realtime scans of your entire online presence. Browsing history, social media, everything.

'Picture yourself at a party. There you are, looking around at all the different guys, wondering whether you have anything in common. You open Blank, search men in my vicinity, aged between eighteen and forty, who are single and like books. Or you could be way, way more specific. The algorithm gets to work, instantly processing sites recently visited by relevant users in the area. Their Instagram, emails, whatever. It sees that I recently posted a quotation from *Anna Karenina* on Twitter, that I ordered a Russian novel on Amazon. My name and picture come up, so you know you can approach me confidently, without fear.'

'Mm.'

'Next, the pub. I want to play pool but am on my own. Imagine I am also learning Arabic. I open Blank, search for guys in my vicinity, platonic mode, age range whatever, Arabic speaker, likes pool. Blank might propose me someone based on as little as a previous photo of them at a snooker table. An article read or an email written in Arabic. We then connect.'

'But what if… '

'Or work. I need funding so I attend a generator event, where I load up Blank and apply the desired filters. Very basically: tech angels specialising in social. I then get a list of hits, which is to say other users in the room who fit my criteria, and thanks to their digital CVs, press articles about their most recent deals, I know who to be seeking out. Conversely, if one of the VC guys is a user, he wants dynamic entrepreneurs with social product. Bingo, his search yields my profile, allowing him to fire me a message saying hi this is Vince from Picpus, we should touch base.'

'Picpus, who are they again?'

'Big VC firm. Huge. And if you're too timid to make the first move you can zing off a poke or a prod to put the feelers out, so to speak. But you're still – and this is what distinguishes us from your everyday dating platform – trusting in the human approach. The natural connection.'

'Right.'

'But like I said: parties, networking events, your commute to work. Even a queue at the sushi place. Potentially fruitful meets are everywhere, the scope is as good as infinite. This is the future of social.'

'Mm.'

Julie was picturing his penis. Probably he would be superb in bed. Lousy as a freelance brand consultant, lousy as an entrepreneur, lousy even as a human being, but superb in bed. Innovative and aspirational. Something about him aroused fondness, an unthinking quality that suggested companionability. Similar to a spaniel, in that way. And after nearly seven years spent living with the very cattiest of cats, Julie was bored of their manner.

That particular cat had been permanently looking down his nose at her, as if in denial about the fact that he was a domesticated little bastard who would be utterly lost on his own. Which he did then prove to be. Cats made you work for their affection, purring in your ear one minute then parading about with their arseholes in your face the next. A dog was what she wanted. A dog who would trot up with his tongue out, who would clamber onto her bed and paw at her pyjamas. A dog who would want her always and keep coming back, even when she locked him outside or twatted him with a broom. Not that she would ever mistreat an animal.

By now she had decided that Luke would be coming back and at the very least going down on her. The rest would depend on whether he had condoms. Before that, though, she wanted to mess with him. Not to humiliate him, but to show him who was in charge. To pretend to throw a ball, then not in fact throw it and watch him bolt, before padding back sadly towards her. She asked:

'What do you think of Gogol?'

'Google?'

'Gogol.'

'As in Google?'

'As in Gogol.'

'The search engine? Google?'

'Nikolai Gogol. The writer.'

'Oh,' said Luke. 'Gogol. I thought… yeah.'

'Are you a fan?'

'Oh yeah, I mean how could you not be?'

'Right? Wow, I can't believe you like him too.'

Julie leaned in and smiled. She got up to go to the loo, giving him time to google Gogol. Walking away from the table she performed le bum wiggle. When she returned, Luke looked up from his phone.

18

'Yeah,' he said. 'I reckon we can all agree that everything begins with Gogol. What was it Dostoevsky said? We all came out of his Overcoat?'

'Yes!' said Julie. 'Yes, oh my god, yes.'

He might have been a goon, but he had done a good job of googling Gogol. She was losing the desire to even hang around and embarrass him, because each second he spent faking a knowledge of Russian literature was time not spent pushing her against a wall, sliding his hands up the backs of her thighs.

'What would you say is your favourite?' asked Luke.

'Favourite what?'

'Favourite book.'

'By Gogol?'

'Yeah.'

'Oh,' said Julie. '*Dead Souls*. Incredible.'

'Yeah no I've not read that one. Just some of his, uhm, short stories.'

'Mm,' said Julie. 'Also very good.'

'What's it about?'

'*Dead Souls*?'

'Yeah.'

'Uhm, well, basically you have this guy, Chichikov. He wants money and status so he goes around Russia, calling on landowners and buying up their dead peasants.'

'But so what do you mean when you say buying them?'

'How to explain… Russian society at the time was divided between landowners and serfs, right? Every so often there was this census: the government counted the number of serfs a landowner had working for him, and he then paid a per capita tax on them, fixed until the next census. Imagine he starts with a hundred, but after two years twenty are dead. For the next eight years the landowner is stuck paying… '

'Twenty percent more tax than necessary.'

Julie nodded. Not so stupid, perhaps.

'Exactly,' she said. 'So what Chichikov does is go around these landowners, persuading them to transfer their dead souls to him by deed. Makes no difference to them, whereas he can start pointing to a long list of people who now technically belong to him.'

'Yes,' said Luke, who was by now looking quite genuinely riveted by the idea of Russian literature. 'Yes, I think I would find that extremely interesting. It sounds… I mean, that is genius. Genius.'

'If you really want to read it I've got a copy. Back at my place.'

'Interesting.'

'Will you take care of it?'

'Absolutely,' said Luke. 'I do sometimes love just bending the spine right back though. Giving the thing a good and proper read.'

Julie was going to hate herself in the morning.

'Yeah,' she said. 'Shall we go back to mine then? You'll probably be wanting it straight away.'

'Yeah. I've just realised though: I left my wallet at home.'

edward:gooderham

chapter:three

The windows of the building opposite are still lit. Then again, they are always lit. Twenty four hours a day, seven days a week, three hundred and sixty five days a year. The only exception is Earth Hour, when once a year and for sixty whole minutes, companies show their commitment to saving the planet with a partial blackout.

Chris has never known what goes on over there. The rooms are set up for meetings. They have flip charts, projector screens, spider phones in the middle of the tables. People come and go throughout the day. They pace around making earnest and forthright gestures, or stand at the window looking down to the street, some like gods, surveying the mortals below, others weighing up the jump.

Whatever they do, rarely are they still doing it after nine. Once every few weeks, perhaps, Chris gets to leave that early. On those rare nights, he rides the bus up Kingsland Road, watching as people spill out of pubs or queue for a Vietnamese. If his hours were just a tad more predictable, he thinks, he would be doing these sorts of things himself. Arriving home, he removes his suit trousers and orders something greasy. He gets into bed, watches an episode of whatever, then not a second more porn than is absolutely necessary before finally falling asleep. Coming down Kingsland the next morning, he realises that he should have made an effort, should have gone somewhere or met someone, and he now might have to wait a fortnight before once again rejecting those options in favour of a burrito and a wank.

It has just gone eleven. He is the only lawyer still lawyering on his floor. There will be others downstairs, in Project Finance, in Asset Finance, in Real Estate Finance, in Banking. Below them the document reproduction women will be mechanically typing away. A cleaner comes into his cubicle.

'Hello Jacob,' says Chris. 'Hi.'

'Mr. Chris,' says Jacob - sort of first name terms. 'How are you?'

'Not good, Jacob. Bad.'

'Oh.'

Jacob makes his way behind the other desk in the cubicle, where Nigel sits between the hours of eleven and five, before squashing himself into his Range Rover and fucking off back to Surrey, where he lives and steadfastly refuses to die. Nigel runs the Corporate Finance department. He will be seventy next year. The idea that Chris might still be doing this or indeed any job at seventy, forty years hence, makes him wish Jacob would suffocate him with a bin bag.

Six hours is not a long day, but in that time Nigel manages to get through one whole pigsty of bacon sandwiches and a plantation of Lapsang Souchong. He smacks his lips, he slurps his tea, and what feels like every five minutes he calls and coos at one of his dozen granddaughters. Some day, when the time is right, which is to say once the last of them has absolutely categorically turned sixteen, Chris will track them all down, seduce them, and, having obtained their written consent, shag them.

Jacob picks up the keyboard, turns it over and gives the base a few good taps. Crumbs snow down into the open black liner.

'Lots of sandwiches,' says Jacob.

'All the sandwiches. Fat fucking arsehole.'

'Your boss?'

'Everyone here is my boss, Jacob.'

'No,' says Jacob. He refuses to believe that.

'Not everyone, no.'

Jacob laughs, a big laugh from the belly. Chris now knows this as the laugh Jacob laughs when he has not really understood but wants to be polite. The laugh fades into a smile, which remains on his face while he empties the recycling, while he changes the bin bags. The noise of his vacuum cleaner smashing into the skirting board, smashing into the door, smashing into the desk and the boxes and the shelves – that noise sounds to Chris the way life currently feels.

'Good night,' says Jacob, leaving the cubicle.

'Good night Jacob.'

'Good luck.'

Jacob is from a small village in northern Nigeria. Five years ago he made his way to London. Chris has taken these two pieces of information, put one and one together and made nine. He imagines Jacob narrowly escaping a pillaging at the hands of Boko Haram, being trafficked across the desert through sandstorms, ambushes, all sorts. Jacob, camped out for months on a Libyan beach, praying that the cross tattooed on his wherever does not get him decapitated by some rabid Islamist. Does he hand over all his money for a berth on a boat across the Mediterranean, despite not knowing how to swim? Probably. Does he get mauled by dogs as he makes his way through France? Contract pneumonia? Does he stow away in the wheelhouse of a lorry to reach England? Certainly he does nothing so banal as just land at Heathrow. Either way he now resides in Woolwich, where Chris presumes he shares a bedsit with seventeen other men, whence he commutes to his eleven different jobs across London, all of which bring in less than Chris spends on porridge and smoothies each month.

This is how bad Chris assumes Jacob has it, yet it is Jacob who wishes him luck. Chris hears this and wants to disintegrate into nothingness, to disappear up the hoover along with everything he has ever touched and everyone he has ever known, except of course Jacob. This is how bad Chris assumes Jacob has it, yet still when he thinks about the current state of his life, he tells himself that trading places would constitute an upgrade.

There is the fact that he will soon be turning thirty. The fact that he is fatter than he should be and basically bald. The fact that he has been dumped, apparently irrevocably, by a girl who according to his own but also any other standards is out of his league. That Julie did once love him, that she has now dumped him, means he has obviously but unwittingly done something or more likely a series of things to make her unlove him. Which is also a fact to be taken into consideration. Two facts, in fact: the fact that he has done the things, and the fact that he has no idea what they even are, because she left without giving reasons. Or rather, she left giving reasons that he considered unreasonable.

Then there is his job. To say that Chris resents his job would be an understatement. It would be like saying that his colleagues, his friends, and his family resent Brexit. He hates what he does with the same dreadful fervour that they predicted a total fucking apocalypse of shit, the moment Britain ceased to be a part of the European Union. He hates so many different aspects of it, hates them all equally, and has by now lost any respect he once had, for himself of course but also for the legal profession. Worse than that is the bitterness born out of realising that nobody else does either, not anymore.

Chris has been duped. The world in which he grew up considered lawyers to be people of pedigree. Bastards, fine, but bastards of pedigree. Suddenly though, having invested four years of study and four more of work, Chris now finds himself in another world, one which cringes at the very idea of the suited professions, and considers anybody who has voluntarily qualified into them a bonehead. The equivalent would be saving up for eight years to buy what was widely acknowledged to be the sturdiest vehicle on the market, a green Land Rover Defender, timeless and very performant, only to pay up, drive home, then turn on the television and see a woman in an anorak in front of a large factory with a graphic along the bottom of the screen reading: *end of the road for Land Rover*. The next headline reveals that Parliament, in a miraculous show of bipartisanship, has voted to ban diesel. After the sport and the local news and the weather forecast comes a documentary about Tesla, the general gist being that anybody without one is a moron.

He is tired of being laughed at when he says what he does, borderline ashamed of it all. Ashamed of having worked hard at university. Ashamed of having wanted a conventional, prosperous career. Ashamed of not being an entrepreneur. Ashamed of turning up late to bars or restaurants or parties, wearing his formless creased suit, only to find everyone else bowing down before some tosser in a tracksuit who has just sold his company for three million pounds. His company that stencils cartoon animals onto vegetables, so children will want to eat them.

Chris is realising that this is what people need. Not the vegetables – nobody could care less about vegetables. They need the story, to believe that they too might be special, instead of what they are, which is superfluous. It makes him angry on so many levels. There is the surface crust of anger, because this tosser has succeeded, above an outer core of rage, because Chris would also quite like to be special. Underneath that lies the inner core of molten, bubbling fury, because he knows he is destined not to be.

And the tossers are not actually the worst. The worst are the guys who when asked what they do reply sales, which means they began as estate agents whizzing around London in midrange hatchbacks, then five years and seven jobs later there they are, flogging digital advertising space for six figure salaries, working nine hours a day and mostly from home. The guys who ask Chris what he does, and when Chris says lawyer they look at him as if he just told them he watched his parents screw each other to death.

He was at least supposed to be handsomely paid, but he is not even that, not really. Last month he worked a standard three hundred and seventy hours, so he effectively brought home fifteen pounds an hour, which he then had the privilege of paying top bracket tax on. Eight pounds net, just a few pence more than the statutory minimum, and about what he would be getting to ride a bike around the city delivering falafel, without the boundless sense of freedom he mistakenly assumes that entails.

He at least earned more than the creative types he used to meet through Julie, although not always, because there was the occasional trust fund wastrel who confused his laboriously constructed but basically aimless bohemianism with the more or less legitimate title of artist. And in any event, these characters had the luxury of doing nothing with their days, of watching people go gaga when they said they were poets or painters or pianists. Frequently Chris found himself looking around her friendship group for an accountant or a management consultant – anyone whose aura glowed the same shade of boring beige. There was one doctor, Ram, who people pitied perhaps even more, because to be a doctor you had to be genuinely clever, and there was the sense that to choose NHS over Goldman or Google can only have been because of some psychotic disorder. But nobody disdains doctors. We are not yet there.

The fact that Julie wanted to be a writer had once excited Chris greatly. Dating an artist set him apart from his law school peers, whose girlfriends or boyfriends were invariably also lawyers, and back then it was easy to believe that their differences were an asset. He had not yet started as a trainee solicitor, but still he enjoyed considering himself her patron. He paid for their drinks, invited her to dinner, and no sooner did he begin earning than the weekend breaks began. They went to Berlin. They went to Barcelona. They went to Rome. During the day he would feign an interest in Heinrich Heine or Catalan Modernism or whatever, before retreating to the hotel for all the blowjobs, which felt like a fair deal.

One year later Julie moved in, and it was agreed that she would pay no rent, only bills. She was working in a gastropub and had finished her first novel. It had not been published, and Chris believed her when she explained why. He repeatedly reminded her of JK Rowling, who had been clinically depressed and on benefits but was now worth three quarters of a billion pounds. He knew zero about fiction but was convinced she had talent, and he adored the idea of one day being able to say that he had been a rock while times were tough. By then there would be movie rights, the whole caboodle. He would no longer need to work, while still meriting regular oral for all the support over the years. Julie would dedicate her books to him, her first reader and best friend. And yes, perhaps it was not too much to think that yes: he could be her muse.

Three years later his patience was being tested. Still she was not published, and the stuff she was giving him to read… well, it was drivel. Her first novel had at least had a plot. The latest was just sections of senseless interior monologue, which she said were supposed to evoke the patterns of menstrual flow. Had the tampon not been invented for a reason? He came to fear the inevitable rejections more than she did, because it would take all his strength not only to console her, but to continue persuading himself that she might some day succeed. Meanwhile he was working more hours in one week than the average Frenchman was required to work in three, and who was supporting him?

Her cultivation became a problem. This was trivial, that was naff. If he made the effort to mention a book featured by the BBC she would half listen before saying something disparaging. They struggled to find things they could both watch. The only movies she was interested in were black and white or foreign or about rape. It was without relish that Chris agreed to begin *Orange is the New Black*, but he did it, because relationships are about compromise, then after each episode he would have to listen to some nonsense about patriarchal structures, about disrupting the prevailing influences of postfeminism and neoliberalism, about the fallacy that superstructures of oppression are no longer enforced in Western society. Who the fuck gives a fucking fuck?

The one topic he vowed never to get annoyed about was money. Then, he began to get annoyed about money. It was unavoidable, what with the historically noble idea of supporting a woman now mired in shit. He looked around at his colleagues with their very emancipated, very corporate significant others. He saw the fruit of that double salary purchasing power, and he knew that it was good. They were buying houses, these arseholes, and furnishing them at John Lewis. They were going to Coachella. Ashrams in Goa, pistachio farms in southern Iran. Val bloody Thorens. Meanwhile the only destination Chris ever seemed bound for was the Stanhope family home in Dorset, because Julie loved to write there, and she never had enough money to go anywhere else.

She never had enough money full stop. She could just about afford half of the food, some of the bills, and the five thousand paperbacks she required each month. Chris calculated that if she just switched to a Kindle, within one year she could have saved enough for a return ticket to New York. But no, because there was the feel of a book, the smell of a book, blah blah blah. How was that of any relevance? Foodies were bad, but none ever went as far as praising the way burrata was spelled or chorizo sounded.

Even when he left her the cash, she would never do the shopping. Frequently he would come home late, salivating at the prospect of a bowl of triple chocolate crunch granola. Then he would open the door, see his money where he left it on the table, and look in the fridge to find no milk. He would go upstairs, wake Julie, and ask whether she had remembered to get milk, as if she might have put it somewhere other than the fridge. She had not had a minute, she would mumble. Not one minute to walk forty metres to the Tesco Express, not one minute in the fifteen hours since he had left her, during which time she had supposedly been confined to the flat, writing like a motherfucker. But he could say nothing, because being an artist was not like having a corporate job.

Amen. Tonight he has at least another three hours of work ahead of him: a suite of eleven documents to send out for review, only seven of which are ready. Venture Capital can be extremely complex, and the contracts Chris drafts are its backbone. They define the relationship between startup founders and his clients, the funds, for whom small details can mean the difference between a successful deal and disaster, as Nigel is forever reminding him.

NDAs, Stock Warrants, Options. Convertible Note and Note Purchase Agreements. Restricted Stock and Founder Agreements. SAFEs. Funding Rounds, Exits. None of it interests him, not even in the slightest. Once upon a time his sole concern was the wordless collation of all this paper, and he loathed it. But when after two years his clerical limbo came to an end, when Nigel started obliging him to read or write or think, Chris began wondering whether it was the closest he had ever come to pure happiness.

He hates the responsibility, the pressure. He has no ambition. He would prefer not to contribute in seminars, or discuss equity crowdfunding, or have deadlines, or update his LinkedIn page. He cannot face the idea of speaking to people on the phone or seeing clients. From each departmental meeting he almost does depart mental. None of the vocabulary means anything to him, the strategies and the synergies and the business development frameworks. Which is a worry, seeing as it has crept into every single domain he might ever stand a chance of earning a living in. Because Chris is not creative. He is not *a creative*, not even creative enough to forge a creative life for himself, creatively out of nothing, like the tens of thousands of uncreative Londoners who call themselves creatives. He thinks he might be happy just inputting data eight hours a day, with an hour for lunch and no phone.

Nobody will ever actually read what he is working on, least of all his client. Vincent Froissard at Picpus Partners. Extremely unlikely that he will even acknowledge the email, but should it not be there when he checks his inbox tomorrow, he will call Nigel and have Chris publicly guillotined. This is how it goes. This is the law.

chapter:four

One more line, dance that shit off, then bedtime. Vince has meetings all day tomorrow. Trying to turf these cretins out the flat will be interesting. There are easily fifty people in his living room, and he knows about twenty of them. Midnight on a Wednesday, standard. Voila what happens when Fabrice gets behind the decks. Vince stands next to him at the MacBook, prepping two slugs and dipping into a funky sway. He looks at the screen: Gilberto Gil, *Toda Menina Bahiana*, absolute boomer.

Woo. Woooo. Wooooo. Vince hands the twenty to Fab. French touch *bébé*. Most of the crew have made it - there must be more Parisians here than at any party in Paris tonight. Earlier this afternoon, Vince was wishing one of them would volunteer to host for a change. He wanted to go home, take it easy, sleep. Then he remembered he was not a fucking pussy. Vico was launching his new label under a railway arch in Clapton. Couple of beers there, then a convoy of Ubers back to Shoreditch. Vince has the loft, Vince has the views. Vince has the sound system, Vince gets the good gak. Two grand a week he pays in rent here. Even if the rest of them had a whip round, still they could never afford it.

No way could he live their lives. In their thirties, sharing flats, arguing over the cleaning rota. Taking the bus. Shopping for clothes at

Zara. Eating in or ordering the second cheapest wine on the list, going halves and thirds and quarters on a measly gram. Worrying at the end of each month and still needing handouts from papa. *La misère totale.*

Nice little Asian chick over by the pillar, talking to his neighbour Eugene. The only other true baller in here. Must be in his late forties, goes around dressed like the Korean Miley Cyrus. Neon wifebeaters, spandex, the works. Just sold his website for eighteen million.

Vince goes over. He bumps fists with Eugene, who introduces the little Asian as Lucy. She is standing straight, casually dropping her shoulders with the beat, moving her hips. She looks Thai, maybe Vietnamese. Tight jeans with a baggy tee tucked in. Insane body. And if eyes truly are the window to the soul, this soul likes to party.

Eugene is telling Lucy about being young in the Eighties. How hard it was to masturbate before the internet. Used to sit on his bed in San Diego, watching MTV with his hand on his pecker, waiting for the right video, letting the anticipation build. Claims he once managed to ejaculate twice in the four minutes it took for Madonna to sing *Like a Virgin*. Lucy is sort of amused but mostly disgusted.

Vince asks who she knows, why she is here. She works with Manon, at the Tate. Does cultural outreach there. But also and principally she is a writer. Vince has no idea what cultural outreach is, but it reeks of minimum wage. He has a soft spot for these artsy, feminist types. Enjoys watching them shelve their principles for long enough to earn the AP bodysuit, the red soles, the weekend in Mykonos.

He asks if she has everything she needs in terms of blow. Some ketamine she would love. Vince leads her away from Eugene and towards the window. He promises to be right back and is, divvying up some K on the repurposed granite sill in no time. One for her, one for him. Not too much, just enough. London looks cruel and awake in the background.

He asks where she comes from and she says Guildford, but he means originally. Originally Guildford. Finally he learns that her father was English but her mother is from Laos. He says he has been to Thailand and Vietnam, Cambodia too, never Laos though. It is so beautiful, she says. Luang Prabang obviously but also Vang Vieng and the temples, the waterfalls. The food. She sounds nervous - this will calm her right down.

Vince takes a fifty out of his pocket, rolls it up and passes it to her. She stoops towards the drugs and he rests his hand on her back. He feels her muscles contract as she snorts. She straightens, rubs her nose, returns the note, blam. Fab mellows things down with some Chairlift, *Bruises*. Just what this needed. If the guy was half as good at web developing as he was with a playlist he might actually get somewhere in life.

Lucy asks Vince where in France he is from. He makes a joke about his accent, about it being that obvious. She laughs. He tells her Paris, which naturally she adores. Grew up around Trocadero, could see the Eiffel Tower from his bedroom window. He enjoys imagining just how wet this information has made her.

Paris, lol. If Vince had a pound for everyone who told him how fantastic it was he could probably buy the place. The funniest are the ones who say Brexit spells the end, who see Paris or Frankfurt replacing

London as a global financial centre. Lolol. Okay, not totally impossible, in the way that Rome rebuilding its empire is not totally impossible. After all, half a million people live in Frankfurt, and history shows what happens when a small minority of Germans really put their minds to something. As for Paris, its brightest half million are almost certainly no longer living there. They are here, they are in New York. They are in Seoul or Shanghai or Singapore or Tokyo. Basically they are anywhere but there.

Here comes Macron though, rolling out the red carpet for businesses! Until that carpet is dyed with the blood of Union bosses, stitched together from their abandoned flags, nobody with two brain cells is walking anywhere near it. Try explaining French employment law to a CEO without being laughed at. Try explaining corporation tax, income tax, wealth tax. Nothing against Manu – Vince was at Sciences Po with him, the guy could have been a killer. But he was a moron for going into politics. He should have stayed at Rothschilds and made partner. Might have tasted some actual power.

Paris, rofl. Vince struggles to believe that anybody might actually want to live there, apart from the odd fat American. Oh my god I love the Opera. Oh my god I love Montmartre. Oh my god I love the Latin Quarter. Perhaps if the States had not been so devoid of culture, so bereft of history, Paris might have escaped becoming imprisoned in its own. Nothing moves there, nothing happens. Imagine a boring museum with a few million people crammed inside, then chuck rubbish everywhere and diffuse the smell of piss. Ensure that nothing supposed to work actually does. Serve up some tired old recipes in the cafeteria. What you have imagined is Paris.

If Vince ever finds himself back there, he will know he has failed. Failed because he needs free healthcare or benefits. Failed because in any event, only losers end up back where they started.

Marvin Gaye, nice. *I Wanna Be Where You Are*. Lucy is dancing now. He has given her just enough ket to keep things slow and loose without sending her into the hole. Everybody loses if she goes into the hole.

'What do you do Vince?'

'VC. Venture capital.'

'Cool.'

Yeah, it is cool. But you gotta earn that shit. Gotta be present, gotta perform. Gotta be a pro, and Vince is. The minute he walks through that door, the partying and the bitches disappear. Coke he only ever does before the very big meetings, and even then just a bump, just a key to keep focused.

Picpus might not be the biggest fund, but it is the best. Since 1993 it has been partnering at every stage of growth with the founders of companies that now have an aggregate value of nearly one trillion dollars. Vince is half troubleshooter, half strategist, holding their hands and walking them through however many funding rounds prove necessary to get them to where they need to be.

He excels at his job because he understands the pressures an entrepreneur faces. Straight out of business school and alone, he created what went on to become the third biggest holiday rentals website in France. Other operators who bounce in with a straight finance background never last long. Too obsessed with playbook modelling and seminar bullshit, none of which works in the real world, where you put out fires with whatever you have at hand. Smooth this out, tidy this up before you go live, they tell founders. Wrong. Ship product, always be shipping product, and worry about the rest later.

Jamiroquai, *Alright*. Vince feels his body begin to thrum with energy. He rubs up against Lucy, dancing her from behind, hands on her hips and head lurched over her shoulder. He makes eye contact with Vico across the room, and there is an acknowledgement that this is great, that they are great.

Today Vince has sent a dozen emails to hopeful founders, telling them their products or their business models or they themselves are substandard. One guy made the mistake of taking out a patent and thinking Picpus or any other VC joint would give a shit. Apple, Google, Amazon, whoever – the best rarely do it first; they simply come along and do it better. Patents mean nothing in a free market, and even less on the internet. Besides, where are you finding the cash to cover the costs of enforcing that IP? The most incompetent of associates at the law firm he uses gets billed out at three hundred an hour, which is three hundred more than you currently make, three hundred more than you have left to your name, because every single cent better have gone into creating the best product around. Good luck offering the lawyers equity. Good luck getting Vince to pay. He wants to see you on the attack, not worrying about defence. He wants you to score, to win at all costs and win large, otherwise you might as well lose ten nil.

Three emails were to engineers, telling them they were wasting his time talking about tech. Talk about how the tech *makes a difference.*

Talk about how it creates an unfair advantage over the competition. Break the idea down into the simplest possible terms and sell, sell, sell. In the last few weeks, only one guy has come at him with anything even resembling an interesting pitch. One guy in more than fifty, which is about normal. Jobs put it brilliantly when he said talent hits a target no one else can hit, whereas genius hits a target no one else can *see*.

This guy was pushing social product, a tad messy round the edges but potentially huge. Vince began paying attention when he read that Blank would not just echo the impact of Facebook, but eclipse it entirely. Bold bastards Vince encounters on a daily basis, but even he had to admire the bigness of the bollocks required to believe you could bypass a beast whose metrics were measured in billions. What remains to be seen is whether the guy can scale up his user base during the pre-revenue phase. The valley of death, Vince calls it. Climb up out of that and you might be okay, but only the toughest survive. What, you want sympathy because becoming a billionaire is hard?

HUMBLE, Kendrick Lamar. Vince asks Lucy if she wants to do another line in the master bedroom. She says yes. Vince can feel the blood pumping around his body now. Very improbable that he will be able to stay hard, but whatever. The best mornings are the mornings when you wake up with your dick in the mouth of a girl whose name you cannot remember, and whose face you will soon forget.

chapter:five

One of the greatest myths in the fruit world is that by eating pineapple a man can improve the taste of his semen. For some reason you remember this whenever you drink a smoothie. And here you are, in an independent coffee shop on Columbia Road, ordering something called a Heart Beet. Watermelon, beetroot, orange, spinach, pineapple. Unfortunately the taste is already in your mouth, but in any event the semen is not yours and the myth is just a myth.

Worse than the taste is the shame, and no seed or berry or vegetable will rid you of it. Then there is the headache making you wish you could remove your brain, bin its bruised majority and get on with your day – hence the watermelon. It contains tryptophan, which will boost your reserves of serotonin, currently as depleted as the scrotum of the guy whose flat you just left. Beetroot is a source of fibre, oranges need no introduction, and spinach you know is essential but can only stomach like this, which is to say blitzed beyond all recognition and drowned out with less shit flavours.

To accompany your smoothie you order eggs on toast. They can write Blue Legbars poached on sourdough with avocado and coconut sambol, but everybody knows this is eggs on toast. You also ask for a chai latte, and the waiter tells you the house blend is Fair Trade, a rich and premier melange of cinnamon, cardamom, star anise and ginger. The words rich and premier melange remind you that you have just cheated on your boyfriend, for the first time and with a French millionaire.

The waiter goes away and you reach for your phone. Your most necessary possession, even if right now you would eagerly trade it for a clean pair of panties, a bottle of mouthwash, and a magic box of retroactive condoms. You look at the screen: no redemption there, only Ram. One arm around you, the other outstretched in selfie mode, Angkor Wat in the background. You swipe your finger, as if it might be possible to efface that moment, that whole holiday in Southeast Asia, your whole relationship. You send an email to your boss saying you are feeling really quite sick and will be working from home today, which is only half untrue, because you will not be doing any work. You also message Manon saying something about covering for you, stomach cramps, whatever.

You turn your phone over on the table. What the fuck are you doing with your life? In fact no, dozens of more basic questions will need to be answered before you can even begin to contemplate that very core one. You decide to work backwards chronologically.

New first question: why the mouth?

You slept in a Kooples tee that Ram bought for you, because it felt improper to be totally naked in bed with this stranger. Already this logic is ropey, but go on. Ram still loves you in that tee, and for this French millionaire to have pulled out and soiled it would have been adding insult to injury. Then there was the fact that he asked, and to oblige seemed not polite necessarily but at least the right thing to do.

44

Which seems ridiculous now. Which makes you cringe now. You should have told him to come on the floor, but that was unthinkable, and there is something traceless about the mouth, something of the river in that it is always changing, always the same but never exactly the same. So you did it for the same reason people throw plastic in the Mekong. You thought it would be carried away, that there would be no repercussions, that it would wash into the wider oceans of wrong where it would become indistinct. Besides, the only alternative was inside you, which was no alternative at all because he was riding bareback.

Question two: why did you consent to unprotected sex? And not even when you were high, but the next morning. When you were low.

The betrayal had been sealed. You had already decided to go to bed with the French millionaire. Of that you would be judged guilty, of that you were indeed guilty, in which case why not indulge in the bigger crime, the one everyone would forever accuse you of anyway? You told yourself you would never be here again, neither in this bed in this apartment, nor in this situation or even one vaguely resembling it, because the shame you would be feeling in a few hours time – the shame you can attest to now – would be too great.

Next: did it feel good? Questions getting harder now. You look at your juice, pick it up and take a long sip. It tastes sweet, of nothing in particular, but each and every one of its ingredients is clearly there.

Good is perhaps not the right word. Vince is certainly hot though. He looks like that French guy from *The Beach*, with the tousled hair, whose girlfriend cheats on him with Leonardo DiCaprio. Which is ironic. There was something about his manner, an arrogance and an obnoxiousness that you found alluring. These were the qualities that first attracted to you to Ram, qualities you have not seen in him since university, but not really since school. Vince came up to you, pulsating with the same kind of life that has been dying in your boyfriend for a very long time.

In fact yes, it did feel good. You taste the chai latte and grimace; you have never learned to properly appreciate this beverage. It felt good to watch someone discover your body for the first time. The urgency of it all. Everything new, everything different, everything a surprise. But then you wanted intimacy. You were crashing down off the drugs, you wanted to hear that everything would be okay, and instead this Frenchman starts pleading to come in your mouth, wriggling up and straddling your face, creasing into spasms while the semen built up, while all you could do was gag. Then suddenly he climbed off and disappeared, leaving you there alone, lying on his bed all alone, with only that taste for company and the shame, so much shame, and this was what it felt like to sleep with somebody else, all these years wondering and finally you knew, and in fact no, it did not feel good.

Also the drugs. At what point did midweek ketamine become normal? Coke is one thing – coke and MD, fine, two things. Ketamine though? You suspect that you are bringing your brain to its knees, razing the villages of its extended amygdala, fragging the tunnels of its basal ganglia, napalming whichever of its jungles shelters your bedraggled troops of memory. Drugs cost money you do not have, unless of course you opt to sleep with the guy providing them. Then there is the fact that your pills are being made by children in Chinese factories. Your marching powder is categorically not Fair Trade. There is no Columbia Road artisan cocaine shop, battling to ensure that farmers get the best possible deal. Learning that the eggs here are not free range would genuinely depress you, yet human beings are dying for your highs, dying the most atrocious deaths imaginable, and still you love your drugs.

Is this all because you will soon be turning thirty? You worry you have done nothing with your youth, worry that wasting it entirely would have been better than what you have done instead, which is nothing. You wrote a novel that will never be published. You travelled to some places, the same places as everybody else. Perhaps your riskiest feat to date has been a motorbike ride in Vietnam, and even that required travel insurance and safety briefings. You have only ever been with one guy, have been with him for more than a decade, and he is no longer the same. Now he wants to get married and have children, whereas you absolutely fucking do not.

How can you even contemplate starting a family? You are still busy trying to work out who you are. You have no idea if you are British, or Laotian, or both, or neither. You wonder whether the real you is the you happy under a rug watching *Friends*, or the you rereading Kierkegaard; the you who likes wet woodland dog walks, or the you desperate to attend Burning Man. Is it the you interested in fine teas? The you who likes Fanta? Could it be possible that these are all the same you? Perhaps you are the you who chose to tattoo something Simone de Beauvoir said across your ribs, that one is not born but *becomes* a woman. What kind of woman, then, have you chosen to become? The woman who shouts at her doctor boyfriend for mansplaining complex

47

surgical procedures, or the woman who lets a stranger come in her mouth because it feels like the right thing to do? Seven hundred pages of heavily autobiographical fiction have not helped you figure out the answers to all these questions. Seven hundred pages of heavily autobiographical fiction have not helped you figure out what the questions even are.

And so, you take drugs. You take drugs because they make you feel better than you otherwise do. You take drugs because they alter the voices in your head, the voices asking the questions, and the questions about what the questions are. Suddenly they become a congress of yesses, before which every proposed plan is workable, unless it entails going home and to bed. Suddenly your head resembles a simmering central square, somewhere in Latin America, and the voices are those of your million supporters, standing under your balcony crying Viva Lucy in unison. You can stop worrying. You can stop being scared about just how wrong things could go if you decide to leave Ram. You can stop feeling awkward about introducing yourself as a writer, even though it has been over a year since you last wrote anything more substantial than an email.

Here are your eggs. Your headache has not abated, not in the slightest. Also what the fuck is coconut sambol? You wonder why you felt so confident ordering what might have been a coconutty variation of anything. Fish or risotto, marmite, anything. It looks like wood shavings. After three mouthfuls you decide to abandon this charade and ask the waiter for some ibuprofen. You would love a can of Fanta as well, but there is zero chance of this place stocking fizzy drinks, so you decide to salvage the tiniest scrap of something we should avoid trying to dress up as dignity. The waiter says he will have a look, asks if last night was a big one. Before this breakfast is through he is going to ask for your number. His grin supposes that all big ones are comic and essentially harmless. There is nothing in that grin to suggest that a big one could conceivably end in disaster, or at least a girl sitting on a bench in Boundary Gardens, crying in the rain.

Just a normal headache, you say. Dehydration, whatever. He goes off and you stare at a chalkboard on the other side of the room, on which it is written that this brunch is feeding your appetite, but not only. It is also feeding the food evolution of this establishment, helping it stay true to its Sri Lankan roots by supporting local growers. Local growers in Hackney, you presume, rather than in Sri Lanka, as confusing as that is.

This, if you ever do write anything again, is the tone you will have to ape if you want success. This is either as much as people want to read anymore, or as much as they are capable of reading. None of which matters, because you have nothing to write about anyway. Nothing but this. Nothing but the rambling thoughts of a confused young woman in an increasingly unfathomable world, which was more or less the premise of your massive failed novel.

The waiter returns with a glass of water and two paracetamol. You take them and ask for the bill. He looks disappointed. He volunteers to box up the eggs and transfer your chai latte to a takeaway cup. You would rather never see any of it again, but you also would rather have told Vince to come on the floor, so you say yeah that would be great thanks.

He comes back with the bill and it is nineteen pounds. London. Basically you have paid five pounds per paracetamol, which right now seems money well spent, and another nine for some blended fruit and a sip of tea. Luckily you can pay contactless and scram, otherwise a tip would have been necessary, to compensate for refusing to be seduced. But in fact you manage to gather your things and leave the coffee shop, all without being asked out. The waiter simply smiles, and as you walk down the middle of Columbia Road, where the roses go six for a fiver on Sunday afternoons, you wonder whether your beauty has wilted. This will be your life on the other side of thirty: no longer knowing whether a guy fancies you, not being fancied full stop.

In Haggerston Park you encounter a homeless man. His puffa jacket is sodden through. In his hand is a can of lager, so no point even offering him the tea. You take the eggs out of the bag, which is when you see that Alex has written on the box. You now know his name is Alex, because it says call me if you ever fancy a slightly more chilled one, followed by his phone number, followed by Alex, followed by a smiley face. You feel relieved in a sense but otherwise profoundly sad, not for Alex but for men generally. Sad that this is what it has come to for them.

You hand over the box. The tramp looks puzzled, so you say eggs on toast. You stop waiting for him to thank you and continue on your way, wondering whether he will perhaps think that you are Alex, that the message is meant for him. If he has either the means or the desire to get in touch, perhaps he and the actual Alex will arrange to meet up for what would be a very disappointing chilled one, for both parties.

You walk along the canal in the direction of Broadway Market. To your left are dreary grey council blocks, places with grimy windows and sandblasted balustrades, places named Something Court, Something View, Something Estate. These resemble the building that you actually live in, as opposed to the kind you dream of living in, the converted warehouses that line the opposite bank and are named Lock Mill or Dock Wharf or Aqua.

The cold is penetrating your bones. Your DNA is all wrong. Clearly you have inherited the Laotian sensibility to low temperatures, and the English talent for moaning about these and indeed all weather conditions. The worst of both worlds. Really the ideal would have been the ability to go around tightless in January, and the Southeast Asian aptitude for just shutting the fuck up and getting on with things. Perhaps if you could figure out who you are, you would know in which kind of climate you were destined to thrive. You could travel around the world summering here, wintering there, always maintaining optimum writing conditions, hopping from one place to another in a shimmy of rootless manoeuvres. If you could just figure out who you are, then you would be free.

Where are you even going? Ram will be at the flat so you cannot go there. He is on lates this week. He will have come home at about ten, a few hours after you were supposed to have left for work. If you go there now, he will wake up and you will have to look at him and lie. You will have to lie that after the label launch there was this house party that went quite late, and you ended up staying with Manon in Walthamstow. This clustered lie will explode into lots of other smaller lies, each with independent capacity to maim and destroy. Lies about not showering, about turning up for work dressed like that. Luckily you are employed by a cultural institution, so this last part is not wildly unbelievable. There will be the lie about not feeling well, not because you feel in any way well, but because the reasons for your malaise will not be the ones given. You will lie that your boss sent you home, and here you start entering into the territory of the dangerously verifiable and conflicting lie. Ram will want to kiss you, to huddle under the covers and cuddle, and when you refuse even this will be lies, because you will appear lurgied and unwilling, whereas in fact nothing will seem more necessary than holding him tight and wailing sorry.

So you cannot go home, but nor do you have the resources to be spending twenty quid in coffee shops. You could seek refuge in a pub, let a Fanta and a packet of crisps see you through until nightfall, but you are not sure you are strong enough to be that person, the person who sits alone in the pub on a midweek afternoon, nearly thirty and playing truant not just from work but from everything, from life. You must find a way of getting inside though. You consider riding the bus, perhaps this approaching one, all the way to wherever it is bound and back. All the way to Finsbury Park Interchange and back. If the driver stops you will do it. She does not stop.

If the West End was not such a mish you would make your way there and go to the National Gallery. You would sit immobile in front of your favourite painting, *The Execution of Lady Jane Grey*. If you were to admit that to your colleagues, they would laugh you right out of the Turbine Hall. The work actually required some drafting skill, its finish is immaculate, and it tells a gripping story. But it is a straightforward salon

52

job, not in any way challenging and therefore certainly not cool. The artist, Paul Delaroche, was French, which is not what you need right now, but looking at his canvas has always soothed your inner melodrama. Jane has been dethroned and sentenced to death. She has mounted the scaffold, been stripped down to her undergarments, and now she gropes blindly for the block. The tension is terrific. Everybody in the composition averts their eyes, but you can never bear to look away. The horror of knowing what comes next.

You both pity and admire poor Jane. At the moment you even feel a little like her, stumbling blindfolded towards a grizzly and painful denouement, not really sure how you got yourself in such a pickle. You turn onto Mare Street, and for a moment you imagine claiming shelter within a Foxtons. You could dupe the most handsome lettings agent into thinking you are keen to move. You could give him an astronomical fake budget and he would fetch you a fizzy drink from the fridge in reception, before talking you through reams of glossy brochures. The light here, the space there, the fixtures, the fittings, the views. Then there would be a ride around Hackney in his branded green Mini. He would park illegally under a glass tower of skyhouses called Indigo E8 and whisk you up to the penthouse. You would ask him questions about the concierge before dropping down to the reclaimed parquet flooring and politely asking him to fuck you from behind, while you gaze east towards the Thames Estuary and, in the very far distance, Laos. At this point, all bets are off as to what you would and would not do.

You realise that you are not far from The Chesham Arms, the pub where Julie works. You decide to go there. Somebody needs to hear what you are going through. If she is not on shift you will go to Waterloo and catch the train to Woking, where your Laotian grandfather is in a care home with late stage dementia. You can ask him to tell you about his flight from his native land for the thousandth time, then talk at him about everything you think is wrong with you. Make your way to Guildford, call in on your mum, ask her to run you a bath. Spend the night in clean, crisp sheets, have dinner and a proper breakfast for once. When you say you went to visit Grandad, she will be so moved that she will offer to reimburse your train fare, and you will protest before telling her it was more than it actually was, coming back to London unburdened and enriched. But this is very much Option B.

Luckily Julie is there. She is thrilled to see you, and ushers you towards the beer garden for a cigarette break. You cannot fathom that she or indeed anybody else would want to smoke. In the last year you have experimented with pretty much every Class A on the market, drawing the line only at heroin, but it both mystifies and concerns you that somebody could fail to grasp the harm done by smoking tobacco.

First, of course, you have to hear about her. You have to hear about the latest step in her miraculous journey from old Julie to new Julie. Last night, she reveals, she slept with Luke. It was great. It was really, really great. That your best friend is managing to move on from her boyfriend of so many years should embolden you, but instead it embitters you, because you doubt your ability to ever do the same. That you set them up makes it worse, because she was supposed to be the one in turmoil, you were supposed to be fine, and in just one night you have managed to engineer not only her triumph but also your own downfall.

54

Nor, you now realise, can you tell her about Vince. Julie worships Ram, you know she does, and the plan was to pitch this confession as a consolatory bonding opportunity. Best friends, wallowing in collective misery. Her buoyancy has ruined the whole dynamic.

In case you forgot, she is also putting the finishing touches on yet another novel. She reminds you that tonight there is that house party, the one you promised to attend. Hosting is an agent named Ola, a friend of a friend who has read her first few chapters and supposedly rates them highly. Fuck your life, basically.

chapter:six

Ram lived above Paradise, a Halal butchers on the Lower Clapton Road, which was no kind of paradise at all. The haunt of gangsters, fools. Murder Mile they used to call this street. Gentrification had brought knitting boutiques, craft brewers and independent coffee shops, one of which doubled as a vinyl emporium. Anybody deranged enough to have bought a townhouse here in 1990, the year Ram was born, would have technically become a millionaire, simply by surviving.

Which was not in fact so simple. Property prices had rocketed but so too had the violence, which Ram knew because he spent his days sifting through its harrowing debris in the Emergency Department of nearby Homerton Hospital. For every hipster needing his stomach pumped there were knifings, there were shootings, and Ram had long lost count of the victims he had watched die. Just last week it was a teenage girl. He flapped about trying to apply compression to her stab wounds, which is always difficult when they number seventeen. She was never going to make it, he was not to blame, but still when he went to tell her mother he felt like Death, the destroyer of worlds.

Ram set off, nodding to the owner of Paradise. He passed behind the hospital through residential backstreets. Lifeless branches shot up from the stubby shorn trees like troll hair, as in the trolls that Ram used to wedge on the end of his school pencils, not the feral internet kind who could call a man a terrorist simply for tweeting the batting average of Virat Kohli. Now a girl walked past, wearing silver leggings and flamboyant trainers that looked like two big Battenberg cakes. Next came a boy, in a black beanie with BAM and then a fourth letter, either an F or an E, emblazoned across the fold in block white capitals. Between Bad Ass Motherfucker and Black Asian Minority Ethnic, Ram was torn as to which was more mindless. Each time somebody conscientiously referred to him as BAME, he had half a mind to correct them, to tell them he preferred the term paki thank you very much.

He needed out of this city. He needed out of all cities, but this one would do for a start. Tired of London, tired of life, it was said, and Ram suspected that was indeed the case. He was fed up being at the forefront of things. Bored of trends, bored of change, bored of permanently peering over the precipice of progress. Whenever a guy zoomed past on an electric whatever, Ram secretly wanted to see him stack it, to stand back and say nothing while kinder but clueless pedestrians asked if anybody knew first aid. Whenever a girl walked solo down the street, snapchatting herself or storytelling, Ram yearned to see her collide with a lamppost or disappear down a manhole. A womanhole, a personhole, whatever.

The Tories riled him. Labour riled him. Leavers riled him, Remainers riled him. Everything riled him, all the arguments and the tension, the permanent atmosphere of conflict. Riled by ignorant bigots, riled by radical Islam, as riled when Muslims called him racist as when racists called him Muslim. In the aftermath of the Westminster attack, an obese Lonsdale heathen told him to get off a Metropolitan Line train, to fuck off back to wherever he came from, which was awkward because by not moving he would have eventually ended up there, in Amersham.

Ram was not Muslim. Ram was not even Hindu. He was a product of the Home Counties, which had their own religion entirely. He was so English that he had once actually baked a Battenberg. He had won a scholarship to a public school formerly known as the East India College, an institution that prepared young civil servants for a career of commercial exploitation overseas, back when the ancestors of obese Lonsdale heathen were just nameless poorhouse ragamuffins who rarely ever lived beyond thirty. It was difficult to determine whether class no longer meant anything in Britain, or race simply meant everything.

If politics upset him, it was because it had become nothing more than a circus of distraction, entirely divorced from the actual issues, such as the clusterfuck that confronted him on the ward each day. The rising murder rate was bad enough, but in what world was it normal for twats to scoot around launching acid in the faces of randoms? Not even in Sinaloa did they do that. They just shot you in the face, which was perhaps less cruel.

Ram longed to practise his trade in a calmer, leafier place, where people inflicted upon themselves and each other a more vanilla kind of trauma. If he could just persuade Lucy to move to the suburbs, he would encounter nothing more barbaric than a crash victim, and the occasional weirdo with a bottle up his arse. Growing up he had hated Amersham, hated its monotony, but eleven years in London had seen to that. Now, in his mind, all county towns looked like sparkling Camelots, where the living was easy and the only thing that could kill a man was a tumble down the stairs of his mansion.

And everything was so expensive. Unlike Luke, unlike everyone else he went to school with, his parents were not rich. Probably the only person worse off than him was Lucy, whose parents had sacrificed everything to send her to a good sixth form. But when her father committed suicide he left the family finances in a slight shambles, in the same way that the British withdrawal from India had been a slight shambles. The chances of them ever scraping together enough for a deposit were therefore nil. No help coming from his parents, no help coming from her mother, and since they had started renting in London they had saved precisely zero pounds.

All of it went on… there was no knowing what it all went on. Council tax. Student loan repayments. Macchiatos, macchiati, whatever. Existence. Which might have been tolerable if they did anything cool. Lucy did, fine. She went to label launches and exhibition openings and house parties, to which Ram was usually invited, but more often than not he was working. And if he ever was free, he found that the mojo had been sapped right out of him, as it so often can be when watching teenage girls bleed to death. So he stayed in, which might have been tolerable if they lived in a cool place, but they lived in a squat and paid three hundred pounds a week for the privilege.

There was a bedroom, there was a bathroom. There was an open plan kitchen and living space. So far so normal. But the bedroom shared the exact same dimensions as a Super Kingsize mattress. Their own was a regular double, and moving it in had required feats of logic from Ram that made his Statistics Module look like a times table singalong. Additional furnishings were necessarily limited to a bedside table a trunk and some shelves. The bathroom was home to every kind of mildew imaginable. On the walls, on the floor, in the silicone, in the grouting. The shower had to be held in place, and the extractor fan made more noise than a train pulling out of Calcutta.

Some more about that kitchen and living space. The maroon melamine table. The zigzag rug. The hideous fabric sofa, still just about white, in the way pavement snow is still white, four days after falling. The kitchen itself must have been installed before the first wave of immigrants had thought up chicken tikka masala, back when the English still believed spaghetti grew on trees. Just about enough worktop space to open your tin of whatever. White goods that were actually white, plastic wallpaper – no, it was grim. And as for the smell drifting up from Paradise.

Ram spent significant amounts of his insignificant leisure time browsing property websites online. He sussed what could be got for what where, and the results were always stupefying. For the price they were paying now, they could have a two bedroom cottage in Tring. Light, spacious, full of charm. There was a fireplace. There were sash windows. There was a pretty garden filled with shrubs and bushes and trees, whose names they would quickly learn. It even had a patio for outdoor entertaining, and Lucy would be able to turn the wooden shed into a study. Ram had done some googling and discovered that Roald Dahl and George Bernard Shaw had both written their best work where? In garden sheds, in the Home Counties. And when those two behemoths failed to convince her, from up his sleeve he revealed this zinging factoid: Virginia Woolf, so commonly associated with Bloomsbury, had in fact felt nowhere more productive than in her Sussex potting shed.

Lucy protested that Tring was the arse end of nowhere, that nothing ever happened there, that it was a cultureless hole void of interest or history. Which was simply not true. Tring had been mentioned as far back as 1086, in a little known publication called *The Domesday Book*. Had a Tring resident not gone to America on a trading expedition, stayed there and had children who then had children who then had children, there would have been no George Washington, no America and therefore basically no anything. No Vietnam War, Lucy had pointed out glibly. But there was a branch of the Natural History Museum in Tring. Right through town ran the Grand Union Canal. And if Lucy wanted to keep her London job, that was a mere forty minutes by train. Otherwise, there might be similar opportunities locally, such as with the Court Theatre at Pendley, which had just staged the opera *Samson et Dalila*, in French and with subtitles. As if that was not culture.

Ram arrived at the restaurant. It resembled a Victorian pub but was now an Italian eatery called Venerdi. Inside, the whole side of a Fiat 500 had somehow been fixed to the wall. Luke was nowhere to be seen. Ram was shown to a table of mismatching chairs and given a menu to peruse. Here they apparently adhered to the venerated Venetian brunch tradition of scrambled eggs and avocado with bottomless prosecco. In Tring there was a Prezzo, there was a Costa, and he struggled to see how this place was any different. Each offered pizza, each served cappuccino, only nobody in Tring felt the need to be a twat about it, or charge you the GDP of Calabria for three courses and wine.

Ram was reading about the classic thin crusts and authentic wood oven when he felt a vintage Luke pat on the back.

'Alright mate?'

'Yeah mate, you?'

'Yeah mate all good, all good. How you been?'

'Yeah mate not too bad, not too bad. You?'

'Saw Julie last night,' said Luke.

'Oh yeah, how you get on?'

'Quite relentlessly well actually. Ended up back at hers.'

'Mate, tremendous,' said Ram.

'Yeah, no, took me fully by surprise. One minute we were talking about Russian Literature, then suddenly we're back at hers listening to Bon Iver. The scented candle's burning and I'm fingerbanging her on... '

'Buongiorno ragazzi,' said a waitress. 'Benvenuto to Venerdi.'

'Uhm,' said Luke, 'Grazie?'

'Buongiorno,' said Ram, uncertain.

'You have made your choices,' she stated.

'Not yet,' said Luke. 'Uno minuto.'

She went away.

'Dude,' said Ram. 'No way is she Italian.'

'Very unlikely,' said Luke, studying the menu. 'Shall we get a bottle?'

'I have to work.'

'And?'

'And there is a problem with me treating patients after half a bottle of Barolo.'

'Fine,' said Luke. 'Well this is very much a celebration, so I will choose and drink the wine, and you can have a dribble to join me in a toast.'

'Whatever.'

'What do you think they have in the sort of meat feast pizza realm? Oh yes, look at that: ham, chorizo, pepperoni, salami.'

'What is the difference between pepperoni and salami?'

'That, my friend, is an excellent question. One our waitress will no doubt be delighted to answer. Speak of the diavola… '

'You have made your choices,' she announced.

'Yes, we did just have one query,' said Luke. 'We were wondering what the difference was between pepperoni and salami?'

'I will ask the chef,' she said.

'No need,' said Luke. 'No need. I would like one large Caserta.'

'Pizzas all the same size.'

'Then I would like one Caserta.'

'For me just a Margherita please,' said Ram. 'Which part of Italy are you from?'

'No. Romania,' she said. 'Drinks?'

'Yes, uhm, your finest vintage of tap water, plus one bottle of… hmmm. Something white, something dry. The dryer the better. Something a bit minerally maybe. What do you propose?'

64

The waitress shrugged and pointed to a wine with her pen, a wine which Luke then rejected in favour of what Ram assumed was the second cheapest on the list.

'Grazie mille,' said the waitress, seizing their menus and disappearing towards the kitchen.

'There was never any way she was Italian,' said Ram.

'Never.'

'Anyway, tell me more about Julie.'

'Ram, as you well know I am a gentleman. I do not go around sleeping with women and bragging about it.'

'So you slept together?'

'We did.'

'I refuse to believe you,' said Ram.

'Why would I lie? What are we, sixteen?'

'I just did not picture Julie putting out on the first date.'

'Oh she put out. Oh she put all the way out.'

'Who tastes?' asked the Romanian waitress, brandishing the wine.

'I taste,' said Luke.

She eased out the cork, poured a drop into his glass, spilled some onto the table and awaited his verdict.

'Mmm,' said Luke, smacking his lips richly. 'Oh yes. Oh that is very fresh indeed. You can pour my friend a glass of that.'

'No, thank you.'

'Ram.'

'The tiniest drop.'

'Magnifico,' said Luke. 'When in Romania, as they say.'

She filled each of their glasses to the brim and thrust the bottle into an ice bucket.

'A toast,' proposed Luke.

'To Julie?'

'Julie shmulie. A toast to our future success.'

'In what?'

'Very soon, amico mio, you and I will be drinking wines like this one on a terrace overlooking… on a terrace overlooking Falanghina itself. In my mind there are cypress trees, little busts spaced along the whatever you call it.'

'What are you on about?'

'I invited you to invite me here today with a business proposition.'

'Mate I'm not buying your lunch.'

'Today you are, but as you will see, I'm going to be more than paying you back.'

'Please just tell me what you want. I'm very tired. Right now, as much as I love you, I would prefer to be in bed. You said it was urgent.'

'Urgent is exactly what it is. Urgentissimo.'

'And it's not about Julie?'

'No, although she did give me the idea.'

'And what would that be?' asked Ram.

'What I am about to discuss is strictly confidential, okay? Not even Lucy can you tell. I hereby invoke the hippocratic oath.'

'The hippocratic… fine, go on.'

'Right,' said Luke. 'So, you will recall my new app.'

'Yeah, you mentioned it. Just the hundred billion times.'

'Basically what it does is streamline your internet presence. You want to walk in here and find – no, better, listen: our core challenge when it comes to innovation is connecting people with opportunity. Every day and everywhere there are enriching exchanges to be had, but don't you think we could be engaging in them more efficiently? What I want to do, what we are going to do, is maximise encounters. I want to find that crucial common ground, to connect us with the right people in our radiuses. Radii?'

'Yes, but what does it do?'

'Essentially it sifts through online footprints to find precisely the kind of people you want.'

'Tinder for paedos.'

'Hah. Okay, imagine this: You come in here, on your own, and while you eat your pizza you want to sit and have a chat with someone about cricket or that Elephant God with all the arms or whatever.'

'Ganesh.'

'Ganesh. You want to have a chat about cricket or Ganesh.'

'Mate… '

'Shut up, shut up, just pretend that you do,' said Luke. 'You turn on Blank, type in those two things, and it starts searching through the internet history and social media profiles and emails of all the other users in here. That guy over there has pictures of that festival with all the coloured powder on his Instagram, he follows Sachin Tendulkar and used some website to stream an IPL game. Ping: his picture pops up on your screen. You go over to him, you have your intro. And all of that legwork has been done instantly.'

'You know Luke, just because a guy has brown… '

'You know what I mean, you know what I mean. And that is obviously a social example, but you could do it for work, as in someone comes in here with an itchy dick, they turn on Blank and find out that as well as being a doctor you also have longstanding experience of being a dick. They can come straight to you for advice.'

'Mm. One question: surely this thing requires an absurd number of users to make it even remotely worthwhile?'

'Yes, it does. Like Facebook, and the last time I checked they were doing okay.'

'Right, but how do you plan on getting billions of people to download your app?'

'The point is not to worry about the billions. You concentrate on getting the first few thousand and you scale.'

'Fine, but where are you finding the few thousand?'

'Aha. This is where you come in.'

'How, precisely?'

'You wouldn't actually really be doing anything. But you would be earning some equity in my company, and therefore almost certainly be getting rich. Just think: a cool few hundred million sitting in the bank, and if shoving fingers up arses still floats your boat you can go off and be a GP in the Cotswolds. Wherever it is you want to live.'

'Right.'

'Turn that frown upside down friend. I'll have you know that a very prestigious Venture Capital firm is in the process of giving me investment. Six figures. One of its senior partners, a Frenchman no less, said and I quote: zis is potentially ze future of social media. Not my words Ram. His words.'

'Nice.'

'At which point I would like to tell you the story of a little known street artist called David Choe. Do you know who that is?'

'Yes.'

'David Choe is the man who decorated the original offices of Facebook and chose to be paid in stock rather than... '

'I just said I know who Dave Choe is.'

'Well then you know that when Facebook went public, Dave Choe cashed in to the tune of $200 million. Which is real money mate. Real, real money. And I'm offering much more than that. The number of shares they gave Choe was, like, minimal, whereas what I'm talking about is signing over, to you, a full 1% of the equity in Blank. Let's imagine that I one day become as big as Facebook, which currently has a market cap of just over $530 billion, that would leave you, Ram, with a casual $53 billion.'

'$5.3 billion. $53 billion would be ten percent.'

'Okay, still: $5.3 billion. All yours, and for the equivalent of a paint job.'

Ram closed his eyes, imagining his father the endocrinologist, imagining his grandfather in Calcutta, all of them together imagining the sum of $5.3 billion. He thought about his miserable apartment above

Paradise. He thought about Tring. For $5.3 billion he could buy the place, perhaps the whole county of Hertfordshire. He would make it his, force everyone else to fuck off, either up into Bedfordshire or down into this polluted shithole of a capital.

'What would I have to do?' he asked.

'Very simple. My investment is, as I said, contingent on having a user base of at least one thousand. Currently I have zero, so I'm not really in a position to go live. I will be once I have the cash of course, and then it should be pretty plain sailing.'

'Yeah but where do I come in?'

'Okay, so, what you would have to do is bring me those users.'

'How?'

'Right, this is where conceptually it gets a little bit odd, but bear with me.'

'Mm.'

'You work in a hospital.'

'I do.'

'In a hospital there are, at any one time and on a regular basis, many dead people.'

'There tend to be, yes.'

'What I would need is for you to procure me the names and email addresses of as many of those dead people as possible.'

Ram raised his eyebrows.

'I mean I've phrased that poorly, but this morning I took the liberty of obtaining some advice, and there is nothing illegal about it. The dead are not protected by any data laws, not even the GDPR, so it's fine.'

'Are you out of your mind?'

'No, no, but listen to me Ram: this is legit. This is honestly legit. You would just, I don't know, like get on the computers or whatever and print me out a list of all the dead inmates.'

'Patients.'

'Yes, all the patients who've died. Who are dead. This is already agreed with the VC guys. And legal counsel, like I said.'

'They asked you to steal the names of a thousand dead people, to pass off as users so they could invest money in you?'

'No, not... What I mean is that they want to see users. It doesn't matter who they actually are or how they interact with the app. But if people are supposedly on it then advertisers might feasibly want in, at which point my Frenchman sees the potential for it to go big. He invests, and suddenly I get a marketing budget to go out and target a proper wodge of actual users. See?'

'Yes.'

'Great, so you'll do it.'

'No. Not even if you paid me would I do it.'

'Technically I would be paying you.'

'Mate, I would lose my job.'

'Mate, check the GDPR. It stipulates that personal data relates to a living individual who can be identified. Which is to say that the protection ends at death, which is to say that what you would be doing is not illegal.'

'Never mind legal. Doctors are bound by an ethical code mate. Which as far as I'm aware does not condone pilfering the data of dead people for my lunatic friend. Who wants to create Tinder for paedos.'

'Ram, I love you like a brown brother, and I appreciate you taking me out for lunch, but this is a big mistake. You're making a big mistake. You're turning down the chance to become a billionaire, to change the world, all because of some ethical code that will very soon be obsolete. Sometimes you have to think outside the box to get things done. Imagine, right, if just because it went against his ethics, Gandhi had refused, you know, to do the things he did, to free the country of your forefathers from the colonial yoke of my forefathers.'

'The nonviolent civil disobedience.'

'Precisely, the nonviolent civil disobedience. Where would India be now, if one man had not had the bollocks to put his ethics to one side and civilly and nonviolently disobey?'

edward:gooderham

chapter:seven

Elon Musk, the space baron, hands Luke a bazooka. Never would he have imagined that such a weapon could be so light. The setting is generically Californian, the beach long and wide. The surf is breaking with a din. A salty vapour and the caresses of a breeze keep things refreshing.

A car appears, trundling through the sand before coming to a stop about a hundred metres ahead. Luke recognises this car. The old family saloon, a bottle green Ford Mondeo, two hundred thousand big ones on the clock. Vehicles like this, they quite literally do not make anymore. In the back of her, a younger Luke was chauffeured back and forth from cricket nets and cricket trials and cricket games. With her he has travelled the length and breadth of Albion, to the Norfolk and Pembrokeshire coasts, up peaks and down dales, north as far as the Highlands and south beyond Somerset. She even entered Liverpool, this elderly runaround, and emerged unscathed.

She has been a fantastic servant, but her time has come. She is diesel and the future is not. Two henchmen get out and exeunt, stage right.

'Just this silver button, yeah? There's no like safety or whatever?'

'Luke. Man did not make it to Mars with safety catches.'

Luke pulls down the smart visor on his smart helmet. The car is in his smart sights now, and the smart crosshairs lock straight onto the petrol flap, the petrol flap whose orientation was responsible for that whopping row between his parents, in an Esso forecourt on the outskirts of Hitchin.

'Blow her to smithereens buddy.'

The whoosh is spectacular. A shaft of silvery smoke traces a straight line towards the boot, then up she goes, up in a satisfying cauliflower of flame. The henchmen reappear to extinguish the fire and dispose of the wreckage responsibly.

'Walk with me Luke,' says Musk. 'Actually no, let's take the quad.'

'Are quadbikes not notorious gas guzzlers?'

'Not this one. Fully solar. Three of these mothers are on their way to Saturn as we speak, so we'll see how that goes. I've also sent a reinforced fleet to Cuba, to help with the hurricane detritus, but January is a month of essentially total cloud cover over there, so it may be a while before we see any impact.'

Luke, riding pillion, goes with his instincts and puts his arms around Musk, feeling an enormous sense of wellbeing as they rampage across the sand. A woman appears ahead. She wears a crimson swimsuit cut radically high, the kind that elongates the silhouette, exposing maximum thigh and tolerating not a single pube. She looks tremendous. Musk brings the vehicle to a complete stop before her, cutting the engine to save energy.

'Emily Ratajkowski,' says Luke. 'I'm a huge fan.'

'Hi Luke. That really is a coincidence because I've long been wanting to meet you. I think you're nothing less than a pioneer. Your app has revolutionized both my social and professional life. And contrary to what some say I think your nose really suits your face. What are you guys up to?'

'Elon and I were just blowing up my parents' Ford Mondeo.'

'That sounds awesome. Would you like to join me for a juice?'

The two males confer and agree, leaving the quadbike there and following Emily towards a rundown shack. Luke turns to Elon Musk and picks up their earlier discussion about the nature of reality.

'So to get back to your theory: you believe it's possible that we are living in an entirely simulated universe?'

'More than possible, Luke. In fact, if I can turn that around on you, I would argue that the prospect we are not is... well, it's as good as impossible. Allow me to explain.'

'Please.'

They sit on bamboo stools around a painted oil drum, under a thatched roof. A pint of green juice appears before each of them, and Luke watches beads of condensation trickle steadily down his glass.

'If we start from the basic concept of the Fermi Paradox... '

'May I just confirm that I have properly understood the Fermi Paradox?' interjects Emily.

'By all means,' says Musk.

'What we are saying is that there are billions of stars with a similar nature to that of our Sun, many of which are billions of years older. In all probability, orbiting around some of these stars will be planets like our

77

own, and if the Earth is in any way typical, many of those planets will have developed intelligent life.'

'Correct so far,' says Musk.

'So we should imagine that some of these civilizations have developed interstellar travel, as you yourself Elon are investigating now, for us. And even at the relatively slow pace that you and your peers currently envisage, the Milky Way could be completely traversed in a few million years. Which begs the unanswerable question: why have we not already been visited by an extraterrestrial life form?'

'Well done,' says Luke. 'I reckon that was bloody well summarized.'

Emily smiles at him and he takes a gulp of juice.

'So if we start from that basic paradox,' continues Musk, 'Let us assume that we have already been visited, long before we even existed. Not only did those extraterrestrials create our conditions for life, but they continue to set its parameters.'

'Aliens as God,' says Emily.

'Precisely. But there is another possibility, one that I prefer, which is that some very advanced future civilization – us but in however many thousand years – has developed the ability to perfectly simulate the past.'

'And by the past,' says Emily, 'You mean our present.'

'As well as all the other previous presents that now constitute our past. Which is to say that the totality of human life and history have been one gigantic virtual reality experience.'

'Intriguing,' says Luke.

'And as good as certain. When you think about the current pace of change, the difference between computer games, say, fifty years ago and computer games today, it becomes almost impossible to think that in a number of centuries there will not exist the capability to create an entirely fake you, an entirely fake me, an entirely fake Emily.'

'It would have to be quite a machine to engineer something as flawless as Emily.'

Laughter and smiles, some blushing, then a cool sip for Luke.

'Which it would be though Luke,' says Musk, serious again. 'Which it would be. If you assume any rate of improvement at all, when you think what the last twenty years alone have brought, surely in X number of years games will have become indistinguishable from life. Utterly indistinguishable. And even if that trajectory of progress drops by a thousand percent from what it's at now, it should still only take a few millennia at the most, and that is a relative speck on the evolutionary scale. The conclusion therefore has to be that the chances of this, here and now, being base reality... Well, they are about a billion to one.'

'You make a convincing argument Elon. I'll give you that.'

'Luke could you rub some cream into my back?'

'Sure.'

Luke takes another swill of juice and gets to work with a little factor thirty number, starting with a few rounds of the shoulders. Emily closes her eyes and rolls the blades with him.

'Mmm,' she says.

'What I would like to know though, Elon,' says Luke, 'Is whether I should be picturing a type of supreme being, one machine, or billions of more minor sort of video game players, as it were. Who or what is controlling us? I would love to get your take on that as well Emily.'

'It's the right question,' says Musk. 'And I must admit I don't know.'

'Down the sides as well please Luke. Yes, there, above the ribcage.'

'I tend,' continues Musk, 'To lean towards the billions of mini gods. But that's just a hunch.'

'And to simulate, you know, the smell of the lotion on Emily's skin, the warmth of that skin and the refreshment of our juices, the throttle of your quad – all of that must require an almost preposterous amount of data, right? So where are these little gimps storing it all?'

'You're quite right,' says Emily, rounding her back. 'And in fact, I would bet good bitcoin that in the whole known universe there aren't even the requisite number of particles that it would take for a simulation of that size. Besides, your hands feel so good they simply have to be real.'

She turns, he laughs, Musk strokes his chin.

'Yes, well, you've got me there. Anyway, I don't know about you guys, but I could definitely be tempted to a quick bit of kiteboarding. Thoughts?'

'I'm game,' says Luke.

'Okay but not too long,' says Emily. 'Actually there's this documentary about puffins which is supposed to be excellent, and I was wondering Luke if you might like to come back to my place afterwards and watch it with me.'

'With great pleasure,' says Luke.

He downs the rest of his juice, feeling the liquid run through him. They stroll towards the water. Conveniently, here are their boards and wetsuits. Luke helps Emily into hers and she zips him up from behind, complimenting him on how his buttocks really fill out the neoprene seat. The water is cold, surprisingly so. Luke decides that wetting himself is the way to go – warm things up a bit. He paddles away from Emily, and suddenly Musk is up and away, gone with a gust of wind.

'Babe,' says Emily Ratajkowski. 'Can you just give me a push up onto the board. I can't quite... '

Luke turns and sees the back of Emily. She is bent over her board, bottom in the air. She really does appear to need his help. But Luke can feel the piss coming now, rolling towards its exit. The process has begun and there can be no reversal.

'Yep, I'll be there in a jiffy, I've just... '

Ugh, this is going to be the greatest wee of all time, a real belter, but for some reason it refuses to come, and Luke, for the life of him, cannot figure out why.

He wakes just in time, jumping out of bed, clattering into his bedside table, rebounding off the wall, finally getting through the door. From here it is seven or eight steps to the toilet but he covers them in three big bounds, fumbling for the light switch while bending his knees and rocking his hips back and forth. The bulb is still flickering into life as he lifts the loo seat, quivers running from his toes right up to his neck.

'God, Jesus, fuckery, ughhh,' says Luke, his face creasing into grimace. The light is on, but in freeing himself from his boxers he realises he is halfway hard. With the contents of what feel like all the bladders about to pour forth, he troubleshoots, dipping into a curtsey and adjusting his swollen nozzle. Out of him, excruciatingly and unexpectedly, spurt two separate trajectories of piss. The dominant one careers across the void and splatters into the underside of the seat. A more languid parabola drops off in tributary towards the floor. He tries to hold it in, charlestoning on the spot, dipping and bobbing, splashing urine on his walls and into the sink. The idea comes to try and interrupt the flow for long enough to sit, but that takes an unholy amount of restraint, and inevitably the door gets sprayed. Finally perched above the cold porcelain of the seatless bowl, there is still the matter of trying to periscope down, and soon he is leaning forward a full ninety degrees, forehead almost touching a mercifully unbepissed patch of linoleum.

It ends and Luke stands up to take stock. He remembers now, remembers returning home from his business lunch with Ram. There was the bottle of wine, the pot of chamomile tea. Feeling rather woozy, he decided to take to his bed, and here horniness hit him hard. Having chosen not to shower he still smelled richly of sex. There were traces of Julie on his fingers, and the showreel of their exploits remained vivid and detailed. It was an explosive wank, over very quickly, and Luke then swooned into siesta, leaving his pee passage packed with a polyfilla of cementing semen.

He is not friends with Elon Musk. Emily Ratajkowski was not being coquettish with him. But the dreamscape was so flush with specifics this time. He remembers quite clearly the sun cream bottle: its logo, the factor, the splurge and splooge of it splatting into his hand.

Luke begins the cleanup, making mittens of bog roll and windmilling his way around the bathroom, wiping at the wet patches. By the time things are just about acceptable from a sanitary perspective, he feels mere minutes away from becoming irreversibly hypothermic. He retreats to his bedroom and shrouds himself in duvet, lying rigid as an icicle and allowing his teeth to chatter. The toggage feels inadequate – has felt so ever since he turned off his radiators to save money. He decides he needs layers, and with his arms swaddled across his chest, he moves around the room gathering clothes. Two pairs of tracksuit bottoms, three socks only, a denim shirt, one hoody, his towelled dressing gown.

Back in bed, his spasmodic shivering eases into a more gentle tremble. Never in his life, not even when he bungee jumped off a bridge and into a ravine in New Zealand, has he been so totally awake. He reaches for his phone, which lays charged on top his Steve Jobs biography, a fixture of his bedside table. 147 unread messages.

Luke reads through his correspondence, engulfed in a personal halo of white light. Aha, classic, an absolute belter of a video has been shared on one of his six Lads Groups: some chav receiving a metal chair in the face. He forwards it to the other five. In another, a friend is being sort of mocked but basically worshipped, for having rimmed a stripper while in Vilnius. Luke reads the words chowing on her fartbox and snorts with laughter. He knows though that one day all this monkey business will have to stop; there will be the share price to think about.

More messages, including from his mother, including from his uncle, but Luke resolves to review them all later, more in the mood for visual stimulation. He opens Instagram and scrolls and clicks to like, scrolls and clicks to like, scrolls and clicks to like. His focus blurs and clears, blurs and clears, blurs and clears. Down and down and further he goes down, as if something might miraculously emerge from these metres and metres of pixel, something powerful enough to pick him up and carry him back to that Californian beach. His rhythm is interrupted as he pauses for a timelapse: four men building a pizza oven. Oh and here is Emily now, sitting up in bed with the sheets pulled over her nipples. Not even a goose pimple of areola will yield to his mighty zoom, and to think that just a short while ago under that thatched roof his fingers were sidewinding those babies, and now – but no, it was not real, none of it was real, and how annoyingly predictable when an erection begins to clamour for its freedom from underneath his two tracksuit bottoms and the belted robe.

It will not be denied, so out it comes. But his phone is still in his other hand, and a newsflash pops up to say that dozens of Syrian children are dead. His boner is instantly pacified, and he returns to the messages. Lots has been written on his chat *Village App Generator (VAG)*. Once a week this group of likeminded guys meets at the pavilion in Victoria Park, where they discuss innovation and bounce ideas off each other. Andy is being feted by the gang for having secured Series A funding for his waterproof rucksack startup. Luke is happy for him, sort of. Nick has apparently won a place in the most prestigious incubator in London, and for his piece of shit sports app. Not even sports – all it lets you do is find people in the same pub who want to play darts or snooker. Blank spaffs on that, absolutely spaffs all over it. Blank can tell you if anybody wants to play darts *who is also* single, or who speaks Hungarian, or who likes Radiohead, whatever. Blank is in another league, yet it was rejected by the very same incubator.

Mate, that, is awesome, types Luke. *Confetti emoji, confetti emoji, party popper emoji, party popper emoji, money with wings emoji, money bags emoji, money in the eyes and money in the mouth emoji.* Luke turns his phone over and thinks about how much of an arsehole Nick is, how unfair it is that he suddenly looks set to make it, and with an idea of such staggering mediocrity.

Then, he sees. The brightness of his screen is casting the bedside table in a weak glow, illuminating the pensive and hawkish face of Steve Jobs. In an instant, Luke remembers the italicized words of his idol: *Sometimes life hits you in the head with a brick, but do not lose faith.* He looks at Jobs and vows not to, not even if he is hit in the head by a hundred Nicks. How many must Jobs have seen off in his time, and not by sitting around wishing they would die. By working harder, going further, being better.

Luke springs out of bed. He will spend the rest of the night pacing around the living room, creating the backbone of what will one day become the vital chapter in his own biography. *Turning Point*, or perhaps *Forgotten Rivals of VAG*. It is very, very cold outside the bedroom though. Luke finds his green bobble hat by the front door, pulling it down over his ears before embarking on his thinkpace, hands linked behind him. Partway through his third circuit, he deviates back towards the hallway and finds a scarf, wanging it around his neck to keep out the draught. It clashes with the hat and the vermilion trackies, but those do at least jive nicely with the yellow robe, and in any event: greatness has no dresscode.

Ram, the absolute bastard. Not that his qualms have forced Luke to query whether his plan is legitimate. If anything such resistance has filled Luke with even more chutzpah, because even the very biggest names, even Jobs and Zuckerberg began with niggling doubts as to whether their next move might wind them up in court. Success is not the result of spontaneous combustion; you have to set yourself on fire.

When Luke left Julie this morning, it was with *Dead Souls*. She had forgotten all about it, but he had most certainly not, and when he jogged her memory over coffee, she looked at him in surprise and then sweetly. It was a look that said: you can stop pretending to like books now that your tongue has been on and around my vagina.

But nothing about his request was an act. If her description of the plot had been even halfway accurate, he needed that book. When he got home he made himself a mahoosive mug of tea and devoured the thing, cover to cover, which is to say he read the first seven pages and the last page, before abandoning all efforts and turning to Wikipedia. Seriously though, it was unreadable. There was no way to discern what was happening, if anything was indeed happening. The names were a bad joke; each character had about seven. Until this morning, Luke has always looked on novels and readers of them as harmless relics. But after giving this baby a whirl, he wonders whether those culture vultures, the sort you see in the news saying only literature can save us, are not in fact dangerous mentalists.

He googled Gogol and was confronted by dozens of articles claiming that *Dead Souls* spoke to our moment, that it spoke to all moments, to the past and the present and the future. These were not even teenage YouTubers, rambling at their bedroom desks. These were academics writing for supposedly respectable publications. No wonder experts were on the way out. Luke scrolled down perhaps a mile of guff about the artistic achievement, trying to glean as much as he possibly could about the plot.

Which, to be fair, was magnificent. Pretty much as Julie had described it. The main character, Chichikov, shakes things up by arriving in a small Russian town and proposing to purchase its numerous dead serfs. They still count as property on paper, and are therefore useful in helping him achieve his mostly admirable final objectives. Chichikov intends to leverage them, thereby acquiring funds for his own estate. He charms his way into the houses of local landowners and pitches them cold. He encounters many obstacles but is always resourceful, and to Luke he embodies the great founder spirit.

Almost immediately he had the idea of approaching Ram. Hospitals were basically bottomless pits of unmined data. All Luke needed was a list of a thousand dead people and their email addresses. He would then claim they were Blank users and go back to Vince at Picpus. Nobody would ask any more questions, and he would get his injection of cash.

Ram was an old friend, a good friend, he was poor, and so Luke fancied his chances of persuading him this would be worth his while. Luke insisted on lunch and won out in the end. He spent the next few hours honing his proposal, ironing out his spiel, and by the time he turned up at the restaurant he had convinced himself that it was foolproof.

Ram, unfortunately, was a fool. People refused Chichikov for a number of reasons, but in his detailed reading of everything around the book, in his reading of everything except the book itself, Luke could find no evidence of anybody opposing on ethical grounds. Some of the characters spurned Chichikov because they were too greedy. Some because they are too corrupt. Some because they were too paranoid. But not a single one turned him down because his proposal struck them as not very nice. Ram is obviously adamant on being a fanny. So how to gerrymander the required number of users without his help?

edward:gooderham

chapter:eight

Michael knows about pissing the bed. Back in the day he used to wake up soaked, run tell his mum, watch her change the sheets, then fall asleep and piss it all over again. He still remembers the smell, knows a bedwetter when he sees one, and this wasteman is the very definition. Hackney is home to some strange individuals, but never has Michael seen anybody quite like this.

The address was a short cycle from the chip shop on Well Street. He rung the bell and suddenly standing there in front of him was the Michelin Man, swaddled in the colours of Ghana. It is colder in this flat than it was outside, colder than the freezer room at Subway. Reeks of piss too – the robe this buffoon is wearing even looks like piss. He takes the bag of food, says okay cheers mate thanks bye, and swings the door shut.

He unlocks his mountain bike, a blue Pinnacle. Just last week, a policeman walked up and asked if it was stolen. Michael shook his head and the cunt laughed, said he was joking. Feds and their funny fucking jokes. That hilarious routine stop and search. Wonder when they last pulled that one on a white delivery rider. Oh yeah man, guilty as charged, silly me for choosing this silver jacket and glow in the dark backpack to run my guns and drugs round East London.

He checks his phone and accepts a job for the Turkish wrap place near home. When Michael was a boy there was no such thing as a Turkish wrap place. Kebab shops there were plenty, but none would have had the audacity to brand themselves as Turkish or their food as wraps. Some things stayed the same, though. The church was still there, St. James, where his mum still went every Sunday. The church where he had been baptised, confirmed, and forced to go for years. The Clapton Arms was still there, even if the punters who frequented it had mellowed, and the simple fact of being black was no longer enough to get you glassed.

Baden Powell Primary was still there, where Michael had learned to read and write. Where he had first had it drummed into him that black meant inferior. Of course nobody told him so, except the thugs outside the Clapton Arms. No teacher stood him up and said Michael you are a coon, and therefore count for nothing. But years later, when he googled the man who his school had been named after, a man who presumably radiated the values of this society Michael was supposed to be part of, he encountered a racist imperialist whose favourite book was *Mein Kampf*. To have a school named after you, many schools in fact, and statues built in your honour, it helped to write things like this:

The stupid inertness of the puzzled negro is duller than that of an ox; a dog would grasp your meaning in one half the time. Men and brothers! They may be brothers, but they are certainly not men.

Baden Powell, Michael also learned, had been part of the expeditionary force that pitched up on the Gold Coast of Africa with machine guns, turning his ancestors into immigrants. So to win the accolades in Britain you apparently had to be one of the baddest motherfuckers in history, meanwhile the Prime Minister was bollocking Radio 1 because rap encouraged teenagers to carry knives.

Not that Michael cared about any of this back when he was at primary school. He had other things to worry about. Pissing the bed, for a start. Being hungry. Still today he goes to sleep with a can of Sprite beside his bed, scarred by all those nights when he woke up not because of the piss, but because of the angry hole in his stomach. We need a sugar tax, lol. Tell that to the kids doing what he used to do, training for a few hours in the freezing cold, then smashing a bag of Haribo on the bus back home, just to get enough calories to keep them from fainting. Hike up the price on sweets, hike up the price on drinks. Hike up the price on the only things they can actually afford. Let them eat Turkish wraps.

Michael enters the restaurant. If it was summer he would have cotched outside. He would have sat on a bench by Clapton Pond, waiting there until the order was ready. Not in this weather though. He nods at the manager and stands in the doorway. The walls are tiled. The plumbing and the wiring is exposed. The bar and the tables are made from compressed wood chip. The food is served on white enamel plates with a blue rim. Michael looks at the menu. He earns seven pounds an hour, plus one pound per drop, plus tips, which average out at about zero point zero. In a very good hour he could earn enough to buy himself a veggie special here. Charcoal grilled aubergines, mixed peppers, garlic, onions, tomato, and halloumi. Probably a net deficit of calories. Two very good hours and he could afford a mixed grill with rice and salad. If he worked all night he could bring his mum for dinner.

People are looking at him uneasily. They would prefer him to wait outside. If it was a little bit warmer the manager would probably insist on it. Not because he is black, but because he is a delivery boy. No hip restaurant wants to accept that its job is as simple as feeding the hungry. No hip diner wants to accept that the establishment they have chosen exists principally to make money. They come for the ethos, for the vibe. Deliveries are just revenue, an ugly and unfortunate sideshow they would prefer not to see, like the slaughtering of their lamb.

Michael starts a game of Candy Crush. Level 2745 he needs to get to, but then a waiter thrusts the bag of food in his face and says alright mate cheers bye. The address is ten minutes away in Walthamstow, past the Lea Bridge Roundabout, where at any one time a minimum of six bus drivers are all trying their absolute hardest to turn a cyclist into roadkill. When he was younger the game used to be running through the traffic, from the church to the island in the middle, from the island to the mosque and then back again. That was before Candy Crush.

Emerging unscathed, he gasses it along the Lea Bridge Road, turns left at the big crossroads, and just after Walthamstow Central makes a right. Continuing straight would take him to Wadham Lodge Sports Ground, where he and fam started out playing football. That was on Kitchener Road, incidentally. Not named after the Trinidadian calypso singer Lord Kitchener, but the Field Marshall whose face graced that famous old recruitment poster. *Your country needs YOU.*

Michael was four when he first kicked a ball. By the time he was eight he was better than his older brother George, better than kids who were five years his senior. Better because he was bigger, stronger, faster, more determined. Better even though his mum bought boots two sizes too big, so he would stop outgrowing them so quickly. The only thing that mattered was football. Outside of school he could usually be found either playing or watching it. He was and will forever be a Spurs fan. Back then, his favourite player was Tom Huddlestone. He could play in defence, he could play in midfield, he could pass, he could score. Loved a tackle and always looked composed on the ball.

Not many magazines came with posters of Tom Huddlestone stapled into the middle, nor would Michael have had the money to buy them, but somehow the bedroom ended up plastered with his image. Huddlestone in ten different poses and with ten different hairstyles, but always in a Spurs shirt. He was the player that Michael modelled his game on, and it obviously worked, because at nine Michael was scouted and signed by the Tottenham Academy. A year later he actually met Tom Huddlestone, who congratulated him on a solid midfield performance, posed with him for a picture, and when Michael got home he sat on his bed and cried.

He arrives at the delivery address in Milton Road, a redbrick semi with a tiny garden out front. Inside its big bay window are chunky white shutters. Michael has not even had the chance to open the painted gate before the guy is outside, guarding the porch like a pooch. He wonders whether he will ever turn up somewhere and be invited in. Okay cheers mate thanks bye have a good one, says this guy here in the real world.

Fucking freezing it is. Michael has a hat and a hood and a snood, but they are not enough. His gloves are the pathetically thin sort foreign players wear when they come to the Premiership. And whatever warmth they might have retained evaporates each time he removes them to check his phone for job details or directions. At the end of every shift, when he gets back home, he fills a mug with hot water and sits with his hands cupped round it until something resembling feeling returns. By the end of each winter he is a shambles. Skin shot to shit, chapped lips, bad knee aching permanently.

He takes a job at a pizza place back by his old school in Homerton. He goes back the way he came, then all the way up Chatsworth running reds. The restaurant is called Venerdi. It was just an abandoned pub back when Michael was at secondary school. Posh now. He goes inside and the waitress says something to him, but with headphones he cannot hear. He takes them out.

'Sorry?'

'Buona sera.'

He shows her the order on his screen.

'Wait here,' she says.

The warmth is magnificent. Michael puts his headphones back in, closes his eyes, listens to some music. Skepta, *Madness*.

His old school is just the other side of the hospital. The City Academy, on Homerton Row. This was not a place where Michael thrived. Which is not to say it was a bad school, or that Michael was a dunce. In fact it was an excellent school, and he started out as a bright student. He enjoyed and was good at maths. He enjoyed and was decent at geography. Neither chemistry nor physics posed him any problems. But football started taking priority.

'Okay grazie ciao,' says the waitress, handing him four pizzas.

They are going just around the corner. Down Link Street, under the railway arches. Michael decides to go the long way, looping round Homerton Overground. He avoids that underpass at night, after what happened to Israel. They were not mates exactly, but they had played football together, and Michael knew people on the estate he was from. He was a Gooner, Israel, but he was alright. Cycling home one night, minding his own business, then two guys come at him with hunting knives, leave him to bleed to death under the bridge. Eighteen, standard.

Michael locks up his bike outside a pricey development. The Textile Building. He buzzes the delivery address, then somebody comes on the intercom and says third floor and opens. In the lift Michael looks at himself in the mirror, moving his head from side to side, glaring. He walks all the way along a landing, his tracksuit chafing against itself. The door is ajar. He knocks and a female voice shouts to come on through. He follows the corridor down, past about twenty pairs of insane creps. Black Air Prestos, Black Cement Jordans. Three different colour combos of the Skylon 2. Magic Stick Air Force Ones, Pharrell Adidas Blank Canvases, Bape Bapestas, even a pair of murdered out Balenciaga Triples. Yeezy 700 Wave Runners. Creps to the tune of about ten grand.

Michael walks slowly through, as if dazed, and eventually the flat opens out into a large living room. Exposed brick walls, huge warehouse windows. Kendrick in the background, rapping over *1 Train*, and in the middle of the room a dozen white folks are sitting around a coffee table, playing scrabble. One girl has arranged the letters on her rail to spell SCROTAM. Empty wine bottles everywhere. There is coke. It is a Thursday. Technically it is Friday morning, but either way this is not the weekend. A guy gets up, takes the pizzas off Michael and chaperones him to the door. Michael points at the Wave Runners, says nice creps, and the guy says yeah, then okay cheers mate have a good one, before closing the door.

Michael wonders what these people do to make money. He wonders how it is that only twenty metres from where Israel got slashed up, these wastemen are sipping wine and playing scrabble. Until now, he would never have imagined that anybody in Hackney had played scrabble, ever. This used to be hood. It still is hood. Yet here are this lot, softer than a Bake Off dozen.

He decides to do one more delivery, then go home and kip. The order is to be collected from somewhere called Temple of Seitan, just around the corner on Morning Lane, and dropped on the other side of Kingsland in Dalston. The restaurant turns out to be a vegan fried chicken shop. Fried chicken, that is also vegan. Two of the men waiting in line are wearing little woollen watch caps, the kind that look like yarmulkes and keep the head about as warm. Michael pushes his way in and announces himself. The vegan chicken is too much for him to handle, and he leans against the wall like a schoolboy, giggling at the fact that nobody here is giggling. A sign explains that the burgers and nuggets are all made from a type of wheat protein that has a very similar texture to chicken. Michael discretely snaps the sign, then moves the camera to his face, which pulls a puzzled pose. He spends the rest of his wait editing the footage, superimposing onto his own nose the beak of a chicken, and writing beg beg beg beg across the screen. He sends the snap to everyone he knows, collects the food, and leaves. The night has at least yielded some comedy.

He canes it along Graham Road and crosses Kingsland. If he takes a right there and keeps going straight he ends up at the Lane, home of the pride of North London. Instead he turns left, then right into the backstreets of De Beauvoir. Plush round here, except for the estate itself, which is bad bad bad bad news. Lawton Road though, where he is dropping off his vegan payload, is nice. The period houses stretch out in uniform, rectangular blocks. The trees are all dead but the gardens are looked after. He jogs up the steps of number 55 and gives the knocker a rat a tat tat. He waits for somebody to come to the door, breathing out, watching it plume like smoke into the night.

'Hi,' says the girl who opens. Buff she is.

'Yeah hi,' says Michael. 'Got your food yeah.'

'Yeah amazing thanks,' says the girl.

'So what, the chicken is like vegan yeah? That is mad.'

She smiles.

'Straight up mad, nahmean? You are some very strange individual, a nice black girl like you eating vegan chicken. You oughtta be ashamed of yourself, namsayin?'

All of this he says with a smile, shuffling from side to side on the spot.

'I know,' laughs the girl. 'I know.'

'Yo, you got a name?'

'Ola,'

'Michael. Nice to meet you Ola.'

'Nice to meet you too. Okay thanks have a good one Michael, bye.'

She moves to shut the door, then hesitates and opens it wide again.

'Michael wait,' she says.

He had set off down the steps, but now he stops and turns around.

'Yeah, wassup?'

'Do you… You don't have any weed you could sell us do you?'

'Ha, jokes. Sorry, ain't no roadman. Good boy innit.'

'Of course, sure, of course.'

'Yo, you got snapchat?'

'Yeah,' she says. 'Ola Akerele. Add me.'

'Maybe I will.'

She thanks him again and shuts the door. Weed, lol, fml. There was Michael, sure she was about to ask him up to her bedroom, and all she wants is weed. Man, she was buff though. Two more girls now walk straight past him, through the gate and up the steps without so much as a hello.

Michael sets off in the direction of home, along Dalston Lane towards Hackney Central. He passes Mare Street again, like he has ten or twenty times a day since the summer of 2011. Since the riots. The big bad riots. Michael was fifteen at the time. His brother was eighteen and had just sat his A Levels. Unlike Michael, George was still bothered about school. Two weeks later, two weeks too late, he would receive his results: two As and one B. Fam was a veritable genius, but he was so angry. An angry, angry individual. Angry because the police got away with murder. Angry because the politicians got away with murder. Angry because the bankers got away with murder. Angry because there was never enough money, never enough food on the table. Angry because his mum was working like a dog, being treated like a dog. Angry because his dad was a cunt, because he ran out on them, like a cunt. Angry about austerity. Angry about spending cuts, about funding cuts, about all sorts of cuts. Angry about tuition fees. Angry because as well as he did in his exams, he knew it would never be good enough to win a grant. Angry because he told himself he would never get to go to university, angry because he had worked hard and he wanted to work hard but it all meant shit. Angry because just down the road they were spending ten fucking billion on the Olympics, but nobody would ever give him the twenty grand he needed to study. Angry because he would end up spending his life behind the till at a KFC. Angry because he was poor. Angry because it was unfair.

Their mum was at work when it reached their ends. Michael tried to persuade George to stay upstairs, in the flat. He had a match the next day, a match that would be cancelled, but he knew that nothing good could come of that mess. George refused to listen. He went down into the street. The police had shields. They started getting rowdy, started shoving. George ended up getting pushed, thought fuck this, and joined a mob of about two hundred heading up Mare Street. Just because.

Everywhere not shuttered got run into. George followed a gang of looters into an Iceland, and without really knowing why, he took two frozen chickens. Two frozen actual chickens, not vegan ones.

Their mum nearly threw him out the window when she found out. For the next two months nothing happened, but all anybody was talking about in the papers and on the telly were the riots and what had caused them. Then one day Michael went into the McDonalds by Hackney Central and saw his brother staring back at him, his mugshot part of a collage of fifteen different wanted. *Your country needs YOU.* Somebody obviously grassed him up, because two weeks later they came knocking, walked him out the flat in handcuffs. He copped five different charges, four of which were a case of mistaken identity. They also claimed he was going around armed, as in with a weapon, rather than with frozen fowl.

The judges sat in session round the clock. To send a message they rejected all reasonable sentencing guidelines, handing out two thousand convictions amounting to two thousand years of jail time. Which was two thousand more convictions and two thousand more years than the same judges had just a few years earlier doled out to bankers, for driving the world economy into a brick wall. Teenagers did actual time for stealing multibags of crisps. One got six months for jacking a bottle of water. For milk, another got twelve. A student got ten months – a criminal record and three hundred days of prison – for stealing mismatching shoes. And George Ansah got two years, for a couple of offences he did not commit, as well as one which he most certainly did: the theft of frozen poultry worth thirteen pounds.

Sentencing him, the judge decided to quote a great and exemplary Briton:

You should remember that being one fellow among many others, you are like one brick among many others in the wall of a house. If you are discontented with your place or your neighbors or if you are a rotten brick, you are no good to the wall. You are rather a danger. If the bricks get quarrelling among themselves the wall is liable to split and the whole house to fall.

Baden Powell, blud.

chapter:nine

Ola closed the door, leaned against it, put her head in the hand not holding a bag of fried vegan chicken fillets. She replayed the scene in her mind, hopelessly unable to change her lines or its outcome. Being told by a black person that she was not a real black person, all because she had ordered some chicken that was not real chicken. To make matters worse, she had behaved like a stereotypical white person, stereotypically suggesting he might have had some weed to sell.

The doorbell trilled. She turned around and opened.

'Hi,' said Ola.

'Hi. Julie.'

'Oh hi, yeah,' said Ola.

'This is my friend, Lucy.'

'Hi,' said Lucy.

'Yeah hi, hi,' said Ola.

'We're really late,' said Julie. 'I'm so sorry.'

'No, not at all. We just got some food in.'

Jazz was oozing down the corridor. Ola turned and led the girls down it, into a gigantic room stretching from the front to the back of the house. In the rear was a dining area, where a few people sat around a long oak table, littered with tobacco packets and wine bottles. Giving out onto the street was the living space, where everyone else was gathered on sofas and armchairs.

On the near wall was a colourful canvas, and the far wall was shelved from floor to ceiling, racked with hundreds and hundreds of books as well as photographs and other oddities. Everything was arranged in a manner that suggested carelessness, whereas in fact much thought had gone into the arrangement of the Japanese ceramics, the ginormous exhibition albums. With books, to create the right blend of irony and hauteur, it was necessary to pull some truly radical shit, like sticking Toni Morrison between Plato and the first edition Harry Potters, alongside a framed photo of somebody taking a photo of Princess Diana.

'Diana right there is one of my flatmates,' said Ola. 'And that's Rosie. This is her place.'

'So just the three of you,' said Julie.

'Yeah, just the three of us.'

'I mean it's amazing,' said Julie.

'Yeah pretty cool, right? Rosie's dad bought it back in the nineties. For like, nothing.'

Lucy and Julie were introduced to the room. Ola poured them both a glass of wine and spread food out in the middle of the table.

'Is that a Chris Ofili?' asked Lucy, gesturing towards the canvas.

'Oh my god yes,' said Ola. 'You like him?'

'He's interesting yeah,' said Lucy.

'So Chris, crazily, is one of Rosie's godfathers.'

'Wow,' said Julie. 'What do her parents do?'

'So yeah Rosie's dad is now head of Harper Collins. We all read English together at uni. Rosie and Diana got into publishing but I went over to the dark side,' said Ola, arching her eyebrows comically.

Lucy was beautiful. Really, really beautiful. She had this air of mystery and a whole young Lucy Liu thing going on. Ola immediately chastised herself for that thought. Just because Liu shared the same name. Just because she was the first attractive Asian that sprang to mind. It was a totally sweeping generalisation, basically the same as saying all Asians looked alike, or all black people loved chicken, or all black teenagers sold weed.

'Dig in by the way,' said Ola. 'Not sure if you're hungry but there's plenty to go around.'

'Looks really good,' said Julie.

'So I am going to shock you: that right there is not actually chicken.'

'Err,' said Julie.

'That is vegan chicken.'

'Oh my god, yes,' said Julie. 'The place on Morning Lane.'

'Exactly. Have you tasted it before? It's really, really good.'

'Yeah I love it,' said Julie. 'Lucy have you tasted this?'

'No,' said Lucy. 'Don't think so anyway.'

'Oh my god,' said Ola. 'Right, you absolutely must.'

Ola took a strip, dipped it in vegan mayonnaise, and offered it to Lucy. She guided it right to her lips, keeping a hand cupped underneath in case it dripped. Lucy could obviously think of no politer reaction than to swallow this suspect protein.

'Good, right? Just like chicken,' said Ola.

'Mmm,' said Lucy. 'Mmm, mmhmm.'

'So you went vegan?' asked Julie.

'Yeah I did yeah,' said Ola.

'How long ago? Was it hard? Is it hard?'

'Yeah like a year ago. Not that hard no. You just need… '

'But what triggered it?' asked Julie.

'I was basically already vegetarian, so… '

'But I mean was it more for health reasons or an ethical thing?'

'Both I guess,' said Ola. 'Objectively it's better for you, and I'm not like trying to convert anyone or anything, but I can't see the justification for killing a million animals a minute, not when you consider the environmental impact as well.'

'Yeah I suppose,' said Julie. 'I mean I pretty much never eat red meat anymore. But I'm not sure I could ever totally totally go without. And is it not on some level the natural way? Us as animals I mean, eating other animals.'

'Natural, yeah, maybe. But just because animals behave a certain way doesn't mean we should. Otherwise we would permanently be raping and killing, trotting up to people in the street and sniffing their arses.'

'Ha, yeah, although that basically is what men do. I think cheese is what I'd miss the most,' said Julie. 'Or milk. Which is random I know, but I do love a good glass of milk.'

'Well you've got soy milk. Soy milk is nice.'

'Yeah but… ' Julie appeared to hesitate. 'I mean, soy is like the classic example of the… I read this article arguing that it was actually quite hypocritical to criticise the dairy industry while going around drinking soy milk. You now have these monocultures popping up everywhere. Brazil, for example. Brazil is buggered because of soya.'

'Yeah but the majority of those crops are being grown to feed animals. Animals we then milk and kill.'

'Yeah I suppose. But anyway, I also think, you know, it's all very well if you're Yotam Ottolenghi, shopping in Islington, but there are about eight billion other people to feed. All their fruit and vegetables would still have to be grown in irrigated fields, sprayed with pesticides, sprayed with insecticides, then flown and shipped around the world, so… '

'Yeah, but… Anyway, there are other milks. Almond milk. I drink a basic one from Tesco, just called nut milk, which I know sounds like the grossest thing ever but is actually delicious. Have you tasted it?'

'What, almond milk?'

'No, nut milk.'

Lucy shook her head absently, Julie too.

'Anyway,' said Ola. 'It's a complicated debate and like I said, I'm not judging anyone, I just think it's the right choice for me personally.'

'Totally. I guess I'm just interested in all these different paradoxes, you know?'

'Mm,' said Ola. 'Reading your work, I definitely got the sense that you enjoy polemic.'

'Absolutely,' said Julie. 'Absolutely.'

'Would you call yourself a political writer?'

'Well political I don't know. I try. And ultimately I think even writers who think they're being apolitical, all they're really doing is just, like, reinforcing the status quo.'

'Interesting.'

'If you're not out there trying to subvert power, you're literally just reinforcing it. You're supporting the dynamic of the powerful over the weak, and in the case of what interests me, men over women.'

'Yeah no I thought there were some really powerful feminine voices there, in the pages that Anna sent me.'

'Yeah so you and Anna were at uni together, then?'

'Yeah, old mates. I need to get out to see her actually. She's so great.'

'She really is. So so great. And honestly, I can't thank you enough for agreeing to give my stuff a read.'

'I've really enjoyed it. I'm looking forward to the rest. I'm intrigued to see how the main character is going to develop.'

'Yeah, I mean I hope you'll find her interesting. There's a lot of brutality in there, but I wanted that, you know? Because I see her emancipation almost as more of a physical struggle than a mental one. A physical struggle against herself. All the conflicting expectations of her youth, the culturally inherited misogyny, all that inner dissonance. It's like this prison of Jungian ego has been built up around us, we've locked ourselves in and thrown away the key, and breaking out will take destruction and… yeah, I think violence to a certain extent.'

'Totally,' said Ola. 'And I do think writers have a duty right now, what with everything going on in the world.'

110

'A duty to what?' asked Lucy.

'To be confronting violence,' said Ola.

'Yeah,' said Julie. 'I think to shy away from it would just be a bourgeois way of saying oh no, I don't want to look at it. I don't want to accept it's there. But it is, and I wish people wouldn't just… ignore it, you know?'

'Yes,' said Ola. 'We need more truth in literature. When you see the numbers in which migrants are dying, the poverty, African Americans being shot by police, transphobia on the rise… I just think to not be talking about all this would be, like, a grave cowardice.'

'Yeah,' said Julie.

'I mean, the other day right,' said Ola. 'I watched this documentary about puffins, and… God, this is really embarrassing, but basically there is this one scene where an Icelandic guy brings down his net in this big swoop, and the puffin gets it. I remember I started crying, and I cried for about two hours straight. The barbarity of it. And I thought: this is what people need to be writing about, these are the kind of books I want to be seeing. Not that exactly, obviously, but you know what I mean.'

'Yeah,' said Julie. 'I mean I could not agree more.'

'Girls,' said Paul, a guy at the other end of the table. 'Another round of *Humiliation*. Are you playing?'

'Ugh,' said Ola. 'Fine, sure.'

'What is that? What are we playing?' asked Lucy.

Humiliation was a simple game, enjoyed around tables like these. Everybody named the most important book he or she had never read.

There was a show of hands, and for each person who had read that book: one point. The person with the most points won, but humiliated him or herself for being uncultured. Of course, you could choose a niche or untranslated novel and appear sophisticated, but the more obscure it was, the more likely you were to lose. Everything hinged on whether you preferred winning a pointless game, or retaining a pointless veneer of erudition. Most chose the latter.

Books had been done earlier in the evening, so the proposed category was theatre: plays never seen performed. Ola began by confessing she had never seen *Hedda Gabler*. Paul deemed that an Ibsenity, but it scored a mediocre four. He went next, claiming that of all the plays in all the world, the most noteworthy he had never seen performed was *The Robbers*, by Schiller. One person put their hand up and he pretended to be annoyed. The game then went around the table, and people came out with all sorts: minor or forgotten works by Beckett, *The Jew of Malta*, Calderón de la Barca, not one but two Pirandello plays. Another Paul admitted that he had never actually seen anything by Chekhov on stage, and his namesake looked at him like he had just owned up to necrophilia. Paul Two moved into the lead, with nine points. Now it came to Lucy. The atmosphere was unexpectedly tense.

'*Hamlet*,' she said. 'Never seen it. Never read it.'

Lucy downed her wine. Poor Paul looked like he had seen a ghost.

'Twelve,' he eventually said. 'Twelve people for *Hamlet*, one short of the maximum. Extraordinary scenes. How is that even possible though? Congratulations Lucy, congratulations Akosua, honestly, sincerely. Julie, you might as well not bother, because there is no way you're beating that.'

Julie nodded, put down her glass and leaned forwards:

'So, this is quite difficult actually, because I love the theatre, my parents love the theatre. I've seen a lot. So, I'm not sure if this counts, but I've been meaning to go. It's just whenever I've tried to get tickets… '

'Out with it,' said Paul.

'Fine,' said Julie. '*Hamilton.*'

The only sound was jazz – jazz that was meant to be background music.

'But… ' said Paul finally. 'It's been on stage for well over a year now. Tickets are everywhere.'

'I know,' said Julie. 'I know. But… no, I know.'

'Okay. Hands up who has seen *Hamilton.*'

All thirteen hands went up, Lucy included. Julie looked at her.

'Yeah,' said Lucy. 'With Ram.'

Everyone was silent. Akosua had been in the fourth week of the London run. Klaus knew the words to all the raps. Paul Two listened to the soundtrack while he trained for his triathlons. Rosie and Diana had seen it in New York, gone backstage and met the cast. Ola had cried during the conventionally ballady final minute of *Who Lives, Who Dies, Who Tells Your Story.* It was just so original, so necessary. It played around with the past and the present. It had rejuvenated musical theatre. It had brought the sounds of the street onto the stage. To have not seen *Hamilton* was… well, it suggested a cultural blindspot of almost planetary proportions.

Ola knew somebody needed to say something soon. She turned to Lucy and Julie, shutting out Paul and the others around the table, as if instructing them to return to their own conversations, to move on, and yes it was fucking mad to have not yet seen *Hamilton*, but they were also bound to be civil.

'So Lucy, what do you do?'

'I work at the Tate,' she said, flicking the stem of her empty wine glass.

'Oh great. And what do you do there?'

'Cultural outreach.'

'Lucy is also a writer,' said Julie.

'No… ' protested Lucy.

'Oh great, excellent,' said Ola.

She noticed that Lucy was empty. That her wine glass was empty. She reached for the bottle and gestured to her with it. Lucy nodded, Ola poured.

'So what are you working on at the moment?' asked Ola.

'Well no, honestly… '

'Lucy is being modest,' said Julie. 'She is extremely talented.'

'I bet,' said Ola. 'Please, I'd love to hear about your stuff.'

'I mean, at the moment I'm not really working on anything. To tell you the truth I'm sort of obsessed with Instagram.'

'Isn't everyone?' said Ola.

'What I mean is: I'm fascinated by people turning their lives into these daily, visual narratives. I just… I mean you probably won't agree, but I've come to the conclusion that the traditional novel… Well, I'm afraid it has zero potential to capture the imagination of a generation interacting that way.'

'I see,' said Ola. 'And you think those more visual narratives can replace it?'

'No, not replace it. But… I don't know. I just… If you think back, think about art throughout the twentieth century, right, you had all these movements, all these different artists picking up materials that could never previously have been used to make art. Plastic bottles, broken glass. All these new and different things that make up the world and our lives. I'm explaining this really badly.'

'No, not at all.'

'Well maybe Instagram can be like that. Life now… I mean you can't understand it all. It's too confusing. There's too much going on. Even just to describe one family, on one street, has become impossible. So maybe on Instagram you can just show people the sort of blades of grass that grow between the cracks. In the pavement, you know?'

'Yeah, that's a really beautiful image.'

'Maybe you can use it to show glimpses of something real, and together that can create a whole narrative, one that can speak to an audience as wide as the novel used to.'

'I'm sorry but no,' said Julie. 'Instagram is bullshit. It's total bullshit.'

'Why though?'

'Because it is. Because it's bullshit. It's just a swamp of airheaded vanity. Uninteresting people with nothing to actually say, all saying nothing of any actual interest. What is that next to the depth of a novel?'

'But Julie,' said Lucy. 'Nobody wants the depth of a novel. Not anymore.'

'Well they should.'

Ola was looking between the two girls like a tennis umpire, enjoying this immensely. It was what she had mistakenly thought every hour of every day of her life would be like, back when she had decided to become a literary agent. This was before she even knew that whole books could be written about kale, let alone that she might be the one selling them.

'And,' continued Julie, 'The absolute worst people on there are the ones who pretend to love books. They make hats out of books, they fill up empty baths with books, they pose going in or coming out of bookshops, or sat snuggled in the corner of one. They put mugs on their books, they put cats on their books, they put hedgehogs on their books, they put croissants on their books. They recreate the covers of books. They open up their books and spread them out and lie on them. That is actually a thing, opening up your books and spreading them out and lying on them. Everything is a thing, except for actually once, from time to time, just sitting down and reading a fucking book.'

People laughed, but Julie was not finished:

'Books are now just basically backdrops. Not even props, just backdrops. Are they not supposed to mean something?'

'Why do you resent Instagram so much for existing?' asked Lucy.

'I don't resent it for existing. I really don't. What I resent is that because of it, creativity now means dressing up like Jane Austen and pouring tea from a porcelain pot over a book. As opposed to actually writing one.'

'Why does it mean that though?'

'Because sixty thousand people will actively, eagerly watch you do the Jane Austen tea pouring, they will like you for it, but nobody could care less if you've done something as humdrum as just writing a novel.'

'You really think so?'

'I know so. I know so. It's just full of talentless morons, projecting a fake image of themselves to earn as much money as possible. And that person with sixty thousand followers, whoever she is, a publisher will actually approach her and ask her to write a book, even if she never had any intention of doing so, even if she has nothing to say.'

'You can't honestly be blaming publishers for wanting to sell books though,' said Ola.

'I'm not blaming them for wanting to sell books. I'm not. I'm just... ugh, I'm sorry. I just really don't like Instagram. I think a writer's job at the moment is to resist that culture, not join it.'

'Do you not think it somehow speaks to the moment?'

'Yes, no, that I can't deny,' said Julie. 'That I cannot deny. It's vain, vapid, vacuous, superficial, full of ignorance and hypocrisy, anti-intellectual, all done in bad faith, and in that way it speaks most profoundly to this moment. I mean, these are people who quite literally judge books by their covers. There's this one instapoet who has more than three million followers, right... '

'Rupi Kaur.'

'Exactly, that's her. She was being interviewed and she walked into this bookshop and saw a copy of Kafka, and she said ehhhhrmagaaaaad, this guy is like, the best.'

'So?' said Lucy. 'I like Kafka. You like Kafka.'

'Everyone likes Kafka,' said Julie. 'Except this girl was talking about the guy who designed the cover. The guy who designed the cover was the best. Her dream was to work with that designer.'

'Yeah, but think of all the people who might never have had an interest in poetry but now do thanks to her.'

'Think of all the people who once did but now don't, because of her. I don't even care whether it's good or bad. I make no judgment on the quality of her poems. What I care about is this shameless self-promotion that's… it's just everywhere.'

Julie sat back heavily.

'Mmm,' said Ola. 'It's an interesting debate. And Lucy what are the themes that interest you? What is it that you want to be discussing in your work?'

'Umm,' said Lucy. 'I guess alienation. Modern life.'

'What we are really interested in seeing at the moment are stories about what is other, you know? The stuff that has not always been talked about in literature.'

'Yeah,' said Lucy.

'Take queer narratives, for example.'

'Mm. Which have been around forever, though.'

'Yeah, but I mean growing up gay now, at the moment.'

'Well surely growing up as anyone at the moment is other.'

'I suppose you're right. I suppose you're right. But what I want are stories about roots, about place, about origins. Where are you from, by the way?'

'Guildford.'

'Oh, okay.'

'But my mother is from Laos.'

'Oh super. You see wow, bring me a story about that. Me personally I'm Nigerian, and it has just been so exciting to watch Chimamanda emerge as a global star over the past few years. Her success has said to me: I too have a story that matters, that people want to hear. Good literature, I think, should enable people to latch onto their identities. To take pride in them.'

'So you were born there?' asked Julie.

'No, I was born here actually.'

'But your parents are both Nigerian.'

'My father was, yes. Originally my mother is from Liverpool.'

chapter:ten

As I make my breakfast, Piers Morgan launches into one of his screeching political riffs. There is no more Left, he says, no more Right. Politics is no longer a line but a sphere. Those who look inwards, who reject globalisation, are pitted against those who look outwards and reap its benefits. Explain yourself Piers! Tell him to explain himself Susanna! Students might be watching this. They might put this in their essays.

By god he riles me. What a blowhard. What a terrifically pompous arse. The worst part is, I seem to need all this irritation. My day cannot begin without seeing Piers, before it even gets light outside, ask a transgender person what the difference is between they wanting to be a they and him wanting to be an elephant. I need to hear his thoughts on body image while I butter my toast. I have to hear his stance on cultural appropriation before I drink my orange juice. No cup of tea can taste the same without his eggheaded reflections on patriotism.

He finishes his sermon by mentioning the old Etonian, even if they are all old Etonians. Boris I mean. Bollocks he makes me angry, he really does. And now, in the shower, all I can think about is him, how much of a charlatan he is. My dad used to say that the lad who thieves a bag of boiled sweets grows up to be the lad who thieves a car. So it should have been obvious that Boris would sell us all down the river, way back when he slagged off Liverpool. Never trust anyone that has a bad word to say about that city. The South Yorkshire Police tried it, *The Sun* tried it, even Ringo tried it, and none of them have turned out to be anything other than rotten.

I do miss it like, the north. The people, the sense of humour. I remember when I first moved down to London, how they looked at you like you were barmy just for smiling at a stranger in the street. September 1981 that was. I was 24 and running away. I had been living at home in Bootle, working as a receptionist. That was the summer of the Toxteth riots. Watching them made me so angry, and it led to the most almighty rows with my family. I could only imagine how desperate those people must have been to react in that manner. For my father that in no way justified all the looting and violence. Oh but it did, I argued. They had been deprived of their rights! They had been discriminated against! Socially, politically, economically. Culturally. They were being intimidated and harassed, simply for being black. My mother thought they were ruining the good name of the city, which drove me mad, because obviously she was forgetting her history. All that money, all that former prestige – all of it came from the slave trade. From the basic exploitation of human beings, shackled in chains then bought and sold like cattle. A disgrace, its good name. And now this. It was the fault of the government and big business. They were the ones who had pushed these people over the edge. They were responsible for the poverty, the unemployment. Nonsense, said my brother: they were wogs, and they needed to learn how to behave themselves.

122

Things were said that were never forgotten and, given some of the choices I would subsequently make, never truly forgiven. I was desperate to leave, and London seemed like the logical place to go. I assumed it would be more open, more in touch with the world. I blamed what was happening in Toxteth on what I perceived to be the backwards provinciality of Liverpool. Like lots of people, I only learned to love where I grew up after finally getting away from it. Anyway, the idea that none of those problems could possibly exist in the capital shows just how ignorant I was, because of course they did. Toxteth blew up because it bristled on the edge of the centre. On one side of Parliament Street you had this terrible ghetto, and on the other you had the Georgian Quarter and the Cathedral. In London it was different, because the worst areas back then were far enough away that there was no need for politicians to even acknowledge their existence. We are such awful snobs in this country. We might not force people to integrate as aggressively as they do elsewhere, but only because we see everybody as so inferior that to try would be a waste of time. And the bigger the city, the easier it is to chuck the undesirables in some farflung invisible corner of it, just so Joe Bloggs can get on without having to smell their food or hear their bloody chanting. Whenever people start describing London as some shining example of tolerance, this is what they really mean. Not that they love the other, simply that they never have to see it.

I found a job as an administrative assistant at Queen Mary, and nearly forty years later here I still am, running the Alumni Engagement Directorate. Makes me feel old to say it. Basically the job is to keep former students interested in and engaged with university life, then talk them into giving us their money. Ha! Seriously though, we have to stay on the lookout for new fundraising strategies, to encourage a bit of philanthropy wherever possible. Simple as that, in a nutshell. It really has been a fantastic place to work, and I am lucky, because slowly you rise up the ranks, you know. You sort of get the feeling that your loyalty is being rewarded.

Anyway, at the start I was rooming in Bethnal Green, then after about a year I found myself a bedsit in Hackney. Amhurst Road, a rabbit hutch of a place where the heating barely worked and a mad woman lived upstairs. About a thousand a month it would probably go for these days, but back then I think it was about twenty bob. This place, where I am now on Rushmore Road, I bought for the grand total of seventeen thousand pounds. In 1988, just before Ola was born. A lot for me back then like, but I shudder to even imagine what it would sell for. Probably half a million, possibly more. Which, by the standards of our society, makes my life a roaring success.

Today, like most days, I leave home just after eight, riding the bus down to Mile End Road. Mornings are taken up with admin, emails. Reviewing funding proposals, that sort of thing. To be honest with you, these last few years have been tough. Since the rise in tuition fees everyone seems to think we have money coming out of our ears, which naturally makes them less eager to give us theirs. I took on my current role in 2013, just after the hike came into effect. Queen Mary, like almost everywhere else, decided to set at the tripled cap of nine thousand pounds a year. My feeling at the time was that most institutions wanted to resist, while worrying that lower fees would suggest lower standards.

Perhaps we should have been braver. Because most of these students now, they are emerging almost fifty thousand pounds in debt. Just staggering, staggering numbers.

Nick bloody Clegg! The Liberal Democrats rode that fees promise to their best election result ever, right into the coalition, only to renege. They could have made concessions elsewhere, but instead they chose the very thing that had mobilised the precariat. Young people who for once were actually engaging in politics, who then had to sit there and listen to the government bang on about austerity. The whole thing was a sordid attempt to turn students into consumers, to unleash market forces on the education sector – the same market forces that just a decade ago priced an entire generation out of ever owning a house, riding roughshod over their career prospects to boot. The media hardly had a difficult job persuading them that Clegg and his party were a bunch of bloody sellouts. Along came the next general election and surprise surprise, they took a pasting. Cameron was left with such a paltry majority that he had to promise his hardliners the Referendum, the Referendum that Europhiles like Clegg might actually have been quite useful in having a say in. Which I suppose he did in the end, because he showed Leavers they could tell lie after lie and get away with it.

And wait for the best bit: he has now effed off to America to work for Facebook! Head of Global Policy and Communications! Presumably they hired him because nobody else on planet earth is as good at intentionally breaking their promises then filming an apology with a straight face. If I was writing a novel, never in a million years could I have come up with such an apt metaphor for liberal democracy degrading itself entirely, then holding its bowl out to the rich and powerful. I hope for his sake he was only ever serving the public for a laugh, that he was never too emotionally invested, otherwise he may well have trouble sleeping at night, over there in his seven million dollar mansion.

Because look at the state of us. Without Clegg we might have had a respectable Labour government. Instead we ended up with ten years of the Tories and Brexit. Oh, and Jeremy Corbyn in opposition. As a lefty who came of age in the seventies, someone who has worked on a university campus for forty years, I confess to having heard my fair share of Marxist gibberish. But Jezza takes the biscuit. He just wants a fairer world, fine, but my postman wants a fairer world, and at least he grasps that his job is to deliver letters, not run the bloody country. I shudder to think what he would do to higher education if he came to power. Make everyone read *The Motorcycle Diaries*? Genuinely I shudder to think.

Then on the other side – well, that just beggars belief. Horrid little toads like Michael Gove. 'I think the people of this country have had enough of experts.' That absurd remark sums up quite nicely what his vision of Brexit will do for universities in this country. Our role in research, our participation in Erasmus programmes, our ability to recruit staff and attract students – all under threat, thanks to the likes of him. This is the man, by the way, who when he became Minister for Education decided to write a foreword to the bloody Bible, as if he was God, before spending half a million pounds of public money on sending every school a copy. Not to be trusted he was, never ever ever to be trusted.

Just down the corridor from my office is a small kitchenette. I go there and make myself a cup of tea. Michael Gove comes in useful here, because I like to squish the bag against the side of my mug as if it was his mushy, reptilian head. This is doing me good, the chance to vent. I never really get to because you have to be so bloody careful these days. Anyway, perhaps I should be grateful that by the time things properly begin to unravel I shall no longer be here. But I worry about my daughter, you know? I worry about the next generation.

Speaking of which, I have agreed to speak with a journalist, who wants to talk about the potential impact of Brexit on higher education. Lovely young man, a freelancer working on a longform piece for *The Guardian*. He is perhaps thirty, around the same age as Ola. Liberals their age get a terrible rap, and perhaps deservedly so, zigzagging around with the zeitgeist, permanently looking for a new cause to clamour about, never committing to anything. But so often when I actually meet them I come away buoyed. There is the definite sense that we have left them a broken world, a sense that I share, and I really do think a lot of them are eager to rebuild. Unfortunately far too many of their peers seem to be out for themselves – one of my colleagues says they are civically nihilist. That is what serious young folks like Luke are up against.

Very sincere he is, very honest about his own privilege. Straightaway he confesses to being a product of the private school system, which he describes by quoting that Orwell line – five years in a lukewarm bath of snobbery. He is now a committed member of the political Left, deeply concerned about the state of national education. As long as we retain this apartheid system based on class and wealth, he says, we will never make any real progress. I could not agree more. As long as middle class parents are either wealthy enough to send their children to independent schools, or shrewd enough to ensure they are in the right catchment area for the better state ones, there will still continue to be a sort of *triage* effect. Never a truer word spoken!

Academy schools, he says, began as a good idea under Labour, but now appear to be exacerbating the problem. The Tories are bringing their Free Market tomfoolery into the Education sector, and it stinks. Yes, absolutely it does, and that is absolutely what they are doing. We discuss this for a while. What Luke wants to do, in his article, is forget all the stats for a moment, put the focus back on the children, the students. He is adamant, and this is what a lot of us have wanted the media to start doing for a long time now.

Luke himself is an alumnus of Queen Mary. He tells me he graduated just before the fee hike came into effect. As lucky as he feels not to be saddled with debt, it breaks his heart to think that others might miss out on the opportunities he took for granted. He studied Marketing and Management here and has fond memories. He singles out his Innovation and Entrepreneurship tutor, Evangelos Markopolous, whose influence on philosophies of Digital Strategy he describes as nothing short of Socratic. But that world turned out not to be for him, too geared around money, and in fact the most valuable skill he acquired during his time here was the maturity to admit that to himself. University gave him confidence in his abilities, conviction to make his move into journalism.

As for effing Brexit. He just feels so betrayed. I think they all just feel so betrayed. He recites a Kipling poem to me, which he says has been on his lips a lot since the referendum. *A Dead Statesman* it is called, and it goes like this:

I could not dig; I dared not rob:
Therefore I lied to please the mob.
Now all my lies are proved untrue
And I must face the men I slew.
What tale shall serve me here among
Mine angry and defrauded young?

I really just think that is so appropriate. I must send it to Ola. Anyway, Luke sympathises with the position this shambles must be putting us in. Clearly he has done his research. He knows that universities always need to be thinking about future challenges, and those seem to be changing and multiplying on a daily bloody basis at the moment. He understands that good universities need a diverse student and staff body. They need to be able to lure, develop and retain talent. But how, after Brexit? From where exactly? He is hitting the nail on the head. Most perplexingly, we are supposed to promote a strong global perspective, both nationally and internationally, which means building strong relationships with the very institutions that our pathetic excuse for a government is waging war on. Anyway, Luke is the one I feel sorry for. I sort of allude to the fact that time is short for me, but I think it just goes right over his head, because he tells me nonsense, sixty is still young these days. A real charmer!

The piece he wants to write is about more than just Brexit. He wants to investigate how higher education and perceptions of it have changed over the years. Luke says he has already approached graduates of all ages and from a variety of backgrounds to ask what their degrees have meant to them. It sounds like he has some captivating testimonials. Where he still wants to do some more digging is with regard to the interwar period – to consider the impact university education had on a generation whose real formative experiences took place far from classroom. Which I agree would be absolutely fascinating to get a take on. We have such short memories, and I sometimes think we are forgetting what those generations sacrificed. Their stories might really ram home the message to some of the more apathetic millennials, you know, that never in history has such a wide demographic had anything like the same kind of opportunities, so perhaps they should stop taking them for bloody granted.

The problem, of course, is that anybody old enough to have left university before 1939 would now be at least a hundred. The people Luke needs are all dead, sadly. But he insists if he can just get his hands on a list of alumni he can do his own legwork, piece together the subsequent careers of students and maybe track down their nexts of kin, that sort of thing. Which makes my life easy – just a matter of a few clicks on the spreadsheet then sending him an email.

He promises to forward me the final article, but warns that it may take some time because he wants to be thorough. We agree that now more than ever there is a burden of responsibility on good, honest journalists to be going the extra mile. We discuss Donald Trump. We discuss fake news. Honestly I could spend hours chatting to Luke, but the rest of my day is chockablock so we have to adjourn.

Really very charming, he was. Exactly the type I would love for Ola to meet. She refuses to speak to me at the moment, and we all know why that is. She can be so incredibly stubborn. She refuses to actually *listen* to me, refuses to even try and understand my decision. You know, not to pursue the curative treatment.

The chances are – well, they are shocking quite frankly, and for me it is a question of dying as well as I have lived. The doctors are giving me two years, and they reckon with palliative drugs I could maintain an excellent quality of life. In the summer I will retire, maybe visit a few places I have always wanted to see. I will try and spend some time back up in Liverpool. But I have no desire to lose my mobility or suffer through my last days in pain.

I get home just after seven. I make myself some cheese on toast, lather it with Branston Pickle and sit down to watch *The One Show*. Monty Don is on, listing his favourite gardens in the world. I do like Monty. Then they get a doctor on to talk about flu, and she asks Monty if he has ever had a really bad bout of flu. Of course he has, what kind of bloody question is that? Then some man starts banging on about home improvement, about whether to carpet your floors or use parquet, as if that is the most important decision a person will ever have to make. Monty is pressed for the pros and cons in terms of both carpets and parquet. I mean, it is an absolute farce this programme. Then they have a feature on bionic hooves for sheep, and Monty has to pretend to have an opinion on that as well. What about discussing something important for once? The future of this country, for example.

I switch the telly off and do some reading. I am partway through an excellent book by Madeleine Albright on the dangers of Fascism. I was never her biggest fan, what with that thing she said about half a million dead Iraqi children being worth it and her hate speech against Serbs and her telling Bernie Sanders voters they belonged in hell, but this book is timely and important. You get the sense that she really *understands* Trump. The danger he represents. I get through ten pages or so before going to the kitchen to pour myself a glass of wine. I take it to the computer, where it quickly becomes one of those nights. One article leads to twenty more, all about bloody Brexit.

At the bottom of the screen I see a banner advertising *Guardian Soulmates*. Ola forced me to join last year, and I have been on a few lousy dates. The sheer desperation of it all, two strangers approaching pension age, straining to hear each other over the cacophony of a pub. Straining even harder to find the slightest common ground. I told Ola, I said look Ola I am not lonely, but she said no Mum you have to do it, everybody does it nowadays, plus even if a Guardian reader turns out to be a weirdo, he is highly unlikely to be a murderous weirdo. Which I suppose is about the most you can hope for in love beyond the age of sixty: companionship with somebody who is not a homicidal maniac.

I have a browse. I come across Jim, 68, and realise that I know this Jim. Not personally, but this is Jim Timmons, the author. Famous back in the eighties and now represented by Ola. Unhappily, I might add. She described becoming his agent as the slightly less belittling but doubly annoying equivalent of being relegated to tea duties.

In interviews he always seemed so rude, so cantankerous, so it came as no surprise when Ola described him as rude and cantankerous. I remember reading his first novel just after I moved to London, just because everybody was bloody talking about it. *Quadruped*, it was called, still is called I assume, not that I have seen it on a shop shelf in about thirty years. I think I threw it across the room in anger. Smug, cynical, pretentious, like so many books written by the male literary darlings of that moment. From what I remember, an odious young student struts around Cambridge, calling lots of people the c word and quoting whole stanzas of Milton from memory. I never bothered with any of his other work.

Ideologically we were poles apart. I even have a faint memory of him forming part of what was laughably referred to as a cultural coterie of Thatcherites. Him and Philip Larkin, I believe it consisted of. How intriguing it might be to actually meet the man now though, even just to shout at him for voting Leave, because he bloody must have done, you can tell by looking at his face.

chapter:eleven

Dissipate was the word of the day, according to his bedside calendar. To scatter in various directions. To spend or use wastefully or extravagantly, as in fortune, or talent. It came from the Latin *dissipare*, and entered the English language sometime between 1525 and 1535. Just in time, Timmons fancied, for Thomas More to use it in the context of Christian faith. Before being burned at the stake, whence his ashes dissipated.

Fast forward nearly five centuries to late January 2019. Timmons shuffled to the bathroom, scratching himself in various places. He squinted at the mirror as he slipped into his beige waffleknit robe. Into his white waffleknit robe that had long since become beige. His hair resembled a cheap wig put on backwards then assaulted by hairdryers. His penis, longtime friend, occasional foe, was peeking out the fly of his navy pyjamas.

Timmons recalled Henry Miller once likening his own penis to a piece of lead with wings. Which was typical of that shambolic bald wanker. The worst bits of Lawrence, rewritten for *Sun* readers: that was Miller. Piece of lead with wings indeed. These days, if Timmons did manage to achieve an erection, it looked more like a petrified mouse than anything remotely elemental.

No, if the lead metaphor did have wings, it was only because his hazardous and antiquated organ was by now nothing more than a pipe to piss through. It could piss twice in ten minutes, the fiend. It could piss out more piss than tea and wine and whisky went in. It could interrupt his sleep to piss and piss and piss. As a younger man, a younger writer, Timmons had always avoided getting his elderly characters up in the night to piss, always considered that something of a cliche. But now he was living that cliche, literally pissing it out of him.

This morning, as he was pissing, Timmons mused that not since Rabelais had a writer really given piss its due. Perhaps it was time for him to be that man. Piss as allegory. Piss as his great, defining religious work. It could be... yes, piss as the mythical arc of history, piss on its parabola towards obliteration, piss as age and life and time, piss into water and back, someday, into piss. Piss being pissed then dissipating before being repissed. God as what though, Timmons? God as... yes, God as the great and powerful pissing lifeforce, God as the pissing cock, but God also as the piss, God in the piss, God of the piss. The Trinity? Piss. There was something here, he thought, as he dribbled out his last few droplets of piss.

He washed his hands, rinsed his mouth, splashed water on his face. More and more it appalled him, the face. It had once been described as attractive by an international magazine, the same magazine that had labelled him the Mick Jagger of fiction. When asked what he made of that tag in a later interview with the *Paris Review*, Timmons expressed frustration, saying it was proof that society was buggered, because if anything Jagger should have been referred to as the Jim Timmons of rock music.

Handsome was no longer how anybody would have described it. Angry angular features, puffy skin all blotched and sagging. That was how they might have described it. He had hoped that by venting all that spleen, by putting down his rage on paper, he would spare his face the unfortunate fate of one day resembling the person he suspected he was. He had assumed that writers, like their writing, like their incomes, could only improve with age. Every single thing about the man in the mirror was proof of just how wrong he had been. Looks, talent, wealth: whatever there had once been had long since dissipated.

Timmons yawned, grabbed the sink, and yawned again before leaving the bathroom. Each day, on each stair, he wondered whether this would be the moment his ever increasing heft plummeted straight through the carpet, straight through the floorboards, straight into the vacuum cleaner or a box of old notebooks. He yearned to die such a richly symbolic death, but not yet, not until he had finished the Great Book. The stairs, the body – both would have to hold out until then, which was looking like quite some time, given that the piss fable was about as comprehensive an idea as he had so far had. Age was becoming a factor, but he kept telling himself that Goethe had completed *Faust* at eighty, Sophocles *Oedipus Rex* at ninety.

He took the kettle. Tilting it to almost horizontal, he manoeuvred it over the dirty dishes and under the tap. In amongst the crockery were chunks of carrot and the spines of the small shoal of sardines that had been his Friday dinner. An iffy miasma was hanging over the kitchen. While he waited for the water to boil he considered washing up, then thought better of it when he remembered that Weronika was coming in only four days time to clean. He went on the hunt for a mug, squeezing out a small, shy fart in the process. The receptacle he found was handleless, more of a pot, bounty from the NORSK LITTERATURFESTIVAL 1986. Tea bags and sugar he had, but no fresh milk, so he raided his stash of mini plastic UHT pots. Which was how he preferred it anyway: two bags to a cup, three teaspoons of sugar, milk from a packet. This, he assumed, was how tea tasted at football matches, in factory canteens, beside the motorway. Places he had never actually been, places he did not care to go, but places he had imagined a million times or more as he sat in Hackney, willing himself to go down, down where Joyce had only partway gone, down to forge in the smithy of his soul the uncreated conscience of a race. The trick was to leave the bags in there until the colour was that of wet mortar, then in with the sugar.

Timmons took his breakfast beverage through to the office. This was where it was supposed to happen. This was where it would one day happen. This is where he came almost every day to fiddle around with sentences, in his fifty year career of fiddling around with and talking about fiddling around with sentences. There was a window, but it was directly behind where he sat, so he almost never looked out of it. The clock on its sill had been broken since seventeen minutes past three, many many hundreds of days ago. On the wall above the desk was a framed picture of the pretty village in Provence where his parents had spent their last years. Next to that was a cork noticeboard, which was supposed to be covered with notes and quotations of all kinds. Instead, pinned up was a postcard of a pastel painting by John Singer Sargent, a portrait of Heinrich von Kleist, and a Tesco voucher for Worcestershire Sauce. Books, newspapers and magazines were stacked everywhere, on shelves and in piles on the floor, under the basic wooden desk and next to the electric heater, meaning one big spark and there was kindling enough to send half of Hackney up in flames. Which would be equally richly symbolic.

He turned on his computer and the heater. He listened to both whirr to life, oblivious to the fact that either of these machines might easily have proved to be his downfall, the faggots that lit the humongous pyre on which he was to be martyred for Art. Until only a few years ago he had preferred to work on his typewriter, an olive Olivetti, but by lunchtime his floor would be carpeted with crumpled leaves of aborted fiction. It was not the waste that shamed him but the failure, the ability to get through reams and reams of paper without producing one worthwhile sentence. Easier just to delete on screen. His old rival Will Self had recently written that it was not possible to create quality literature using a computer. What was he, a reactionary now? It was for spouting some similar nonsense that Timmons, back in the early nineties, had first told Self to go fuck himself.

In the time it took his computer to get going, however, it was true that he probably could have handwritten one of those emaciated novellas that Ian McEwan kept churning out. Timmons slurped his tea, trying to remember whether he had ever told McEwan to go fuck himself. Rushdie yes, famously. AS Byatt once, by accident, but not McEwan, not as far as he was aware.

Timmons bent down with a groan, gave his shins a mad scratch, then retrieved a bag of cantuccini biscuits from his desk drawer. These he bought in bulk from an expensive Italian deli on the Southgate Road, and most mornings were spent dipping them into his tea. For him this was beyond alimentary, a figurative gesture, something like his own artistic process: refined, Italianate sensibilities, softened in a cloudy brew of Englishness. Chaucer could not have completed his *Tales* without Boccaccio, Shakespeare might never have written poetry without Petrarch, Milton cannot be conceived of without Dante, just as Timmons without Cantuccini was simply not Timmons.

Passwords though. He seemed to have about fifteen of the buggers. Dante never needed to worry what his username was. Dante never needed to waste time remembering the difference between his inbox access and his login details for the Cloud. For Timmons, everything was some variation of the Joycean compound Nightblue Fruit. But some sites necessitated an underscore, others required caps. Many demanded a number, and so 1 replaced the letter l. Except then he would forget and create new ones elsewhere, changing instead the B for an 8. Others again with both the 1 and the 8. Numbers and letters did not suffice for *The Times Online*, which was how he ended up with the spastic gobbledygook of N1ght8Lu€_Fru1t.

When he finally secured access to his own email inbox, he discovered – among the vulgar pleas to buy or consume something or travel somewhere or add multiple inches to his ageing piss pipe – that he had been sent a message on *Guardian Soulmates*. Something from his agent too, but that could wait, because nobody had contacted him via this dating site since the Greek Financial Crisis. He remembered because he had ended up dining with the woman in question, who had harped on and on about the merciless troika, until he had felt compelled to call her a daft cow. That was years ago, and nothing since.

He clicked the link and *The Guardian* exploded into his vision. They wondered whether Timmons was interested in helping them deliver the independent journalism the world needed right now, for as little as £1. No he most certainly was not. Already he must have been providing the prosecco at their parties, twenty pounds a month for however many years, all because he had heard their database was largely free from the kind of paupers and misfits that as a paper they claimed to be championing. He exited the appeal and now, in front of him, was an empty login screen. He had not visited this domain in months; how was he supposed to remember his password? The bastards, the fake socialist charlatans. Three wrong combinations of Nightblue Fruit later, and his only remaining option was to answer the secret question, gain access that way. He began typing out Langley, the maiden name of his mother, only to see that the question was another. What, they asked, is your favourite book?

Surely he would never have deigned to answer such a derisory question. Unless of course he had responded sarcastically. What was the name of that Hilary Mantel novel, the very famous one? No, his lampoon would have been less obvious, more subversive. He typed in *Lolita*, pressed enter, then had to click on six different pictures with traffic lights in them to prove that he was not a bot. This was absurd. He dropped a cantuccino in his tea, had to go fishing around with his fingers at the bottom of the mug. His answer did not match their records.

He tried *Madame Bovary*. He now had to tick all boxes containing big red American fire hydrants, until none were left. Timmons was raging, smashing the mouse buttons and the letters of his keyboard like a teen gamer. This was supposed to be Britain, a British newspaper. What was the country coming to when a man had to solve riddles and identify foreign fire hydrants just to chat with a filly? His answer did not match their records.

Things had once been very different. Rewind to New York City, the late eighties. There was Timmons, entering his forties, living on Avenue B in the low twenties, with the world, it seemed, at his size tens. He was working on the Big Book, and there was no reason to believe it would be anything other than a booming success.

The debut, *Quadruped*, was published while he was still at Cambridge. Heralded as a 'ruthlessly brilliant sendup' of the traditional bildungsroman, some credited it with changing the genre forever. Timmons then spent a decade as the literary editor of a nationwide newspaper, decimating his peers and attending lots of parties, before making his return with *Hiroshima Tourist Bureau*, a 'speculative and exuberant take on the atomising effects of mass travel, packed with erudition and a dark sense of foreboding.' The critics hailed it as a tour de force, and him as the voice of a generation. He was even longlisted for the Booker Prize.

Soon came the move Stateside. After only a week, Timmons was ingloriously mugged on the Subway. He recounted the ordeal in an article for *The New York Times*, courting controversy with what were deemed sweeping and derogatory generalisations about Puerto Ricans. From then on he was rarely out of the public eye. In between teaching to packed out lecture theatres, gossip had him sleeping with everyone from pop superstar Debbie Harry to the property tycoon Donald Trump.

All the while his agent was at work behind the scenes, announcing that this next book was going to be extremely long and incredibly important, eventually managing to secure a record advance. But the publisher was made to wait, along with everyone else. *Peccabam Pecuniam* took Timmons eight years to write. The idea was to fuse the Great American Novel with the British Comic Tradition, to create a novel of ribald comedy but also deep melancholy, all in the inimitable High Style. *Hiroshima Tourist Bureau* had, after all, had its doubters, and the aim was to bury these goons under the mastery and page count of *PP*.

The critics pilloried it. Frank Kermode, for example:

'[Timmons has] displayed a clear ambition to pick up the silken thread of English satire, the one which extends unbroken from Swift and Fielding through to Waugh and Amis. That he has done so goes without saying. The calamities, however, begin when he tries to loop that thread around a robust frame, the kind synonymous with Bellow at his best, and it comes as no great surprise that the author ends up hanging himself with it.'

And so on and so forth. It was roundly denounced as unfinishable. Harold Bloom argued that its one redeeming feature was a superficially strange originality, but this he accused Timmons of lifting straight from Nabokov. And it was true that while teaching he had developed a mania for (even an obsession with, becoming transfixed by the soaring lyricism and playful razzmatazz, all the other qualities that made Nabokov Nabokov) Nabokov.

Nabokov – another one who had never had to deal with any of this modern crapola. Passwords, the internet. Yes, the great man had been forced to flee his country of birth, to trade the life of an aristocrat for the common trials of an immigrant, only to find himself fleeing once more, this time from the Nazis. But to Timmons this seemed like only moderately more of an ordeal than being obliged to navigate the beastly worldwide web. He longed to return to a time before its invention, perhaps the first half of the Twentieth Century, when Europe was burning in its entirety, but the opinions of a writer were at least given their proper due. When one could keep up with events, however grim.

Timmons imagined buying a newspaper in September 1938, reading that Chamberlain had secured peace for his time. That would then remain the story, until a few days later when he decided to buy another paper, at which point he would be incrementally brought up to date. And when, months later, it transpired that Chamberlain had done nothing of the sort, that peace was just an illusion, Timmons was therefore capable of understanding precisely how and where things had fallen apart. Which the internet had made impossible.

The internet boasted three variations of the Munich announcement before the real one was even made, only for Goebbels to post his own intentionally conflicting version. With Chamberlain still in the air, Laura Kuenssberg would start tweeting that Churchill was refusing to back him, Cooper was refusing to back him, Eden was refusing to back him. Rumours would surface that Chamberlain was resigning, that Chamberlain was staying, that his plane had been shout out of the sky, that the plane was fine and passing over Margate. There would be interviews with people from the Sudetenland, stories of betrayal. And by the time Chamberlain emerged from his plane with his piece of paper, even he would need clarification as to what the hell was going on.

Nowadays, Timmons refreshed his internet page and the news was no longer news. It had been chased away by a blitzkrieg of newer, better news; pushed back towards the beaches, back and into the vast sea of all that has been but is now forgotten. Nothing was permanent, except the very things he would have preferred not to be. Such as, for example, video footage dating from January 1988, when Jim Timmons appeared on American national television for the first and last time.

Invited onto *Firing Line* along with Norman Mailer, the two writers locked horns in a debate entitled *Whither the Novel?* Discussion grew heated. After seventeen minutes, in an unprovoked attack on British culture, Mailer called *Middlemarch* a scrappy hack job. Timmons, apparently drunk, succumbed to a sudden and violent surge of patriotism, leaping out of his seat towards Mailer. Fisticuffs ensued, which the Englishman got the better of, but the establishment sided with Mailer, and when *PP* got its critical mauling a few weeks later, Timmons was cut adrift.

Relatively speaking, of course. Adrift was what he was now, sitting in his pyjamas in Hackney, writing an email to the *Soulmates* team, requesting access to his online dating account. Back then, in New York, he was still dating actresses and socialising with the likes of Philip Roth. His decision to move back to London, where he had zero amici, was therefore baffling.

He took what money remained from the *PP* advance, which fortunately he had been allowed to keep, and bought a gabled Jacobethan house on De Beauvoir Square in Hackney. Nothing Timmons had done up until that point in his career, not all of it combined, had earned him anywhere near the money that this one acquisition would make on paper over the next thirty years. He had bought it outright, which was fortunate, because nor would any of his subsequent work have covered even the measliest of mortgages. He lived off his modest inheritance. His pension was a Basquiat, bought for thirty dollars directly from the artist, who had come knocking at his door one night in need of cash for a fix. That too had soared in value, and was now worth many hundreds of thousands of bags of cantuccini.

Timmons assumed that he would be able to reconquer the British literary establishment, but he assumed wrong. *Only Living Boy in New York*, his book of essays on American culture, was published shortly after his return, in 1991. A total of 423 copies were sold in the first year. As if behind his back, a new generation of writers had emerged. Nor was there any competing with this riffraff, because even a televised scrap with Normal Mailer was lightweight publicity when compared to an Iranian fatwa. None of the new breed ever cited his influence, not one stuck up for him or tried to salvage his reputation. *Au contraire*, some of them went about actively savaging it. After writing a glowing review of *The Remains of the Day* for a magazine called *Fem*, Timmons learned that Kazuo Ishiguro had spoken at a festival of the need for English fiction to 'move beyond the arsey narcissism and bad laddishness of Jim Timmons and his acolytes.'

No, the literary scene was not at all like the raft John Updike had described – Updike, who had been his friend, until calling *PP* a 'shambolic wigwam of postmodernist drivel.' Yes it was a raft, small and sinking, but newcomers did not have their fingers stepped on; they were hauled aboard, at which point they set about killing and eating the oldest or the fattest or the weakest.

The last thing he had published was *Mauve*, a collection of short stories. But it too was a spectacular failure, after which Timmons beat his retreat from society. He began spending all his time at home, living like a filthy, impious monk. He procured some chickens for his little garden. He survived principally on tea and biscuits, toast and eggs, whiskey. But if this was where and how it had to be written, this was where and how it had to be written: the comeback book that would make society tremble, that would carve his name onto the great cenotaph of posterity. It was to be a novel about the artist, about the act of creation as sublimation for the sexual impulse. It would be called: *Daedalus*.

Six years later he was visited by Philip Roth, the only friend to stay loyal through the unravelling of his American fortunes. Roth was in London promoting his masterpiece *American Pastoral*. They went for a walk along the canal. Timmons confessed that he had scrapped his *Daedalus* project and had been writing poetry, mostly while sitting pantless on the toilet, under the *nom de plume* Caedmon. In it he sung about the origins of created things, like man and the world and history. None of it had been published but everything was stacked inside the chicken coop, which had been moved under the stairs after the last of the chickens had perished.

Roth read a few pages and saw that it was not good. Understanding that Timmons was in the middle of a serious mental breakdown, he used his reputation to pull some strings. The best that could be done was a job offer from the Creative Writing department at Brunel University, which Timmons reluctantly accepted. None of the students had ever read his work. Very few even knew who he was.

Twenty years later and there was Timmons, sat in his office, where he still came slavishly to grovel at the feet of the muse. But the bitch was no longer listening. And he had no memory, which ruled out buying time with his memoirs. Proust, the great poofter, had been able to recall the most minute minutiae of a childhood evening at home, or a walk through the rain, yet here was Timmons, unable to summon up a meagre internet password.

He returned to his emails and opened the message from his agent, Ola. How on earth was she supposed to represent him, when she had been born after his great period had come to an end? Whatever pages he sent her way were poopooed, as if she knew the first thing about literature. Recently she had rejected his witty and imaginative proposal that satirically juxtaposed cookbooks with literature:

Paris in the 1950s, reimagined. Elizabeth David and Julia Child as highbrow figures in cafes, fawned over for their groundbreaking philosophies on the proper way to steam a turbot. Meanwhile Sartre and

Camus, anonymously holed up in some kitchen, nattering unimportantly about Being and Nothingness.

For Timmons it was a way of critiquing the publishing world, and how it continued to debase itself by begging celebrities to write about their diet plans. Ola sniffed at it, which, given that most of her other clients were celebrities who wrote about their diet plans, was unsurprising. Timmons would long ago have demanded another agent, but who would take him? Who still cared? Last year he tried to circumvent her by calling two of his former editors directly, but one was retired, living in the Dordogne. The other was dead.

What riled him the most about Ola was the pretence that she objected to his work on literary rather than commercial grounds. When she said she had a problem with the voice, with the consistency of his prose, what she really meant was this: she would struggle to sell a gazillion copies to bozos who recognised his face from reality TV.

He had replied to her previous email somewhat flippantly, by asking her to provide some examples of what she meant when she said *literary quality*. He wished to know, more specifically, what she thought editors were looking for, beyond airport junk and battle trolls. Apparently she had obliged.

Her email mentioned one young writer she had just signed, who she described as having the potential to become a British Laotian Rupi Kaur. Perhaps truth and beauty, she wrote, were now to be found in incomplete but authentic entities, revealed in shards and fragments made more meaningful by their absences, rather than as part of some overwrought unity. For example on Instagram.

Poppycock. Timmons had no idea who Rupi Kaur was, so he googled her. He discovered that she was a poet, discovered that her fame was thanks to the social media site Instagram, discovered the Instagram account itself. Interspersed between pictures of her wearing various barmy *haute couture* outfits were images of plain text on white backgrounds. He hoped, for the sake of the human race, that this was not her verse. He soon realised that it was. He scrolled down, reading at random these brief ditties of affirmation and empowerment.

They were so unspeakably bad that Timmons was actually quite enjoying himself. Then he learned that critics were taking this heinous poetaster seriously, and there followed much blaspheming. This was it for him, confirmation that the world had now been dumbed down to rock bottom, but the real rock bottom, the one that lay several strata below other merely sedimentary rock bottoms. Language no longer conveyed any meaning whatsoever. That politicians should manipulate it to bend the truth was nothing new; that had been the case for millennia. So too were the banalities and inanities of pop music all well and good; they had their mass appeal, and Timmons had always been content to render unto the proverbial Caesar. But to be calling *this* poetry was a quite unprecedented development. Here was the true triumph of populism.

Timmons was livid. He read a ninth, tenth and eleventh article, all about Rupi Kaur. He was putting two unmoistened cantuccini in his mouth at once, desperate to chew. Baudelaire, he thought: *You gave me mud, and I turned it into gold.* This was just mud though. Just mud, smeared on a page and exhibited to the world. But it was accessible, they claimed, as if that had ever been the basis for art. It was honest.

150

Probably it was, to be fair, because culture was by now spinning on such a debauched axis that genuine were the facile grabs for fame, while anybody still claiming to strive for depth was surely a fraud.

Once again Timmons longed to return to a time before the internet, before it had provided a forum for such crassness and superficiality; to a time before the arts had reengineered themselves around whoever could assemble the biggest crowd, around whatever was most liked or most shared. To a time when people were required to at least engage with the challenging. To a time before this merdique silo of social media merde. To the reign of Mary Tudor, ideally.

Ola had also taken the liberty of forwarding a manuscript that, she said, showed promise but needed work. The kind of novel she enjoyed receiving. Timmons opened the attachment and perused the cover letter. Dear Ola, bla bla bla, young girl, bla bla bla, patriarchal oppression, bla bla bla, social commentary of the kind Gogol was aiming for in *Dead Souls*. Timmons grunted. This he would not, could not tolerate. For twenty years he had been teaching this novel to students, for twenty years hearing the same ignorant bluster about social commentary. The forwarded message contained an email address, and Timmons decided that he would do this young writer a service by telling her just how wrong she was.

He went to the kitchen and made another mug of tea, composing the email in his mind. It occupied him for the next three hours. Once it was sent he drafted another to *Guardian Soulmates*, because now he remembered: his favourite novel was *Dead Souls*, and he would be grateful if they went ahead and granted him access to his dating account.

chapter:twelve

There were so many ways to get a healthy start to the day. Tepid lemon water, apple cider vinegar, kombucha. Some did an hour of strenuous yoga, others sat and meditated. Also believed to be beneficial were bracing showers, chia seeds for breakfast, writing a journal. But Julie had no need for such joyless fads, not today. Three fucks last night, another this morning, and she had risen feeling capable of anything. Flush and limber, thoroughly invigorated, without the need for a rollmat or so much as a sip of fermented tea.

A diary might have been useful though, because already her sentiments towards Luke were far from straightforward. They needed working out. Half of her wanted to be done with him, never to see him or be touched by him or have to hear his voice again. He was just so basic. So very, very basic. An average bloke with average ambitions: to start a startup, to be a billionaire.

Julie sat in his kitchen, contemplating his appearance. He was too pale. His nose was too large. He had no arse whatsoever, so his jeans tended to sag and bag and billow unattractively in the behind. Currently he was in chef mode:

'Why do these slags always get buried in the bottom?' asked Luke, rooting around in a red pepper for a wayward seed.

'Don't say slags,' said Julie.

'In terms of shakshouka mine is quite a wet philosophy. Hope that's alright.'

In went the peppers and the pan began to frazz. Luke filled a mug with water and lashed it over the veg. There was a spitting and snarling but soon everything was fully submerged.

'Now you're gonna see the sauciness really come to fruition.'

Julie saw ketchup go in. She saw what she thought was cinnamon go in.

'Tomatoes,' said Luke. 'Get in there you benders.'

Balsamic vinegar now.

'Great bedfellow of the tomato, balsam.'

Luke now hacked a pomegranate apart and let its seeds hail down. Frozen blueberries too, always mixing.

'Our issue though is losing all that liquid. And it has to cook a bit before I bosh the eggs in, so seeing as I have no lid watch what I do. Look, watch.'

Luke thatched a roof of kale leaves over his pan.

'Keeps it nice and moist.'

That he and Julie had nothing in common was already obvious. Yes, they shared broadly overlapping worldviews, because whatever you might think about Luke, he quite genuinely despised it all, the whole sweep of conventional villainy. Conflict, cruelty, inequality. Racism and sexism and terrorism. Prostitution and pollution and, last but by no means

154

least, religion. He wanted to fix it all – believed, indeed, that all of it was there to be fixed. But there were two things that he downright refused to scorn, and they were precisely the ones that for Julie it seemed most essential to.

Money and technology were not easy things to loathe, not like the sandbox scourges of war or xenophobia. To hate money, to hate technology, was to embark on a voyage of rejection that spanned the entire modern world, which was unnerving because you never quite knew if you were a dazzling intellectual navigator, or just massively depressed. To Captain Julie, there had to be somewhere better beyond, another utopia but this time a real one. Luke meanwhile was the hardy young matelot, earpods and dollars locked in a box beneath his bunk, not quite ready to step ashore onto her brave new beach without them.

Put simply: both agreed that planet earth, as it currently was, stank. Julie believed that it could, should and might be excellent if everyone just agreed to hit the reset button, abolish the patriarchy, read more Austen. For Luke, things were and had been steadily improving forever, starting from minus many many million and always generally on the way up. Yes we were still far from perfect, but we would get there in the end, with money as our fuel, with science and technology as our shiny twin engines. In the colossal realm of human ideas past, present and future, these two were only marginally not identical.

But that minor divergence had already caused a first clash. Last night, date number two. Julie said she had never seen the Steve Jobs film, so Luke happily assented to watching it for a fifth time. As the end credits rolled, he opined that the former Apple boss was a worldhistorical figure of equal if not greater stature to Jesus. Julie felt no particular fondness for the son of God, but the comment riled her, so she retaliated by wondering out loud why we insisted on worshipping such wankers. When it came to Steves, she would not have traded one million Jobs for a single Wozniak. He had been a vindictive egomaniac who rejected a daughter, who cheated his friends, who insulted and bullied his colleagues, who never gave to charity, yet we forgave him all this and more because he had built us funny gadgets.

The outburst left Luke not so much angry as deeply hurt. But Julie was off, talking about other biopics now, talking about *The Theory of Everything*, and she proceeded to brand Sir Stephen Hawking a flagrant womaniser. Here Luke drew the line. Everyone was allowed their own opinions, but you did not disrespect The Hawking. Plus, these men were dead. Did she have no respect for the dead? He spent the next hour on his smartphone, dredging up dirt from the personal lives of literary giants, gleefully telling Julie who had been a paedo, who had been a misogynist, who had been a mouthpiece for despots.

But this antagonism inevitably led them to the bedroom, where it did what antagonism does best. Julie might have referred to Eros and Thanatos, Luke their yin yang thing. Because if anything classified as worldhistorical, it was the sex. Luke was the *weltgeist* with an erection, a dreadful and irrepressible lifeforce before which all resistance was futile. Julie was rebounding from years of frustration with Chris, in the same way the French rebounded from revolutionary chaos by following Napoleon to Moscow. Luke carried her from room to room, shagging her with the kind of ferocious abandon with which Bonaparte had put a whole continent to the sword. He picked her up, he threw her down. He tipped her legs behind her head and flipped her over. He whispered in her ear, he shouted at the ceiling, he mooed like a cow. He played with her nipples and tickled her bum. In the hours they had so far spent together, already he had come on her back and her stomach and her boobs. Come on her right thigh, come on her left thigh, come on the pillow. He had come all over the place, so often unexpectedly, as if her bedroom was the battlefield at Austerlitz.

He was in sex as he was in life: boundless, incessant. He was a circle whose centre was everywhere, whose circumference nowhere. Already Julie wanted to hate him, honestly she did, but sometimes she hated life, and just as she felt compelled to keep living it, nor was there any negating this terrific urge to screw Luke. Had he been a true badboy, it might have been easier to cast him aside. It was what he desperately wished to be, she could tell. But deep down he would always remain one of the good guys.

The way he made her laugh! Despite herself he made her laugh, if not with him then at him, but either way she got pounded by the rolling thunder of his relentless banter. God help anybody under that behemoth. Nowhere to hide, not from that kind of firepower. Videos of clumsy penguins, zaney Japanese adverts for dildoes. Amusing factoids about cheese, about bees, about the gestation period of giraffes. Boom, boom, down it kept coming, until eventually you staggered out of your foxhole, morale in tatters, waving the white flag and screaming Luke is good, Luke my friend.

Now he raised the corrugated green roof on his shanty of grub to check everything was in order.

'Oh yes,' said Luke. 'Ohhh yes. Tres damp.'

Luke clicked his hob down to zero. He cracked four eggs into the pan. Bits of shell were retrieved from the sauce, with the same thumb and forefinger that only an hour ago had been vying for her anus.

'The heat of that is going to poach those right through,' he said.

Now he came to the table with plates in hand, teatowel draped over his shoulder, humming a vaudeville.

'Blankshouka, Mademoiselle.'

Julie examined the plate in front of her. It looked like afterbirth. The kale leaves that had been roofing his concoction were there, but now as a floor.

'Is there fruit in this?'

'I told you: sweet and sour.'

Julie unbelted a string of onion from around a blueberry, before snaring the pellet with her fingers then nibbling perhaps a quarter. She proceeded thus, warily, as Luke shovelled in whole forkfuls.

'Mmmm. So many nutrients in here,' said Luke. 'All the nutrients. Do you ever think though... I mean, I was in the supermarket the other day, and I was just like: why do we still eat what are basically plants?'

'In what way?'

'As in, why do we eat them? Obviously I'm not questioning the seven a day, but you just think given how far we've come from, like, the Middle Ages. It's odd, because those guys were probably eating peppers and blueberries that weren't enormously different to these ones, yet they were basically barbarians and we are, you know, civilized.'

'What are you suggesting?'

'I don't know. I was just... Food is ripe for disruption. It would be quite nice if those meal replacement smoothies caught on, you know. The guy from San Francisco, where you can basically get all the minerals and energy you need and you don't have to shop or worry about overcooking the eggs, or whatever.'

'Hmm. the problem here though Luke is that they're very much undercooked. Raw, in fact.'

'Well leave the eggs if you don't like them. I don't care. But you see this is precisely my point. We've overhauled practically everything else to make us more efficient, so why not food? Right now, for example, you and I could just be on the couch with our shakes or whatever. I could be relaxing before my meeting, rather than having to worry about washing up and stuff.'

'What time is your meeting? Weird that it's on a Sunday.'

'Eleven. The working week, as a concept, is dead.'

'Nervous?'

'Not really.'

'Do you have a strategy in mind?'

'Not a strategy as such. I'm just going to show him that in two days I've gone and procured double the number of users he wanted. Then ask him for a hundred grand.'

'And you're seriously expecting him just to give it to you?'

'Yes.'

'Admittedly I know nothing about startups, but that cannot be how it works. It would be like me going to a publisher and saying oh, hello, the name's Julie, and this is my novel about, you know, whatever it's about. Can I have six figures please?'

'Yes,' said Luke. 'Is that not what you would do?'

Julie remained momentarily speechless in the face of such ingenuous ingenuity.

'Is... but... it's not about what I would do. Luke these eggs, really. I don't think they're edible.'

'The eggs are fine. Raw in any event is fine. They reckon the protein is better when they're raw.'

'Do you not think this investor man wants you to show him some steady growth first?'

'Steady growth is for pus... ' – Luke aborted, remembering how verboten that word now was – 'It's for losers, steady growth. That is precisely *not* what they want. Guys like Vince want you either to explode into the stratosphere or disappear. A hundred grand is fucking pocket change to them, and if he genuinely thinks the idea is worth anything he'll give it to me there and then. If he does we'll go away somewhere. My treat.'

Julie could not finish the shakshouka. She ate all of the pomegranate, most of the blueberries, but little of the remaining ensemble had not been contaminated by soggy albumen. She pushed her plate to one side, took a banana and peeled it. The connotations of her putting it in her mouth led to a filthy exchange, and within a few minutes Luke was kneeling beneath her on his shower floor. His tongue and his fingers and the showerhead were all variously and industriously working away at her clitoris and her vagina and her labia and her perineum and her anus. Fantastic it was. Five minutes more and her knees were buckling, her back was spasming against the cold tiles, and then Luke, heroically, was keeping her inert frame aloft. In twelve hours he had given her more orgasms than Chris had managed during the whole six months of his stint as a litigation trainee.

This was what she was ruminating on as she walked down the Kingsland Road an hour later. The temperature was nearly freezing, the sky Macbook grey. Julie wondered whether, in six nearly seven years with Chris, she had even once come as violently as she consistently seemed to be coming with Luke. That shakshouka though, what a calamity. She decided to enter the next coffee shop and have a proper breakfast.

She ordered a soy milk cappuccino and a Wheatgrass Wonder. Also a piece of vegan lemon cake. The barista told her to take a seat, that everything would be brought over when ready. She claimed a stool by the window, looked out at the people walking past, all of them wrapped up warm. The many surrounding Apple products were a reminder that she had not yet turned on her phone. This, more than anything else, spoke volumes about the sex, about all the good it was doing her. She could get several hours into a day without needing a portable electronic device to reassure her there might be a point to it.

Her order arrived. The juice looked like what gathers at the top of a jar of pesto – nearly a pint of that. Julie checked her iPhone, cleaning smudge marks from the screen as she waited for it to power up. Her background picture appeared, the long sweep of Chesil Beach. Now a message from Lucy: Ola had decided to sign her.

Oh, my, god, that, is, awesome, news, typed Julie. *Confetti emoji, confetti emoji, party popper emoji, party popper emoji, book emoji, book emoji, geek emoji.*

Why though? Lucy had no book. Lucy had no idea for a book. Lucy barely even wanted to write anymore. Surely Ola was not intending to send her old novel out for submission? It was crap, it was a piece of crap, even Lucy admitted it was. Never in a million years would crap like that get published. Perhaps she had been right: Ola was a lesbian, and she fancied Lucy.

Julie came away from the house party with that conviction, and also very worried about her friend. The totally incoherent or totally banal mysticisms. The apparent interest in that egomaniacal cesspit Instagram. Lucy had seemed about one motivational quote away from morphing into the British Laotian Paolo Coelho. An ordinary literary agent wanting a piece of that made perfect sense; Coelho probably earned more than the Brazilian football team put together. But Ola had come across as serious. Interested in *serious* fiction.

Maybe Julie also had an email from Ola, offering representation. She checked her inbox. She did not. Here was something though, from an unknown address. She opened the message and took a bite of cake.

Dear Ms Stanhope,

I address myself to you following a conversation with our mutual… agent. Ola has spoken highly of you, and she did me the great honour of sharing some pages from your most intriguing novel Wench. *She wished to know my thoughts; I prefer to share them with you directly.*

My name is Jim Timmons. I am the author of three novels, one volume of short stories and numerous essays. For many years I worked as a reviewer for The TLS, *and in 1985 I was longlisted for The Booker Prize.*

You can certainly write, young lady. During two decades spent teaching creative writing (hélas!) I was obliged to read more than my fair share of doggerel. Enough, perhaps, for a thousand lifetimes. A truly bonne plume *is rare, but I think you have the makings of one. Keep writing, keep reading, and surely you will get there. George Eliot was published for the first time only at forty, and it would be a decade more before she developed the maturity we see her reach in* Middlemarch.

Wench, *I am afraid, is a weak novel. It smacks to me – and richly, I might add – of* poshlost. *What, I hear you ask, do I talk about when I talk about poshlost? Principally all that is stupid, all that is trivial, all that is vulgar.*

пóшлость, in Russian, means a lack of profoundness. A smug inferiority both moral and spiritual. For the most comprehensive definition we must turn, as is so frequently necessary, to Nabokov. Poshlust, *as he wittily coined it, is not only the obviously trashy, but also the falsely important. The falsely clever. Corny merde, vulgar cliches, philistinism in all its phases. Imitations of imitations, bogus profundities. Crude, moronic and dishonest pseudo-literature. Pinning it down in contemporary writing, our émigré Virgil guides us through the infernal bogs of social comment, humanistic messages, and political allegories. Overconcern with class or race.*

My preoccupation stems from your reference to the gigantic Dead Souls, *a novel that mercilessly and majestically trains its poshlight on poshlost. What I most take issue with, Ms Stanhope, is the assertion that in writing it, Gogol might have been eyeing something so grubbily basic as social commentary. A thousand times no. I do not wish to say that the plot is of no significance; simply that the supremacy of style relegates it to a secondary plane. In striving for the epic, Gogol shows us not Russia under the microscope, but something wider. Something greater. The unalterable superficiality of life, if you like. His characters are caricatures; they are what Forster would have called flat, which only adds to their formidable everyman quality. They stop being Russians of their time and become universal. They could just as easily be Wall Street Bankers. What they embody is a fakeness that is everywhere, that permeates everything. The purchasing of dead souls is but a metaphor, in itself ridiculous, because nobody in the real world would ever embark on anything so ludicrous and obscene.*

The great pity with literature today is that we have stopped aiming at anything remotely transcendant. We have been paralysed by the anxiety of influence. Gogol looked to Homer, he looked to Dante. He saw what genius was and strove to attain or surpass it. Meanwhile we merely glance behind us, and are so terrified or repulsed by what we see that we end up ignoring the past entirely. We preoccupy ourselves with angry and didactic manifestos, and have become obsessed with truth. Why? It has reached the point, I think, where the most transgressive thing you could do as a young author would be to create a character and put him or her at the heart of an invented story.

We are obsessed with identity. Why? You refer to yourself as a female author. You have rendered your protagonist in such a way that her tribulations could only ever be those of a middle class English white girl in her late twenties. By doing this you are voluntarily relegating your work to the ghettos of fiction. If Shakespeare had tried such a trick, we would be left not with a corpus that speaks to all people and all time, but the scribblings of a dead white man who spoke most prolifically out of turn about Venice and Denmark. About ambition and love and rage and jealousy. About power. About human nature.

With art, one must aim to sensibilise, not beat people over the head with a stick. What does Dryden say to us? He says that art can be both delightful and instructive, but while instruction is not always delightful, delight is always instructive. I wish you the best of luck in the future.

Yours respectfully,

Jim Timmons

Eugh, who was this twat? Had he been living in a hole for the past two or ten or seventy years? Julie took another bite of her cake, washing it down with more juice and cappuccino. If there was one thing she enjoyed, it was putting patronising old men in their place. She decided to do so immediately. She wrote:

Dear Master Timmons,

Respectfully also, I disagree. You cite Nabokov. Nabokov argued that Gogol is pointless unless read in the original Russian. If we are to take him at his word, then surely to evaluate the translation for anything beyond what happens from chapter to chapter, i.e. anything beyond the plot, would be absurd. I am presuming that you too have read the work in translation, given that you refer to it as Dead Souls *and not* Мёртвые души.

Even if this was just a case of Nabokov being Nabokov, the book seems to me to come straight out of the picaresque tradition. Rabelais, Cervantes. Always we see the same scenario of rascally hero surrounded by flattish characters. In bouncing the hero around amongst them, the authors could illustrate the priest, the shopkeeper, whoever. By doing so they achieved their critique of society, just as Nozdryov the bully or Manilov the sentimentalist are ways for Gogol to explore the greed and complacency that he predicted would be the ruin of Russia.

Please feel free to send me your work, should you wish to hear my thoughts on it. I wish you the best of luck in the future.

Julie Stanhope

Julie hit send. Not even after an hour underneath or on top of Luke would she have felt so good. She went to pay the bill, touching her card nonchalantly against the machine. She walked outside and into the winter morning, cold against her cheeks. Annoying her slightly was the idea that Ola had obviously not thought twice about forwarding what was unfinished work to this Timmons knob. Then again, perhaps that meant she would imminently be proposing to sign her. Julie was smiling at this thought when suddenly, dreadfully and unmistakably, she saw Chris walking towards her.

She looked at the pavement and held her line but it was no use, it was too late. He had seen her. She could feel that he had seen her. Probably he would think she had been smiling at him, which was not true. Or that she had looked away because she was trying to avoid him, which was true. Fuck.

'Hi.'

'Oh, Chris. Hi. I totally didn't see you.'

'Julie, you looked right at me.'

He looked like shit. Really tired, very bad.

'Did I? I don't think I did.'

'You… fine, whatever. How are you?'

Fucking amazeballs. I am about to be signed by a prestigious literary agency. Also I just won my first literary feud. Also about an hour ago I broke a fingernail because I was coming so furiously that I ended up clawing at tile grouting.

Was what Julie decided not to say. Instead, she said:

'Not bad. You?'

'I'm good. I'm really good. A little tired but really good.'

'Why are you wearing your suit?'

'I'm on my way to a meeting.'

'But it's Sunday. Why is everyone having meetings on a Sunday?'

'I know, it's moronic.'

Julie winced. She remembered how Chris repeatedly said the word moronic, pronouncing it marronic, as if of the chestnut.

'You working a lot then?'

'Ninety hours this week. Went home for the first time on Wednesday morning, just to change my pants.'

'Grim.'

'I miss you Jules.'

'Yeah, erm, I miss you too. Look, I've really got to go. My shift is starting.'

'Yeah, no, cool. Are you still at the Chesham Arms?'

'No. I mean yeah.'

'Maybe I'll come by and see you after my meeting's done.'

'Chris, I think that's a bad idea.'

A bad idea generally, but also because she had no shift.

'No, you're right. Look, listen, I'll leave it up to you. You have my number. Whenever you're ready, just reach out.'

edward:gooderham

chapter:thirteen

Never should he have admitted to missing her. And as for reach out. To have told her to reach *around*, to have instructed her to drop to her knees and lick his bumhole and give him a reacharound – even that would have been less disastrous.

Chris mounts the bus, scans his card, goes upstairs. His favourite space is free, right at the very front, as if the bus is a lorry and Chris the man driving it. Yet another job he certainly would have preferred. He remembers, when he was younger, hearing how the cousin of his godmother chose to spend his weekends. Martin, an accountant, would leave work on a Friday evening and make his way to Dover, where a freight company would assign him a heavy goods vehicle and tell him which corner of Europe it was destined for. Late Sunday night he would board a plane, and the next morning he would be back at his desk in accountant mode. Not infrequently he would spend his holidays making even longer deliveries. Chris used to think this made him the single weirdest man on the planet. But now, in Martin, he sees heroism.

Back to those front seats on the upper deck of a London bus: fucking superb. Sitting there, for Chris, goes some tiny fraction of the way towards recapturing that grand, panoramic thrill of the cockpit visit – a

171

highlight of his and so many other middle class childhoods in the nineties. Too poor and you were not flying anywhere, not yet. Too rich and such experiences were banal. The stewardess beckoned you through, marched you down the aisle, and suddenly you were in there. Strangely small, it was. But the uniforms, the dashes, the dials, the sky, the sky. The captain let you handle the joystick. He looked at you and said there you go, son: you are now flying this aircraft. And you believed him.

Many are the reasons to pity somebody being born in the year 2019, none more tragic than the fact that he or she or they will probably never set foot in a cockpit. The terrorists have seen to that. To be fair, theirs was an extraordinary idea, and had Chris known just how much he would go on to hate himself for becoming a shitty corporate lawyer, for somehow losing the love of his life, he might have had it first. If he had known that standing in the cockpit of a 747 was as good as things were ever going to get, he might have jammed his colouring pencils in the eyes of the crew, locked the door, and taken that baby down.

Chris sort of takes his hat off to them. Terrorists. The problem, though, is that they never show up at a time or in a place where they might actually serve a purpose. For example on a bus going down the Kingsland Road, on a Sunday morning, him set to work his hundredth hour of the week. For example outside Tesco Express, again on the Kingsland Road, him about to tell his ex that she has his number, that whenever she is ready she should just reach out. Both impeccable moments for a humungous bomb.

But it seems to be going through a relative dry spell, terror. No attacks in Chris cannot remember how long, not proper ones anyway. Big ones, Western ones. Which might explain why work has seemed even more boring than usual of late. Nothing makes a midweek afternoon pass quicker than dramatic, breaking news. Something worthy of a Live Feed. Normality briefly but gloriously suspended. Red graphics everywhere, exclamation marks, and just for a moment, very much the feeling that anything could happen. Chris may be sent home. He may receive something for free. He may have to fight his way onto a spaceship bound for Mars.

Quickly it becomes important to know what sort of numbers we are dealing with. How many dead, how many gravely wounded. One bystander reports seeing bodies on the ground. Another has seen blood, lots of blood. Soon there are rumours of video footage, and Chris thinks: where can I find this video footage? Precisely how graphic is this video footage?

Not that innocent people necessarily need to lose their lives. Donald Trump winning the US Presidential election, for example, made for a very painless day at the office. All that opinion to read. And absolutely nothing had excited Chris more than the prospect of a No Deal Brexit. The days following would without question have been the most eventful of his career. Tanks on Bishopsgate. Canned food. No internet. Nigel ends up dying simultaneously of hunger and thirst, with all the bacon trapped at Calais, and crates of Lapsang at the bottom of the Thames Estuary. Ingrid in Project Finance, worried she may be deported back to Sweden, drags Chris into the stairwell and begs him to fuck her. There is a fire alarm, nobody knows why, but Jacob arrives and herds them both to safety. The relevant officials happen to be in the vicinity, and

Jacob is given instant citizenship for his courage. Also the Range Rover that used to belong to Nigel, as well as his Surrey pile and all the money too. The next day everyone is instructed to work from home. Julie calls and says Brexit has really put things in perspective: she wants Chris back, she is determined to stop smoking and promises to read fewer books.

There is still a chance they will get back together, thinks Chris. Julie did not look at all well. He wonders whether their encounter counts as a victory for him. She made a fool out of herself by pretending she had not seen him. But then he a) admitted to missing her and b) let slip that embarrassing *obiter dictum* about reaching out. Fmfal. No, at best it was a draw. Probably though it was a heavy defeat.

Frustratingly he has no way of knowing how she is really faring. She has no Twitter, no Facebook, no Instagram. Stalking a nun would be more straightforward, more revealing. It would be devastating to see some inspirational post about moving on, to see a picture of her smiling or with her arm around some Latin sewer filth. But the not knowing is ten times worse. A thousand times worse

Really what he needs is the green light from one of her friends, divulging just how miserable she is, relaying her secret desire to give things another shot. There would then be a channel through which he could commence negotiations. The likelihood of him being totally humiliated would be almost zero. But none of her friends can stand him – he knows that. He never made any effort with them, never attended their parties, and now not a single one will be fighting his corner.

Chris reaches for his phone. He swipes back in time through his own Instagram, back in time to when Julie starred in it. Here she is, with her hands wrapped around a latte. The emotions triggered by just this one picture are – what even are they? He hates himself, certainly he hates her, yet apparently he loves her too. Suddenly all feels heavy: his clothes, his stomach, his life, but also the bus and the traffic and East London, as if he carries these things on his shoulders.

Next comes Julie, standing on Chesil Beach, turned away from the camera and looking out to sea. Day is ending and night is on the way. The sky is a mix of different colours. Peach and tangerine, grapefruit flesh. Blue, not commonly associated with sunsets, is here still playing a major part – a light and silvery blue. Silver, gold, bronze. There are mauves, lilacs. There are turquoises. One of the pinks is so pink that it is almost fuchsia. Then there is the shingle with its blacks and browns, the sea with its inky purples. Perhaps for only one second, perhaps for less than a second will the whole scene remain that exact shade of evening. And yet Chris has managed to capture it. The picture is so beautiful that he has forgotten the massive row that marred the walk out there and the walk back. He has forgotten that probably what Julie is thinking about, as she gazes along the horizon, is the most humane way to dump him.

Next comes their trip to Paris. Remarkable really how much they managed to fit in. Incredible how the cameras on these newer iPhones manage to capture even the buttery gloss of a croissant. No filter, none whatsoever on those boulangerie shots. Julie smiling at cheese. Julie walking away from him and vaguely towards the Eiffel Tower down a busy shopping street. Julie inspecting punnets of cherries. Julie in front of a painting. Julie in front of a sculpture. Julie staring up at a mural. Julie in the Marais. Julie by the river. Julie in a bookshop. Julie in another bookshop. Julie looking at old ashtrays. Julie looking at old books. Julie smelling old books. Julie asking some French fatso the price of old ashtrays and old books. Julie smoking on a terrace.

The whole long weekend began to distill down into a generally pleasant event, whereas he had, in actual fact, suffered through it miserably. As usual she had belittled him, for example when he claimed that one of the great films set in Paris was *Ratatouille*. He had browsed what felt like every flea and food market in France, every bookshop too. He had spent much of the Friday holed up in their Airbnb, working. He had trudged his way around four different museums and listened to the life story of Simone de bloody Beauvoir, none of which came under his personal definition of Good Times. Just two things had he really quite wanted to do there: dine at that place Anthony Bourdain loved and have anal sex, neither of which had been possible because her lunches had sat too heavily. But the pictures, the comments, the likes – everything combined to contrive the same lasting impression, that the trip had been a blast.

Plenty of people went on Instagram, saw fake glimpses of fabricated lives, and duped themselves into thinking they were worse off. But this is Chris, duping himself about Chris. This is his own bogus remembrance of his own things past. This is Chris willing back times and places that never actually were. Jealous of versions of himself and his life that never even existed.

Almost certainly she has still not been published. If she has, he can wave goodbye to the last of his chances. Her continuing failure – by which he means her own sense of continuing failure – is crucial to him remaining desirable, or at least necessary. Maybe he should offer to publish her. Effectively he would be paying to be her boyfriend again. He wonders whether this is beneath him, realises that he is now crying. He notices the little red hammer, mounted beside the window. *Use in the event of an emergency.* What about in the event of severe depression? *Remove the hammer to break window glass.* What about to break his own knuckles, to smash his own face in?

Here comes his stop. This woman, the recorded woman who has told him to alight for Hoxton Station and the Geffrye Museum, who is telling him now to alight for Shoreditch High Street Station – she too has known pain. Chris can hear it in her voice. When she says please keep track of your belongings, she understands that things can get lost along the way. Girlfriends, for example.

Chris gets off the bus. The pavements fronting Boxpark are busy. Chris looks in the windows to see how obvious his crying is. He is about to enter the penthouse apartment of a man for whom weeping is anathema, a man who quite probably has not shed one single tear of sadness in his life. He reaches the building and enters the code he has been given, sees in the reflection that his eyes are indeed red.

Now he has a brainwave. He could actually gain some kudos here by blaming it on cocaine. He could claim that he was so busy fucking and snorting that he simply forgot to sleep. Vince knows how it is. He will tell Chris to sit down in his big black leather chair, the kind with the wooden frame and matching poof. He will pour him a prestigious single malt, they will clink glasses, then Vince will offer to take his own minutes. He will draft his own term sheet. Chris should drain his whisky, go home to all the bitches and the drugs.

Reality though now, and Chris is in the lift. The woman announcing what floor they are on, the general direction they are heading in, what the doors are doing – she has also known pain. She announces their arrival, the lift opens and Chris emerges onto a landing. This high up, in buildings like these, there is only ever one apartment per floor. There can be no confusion, and in any event the door has been left open, as Vince said it would be.

Chris knocks and enters. Sitting in the big black leather chair is a guy about his age, who springs to his feet and introduces himself as Luke, founder and CEO of Blank. He looks familiar. He looks like a tosser.

Luke makes the smallest of small talk: about the palatial surroundings, about the iconic artwork – Steve McQueen sticking up two fingers to the crowd at Le Mans. Then he mentions how cold it is. Milder tomorrow though. Being basically a slave is bad enough in itself, but Chris wonders whether it might be more tolerable if his masters were not such cardboard cutout cunts, if just one would reveal himself as the magnificent specimen of some superior race.

Think of the devil and he shall appear, as Vince does now. And just as the devil was the most beautiful of all angels in heaven, so too does Vince look divine in his running gear. His visible muscles, which are all the arm ones and most of the leg ones, are taut and glistening. His hair is thick and tousled with sweat. His face is flush. He looks like the attractive Frenchman from *The Beach*. Outside it is barely one degree, but still his schlong remains a factor in the short shorts scenario. He is breathing heavily but also singing what sounds like the chorus to *New Rules* by Dua Lipa. Singing until he yanks out his earphones and crows:

'Bonjour bonjour my little pussyholes.'

'How far did you get?' asks Luke.

'Thirty K.'

'What's that in miles?' goes Luke again.

'Eighteen. Point six or something.'

'Jesus,' says Chris. 'What time were you up?'

'Sundays I always always get up at six. To be honest I sleep very little, rarely more than four hours a night.'

'Wow,' says Luke. 'I mean that's half what they reckon is necessary.'

'Thatcher got four hours a night. Tom Ford gets three. Macron is sleeping very, very few hours. If you want to win, you've got to be up and playing the game. And Sunday morning jogs are non-negotiable for me. They're the one moment of the week where I really disconnect.'

As he says this, Vince removes his phone from its arm sheath and uploads details of his run to Strava. Fellow users will now be able to see his route, his time, his average and minimum and maximum speed, his average and minimum and maximum heart rate. Vince will be able to judge himself against their efforts.

'One thing,' says Vince. 'We're going to have to think about how your platform integrates with Strava.'

'Yeah, no, I know,' says Luke. 'I'm already there. This is what I'm envisaging: some sort of qualitative calibrating, where you search Blank looking for runners to head out with in a new city, and according to your own metrics and what you yourself as a user deem competent, the beast dredges up only joggers capable of, say, five or six minute miles. Or let's say you're using it to find girls, then automatically it knows to adjust those numbers down slightly.'

'Nice,' says Vince.

He peels off his shirt. This is now the closest Chris has yet come to wanting him dead.

'I'm going to grab a shower. Chris in the meantime if you would walk Luke here through the ins and outs of what our Term Sheet is going to look like.'

'But... I...'

It comes out less confidently than he was hoping for.

'Yes? You?' mocks Vince.

'You and I will need a brief chat about numbers, no? Before I can suggest to Luke what his obligations might be under any potential Term Sheet. No?'

'Oh, ya, numbers, hang on I've got those here.'

Vince puts his hand in his pocket and already Chris knows: no numbers are in there. Sure enough when the hand emerges, its middle finger is cocked in an offensive gesture. Vince laughs.

'What I mean is just talk to him vaguely about the next steps. Okay?'

Chris nods and Vince disappears to take his shower. Chris wants to follow him into the bathroom. He wants to explain the probably apocryphal but nonetheless interesting legend surrounding the origin of that hand gesture. Apparently, just before the Battle of Agincourt, the French threatened to take every English archer they captured and cut off his fingers so he could never fight again. The French were overwhelming favourites, but being useless French dicks they somehow ended up losing. Those who managed to escape being slaughtered with arrows had to look across the battlefield and see the English longbowmen, waving their middle fingers at them.

Instead, he prepares to talk Term Sheet with Luke. But Luke is dazed, because he has just been Vinced. Chris has seen this technique many times. An old one, used on entrepreneurs too young or foolish to have shopped around elsewhere, which goes like this:

Once Vince has already decided to make an initial investment, the founders are lured to his apartment at the weekend. Before the meeting he gives off the impression that he is still on the fence, that they will have to pitch him hard. He turns up a few minutes late, having let them stew a little in the opulence of his digs. Then suddenly boom: he has committed, and the poor saps are euphoric. They are on the back foot, right where he wants them. At some point he leads them over to his window, looks out over the City, and says soon they too will be living in a place like this. They are so overawed by the whole experience that they eagerly sign whatever terms Vince feels like proposing. Which he has usually had the decency to run by Chris beforehand.

'So very basically,' says Chris, 'The document is just Vince and Picpus setting out the terms of the investment they want to make in your company.'

'Do you think he takes a lot of vitamins?'

'Vince? Yes, I suppose you could call them vitamins.'

'To have that sort of energy off the back of four hours is… '

'Yeah. There are all sorts of pharmaceuticals at work I think. Supplements, stimulants. So what I was saying is that you are going to be giving over to Vince, to Picpus, what are called convertible preferred shares in Blank. This is just stock essentially, stock that can be sold on his eventual exit from the company. Into the Term Sheet will go all sorts of provisions detailing how that percentage of stock might increase, depending on whether or not you hit certain targets.'

'Yes, yep, absolutely.'

'Vince is also going to want to retain vetoes over certain corporate actions that could affect his position. Not necessarily how you use his capital, but more generally where you are taking the company.'

'Naturally.'

Cue Vince. He is wearing a tracksuit now, drying his hair with a towel.

'Also Luke, and above all,' says Vince. 'What this document is looking to do is lock you in. Because what I'm investing in here is not so much the product as you personally. Here, come over here.'

Luke walks over to the window. Vince rests an arm on his shoulder and they look out over the City together.

'Soon you too will be living in a place like this. I'm sure of it.'

Chris lets his eyes close, opens them.

'Anyway,' continues Vince. 'What are you doing tomorrow?'

'I'm building a fucking unicorn,' says Luke.

Chris lets his eyes close.

'Good answer. Now one thing I've taken the liberty of doing is renting you some space at WeWork over on Bishopsgate. This is something I do for all my seedlings, because I want you in an environment where I can keep an eye on you, where you can really thrive. That's on top of your capital – call it a goodwill gesture. But these first few weeks post-injection, I mean I cannot describe how crucial they are going to be.'

'Yep, yep, absolutely. Absolutely.'

'The important thing to remember is that there are always significant punches to be rolled with along the way.'

'Good. So now Chris and I are going to have a chat, and he's going to get you that Term Sheet by the end of today. What I will need for you to do is sign and get it back to him. Understood?'

'Yes Vince. And look, I just want to say... I just want to say that you are not going to regret this. I feel confident in saying it will be the best investment you have ever made. I mean it. Together we are going to take Blank to the very, very top.'

The handshakes now. Vince goes with his classic, a shake that says get out there and build me that future, kid. For Luke this is clearly a moment loaded with import, but he blows his shake. In wanting to appear excited by the challenge but also slightly daunted he comes off weak. Now he approaches Chris and tries to fob him off with the worst of all shakes – the condescending respect shake, the grateful for all your hard work shake. Chris lets his own hand go limp. This is his fuck you shake, his fuck it all shake. His wish I was home wanking shake.

Luke shuts the door. The lift woman can be heard announcing his descent and now Vince turns to Chris.

'What do you think?'

'What do I... about what?'

Never has Vince asked for his opinion on anything.

'About him, about the company.'

'What... me?'

'Yes, you.'

'Well... honestly?'

'Honestly.'

'I think it's a piece of shit. I think it's worse than a piece of shit. I think he hasn't got a clue.'

Vince walks back over to the window, running his hands through his hair.

'His numbers are... ' Chris continues. 'I mean, there are basically no numbers in his literature. There is a gaping lack of numbers. Basic stats like CAC and LTV are very, very absent. There's nothing concrete. It's all just speculation.'

'Speculation is the name of the game Chris. The absolute name of the game. There's something about the guy I like. And look how quickly he brought me those users.'

'Yeah well I think there's something fishy there as well.'

'Okay, that's enough thinking for you for one day. The point is it sucks data, and if it sucks data, I'm in. I want you to have me a Term Sheet to look at by dinner time, if that's alright.'

That most certainly is not alright. That is a fucking holocaust of not alright. That is Chris missing all of the City game and at least the first half of Watford vs Stoke.

'Alright.'

'Good.'

'And, I mean, numbers?'

'I'm feeling charitable. Go with five scaling to twenty-five and water down the liquidation prefs that we put in for Moob. In fact no, cap at twenty.'

'Cap at twenty?' asks Chris, scribbling but incredulous.

'Twenty. Like I said, I'm feeling charitable. There's this... I'm fucking this chick at the moment and she's... Chris, she's insane.'

'That's excellent news. Twenty percent though, are you sure?'

'You know when you're fucking so hard you can actually feel a girl's bones?'

His silence suggests not.

'Anyway. She's on her way over so let's round things up please. Twenty, like I said. But rape him as hard as you like on vetoes and the tag and drag alongs. Then get it over to me asap. In between blozzers I'll try and cobble some comments together.'

chapter:fourteen

London, Monday morning. People have their passes at the ready, on their trousers or around their necks on lanyards. Waiting for the bus, waiting for the underground, waiting for the overground. In taxis and walking and jogging and cycling and scootering. Miserable midwinter weather: not too cold, not too wet, just drizzle. Miraculous how it barely even dampens the face yet still soaks through to the soul. Headlights brakelights streetlights bikelights all tripled and quadrupled in the slick streets, distorted by the damp. Is it not yet fully light, or already starting to get dark? And the noise, the noise. If the capital has a sound, that sound is a big red bus, swishing through surface water, overtaking with a furnace roar, pulling in with a screech. That or a tube train, hurtling into its tunnel with an iron shriek: the sticking and slipping of wheels on rail, the tormented ghosts of nine million living dead.

Smartphones everywhere. Smartphones in Mayfair, smartphones on the Old Kent Road. Smartphones up the river in Richmond, charting morning runs and rides around the park; smartphones down the river at Greenwich, where commuters check the time of the next Clipper. Smartphones on Hampstead Heath, smartphones on Clapham Common. Smartphones on snooze. Smartphones ordering Ubers, smartphones navigating Ubers, smartphones rating Ubers. Smartphones in the back seats of Ubers, reading articles about Uber or the latest smartphones. Smartphones in the ears of this bored and furious city: podcasts, music, radio. Smartphones buying books, smartphones reading books, smartphones listening to books. Smartphones in the faces changing from Bakerloo to Central at Oxford Circus, numbed with distraction. Smartphones watching films, watching series, playing games. Smartphones tapping in, smartphones tapping out. Smartphones in the free hands of people picking up papers; smartphones in the free hands of people passing them out. Smartphones in The Savoy and smartphones in Greggs. Smartphones reading I love you, smartphones saying I hate you, smartphones asking whether the pharmacy had it in stock. Smartphones wanting debriefs, smartphones thinking lunch. Smartphones organising pints, smartphones plotting wine, smartphones needing the strongest gin and tonic ever poured. Smartphones swiping winter sun, chatting winter sun, booking winter sun. Smartphones taking pictures of Trafalgar Square. Smartphones taking pictures of porridge. Smartphones framing Monday selfies: hair a mess, hello Soho, coffee vibes. Smartphones turning in full circles on Tower Bridge and London Bridge and Waterloo Bridge. Smartphones filming Big Ben, as the clock strikes nine.

Nowhere are there more smartphones, and nowhere are they smarter, than at WeWork. The name is appropriate for here come many groups of people to work, people grown wary of the conventional but outmoded concept of putting unnecessary space between things. Words, for example, or colleagues. Space means distance, and distance means a lack of connection. Space is literally the past. Space is us seeing the moon and the planets and the stars as they were before their light reached us, as they were seconds or hours or billions and trillions of years ago, back when the universe was young. Back before there were smartphones.

'Vince has signed you up to Labs.'

'Labs,' repeats Luke.

'This is what we call our global innovation platform, powering the next generation of industry transformation by helping start-uppers like you create the future.'

Luke lets the seriousness of that challenge sink in. He sees himself as a shaper of ideas, a driver of change, raised on a plinth and staring into the middle distance of a Valley dreamscape, a very rich man. As he follows this woman around Bishopsgate WeWork, semicircular stares seem to trace his progress, just as they will in the Stock Exchange on the morning of his ginormous IPO.

'We want to help you turn creative ideas into scalable solutions,' continues the woman. Luke cannot remember her name. She is unimportant though, not so much building the future as making sure the internet is working for the others who are.

'And I have heard that the coffee here is excellent. Does the Labs package come with free and unlimited access to coffee?'

'Yes,' says the woman. 'Our coffee is micro-roasted.'

'And the carafes of water with little bits of cucumber and mint?'

'Yes, fresh fruit water, yes.'

'There are also rumours about top notch beer.'

'Craft on draft, yes.'

'And I have access to all those things?'

'You do. Above all what we want to do for you is humanise the process. One of our founders grew up on a kibbutz and the other on an Oregon commune. That same spirit of collaboration is very much the vibe here.'

Finally she leaves Luke alone, and the future has begun. He is now a man in charge of a company, his own company. He can work wherever he wants, whenever he wants, however he wants, but the measureless sum of different possible things he could or should be doing has momentarily left him paralysed. Investigating this micro-roasted coffee situation seems like a sensible first move.

People are loitering around the machine. So far so identical to every office in the known world. Luke can feel a cheeky little bit of collaboration coming on. He waits his turn, behind a girl and a guy in deep discussion. The guy is American, the girl has not yet spoken. She takes notes while he gestures expansively.

'Yeah, yeah, yeah,' says the American. Now his arms go up and his hands move out, as if plastering an imaginary heading on an imaginary board.

'So that'll go up there,' he continues. 'Like that. And what I'm thinking is something along the lines of this, wait for it: *The Brand Reigneth Over All.*'

'Reigneth?' asks the girl.

'Yeah, reigneth. It's old English. You'll have to look up the spelling but I think it's just t h at the end.'

'Could we just put reigns? The brand reigns over all?'

'No. No. I want the drama of reigneth. I think reigneth evokes drama.'

They move off, clearing the way for Luke to choose his coffee. A colour screen tablet is built into the panel of the machine, and Luke considers his options. The mocha looks voluptuous, extravagant, three whole tiers of beverage. Never would he spend his own money on something so frivolous, but this is not his own money. This is not even money at all. While his beans are being ground, Luke hears chatter behind. He turns around to see two guys roughly his age, locked in debate.

'What about – hey, hi mate – what about Athena?'

'Athena as in the goddess?'

'Yeah.'

'Meh. What about Eruke?'

'Eruke?'

'Eruke. Eruke.'

'What does it mean?'

'Nothing I don't think. But it does resonate.'

'Yeah but we want something more... what about ZealPro? What do you think about that? ZealPro?'

'It just sounds a bit bonkers, you know? I have to be honest I like Sparsh.'

'Sparsh, what was that again?'

'Sparsh. It means touch, in Sanskrit.'

Luke leaves them, taking his mocha and moving in the direction of the breakfast bar. Perhaps here he can engage in a profitable exchange, something to get his creative juices gushing. Perched on stools are four more guys, all again roughly around his age. Luke, to his embarrassment, realises he is wearing the same shirt as one and the same shoes as another. He has the same rucksack as a third, who is wearing the same shirt as the fourth, who has the same shoes as the first, who has the same backpack as the second. All five have the latest iPhone.

Present are Tim Price, an entrepreneur, Tom Atkins, an entrepreneur, Tim Bateman, an entrepreneur, and Tom Owens, an entrepreneur. Price is yawning, hunched over what looks like a cappuccino but could well be a flat white.

'The tube was absolute AIDS this morning. Absolute AIDS,' he says.

'Mate,' says Bateman, 'You're a mug. Cycle.'

'Yeah but I don't want to get all sweaty though.'

'Shower here you bellend. Shower here.'

'Also can't be bothered. Also these babies make it just about bearable.'

From his Sandqvist backpack, Price pulls out a pair of headphones and places them on the bench.

'Feel how light they are though, honestly.'

Atkins picks them up. His facial expression confirms it: these are light.

'Is that the… ?'

'Sennheiser PXC 550. Wireless. The absolute daddy, ask any true music buff.'

'Price?' asks Atkins.

'Yeah?' replies Price.

'No, as in, how much?'

'Oh. £249.99 RRP, but I managed to find them online for £220. And obviously totally noise cancelling. Look, listen.'

He invites Atkins to try them on. Atkins obliges. Now, by the look on his face, it is clear that peripheral noise has been isolated. He has entered cocoon mode. Price then presses play on his Spotify *Made For You* page. Atkins bites his lip and really begins to concentrate, nodding his head.

'Yeah,' he says, removing the headphones and handing them back to Price. 'The levels are good, but the noise cancelling doesn't do it for me. Try these.'

Atkins reaches into his Sandqvist backpack and pulls out another pair of headphones. The last ones were black but these are grey.

'Oh nice,' says Bateman. 'Very, very nice. Is that the… '

'Bose. QuietComfort 35.'

'The latest one? With the update for Google Assistant?'

'Oh yeah,' says Atkins.

With a tinge of rancour, Price retrieves his own headphones and puts them back in his Sandqvist rucksack.

'Yeah, no,' says Owens. 'You simply cannot beat Bose when it comes to pure noise cancelling capability.'

Luke senses an in:

'Yeah,' he says. 'Bose are generally considered to be the best, when it comes to noise cancelling.'

They all nod in his direction and Luke nods back. With a tilt of the head he makes it clear that he is here to get involved in rather than interrupt the conversation.

Atkins now, and he cannot resist. He offers his headphones to Price, urges him to try them. Price takes them, places them over his head. He can shrug all he likes, but he knows they feel good. Atkins activates the noise cancelling and Price shuts his eyes. Probably he does not mean to, but still he shuts his eyes. Everyone around that breakfast bar understands: Timothy Price is right now living the dream, cut off completely from all the noise, all the toxic and relentless bullshit of his fellow human beings.

'Try the assistant,' mouths Atkins, contorting his face as if in communication with a deaf person. Price nods.

'Ok Google,' he says. 'Fuck Mrs. Atkins.'

Everyone but Atkins laughs. A pause, then Price laughs too, presumably at the response of Google. Atkins reaches for the headphones back.

'The only thing,' says Owens, reaching into his own rucksack, a Herschel. 'The only thing is when it comes to the music quality, Bose can let you down a tad. I always find their bass a bit squiffy. Try these.'

Onto the breakfast bar he places a pair of grey headphones.

'Shit the bed,' says Bateman. 'I didn't even realise these were out yet.'

'They're not mate. Not here anyway. My dad was just in Tokyo.'

'Oh my days. How much?'

'Not cheap. That I can tell you. But worth every yen.'

'Sony,' says Atkins, dazed. 'The WH-1000XM3. These as good as they say they are?'

'Be my guest,' says Owens. He knows they are.

Atkins dons them. Everyone waits. Owens turns on his bluetooth and connects his phone. He goes to his Spotify *Made for You* page and scrolls down a little until he finds the same song Price used to test the Sennheisers. *I Will Wait*, by Mumford & Sons.

'Oh, fuck,' shouts Atkins. He has to shout, because whatever preconceptions he had about how good sound could be have just been bulldozed. 'That is tasty. I mean those levels are *insane*. You don't usually associate Mumford & Sons with bass but that is absolutely banging, perfect.'

This is loud from Atkins, and other WeWorkers are looking over now, some of them very irritated. Owens adjusts an imaginary volume dial with his fingers and thumb, telling Atkins to quieten down. Atkins takes off the headphones.

'Sorry, was I shouting?'

'Yeah a little,' says Owens. 'By the way, with those you're looking at *thirty hours* battery life. Absolutely spaffs all over the Bose on that front.'

'Yeah those are some seriously nice headphones,' says Luke, taking one big stride forward. 'Check these out though. They were a Christmas present. I really like them.'

Luke reaches into his own Herschel backpack and pulls out a black neoprene case, about the size of a pair of headphones. He edges towards the middle of the group and puts the case on the bar. As he zips it open there is absolute silence.

'Fuck me,' says Price. 'Are they Bang & Olufsen noise cancellers?'

'Yep,' says Luke. 'Beoplay H8.'

The black headphones are tucked snugly into the black case, secured behind a sleek black band. They collapse flat, wonderfully ergonomically, a far cry from the clumsy contortions needed to fold away the Bose. Velcroed to the roof of the case is a black mesh bag for assorted cables, not like the messy melee inside of the Sony pouch.

Owens is fuming. He refuses to look at the headphones on the breakfast bar in front of him. Refuses to look, because he knows they will be the most magnificent fucking headphones he has ever seen in his life.

Slowly, dramatically, Luke removes them from their housing. The lines are sleek and clean, the branding tasteful and discreet.

'Is that real leather? On the band?' Price wants to know.

'Real, yeah. Lambskin. Feel the weight in them. Go on.'

Price hesitates, not sure whether Luke can really mean that. The two of them have only just met. But Luke insists. Price picks up the headphones, moves them up and down to gauge the heft, like he might a bar of gold bullion.

'Not very practical,' snaps Owens.

'Practical no,' says Luke. 'But I like them. I really only wear them while I'm working. Which is basically all the time.'

Everyone laughs. Owens too, guardedly.

Luke decides to make his play. Like the magician at a wedding, like the motivational speaker, Luke knows what he has to do: neutralise the principal cynic.

'Try them,' he says to Owens.

Owens takes the headphones, with no small amount of reverence. Luke sips his mocha, then says:

'They're on a proximity sensor, so the minute you put them on your head the audio should start.'

Luke watches Owens. Everything beyond the breakfast bar now feels far away. Nobody exists, not outside this immediate group of five. They could be anywhere, in any of the five hundred WeWork sites across the globe. Luke gets his first sense of just how thrilling life is going to be within this community. This is what he has always imagined, whenever he has heard the phrase *esprit de corps*.

Back to the headphones. Everyone seems to be willing Owens on, waiting for him to enter that sacred space of pure isolation. He puts them on. The speed with which sound is both blocked out but also brought careering into his ears clearly takes him by surprise. His eyes open wide, and Luke gives a thumbs up.

'On the head they look completely and utterly sick,' says Atkins.

About a minute goes by before Owens removes the headphones. He breathes out and nods his head. Everyone awaits his verdict.

'Yeah, I mean what can I say,' he says, handing them to Bateman. 'The isolation is top notch. Really top notch. The audio is smooth, pretty warm. They feel like butter on your ears, that's what's crazy. They're just gorgeous. Gorgeous man. Are you listening to Isaacson's Steve Jobs biography on there?'

'Yeah,' says Luke. 'I mean I've already read it a bunch of times, but I like to listen back to certain sections.'

'I know what you mean, some absolute pearlers in there. "Picasso had a saying,"' quotes Owens, quoting Isaacson, quoting Jobs. '"Good artists copy,"'

'"Great artists steal,"' completes Luke.

Luke knows he is on top. The trick now is to not appear too eager, to leave them wanting more.

'Guys I've just got to go and fire off a few emails,' he lies. 'Feel free to have a play around, then bring them over when you're done.'

'Are you sure man?'

'Yeah, yeah. No worries. I'll just be over there.'

'Where?'

'Just there, underneath that orange girder. There, by that mural. *Get High on We.*'

'Ok cool man,' says Owens. 'We won't be long anyway. Pricey remember we're meeting Fisher in twenty.'

Price nods but he has not heard and does not care. He is on his own now, lost in a world of flawless Danish design, lost in the story of Jobs cheating Steve Wozniak out of a bonus during their time together at Atari.

Luke picks up his mocha and his rucksack and walks to the other side of the room. The bluetooth range of those babies is about two hundred feet, so Price is hunky dory. Luke opts for the mass of faded leather poofs, lazes down into them. Oh yes, very civilised – he could get used to this. He feels like a Roman, like a senator. Like a consul? Perhaps it would not be a stretch to describe that ancient empire as a precursor to the start-up nation. Now he understands where they got all their oomph: reclining.

What time is it? Just gone ten. Luke has achieved nothing in his first hour, but this is such a pleasant place to hang out that he has no issue with being here beyond midnight. In any event, what bigger achievement than socialising? Why is he here after all? What is the end goal? To connect people. And the rule of any successful business, the absolute golden rule, is people product profit. In that order. Try shuffling it around and you will fail. Investing in the right people creates the culture, and if you get that sorted the product follows organically, and if you get that sorted then say hello to a shit ton of profit.

Luke takes out his laptop, takes out his phone. He can see now, written on his screen, the long list of things he has to do. It makes for horrifying reading. To start with he needs a good developer, he needs a good programmer. There is also the minor matter of signing that Term Sheet, getting his hands on le money. Yeah, do that first probably. Sort the money out, then worry about building a team.

Luke finds the email from Chris. Sent at 1:14am, ouch. He opens the attachment and scans the provisions that various blogs and websites have warned him to watch out for. These, they say, are where an investor will look to shaft him. Not Vince though, not Picpus Partners. Although hang on, that percentage right there is not going to work, no sir. Twenty percent is simply too high. By this maths, Vince is valuing Blank at a measly half million quid. Zuckerberg gave Peter Thiel only ten percent of Facebook for half a million, and here we are talking about a potentially way bigger return on investment. Luke knows Vince knows this. He knows Vince knows he knows. He knows because Vince showed his hand by appearing so keen yesterday. Not the slightest hesitation, which means he realises this mother is about to explode. Well, if he wants in he will have to come a long way down. A hell of a long way.

Luke calls Vince. The phone is ringing and Luke is shaking his head. Three rings, four rings, and now Luke sees another egregious number in the clause below. Fucking French bastard. Perhaps his Grandad had been right to vote Leave.

'Hello yes Vince?'

Now Price and Owen are walking over with his headphones. The lack of privacy suddenly becomes a pain, because really Luke would have preferred to remain polite, but now he will have to impress his new friends. He will have to give Vince both barrels.

'Well, Vince,' he continues, 'I'm sorry you're in bed, but if Picpus is serious about this investment then you're going to have to start pulling your finger out. I have plenty of other investors interested and these numbers are just unacceptable. *Pas acceptable*. And what happened to only needing four hours a night?'

Luke looks at Price and Owen, who are now standing in front of the poofs. He arches his eyebrows and neighs his head, as if to say: you lads know how it is, dealing with these highly prestigious Venture Capital firms.

'I see, I see,' says Luke. 'You're not sleeping. I… right, well, no perhaps you should give me a call back when you're… a little later, I mean. But I'm really not happy about these numbers Vince. Really not happy.'

Blanks hangs up. He weighs up the moment, tries to grasp the mood, evaluates all the different contingencies of this next bit of banter. Yes, he decides: they will enjoy it.

'These money men,' he says. 'They really are something else. The guy's trying to negotiate my seed while getting noshed off.'

about:blank

chapter:fifteen

Here you are again, back where you vowed you never would be. By here we mean a physical place, the bedroom of a penthouse, but also a metaphorical one, far less plush: the hell of unrepented sin, as described by Dante. Here you are on his loud and stormy sea, over which and in the dark you are forever being blown back and forth, like a bird on the wind. The description is a pretty good one, not that far from how you currently feel.

But probably your own hell would be a far shitter place. That one was for lovers, and you and Vince are not lovers. No lover would answer the phone, not while his lover was going down on him. No lover would actually come out and say, on the phone, that his lover was going down on him. And no lover would keep going down on her lover, not after all that. The fact that he did, the fact that you did, all strongly suggests that you are not lovers, that this is not love. Perhaps it is boredom. Boredom might explain it. You are beginning to remind yourself of a character from a Dostoevsky novel. Tired of life, tired of living, miring yourself in filth for nothing but the lack of a reason not to.

There it is, that taste in your mouth. Without getting ourselves bogged down in all that again, it never improves, that taste. You collapse back onto the pillow and pull the sheets up over your chest. You want to go to the bathroom but cannot, not immediately. That would be rude. Not quite as rude as him forcing your head down, as him broadcasting this blowjob to the world, but rude all the same. You close your eyes, and now that you can no longer see him, his noises sound like the noises of a primate. He grabs hold of your thigh. Much to your dismay it feels nice, having his hand there.

Seconds later he gets up, walks to the window, and says:

'The irony is, I only respect people who stand up to me. Then when they actually do, I immediately get the urge to crush them like ants. Know what I mean?'

Never have you found yourself in such a state of moral confusion. Vince, you think, is probably pushing Stalin for the honour of worst person to have done something genuinely great. As in ridding the world of Hitler, as in fucking you like a wizard. Apart from that he is surely irredeemable, down with the most atrocious dregs in the whole of human history.

It has just gone ten. You are late for work. The Tate and cultural outreach are a joke, but still the amount you are late for or absent from work is beyond a pisstake. Lately you have tired of the job, which comes as no great surprise because as we said, you have tired of everything. There is a Jenny Holzer exhibition at the moment, and pretending you have even the slightest interest in her work has proven a chore. Your colleague, in the brochure, has written that words are central to her work, whether pasted on a wall or flickering from a sign or carved in granite or stitched in wool. She has written that her texts can be forceful and apparently simple, but so often contradictory. Perhaps you deserve your own retrospective then. They could just sit you there, in the middle of the Turbine Hall, for everyone to look at. Very simple, very contradictory.

As well as Jenny Holzer, more pressingly in fact, there is Manon to be faced. Again you will be obliged to talk about Vince. The revelation that she has also slept with him, that most of her friends have slept with him too, has already crushed you with the weight of its awful predictability.

Now you tell Vince: you have to go to work.

'I have to go to work,' you say.

'Yeah, yeah, cool,' he says.

Still he is standing at the window, slapping his penis and deep in thought, if that is what it is.

'I'm going to take a shower,' you say.

'Yeah, cool.'

The shower is powerful, fantastic. It soothes your head, but still your heart feels like a low piano chord being pounded on repeat. Pound, pound, pound. Probably that has something to do with the coke. Nose and throat have both seen better days, but if you just keep standing here, under warm water, everything might be fine. But then everything has been washed, everything washed again. Everything is as clean as it is ever likely to be, yet still you are standing there. Gallons and gallons of hot water, literally down the drain. About Vince and his energy bills you could not give less of a toss, but there is the planet to think about. Destroying yourself is one thing, the planet probably another.

You cut the water, wrap your arms around yourself, tuck your chin into your chest. Drop after drop drips down and into the drain. Finally you reach for the towel and smother yourself in it. Strewn on the bedroom floor is the lingerie he bought for you, the black bra and the black panties and the black garter belt and the black suspenders. You have no choice but to leave it all here. You can hardly take it home, hardly pretend you bought it for yourself or for Ram, not when it cost what both of you make in a month combined. More than how it felt on, more than the quality of the lace, what really smacks of decadence is you donning then discarding something so dear.

You step into your Asos basics thong, slip into your Asos basics bra. The way they feel in comparison, they might as well be made out of cheesecloth. Your clothes are not even here. Your clothes are in the living room. Your clothes are by the front door, which shows how quickly you were out of them. The apartment is hip, it looks unlived in, and as you walk through it in your underwear, you feel momentarily like a woman in an advertisement for body lotion. You could put your foot up on the arm of this sofa, point your toes downwards, marvel at the smoothness of your legs.

Vince has come into the living room but still he is naked, still standing by the windows, all of which he has opened wide. To be fair it is hot in here, far too hot, but this is January. You wonder what would be wrong with just turning down the heating. Why not just do that?

'Why not just turn down the heating?' you ask.

He turns around. The way he looks at you, you may as well have just blamed him for a suite of French atrocities in Indochina. Blamed him personally. Mother of god though, he truly is in tremendous shape. What a pleasure, what an absolute pleasure to spread your hands out and drive them into that chest. Riding this man is like riding something sculpted by Henry Moore, only warm, alive.

You finish getting dressed, return to the bathroom, dreading all the while the impending adieu. It promises to be awkward, so awkward that avoiding it by leaping out of these very high windows seems like not the worst idea. You brush your teeth, you brush your tongue, you brush parts of your mouth that have never before been brushed. This time you came prepared, toothbrush in handbag, because as the saying goes: fool me once, shame on you; fool me twice, shame also still on you.

Now the goodbye. You tell him you are off, half expecting him to stay staring out the window, maybe a grunt. Instead he comes bounding over, naked remember, and you have zero idea what might happen next. This could be you, about to get beaten to death. Instead he pulls you towards him and snogs you like a demon. Deep and intense it is, wet but not too wet, one hand in your hair and the other fanned across the middle of your back, controlling you entirely. You are like a puppet, unburdened by conscience, unburdened by consciousness, freed from the weight of reason. Like a puppet, full of grace. His hands move down, they cup you and squeeze you and draw you closer, and your thoughts grow dimmer and weaker. There is only the kiss. It last three seconds, or perhaps three days. Who knows, who the fuck cares. Perhaps during it you are living. Perhaps in this moment, truly and completely and for the very first time, you are being yourself.

Mercifully he says nothing – mercifully because nothing needs to be said. You walk out the door without looking back. How ironic that the lift is literally bringing you back down to earth, because before you even reach the street, the voices in your head have returned. You resolve to drown them out with music. You put in your headphones and mosey around Spotify in search of something appropriate. None of the dead or distinguished artists that you publicly claim to adore will do. The Velvet Underground will not do. Ella will not do. Not even Joni will do. Nothing that requires any sort of unpackaging will work right now. Right now you need pop. You need direct, easy, plaintive pop. You need Coldplay, just admit it. You need *Fix You*. You need to listen to that on repeat, like you so frequently have since your dad died five years ago. You can do what you always do, clear your search history afterwards, erase all proof, but that song is precisely what you need. Not that it has ever managed to fix you.

This weather is horrific. Your coat is not waterproof. Nor is it sorrowproof. Nor is it disgraceproof. You will not be able to bear these temperatures or this rain until the end of February, probably March, but realistically, what with the increasing extremes of global warming, forever. You should ask Vince to take you somewhere on holiday. This liaison is gathering such overwhelming momentum that you cannot now see a tactful way out of it. Probably you will just go along with it for the rest of your life, so you might as well wangle a holiday. Get him to take you to Morocco, Tahiti, anywhere warm and with sunshine. You can have lots of sex in a sumptuous hotel bungalow, somewhere on stilts perhaps, somewhere with a private infinity pool. Having to put up with his meditations on power and human nature, having to put up with your shame – all of that seems like a small price to pay when skies are this grey. Anytime anybody in London tells you she is going away, you are always amazed, always jealous. Before she even says where: amazing, jels. She could be going to Yemen. She could be going to Kabul. She could be going to Sunderland, but still you would be amazed, still you would be jealous. She has escaped.

You cannot face going straight to work. Anyway, more than an hour late means you might as well turn up at midday. You can blame what will be your third period so far this month. You could have six more but still your boss would say nothing, not if it involved having a conversation which necessitated him using the word period, or any of its euphemisms. You suspect that you could stroll out of the Tate with a Seagram Mural under each arm, and if you cited lady problems poor Gregory would hold the doors and see you into your Uber.

Shoreditch High Street has become Bishopsgate. You have passed under the railway bridge and suddenly trainers and a freelance aura have given way to a more suited severity. You decide to stop for breakfast at a place called The Department of Coffee and Social Affairs. You sit down, alone in the corner, looking across the street at a featureless office block belonging to WeWork. It is green and grey, glass and granite.

One of the ministerial aides or perhaps junior civil servants comes to take your order. You ask him if there is such a thing as just black filter coffee, and he says yes, of course, the V60 method. He recommends either the Autumn Walks blend or Into the Mystic. You ask the difference between these two. With the Autumn Walks – Tanzanian, he says – what we are talking about is a truckload of hidden intricacies. Purple fruit aromas, strong blueberry flavours, strong strawberry flavours. Very rich, very deep. Into the Mystic on the other hand is a Nicaraguan blend, so essentially obviously that means a vibrant but balanced red currant acidity. Ripe citrus is gonna be prospering, with aromatic notes of toffee and baking spice bringing up the rear. Mouthfeelwise this is gonna be medium to heavy, with a moreish milk chocolate finale. Into the Mystic you go, with one blood orange tartlet.

You have to stop doing this. You cannot afford it. Coffee plus pastry plus lunch plus two more coffees is costing you the equivalent of two hours work each day. A quarter of your salary, gone. Then there are all those intangible, invisible gremlins like tax and rent and bills. Your commute. The gym membership you never use. Then factor in the essentials like Netflix, like Spotify, like Uber, like Deliveroo, like Asos, and you have enough left each month for one large glass of Pinot Grigio, plus two or three milligrams of cocaine. Really for breakfast you should be moistening dry cornflakes with sips of Nescafe. Really, mouthfeelwise, your mornings should be a bit more mundane.

One option would be to start doing a weekly shop, to prepare your own meals. But this is no option at all, because it would entail becoming one of those thermos and tupperware people. You would have to get organised, to forge a routine, but forging a routine is tantamount to accepting that the world has trapped and hamstrung you, that you have been harnessed like some browbeaten buffalo in Laos, condemned to plough the paddies for however long a buffalo lives.

Option number two would be to otherwise reduce your outgoings. Buy fewer clothes and shoes, for example. As if you could do that, just buy fewer clothes and shoes. As much as it might sometimes pain you, you were not raised a Buddhist; you were raised a Consumerist, so consume is what you must do, at least if your existence on this earth is to retain any vague semblance of meaning.

Three: start asking Vince for cash. The problem with that, though, is you would literally be prostituting yourself. Already you are to all intents and purposes a coke whore, swapping sex for drugs, but cash would be a whole different kettle of *poisson*. You would be cranking up the shame to not even able to look at yourself in the mirror levels.

Money. The only remaining possibility is to somehow earn more money. Deeply demoralising, how everything in life ends up boiling down to this one dirty fact. Not just some things or lots of things or most things, but absolutely every single thing. Every single thing around you in this coffee shop – the plants and the plant pots, the tables and the chairs and the benches and the stools, the bar and the plates and the cutlery and the napkins, the flour and the sugar in the cakes, the fruit and the chocolate on the cakes, the coffee beans and the various coffee machines, the water and the electricity that power those machines, the wood and the plastic in the floors, the concrete in the walls and the glass in the windows, the heat in the pipes and the light in the lights, the rubbish in the bin and the bin itself, the black bags lining the bin, even the paper those bags came wrapped in – everything has ended up there because somebody somewhere has been paid money.

The good news is that for the first time in nearly three decades, you can actually envisage a relatively painless way of making some. To say that Ola is interested in you would be like calling Pol Pot severe. This girl is forced labour interested. She is minimal food rations, reeducation camps, mass killings keen. She will not stop messaging you. She thinks if you can just get two or five or ten thousand more followers, if you can drum up some traffic with a daily rhythm of aphorisms and quotations and your own personal content, as well as some pictures of books and some others of yourself, she should then be in a position to sell you to publishers.

Last night, you asked her what sort of pictures. *The sexier the better*, she wrote. *Not hard for you*, she wrote. *Winking emoji, winking emoji, blushing smiley face emoji. How sexy is too sexy?* you asked, and she replied *no such thing* followed by four laughing emojis. So you sent her a picture of you chez Vince, dans le bathroom, in front of the mirror, dressed in all that black lingerie. *What about this?* you asked, before switching your phone to airplane mode. You killer you. Who knew you had it in you? The only question now is: for how long are you prepared to let this girl believe you might one day come careering into lesbianism?

You take out your phone. This is who you are now, this thing in your hand. Of course there are your memories, all that weightless data up in the Cloud, but the rest comes in at 129 grams. You feel so much heavier. Everything feels so much heavier. You and Ram have been replaced on the home screen by Lady Jane Grey. Which is apt, not because your plight is at all similar to hers, but because this phone is your life, and your relationship with Ram is no longer on the surface of it.

Apt because Ram has been banished. Still he exists, but somewhere more hidden, somewhere complex, forever a part of you whether you like it or not. You spend between forty or fifty minutes of each day still loving him madly. You spend between forty or fifty minutes of each day thinking it would be simpler if he just never came home. If he just died.

You have messages from Ola. Many, many messages. She likes that lingerie picture a lot. She suggests you dial down the sexiness just a tad, but if in doubt, send any pictures her way for a very thorough vetting. *Tongue out emoji, tongue out emoji, tongue out emoji.* She recommends ignoring Julie and having another look at Rupi Kaur, using her as an example. She exploded onto the scene by posting provocative pictures of herself on her period. When Instagram took those down she berated them for it, the lesson being: get people to notice you. Create a spectacle, grab their attention, then crack on with your own agenda.

Ola is right. The strategy is bulletproof, and a simple matter of shanghaiing the public at large. Playing to the vanity of the people who matter and hoodwinking the idiots. You are looking at Rupi Kaur now, looking at her Instagram. Truth be told, poetically speaking, the girl does not know her arse from her elbow:

i do not need the kind of love
that is draining
i want someone
who energizes me

Art maybe, but this is not exactly Anna Akhmatova. This is not even Ariana Grande. It sounds like the kind of thing Kahlil Gibran might sit down to write after four pints of cookie dough ice cream and seven seasons of *New Girl*. Not even inside the fortune cookies at Wing Hung in Guildford is the sentiment this tinpot and greasy.

Millions of followers, yet she herself follows nobody. She has appointed herself as a prophet and spreads her gospel, never muddying herself with dialogue, never cowering before the haters, sort of like Osama Bin Laden in that way, only less charismatic, less gifted with words, and however hard she tries – because obviously she is trying – far less rich and famous.

Not quite in his league then, but still a mastermind. Yet you cannot just copy her, not least because you would be the millionth person to try. You will have to come up with your very own strategy. So with what material might you be able to shock? Mixed race and the immigrant experience were already old hat when Hanif Kureishi wrote the best British novel of the nineties. They were even older hat when Zadie Smith wrote the best British novel of the noughties. Now they are such old hat that they are no longer even a hat, just worn scraps of felt, and do you honestly think you can do any better than two of the most rambunctious talents that Britain has recently produced?

Next: the menstrual cycle. Well, Rupi has gone ahead and rendered that quotidian. And seeing as you refuse to grapple with your father and his suicide, what else can be mined from your generally uneventful, generally privileged life that might captivate an audience? Come on though, if *Made in Chelsea* can go fifteen whole seasons of primetime television, you should be able to rustle up a few thousand more followers.

The coffee is yet to arrive. Considering you are paying money for it, considering these ministerial aides or civil servants are being paid money to make it, that is frankly a fucking joke. It has been ten minutes, maybe more. You can see him there, standing behind the bar as if it was the workbench of an alchemist. He is fiddling with all sorts of handheld devices. They could be calculators. They could be geiger counters. They could literally be anything, other than what they apparently are, which is necessary to make one small cup of drip coffee.

You take out your book. Dostoevsky. *Notes from the Underground.* You begin to read:

'The author of these notes and the *Notes* themselves are, of course, fictitious. Nevertheless, such people as the writer of these notes not only can but even must exist in our society – taking into consideration those circumstances in which our society was formed. I wanted to bring before the public more distinctly than usual one of the characters of the recent past. He is a representative of a generation that has survived to this day. In this fragment entitled *The Underground*, this person introduces himself and his views, and apparently wishes to explain those reasons as a result of which that generation appeared and was bound to appear in our midst.'

You can upload this passage to your Instagram for a start. If you ever do make it big, you can refer the literary establishment back here, back to the very beginning. You can prove that you were doing it all as a joke – you were subverting yourself and the world and it worked. You were being *ironic*. Finally, here comes your coffee. The ministerial aide or civil servant presents it to you as if he had to ride all the way to Nicaragua on the fin of a shark, as if he had to plan and execute a coup to overthrow its president just to source this one measly beverage. Out of spite you shorten thank you to thanks. You barely even smile at him.

You frame your picture, bending back the book and placing it spine up on the table, beside the little wooden board with your coffee and tartlet on. London is outside, in the background, and as a bus goes past you snap. You exaggerate the red in the bus and soften the lights inside, working in a mellower vibe, strong on the blues and yellows. You sharpen the focus on the orange lettering of FYODOR DOSTOEVSKY. As a caption you write Monday morning, lazy start. You copy out the passage, and now for the hashtags. Ola has told you not to be bashful on this front, so you fill your boots:

#book #books #bookish #bookworm #booklovers #bookstagram #instabook #bibliophile #reading #reader #readallthebooks #readallthetime #instaread #readersofinstagram #amreading #literature #russianlit #russianliterature #writers #russianwriters #goodbookandcoffee #booksandcoffee #coffee #coffeeandcake #cozyvibes #whimsicalmoments #dostoevsky #fyodordostoevsky #notesfromtheunderground #undergroundman #alienation #ennui #nihilism

edward:gooderham

chapter:sixteen

Every Monday, Ola worked from home. She referred to this as her reading day, and to be fair she did read. But she also masturbated like a maniac and spent whole afternoons disappearing down barely believable avenues on YouTube. There were documentaries on life in Siberia and interviews with Spanish Navy cadets. Videos of cows being milked. Clips of the popstar Brandy, backstage before a concert. People plastering walls, people feeding hyenas, people explaining Credit Default Swaps. Eyebrow threading tutorials. Afghani children blowing glass bottles to the tune of *Billie Jean*. Old men doing origami. Top ten Ross moments from *Friends*, top ten places to visit in Ecuador, counting to ten in Xhosa. How to properly slice a mango. How to combat fistula in developing countries. How to sharpen a pencil with a razor. And so on and so forth.

Most of it she found tedious in the extreme, as if she would rather have been doing anything else. The masturbation though: that was pure pleasure, a proper perk. Certainly it constituted the highlight or highlights of her day, arguably her week. What an idea, that even just a fraction of her salary went towards lying on a sofa and touching herself. But even at the office people were doing it. Ola had listened to a podcast about the porn industry and learned that most sites experienced their heaviest traffic when? Monday mornings. Between the hours of nine and twelve, at any one moment across London, dozens of people were probably locked in toilet cubicles, silently rubbing themselves off. Something to think about.

Doing it at work was low though. Tragic in the Greekest possible sense of the word: a desperate act in the name of Dionysus. It was the equivalent of wolfing down a fried breakfast at a roadside Little Chef, with nine hours driving ahead of you and no further prospect of food. Home was the one; that was where you wanted to be. Home was like sitting down to a nine course tasting menu with wine pairings. Silver service and a team of naked waitresses all of whom looked like Rihanna. On the terrace, gentle breeze, unbeatable sea view. Yes please.

The morning ones, still in bed, were the choicest. Waking from your dream into the common nightmare but then saying no, I refuse, I will not. Not yet. Once you were up and about, the trick was to earn it. Ola used masturbation as a reward, dangling it in front of herself like a vegetal orange dildo. She would make herself read twenty cover letters, write ten rejection emails, or get through three manuscripts before even thinking about her fanny.

Today she sat at the long oak table with a pot of green tea and her work stacked in front of her. Her phone was hooked up to the Sonos, running a Spotify playlist called *Productive Morning*. The first manuscript on the pile was called *Stiff Peaks*. Crap did not even begin to describe it. The story of a couple whose thirty year marriage ran into trouble, only to be saved by husband and wife deciding to pursue separate interests. The husband takes up hill walking, the wife becomes interested in baking.

This was what happened when people spouted stupid adages like *everyone has a book in them*. Like *write what you know*. It was a case of too much time on hands that would have been better sticking to pastry. Or masturbation. It was boring, it was badly written. All Ola was doing now was picking out four or five of the numberless flaws. She would then be able to claim, in her rejection, that these needed a bit of polishing up, whereas polishing a turd would have been more feasible. And another thing: why was it, and not just here but in seemingly all fiction, that only black characters had to suffer the ignominy of being compared to sweets? Her caramel skin. His broad back, the colour of molasses. Why were white characters never given thighs the colour of bun icing? Why had she not once read about somebody having the complexion of a Victoria Sponge?

Ola turned to *Chittagong Sunsets*. When Pushpavathi was just one year old, her parents had upped and left Bangladesh, following the rest of her wider family to the market town of Pudsey, just outside Bradford. Pushpavathi wrote honestly and mournfully about her recurring desire to go home, back to the traditional environment of her first twelve months. Could one ever grow up English within a conservative Bengali household? In one tragicomic passage, she phones the Malmaison Hotel in Leeds and begs to speak to Johnny Borrell, lead singer of Razorlight, after her parents refuse to let her attend his gig in the city.

Ola was committed to finding this a publisher. There was a real danger in people only ever seeing the same story, now more than ever, so she saw it as her job to promote as many unique ones as possible. But this was the third draft Ola was reading, and still Pushpavathi had not managed to tidy up her prose. To be honest it was slovenly, flooded with grammatical errors and excruciating similes, as is the Ganges Delta so often flooded, with water.

The chapter in which a young Pushpavathi begins to discover herself sexually, however, left Ola positively screaming for a wank. She described herself lying face down on the bed, grinding against the muzzle of her stuffed tiger toy. Things then went a bit haywire with a metaphor about the jungle, but the overall effect was still highly arousing. Ola had said three manuscripts though, which meant one more to go.

Wench, yes. Ola had been umming and ahing over this for a few days now. Julie, its author, stood out. She could obviously write. Her prose had real bite, real flow, and it kept Ola turning the pages. She tackled themes of sex and oppression. Nor did she shirk from exploring the hidden depths of her characters, even the dark places. Especially the dark places.

It was literary. Julie was literary. She cited Gogol in her cover letter, and with conviction. Here was the kind of book that Ola had once upon a time dreamed of writing. Selling it, however, would have required nothing short of a miracle. In an elevator with a publisher, who would be able to pitch it? Behold the tale of a privileged white girl, very angry about the state of the world, who not much really happens to over the course of ninety thousand words. Ola would be laughed right out of the elevator, in between floors. *Cat witnesses double murder; a silent witness, or is he?* That was what she needed, an angle. *Orphan attends wizard school.* Boom, sold. This was Julie though, who judging by the other night seemed to think all forms of selling were base and beneath her. Ola was therefore going to have to pass.

She stood up, giddy with excitement. Rarely had she been so eager for a session with herself. Yes she had read her three manuscripts, but only a paragraph into *Stiff Peaks* and already she was ruminating over the sexiness of the verb to baste. She escorted her vagina over to the sofa, closed her eyes, and slipped her hand into her pyjamas. She started tracing the number eight around herself, slowly slowly. She pushed the heel of her palm down, pressing it against her. Mmmhmm. Little digit suck, teeny tiny moan, then fingers back to the grindstone.

Phase one was proceeding like a dream, but soon it was time to crank things up a notch. Ola hurried up to the master ensuite, where Rosie kept her Phillips Sonicare DiamondClean. It was thick and pink and had five different cleaning modes. Ola took it, pausing to look at herself in the mirror. She hated her hair, she hated her face, and why did she look so young?

She retired to her bedroom, where she took the head off the brush and slipped its base inside a satiny summer sock. She wiggled out of her pyjama bottoms, got under the covers and activated White mode, a gentle intro aimed at removing surface stains from the teeth. She rested her vibrating bundle against the top of her vagina and bingo bango. Concentric circles, concentric circles, then already it was time to up the ante, to the speedier thrum of Gum Care. Oomph, tingling now, really tingling, and she kept insisting until the smart timer kicked in and cut her off.

No way to disable that sadly, but Ola got back to it with a Gentle Teeth Massage. Still nothing too heavy duty, but the tickle began to spread up and down and around her clit. Time to see how the little madam would respond to Polish Mode. Creeping up to around the fifty thousand brush movements per minute mark here, getting a tad noisy, getting a tad rowdy. If Ola had kept a stash of condoms and a supply of lube beside her bed, that Phillips would have been going straight up her vagina right about now. She considered it anyway but decided it was harsh on Rosie. She sucked her middle finger, slipped that inside instead, then with the thumb of her other hand she put the hammer down: Deep Clean Mode, seven times more likely to annihilate plaque than other leading toothbrushes, according to dentists. Her homespun dildo now sounded more like an airborne drone. Ola arched her back and groaned, a real groan, a deep groan from somewhere around the thorax. Hello to you, Mrs. Forefinger, come on in and join the party. And then the sodding smart timer kicked in, quashing the fun once more.

Ola exhaled in frustration. A fresh approach was needed. She wrapped a towel around her lower half, waddling downstairs to retrieve her phone, waddling back upstairs. She threw herself onto the bed and rammed a pillow between her thighs. She loaded WhatsApp and opened the picture from Lucy. The state of her. The pillow started to get it now, right along the crease. Ola was humping and rubbing, pivoting her hips back and forth. She alternated between looking at the photo and closing her eyes, imagining herself with Lucy in various states of coitus. Them in an office. Lucy draws the blinds of the meeting room, pushes Ola over the table and starts eating her out from behind. Lucy tears out pages from the galley proofs of her debut novel and shuts Ola up by shoving them in her mouth. Them on a farm, scissoring on a barn floor made soft with hay. Also there are rose petals, and Ola makes Lucy ejaculate.

Ola was close now. She ran her hands up and down her body and massaged her breasts and pinched her nipples before returning to her vagina and slaying it like an electric guitar. Then the pillow started getting it again. She bit her lip, opened her eyes, saw Lucy in her lingerie. The look on her face and then oh, that was it. Ola stretched out her legs and clenched them together, rolled over onto her back and brought her hands down over herself, crossed them and kept them there as she jerked violently up and down. Her eyes dilated and crossed then closed, while still she lay spasming in ecstasy. Spasming and spasming as if emptying something out of herself, emptying herself until it was all gone, all of it gone. Slowly the pained expression left her face, her grimace eased into a vacant stare, her breathing slowed. Shivering, she wrapped herself in duvet, then lay there not really awake but not really asleep either, suspended in some blissful otherwhere.

Five or ten or twenty minutes went by, maybe an hour, then Ola took her phone and checked her emails. She deleted three from Expedia tempting her with last minute offers. She deleted one from Reebok. She deleted eight more – why were these not going in her junk?

She opened her work inbox and did some necessary admin, filing away new submissions and typing out some polite rejections with her unwashed vagina fingers. She told Jenny Hannacher that the plot of *Stiff Peaks* was sagging a little in the middle third, that the husband character seemed flat. She told Julie that she could really really write, but while there was so much to be admired in *Wench*, she believed there were other agents out there who would be better placed to represent it. Lastly Ola wrote to Pushpavathi, telling her to show more and tell less, to watch her dangling modifiers, to watch her cliches, to have another look at some of those similes. Also words like crepuscular were best avoided. Also, with the dialogue, lose some or most of the adverbs, e.g. she snarled vaingloriously, he retorted grandiloquently.

After a shower, back at the long oak table, she turned to *The Weight Management Consultant*. This was the first draft of a book that Rosie had already commissioned for Harper Collins, and now she was asking Ola to represent its author. Lucy was 26 and had been working for KPMG. Via her Instagram account, she started documenting how she maintained a healthy relationship with food while working long hours. She posted pictures of herself snacking on nuts and seeds, or grinning from behind a gigantic salad at lunchtime. Midnight bananas became a recurring motif. She shared before and after shots of her abdomen, which had gone from resembling an underdone ham to a packet of hot cross buns. This was a simple message of wellbeing, delivered with a smile, and people quickly connected with it. Before she had even reached the certificate level of her CIMA she had more than fifty thousand followers. Harper Collins wanted a piece of that, so they offered her a book deal, and when a podcast came along as well, Lucy decided to quit management consultancy to focus on her brand.

She had turned her first draft around remarkably quickly – Ola was impressed. This was not her favourite part of the job, though. Frankly she thought the whole wellness industry was bullshit, a sinister ruse.

Because ultimately, whatever she tried, she always ended up feeling like the very opposite. Like badness. She had biohacked and rewilded, disconnected and reconnected, chowed her way through bushels and bushels of ashwagandha, but still she woke up in the morning looking and feeling like Sasquatch after six consecutive marathons through the desert. Meanwhile girls like Lucy could live off pork scratchings and Bacardi Breezers, and even if they were nursing the cystitis of the century, even if they were on not just their period but all the periods, still they looked like a million followers.

Ola wished the whole trend would disappear back down the hole it had somehow crawled out of. It was the new luxury industry: frivolous, snobbish, the reserve of a restricted elite. But there was no derailing this train, not now, in which case choo choo, all aboard. It brought money in, so it had to be seen as an ally, since publishers could then put those proceeds towards a worthier cause. Like government arms sales to Saudi Arabia, in that respect. Ola would have suffered five hundred books about forest bathing and goat yoga if it meant getting someone like Pushpavathi published, just like the future of Yemen and the lives of journalists were small prices to pay for more cycle superhighways.

The Weight Management Consultant was particularly abysmal though. The tests to get into KPMG must have been strictly numerical, because Lucy was literally illiterate. She could not spell and did not know the meanings of words. Was there not spell check? Were there not now apps, to help people with their grammar? Certainly there was thesaurus, because this girl used it with the ruthless efficiency of somebody who belonged in professional services and nowhere else. She had sought synonyms for most nouns, most verbs, every adjective, and this bid for sophistication stripped all meaning from her recipe methods. *Insert the papaya and imperceptibly bruise it by means of the pestle.* Then there was that word, scrummy, which she used far too frequently, aka more than zero times. No, Ola could not deal with this bitch, not yet. Maybe after she had masturbated another eleven times.

Instead she began reading the manuscript for *Dying to Live*, a treatise on medicine and transhumanism. The author was a retired doctor named Bikash Chaudary, and his aim was to illustrate the paradox between the spending of trillions of dollars on searching for ways to prolong life, in a society that has turned its back on the elderly. Chaudary envisaged a bleak future, one in which rundown care homes and hospices would be overflowing with depressed and ignored centenarians. Ola wanted to find this a home. It was a thoughtful and poignant book that addressed difficult questions, like why we live and what for. This was already the second time she was reading it through, and suddenly she realised she was crying. She was in the middle of a paragraph about death, about why we humans seem so hopelessly unable to come to terms with it, and a tear fell onto the page.

Ola understood that it was perhaps time to confront her mother. To confront the large malignant tumor in the back of her brain. But how could she just give up like this? It was selfish, it was cowardly. Ola wanted to grab her head and shake the melanoma out of her. Every day in the media there were stories about celebrities battling with cancer, celebrities beating cancer, celebrities giving cancer what for. They could do it, so why not her? Never once did you read about celebrities taking cancer lying down, celebrities letting cancer show them who the boss was. Celebrities probably thinking palliative care was the best way to go.

She decided to go round to her house. She would write her a letter and bake her a cake. When her mother came home from work, she would read the letter and eat the cake, then call in tears to say sorry for being so stubborn. She would be operated on, and if the surgeons failed there would always be radiotherapy, and if that failed too then chemo it was, chemo to the bitter end.

Ola retrieved the *Stiff Peaks* manuscript and photographed the page where the narrator described how to make her lemon drizzle slices, because as shit as the book was, those did sound bloody tasty. She set off immediately, putting on her headphones and listening to a podcast about ISIS. She stopped at Tesco Express on Kingsland Road to purchase caster sugar, icing sugar, flour, baking powder and lemons. The eggs and the butter and the milk were all organic. Still she felt bad for the chickens and the cows, but this was cancer we were talking about, a *cancerous* tumor. She could forget about her veganism for one afternoon. Besides, her mum had never found anything nice to say about even one of her vegan recipes. Then again, she had never found anything nice to say about a lot Ola did.

As she was putting her key in the front door, Ola was imagining how she might react when she returned home from work. Probably she would do that thing where she put both hands to her mouth then her chest and arched her eyebrows. She would read the letter out loud. She would take the tiniest nibble out of one of the lemon drizzle slices and make that mad noise she made when she tasted something nice. *Miamiamiam.*

Ola hoped her mum had an appropriate baking tray, otherwise the plan was fucked. Had she not had her headphones on she would, by now, have heard the noises emanating from the living room. But she was immersed in the podcast: a man named Abdullah was breaking down in tears, describing the heartbreaking ordeals of thousands of Yazidi women, kidnapped and kept as sex slaves by ISIS.

Ola made her way through to the kitchen to see about the baking tray. To get there, however, it was first necessary to pass through the living room. And when she opened the door she was confronted by the pale, pockmarked and wrinkly arse of an old man. To say his back was covered in moles was less accurate than to say his fatty slab of mole was dotted with spots of back. Worse was to come, because hearing the living room door open, he whirled round in panic, only to reveal the most repulsive erection Ola had ever seen in her life. Like the outstretched neck of a turkey.

All this trauma was unravelling in the most bizarre of fashions, sort of simultaneously but also in slow motion, and now Ola realised that the old man with the arse and the turkey neck erection was none other than her client, the Booker longlisted author Jim Timmons. Cue her mother coming into view, first sitting upright on the sofa, then jumping to her feet. She too was fully naked unfortunately.

Ola dropped her bag of ingredients. Bear in mind, too, that the headphones were still on her head, so all she could hear was Abdullah being interviewed at the refugee camp outside Mosul, divulging the most harrowing details imaginable about what had befallen those Yazidi girls. Ola could barely hear her own confused bleating, let alone the noises of protest and disbelief from her mother and Timmons. Let alone the knocking of whoever was at the door.

There was nothing to do in cases like this, when you had wanted to do something nice for your terminally ill mother but found a man you both worked for and loathed having sex with her, and not just sex but the kind of sex young people had, on a sofa that you yourself had lounged on maybe ten thousand times – there was nothing to do but turn and run.

chapter:seventeen

Michael knocked for a second time. He unslung and unzipped his cuboid backpack and removed two pizzas. Box warmth spread pleasantly across his palm. Still nobody answered so he rapped again, this time for longer. He switched hands with the pizzas, making the most of the heat while possible. Someone was moving towards the door at speed, then it opened and there was Ola.

Before he could speak she was gone, down the steps. Michael wondered whether he had just been made accessory to a crime. Before he could even think about following her, two old white people in dressing gowns came surging through the door. Michael assumed racially motivated sex crime, or lost lynching opportunity fortuitously regained. Then they were past him too, making after Ola.

These were peak happenings for a Monday lunchtime. Peakest of all was the idea that two middle class white folks might literally leave their abandoned door wide open to a random black male. As if the old man suddenly realised this himself, he turned around and walked back towards Michael, shaking his head.

'Yes,' he said. 'Pizza. How much do we owe you?'

'No man, paid innit.'

'Just give me a moment. I'll go and fetch my wallet.'

'Nah… '

Too late. The man disappeared inside the house, and not for all the dollars in America would Michael have followed him. He had seen *Get Out.*

'Yes,' said the man, reemerging with an open wallet.

'Nah, the food is paid.'

The old man looked up, confused.

'How can it be? You just got here.'

'Yeah but no, the app.'

'Yes. We ordered them on the application.'

'Yeah, so it's paid. On the app.'

Michael handed him the pizzas.

'You're quite sure there's nothing further to be settled.'

'Nah. Just like a tip or whatever.'

'So service is not included on the application?'

'Nah.'

'Do you have a receipt?'

'Nah, no receipt. All on the app.'

The old man was increasingly suspicious. His robe was on the point of unbelting itself, and Michael began backing away. Forty or fifty pence would not be worth seeing an old white dick and balls for.

'Wait,' said the man. 'Wait, tip, yes, okay.'

He stepped back inside and delved into the pocket of a hanging coat. Like a zombie he edged back towards Michael, with the pizzas balanced between his outstretched forearms and two weighty fists of change. Robe really hanging by a thread now. The old man gestured for Michael to hold out his hands before raining money into them. Coins the likes of which Michael had assumed were out of circulation. More coins put together than he had received in three years doing deliveries, perhaps eight or nine pounds in total.

'Cheers man.'

'You're welcome. But you're sure that's all we can give you?'

'Yeah, no man. Later.'

Michael decided to leave before anything really sinister could happen. As he unlocked his bike he saw the old woman coming around the corner, visibly upset at not having been able to catch Ola. Michael needed to be on his bike, to have put some distance between himself and these freakshows before they had a proper chance to regroup. Maybe he could catch Ola, see if the feds needed to get involved. Sure, because Pentonville prison was chockablock with old white folks like these, pensioners who spent their Monday afternoons chasing black youths round Hackney.

Pentonville, where his brother had actually spent two actual years, for a no less farcical crime. Pentonville, where Michael had gone twice a week to watch him cry. As time went by, George got thinner and thinner, looked worse and worse, until Michael could only bear it once a month. Between visits he would call instead, but still George cried. He wanted to come home, he wanted to come home – that was all he ever said. Please just ask them, please just beg them. I need to come home.

After each call, after each visit, Michael would get on the bus and go up to the Tottenham Academy in Enfield. There he would prowl hooded into the gym and glovelessly batter a punchbag until his arms were numb, until his knuckles were raw. If coaches were lingering, he would spare himself their concern by taking out his anger on a weights machine instead. He would do eighty or ninety repetitions of the same basic motion, pushing or pulling or lifting until his limbs had turned to pudding. He would sprint uphill on a treadmill, until his thighs and calves were nothing but useless fillets of lactic acid.

Michael bulked up. He got hench, putting muscle between himself and the world. But it was not enough, and the frustration began affecting his game. Michael, who had always been composed on the ball, whose temperament had always been unflappable, became the guy who had to be restrained by teammates. On the pitch he began to look less like Tom Huddlestone and more like a fox trying to tip a wheelie bin. He began shooting from distance, hoofing the ball out of play. He picked up yellows for dissent, reds for mad lunges, warnings from his own coaching staff.

Very probably he would have caused someone serious injury, had he not ended his own career first. In the fourteenth minute of an Academy match against Charlton Athletic, he charged in for a header that he was never going to win, only for his opposite number to duck at the last moment, leaving Michael to ballerina through the air. All that momentum, all that traveling mass, came crashing down onto a crooked right leg. His knee might as well have been the joint of a chicken wing. Anterior cruciate ligaments, posterior cruciate ligaments, meniscus, tendons – everything that Michael could have torn, he did in fact tear. And three weeks later, Tom Huddlestone was sold to Hull City, which just about said it all.

It was thirteen months before he could even walk normally again. Spurs were gutted but they had to let Michael go; his career was over before it had even begun. It was of no consolation, now, to think that it was not his fault, that he was worse off not because he was incapable but because he was unfortunate. That made it worse. That made him twice as mad. But certainly Spurs were right to give up on him, because here he was almost six years later, right knee still aching whenever the temperatures dropped or he pushed himself too hard. Pushed like he was pushing himself now, speeding in the direction he assumed Ola had hurried off in.

He turned onto Mare Street. It was lunchtime, crowded, and Michael realised that his chances of spotting her were minimal. He pedalled three or four times then coasted, pedalled three or four times then coasted, looking from face to face on the pavement. He passed in front of Subway, where he had been given his first job after leaving the Academy. George too, when he finally came out of Pentonville. Both of them became Sandwich Artists, which meant they mopped and swept and wiped tables. They spent hours peeling apart layers of sliced cheese. They counted olives, pickles and peppers. Michael was once shouted at, because a customer had said Chipotle Southwest sauce, not Ranch sauce. Another asked George – and this was irony at its cruellest, irony whipping his back and twatting his kneecaps with a crowbar, then kicking him in the ribs when he was down – if he understood the difference between turkey and chicken.

Michael would take his buns and see how close to the hinge he could cut them, sometimes slicing them clean in two, just as he had formerly sent the odd through ball careering out of play, or straight into the arms of the opposition keeper. By the time he turned eighteen, he thought he would have a shirt with his name and number on the back. Instead he had a cap and an apron, a polo shirt, and a little badge reading *Subway, Eat Fresh*.

It might have been different, had he revised for his GCSEs. At the time though, watching YouTube compilations of Yaya Toure dictating games from midfield, using his strength to create space, threading unthinkable passes – at the time, that sort of studying had seemed like the most literal way of obeying his mother and her pleas to take his future seriously. Which he tried to explain, when he told her he had passed only Maths and Geography, and would not be going to sixth form.

As far as she was concerned, both of her sons were now prisoners. Both of them had committed the most unpardonable of crimes, which was giving society even the slightest reason to keep them down. Boosting a chicken, flunking school – it was all the same. People could claim you had been given your chance and failed to earn your place. You had given the ball away, called the ref a wanker, got yourself sent off. Now you would wear an apron. You would suffer all the secret contempt, all the pathetic disregard with which society treats its artists, sandwich or otherwise.

Michael remembered where Ola lived, or at least where she had opened the door a few nights ago, on the other side of London Fields. Maybe she was on her way there. He cut across Richmond Road, turning right at the Job Centre and shifting down a few gears before pegging it under the railway bridge. Then he saw her up ahead.

The headphones, the chunky green coat, the woke walk – this was definitely her. He accelerated until he was no more than a few metres behind, then stopped pedaling and whistled. Ola continued on, refusing to acknowledge him. A couple were walking their dog on the other side of the railings.

Again and again Michael whistled, a little louder each time. Finally he sped in front of her and mounted the pavement with his bike, skidding to a stop across her path. Ola straightened up. Her eyes opened wide and her hands came up into two palms. Then she recognised Michael and slouched into a more relaxed posture.

'Yo,' said Michael.

'Eugh, rude,' said Ola.

She stepped down off the pavement, as if to walk around him.

'Yo, you okay?'

'Look, just leave me alone. Please. I'm really not in the mood.'

'But… '

'Did nobody ever tell you it's not nice to chase somebody down the street on your bike?'

'What? I was just checking you alright, after dem dressing gown crew.'

Ola was passed Michael now. He turned his bike and started slowly rolling alongside her. She put her headphones back on and looked towards the park. The dog walkers were watching vaguely, as their spaniel bounded after a ball.

'Why you ignoring me? This is mad blud. I was just tryin to be nice.'

Ola stopped again, removing her headphones. She looked at Michael.

'Why do guys always think girls are in the mood to be stopped and harassed? Do we have big signs on our heads saying please, get in my way, start talking to me? Do you think this is cute or something? Do you think you're flirting? You're not. You're threatening me. I don't know you. I didn't ask to speak to you. Did I ask to speak to you?'

'No,' said Michael, looking at his handlebars.

'Would you like it if a guy went up to your sister and started creeping alongside her?'

'No.'

The dog walkers had by now approached the railings.

'Is everything alright miss?' asked the woman.

'Fine,' said Ola. 'Everything's fine, thank you.'

She put her headphones back on and entered the park. Muddy patches marked out all the summer barbecues. Michael could feel the dog walkers watching to see what he would do. He turned his bike around and set off in the opposite direction,.

On one side of Eleanor Road were terraced houses. Glossy painted doors behind trimmed hedges and up railed steps. None of the windows were shuttered; these people wanted Michael to see their expensive furniture. They wanted him to see the tribal masks on their mantlepieces.

The tower block opposite was scaffolded in blue. Probably contractors were in, ripping out the combustible cladding. Probably residents had been told they would need to foot the bill themselves, because the freeholder had absolutely no obligation to. Probably they had been given a choice between finding forty thousand pounds from somewhere, and continuing to lay awake each night, wondering where the fire would start. How quickly it would burn.

The day after Grenfell, George was fired from Subway for finally snapping and calling their boss a fat prick. Estimates of the dead, meanwhile, were mounting. Their mum came into their bedroom one morning and told George to get up, to go and find another job, but George said why, what was the point? It was always the same bullshit. Nobody cared and it was bullshit. London had literally watched a hundred people burn to death, and nobody would get punished. Nobody would go to prison. Not one piece of property development scum, not a single one would go down, even though babies and children had been incinerated because of their greed. No politicians, no local councillors, none would ever acknowledge their guilt, even though whole families had choked to death, huddled together in corridors. Nobody would ever be held accountable, nobody would ever pay the price. Everybody would go back to talking about Brexit, about shit that did not matter, talking around in circles while people kept getting stabbed to death or made a bonfire of. None of them, not one would be punished, just like none of the bankers before, just like nobody was ever punished as long as he was rich and white. You had to be poor, you had to be black. You had to steal a stupid fucking chicken, two fucking chickens, whatever.

Michael wanted to go home. He would do two or three more jobs, then go home and cotch. He pulled off his glove with his teeth and retrieved his phone, swerving towards the curb. He accepted a delivery from an Indian restaurant on Amhurst. He put his snood in his mouth and breathed out, warming his chin. Had he known he would always be this cold, he would have stayed at Subway.

Trapped behind the sandwich counter, hearing about Deliveroo, Michael imagined himself mooching around London on his bike, generally loving life. There he was kept inside and made to perform the same boring tasks, even if he was given a salary and holidays plus one sandwich per day. If he was genuinely sick he could stay home, otherwise he was there to shut up and do what he was told, at least until his role could be effectively performed by a machine, at which point he would politely be invited to fuck off and die.

Deliveroo set him free. They persuaded him that to be anything other than out on the road, out for oneself, was the most degraded form of submission imaginable. Now he was flexible, free. Free to earn less than the minimum. Free to work round the clock without rights or protection. Free to go hungry if he was sick or incapacitated. Free to ferry the rich their wraps, until his role could be effectively performed by a machine, at which point he would politely be invited to fuck off and die.

Michael was locking up his bike outside the restaurant when an Indian man ran outside. He handed a brown paper bag to Michael and said okay thank you bye. Michael held the open bag in front of his face, letting the steam warm his cheeks. Then he remembered the one star reviews he had received for delivering food gone cold. He put it in his backpack and set off in the direction of the Lower Clapton Road.

He coasted for a while behind a bin van, unable to overtake it because of the oncoming buses, forced to breathe in its putrid fumes.

Further and further he followed this van, full of its filth and its rubbish, full of all the things London wanted rid of, until finally arriving at Paradise.

about:blank

chapter:eighteen

'Incredibly,' said Sir David Attenborough, 'His testicles have now swollen to the size of broad beans, as he readies himself to mate. Just one month ago, they would have been no larger than a pair of poppy seeds.'

On screen, a puffin puffed out his chest and beat back his wings, like Victory. The shelf he stood on was stained with moss, splatted with what was presumably his own faeces. The sea beyond was the same slate grey, and crops of wildflowers scattered the foreground. Here was a puffin on the edge, alone but defiant. Except no, because now out panned the camera to reveal hundreds of other puffins, possibly thousands, all perched on this same heartstopping verge of cliff. Some waddled to and fro, looking like old men off for the paper. Others took flight, while Attenborough explained what was on their agenda for the day. Fish, for instance, as well as not getting shitfucked by a marauding gull.

'Whether these final few puffin colonies can survive,' he concluded, 'Depends, of course, on us.'

Sir David fell silent, and string instruments began to chug. Then a French horn, low and rolling. Boom boom, big drums, everything getting louder and suddenly violins. Violins, violins, higher and higher until finally in came the gospel choir. Ram wiped away a tear. They really were up against it these poor feathery bhenchods, and all our fault as usual.

The doorbell rang. Ram went to the door, unlocked the lock, unlocked the mortise and opened.

'Okay cheers mate thanks bye,' he said, taking his bag of food and closing and locking the door again. He went into the kitchen, retrieved a knife and fork, a wad of kitchen roll, and returned to the sofa. The plight of the puffins had left him glum; he needed something inane to eat his lunch in front of.

The library of possibilities fitting this one criterion was Alexandrian. How to decide, with so much to choose between? Ram watched the trailer for a crime thriller set in Montreal. He watched the trailer for a crime thriller set in Bolivia. He watched the trailers for four police procedural dramas. He watched the trailer for *Sense & Sensibility*. He watched thirteen trailers in total, before beginning a documentary on a festival in the Bahamas that turned – the trailer promised – nasty. Ram needed to know precisely how nasty. Already he had eaten two onion bhajis.

So it began, with models in all kinds of swimwear. Halter and bandeau and flounce bikini tops, with string and cheeky bottoms. Full swimsuits too, in every colour of the rainbow. Models running through clear shallow water, dropping to their knees and flicking wet hair back over their heads like elephants might their trunks. But Ram soon realised that the nastiness had to do with financial fraud. There were unlikely to be any orgies taking dark turns, so he put down his foil tray of rogan josh and leaned towards his laptop. He put on an episode of *How I Met Your Mother*, but it was one he had already seen, so this too after eight minutes was abandoned.

The models were still on his mind so he decided to review some porn while he finished his pilaf. He navigated his way to PornHub and perused its homepage, scrolling down. He deliberated, working out what he was in the mood for. Again the choice was overwhelming, a whole Vatican of smut. Horny girl wants to eat throbbing cum. Kinky Czech bitch has an insatiable passion for fisting. Cute Latina roughly fucked and jizzed. Mum facefucks military stepson home on leave. Revenge anal, gangbang revenge. Up the bum on the toilet seat. Amazing slut, filthy slut, dumb slut. Amateur slut demolished by strangers. Slut with size fourteen feet. Do your chores or suck my dick, slut. I give him my ass.

Ram was done with the pilaf. He felt slightly queasy and reproached himself for having ordered and eaten that third onion bhaji. He wanted nothing violent, nothing messy, not with a quart of rogan josh inside him and all that rice. To be honest he would have preferred not to see a penis at all. He put his empty food cartons to one side and clicked on Busty Swedish lesbians allow curiosity to flourish with tongues and dildos. Busty and Swedish were both good; the less they looked like Lucy the healthier this probably was. Or was it the other way around?

Here were these two supposed lesbians then, elaborately lingeried on a bed. One was massaging her breasts, fully visible in an open cup bra. Her companion was licking a long, metallic dildo. This was soon discarded, and the two began aggressively slobbering on each other. Within no time, the vagina of the dildo licker was playing a central role, being pushed and prodded at by the other. She gave it a few quick laps of the tongue then smoothed a hand over it. There followed all sorts of smacking sounds and kissing and licking techniques, as well as some casual observations about the wetness and taste of things. Some spitting. The long metallic gentleman was retrieved and wielded with abandon, but none of it was doing anything for Ram.

Instead he made a prosaic search for clips of an ordinary girl masturbating. He scrolled down until he found a slim brunette who looked sort of like Lucy if he squinted. She was stretched out on a sofa, naked and alone, passing the time of day by noiselessly playing with herself. Just like Ram. He put his hand down his pants and lay there with a glassy stare, but his heart was never in it. He rubbed and pulled but he was too sluggish, too bloated. The prospect of an orgasm nothinged him. He closed the page, deleted his history, and went to throw his takeaway detritus in the bin.

Possibly he would have sex soon anyway. It had been about three weeks, so surely it was due. His fault, but once they moved to Tring he was sure he would recover some libido. Fewer murder victims and all that. He returned to the living room and picked up his phone. He lay back and held it above his face, scrolling through Instagram, flicking at the screen like a bored beggar swatting flies. One of his colleagues was in Malawi. Another was drizzling honey over a bowl of granola. Then there were all the older ones with children, and because yesterday was Sunday there were pictures of the little sprogs in hats and wellies or playing football. Reading *The Gruffalo* or peering through the banisters in their nappies. Independently putting their trousers on or poking a stick into mud. Sitting smugly in rucksack carriers or getting their hair brushed. Feeding themselves out of real life actual bowls, climbing onto the wheels of stationary tractors.

Then there were the Monday morning coffees, the millions of Monday morning coffees. At home and at work and in thermos cups, but mostly in cafes. Lucy too had posted one. Which was odd, because Ram knew this place – the Department for Coffee and Social Affairs. It was hardly on her commute; she had stayed with a friend in Peckham last night. Nor was it normal that she was still sitting there reading at gone half ten. Ram wondered whether it might have been a meeting, then realised that he knew more about what puffins did on a daily basis than his girlfriend of more than a decade. Did she have meetings? Probably. He resolved to start asking her more questions, start taking more of an interest in her life.

Ram read the internet next. He read about an architect with cosmic ambitions. He read about the most dangerous cleaning job in the world. He read about how to compost a human body, and why. He read about the Kangaroo and when it had learned to hop. He read about Hawaii raising its smoking age to one hundred years old. He read about plans to build a moon base. He read about Chinese New Year and the secret trend of fish tossing. He read about Italy and its ghost hotels. He read about grey squirrel being the ultimate sustainable meat. Since buying his first smartphone, Ram had read *Ramayanas* and *Ramayanas* of similar material. Whole *Mahabharatas* of clickbait, just because.

Two more hours before he was due at the hospital. Reluctantly Ram got up, walked over to the television and prepped the playstation.

He owned two games and was in no mood for football, so he inserted *Grand Theft Auto V*. Fifteen minutes after buying it he had already abandoned any pretence of accomplishing missions or following the story to its conclusion. Instead he liked to activate cheats that gave him a comprehensive arsenal of weapons, as well as armoured vehicles and practical invincibility. Only by tank fire could his avatar be killed.

He would usually begin by running up to the nearest unsuspecting pedestrian and beating him or her to death. Others might get their heads blasted off with a bullpup shotgun. The police would then be onto him, at which point it was just a question of scaling up the mayhem. With the entirety of San Andreas law enforcement on his tail, he would drive down into a subway tunnel and wait. Policeman and soldiers would start coming in after him, only to be slain in droves. The pity was that the graphics sporadically regenerated, erasing the Valhallan piles of corpses he would diligently rack up, such that he could never get a true gauge on numbers. But probably in an hour he could waste more than a thousand helpless guardians of the peace, before getting bored and trying to face down their tanks with a hatchet.

Now he stole Porsche and razzed it through the city of Los Santos, before hitting a jump that lifted him onto the roof of a skyscraper. This proved to be a perfect vantage point for the sniper rifle. He picked off nineteen women and children before the first helicopter appeared. This and the next four he blew to smithereens with a rocket launcher, before jumping off and parachuting down to the street, where he managed to massacre one or two precincts of police before stealing one of their trucks and tearing out of the city, losing them in the hills.

Magnificent, this game was. The only way Ram thought it could possibly be improved was if they released a version in which the protagonist was an Indian, the setting downtown Islamabad. He was about to minigun a passing freight train when he noticed a notification on his phone. A message from Luke, then another, then another four, all of them from Luke. Miracle reprieve for the train, which rattled past as Ram opened Whatsapp.

Bro, not sure how to tell you this but I think Lucy is cheating on you

What I mean is, Lucy is definitely cheating on you

So my investor, the French guy, Vince, I was with him and he was like dude let me show you a picture of this Asian (no offence, his words) chick I'm banging

So I was like okay

Anyway, then he takes out his phone and shows me the picture and the picture is of Lucy

Luke was still typing, and more messages had come through while Ram was reading:

Not just like Lucy on LinkedIn or whatever, but Lucy in this guy's living room in lingerie, with like her hand on her hip, all provocative and glaring and shit

I have been to this apartment, it's in Shoreditch. And this is her. It's definitely her.

And already this guy has told me how good she is in bed and anyway it's her. So to be extra sure I start asking all these questions like what does she do and where did you meet her, and he mentions the Tate and writing and he says apparently she has this Pakistani doctor boyfriend

I wanted to tell him you were Indian and that Pakistani was literally the worst thing he could call you

That you were British Indian, I mean

I don't really know what to say man

Ram?

This really sucks man, really

What do you think you're going to do? I'm happy for you to tell her I told you, whatever

Anyway I've now signed with the guy so it's not as if he can just back out of Blank, and anyway I doubt he'd be that angry with me. Lucy maybe, but ultimately it's you I'm thinking of her

*Here. You I'm thinking of here

Ram?

I can see you're reading this, say something

Do you think I should speak to Julie about it?

Ram turned his phone over and sunk into the sofa. He looked up at the ceiling and remained that way for a few minutes before the phone started ringing. It was Luke. He let it ring.

This was it then; this was how he lost her. Ram had always imagined, on and off for eleven years he had imagined, that he would be the one who might eventually grow frustrated. With her clutter. With her refusal to grow up or settle down. With her snobbish resistance to Tring. They might stay together or break up, but he would be the one to decide.

Of course he knew, but never had he really considered that the rest of their lives might depend on anything other than the force of his own will. Never had he really realised that he was only half of the equation. He was not alone, he had never been alone, and now a decade of unwitting selfishness came crashing down on him, as if it was the ceiling he was staring at.

And how about this for weird: more than anything else, what he wanted was to call her and apologise. He wanted to run through everything they had ever done together and ask what he could or should have done differently. His hatred was not the Hollywood kind he had always imagined, livid and out for revenge. Instead it stemmed from how pathetic this contrition made him feel. He hated Lucy precisely because he should have been blaming her, but he could only blame himself.

This Vince character though. Him he could blame. Him he could easily hate, without even anything concrete to go on, beyond the fact that he was obviously an underhanded bhenchod. If he was investing in Luke it meant he was probably rich. If he was investing in Luke it meant he was probably stupid. Probably vain, probably arrogant, probably shallow. Probably blundered through school, probably never worked hard, probably never without his phone. Probably exactly the kind of slimeball that by now served as a role model for half the planet. And what really seethed was the idea that this hatred, the ease with which it came, might have been exactly what drove Lucy away. Ram had spent so many evenings boring her with rants about the Vinces of this world, about their unearned success, that in the end Lucy had felt the need to actually go off and fuck one, just to restore some sense of balance.

Ram stood up. On the television screen was a man standing beside train tracks in the blue hills of a midnight desert. Over his shoulder was slung a minigun, and he would have done anything and gone anywhere Ram commanded. He was ready to maim and kill and destroy. He was ready to run back to the road, slit the throat of a passing motorist, then cruise up and down looking for anyone who even loosely resembled a Vince. Slap him around, stab him in the eyes, shoot him in the dick with a pistol. Without even the slightest hesitation, this animated mercenary would have let rip until the Vince was no more, until he had literally disappeared.

But suddenly Ram had no desire to play. He turned off the television, put on his coat and went outside. He had no destination in mind. He knew only that he needed to walk. He walked past Paradise and the tattoo parlour, the Polish deli and the Turkish picture framers. He passed the knitting shop and the coffee shop that was also a vinyl store. He passed the Carribean takeaway and the Salvation Army. He reached Clapton Pond and the newsagents, the charity shop. The fish bar and the bookmakers and the bike shop and the funeral directors and the laundrette and the pub. He felt the craziness of things being various, the craziness of London. So much more of it than he could ever comprehend. And yet none of it was as hard to grasp as his girlfriend, as one single human being.

Suddenly Ram heard brakes and a horn followed by more horns. He heard a scream from the other side of the roundabout. He heard shouts for help. Ram ran. Traffic was stopped and people were gathering on the pavement. There was an order to call an ambulance. He came around the front of a bus and saw the driver and a few others crowded over somebody on the floor. There was a blue bike between the curb and the road, its front wheel buckled. A Deliveroo rucksack lay face up on the double red lines.

'Okay, let me through please. I'm a doctor,' said Ram.

'It's... the lad he just came speeding through,' said the driver. 'Just totally speeding through, I only saw him too late.'

'It's okay, it's fine,' said Ram. 'You're in shock, I just need you to go with this woman here while I see to him, okay.'

Ram gestured for the woman to take the driver to one side. She too looked in shock, but she did what she was told and led him away. Ram kneeled down, immediately recognising the boy who had delivered his lunch only thirty minutes earlier.

'Right,' said Ram. 'Has anybody moved him? Is he breathing?'

'I don't think so,' said one woman.

'Have you moved him?'

'No, no. We've not moved him.'

'Okay, just if I could ask the three of you to back up a little bit please. Just a little space so I can have a proper look at him. Thanks, okay, thanks.'

They shuffled backwards and Ram was left alone over the boy.

'Hello,' he said. 'Can you hear me? Can you hear me?'

Ram tapped his shoulder. He put his hand on his head and gently tilted it back. There was a significant laceration above the ear from which he was bleeding freely. Ram opened the mouth and lifted the chin with two fingers. He leaned in close but felt no breath against his cheek. He took off his coat and wrapped it over the boy.

'Does anybody have a scarf,' he said. 'I need a scarf.'

Immediately a man handed him one, and Ram pressed down on the wound. He began giving CPR, counting to fifteen under his breath before giving the boy two breaths. He repeated the cycle, checking for a pulse but finding none, checking for some sign of consciousness but finding none. He started again, four lots of CPR punctuated with vigorous bouts of assisted breathing, and still he was performing this routine when the paramedics arrived. Still Ram would not stop, still he could not stop, until one of them crouched beside him and put her hand on his shoulder.

edward:gooderham

chapter:nineteen

What an awful story. Young delivery rider, knocked off his bike on the Lea Bridge Roundabout. He and the bus driver both distracted by their phones apparently. Third cycling fatality already this year. Really very sad indeed.

I turn the page, read an opinion piece. Simon Jenkins on Brexit. I am sitting on my own in an Italian restaurant with a large glass of Montepulciano, some breadsticks, and a copy of *The Guardian*. I did say I would try and care less. Jim thinks I take politics too seriously. Which he would say, because he belongs to that charmed class of people who it never even really affects. The last time he voted was in 1979, for Margaret Thatcher the first time round. Not once since, not even for the Referendum. I mean, what can you say about a man like that?

You ask for his opinion on something political, anything political, and all you get in response are these gnomic abstractions. *Hmm, ya, how ironic that Maggie, a diehard Tory, unleashed the economics that has rendered Conservatism, in the Burkean sense, impossible. Hmm, ya, how ironic that the Progressive Left, once so countercultural, once so interested in breaking taboos, has now become the dominant culture, so obsessed with erecting new ones.* Everything is bloody ironic.

He says I need to live a little in the time I have left. Which is a right laugh, because he told me that in bed. It has all been quite a whirlwind, I must say. He has me playing truant, like a schoolgirl. He calls me the Lady Chatterley to his Mellors. Which is absurd, because he went to Harrow, whereas I am the granddaughter of a docker from Bootle. But these days, he reckons, birth is no more important than ideology when it comes to class, in determining who makes up the elite and who is ostracised. And in any event, upper class middle class working class: everyone now lives the life of the mind, or not even the mind anymore but somewhere on the surface of the mind, somewhere behind the mind. We have forgotten our bodies, Cliffords one and all, paralysed from the cranium down, alienated entirely from the physical realities of our being. These are the kinds of rants a girl can look forward to during a romantic evening with Jim Timmons.

The physical side is really remarkable though, something I never expected. Also I just enjoy his company, because we are so bloody different. Take reading. There is just so much to read, such little time, so for me it has to be in some way *relevant*. For example I am about halfway through a remarkable book by Steven Pinker called *Enlightenment Now*, which is arguing that we need to resist this idea that the world is getting worse. The data clearly show otherwise. You explain that to Jim though and he becomes absolutely apoplectic with rage. Says Pinker is doing to statistics in the name of Liberalism what America did to prisoners at Abu Ghraib in the name of freedom. Torturing them, putting hoods on them, hanging them upside down, generally degrading them until they have said what he needs them to say, all in the service of an ideology he no longer even understands. Meanwhile Jim sits there reading *A History of the Crusades*. Three volumes and nearly a thousand pages of thoroughly debunked, overly romantic history. I asked if he was doing research for a new novel set during the era, and he said only in so far as all eras are the same. I sometimes wonder whether I should book him an appointment with Dr. Thakkar, my neurologist.

I expected Jim to be different. I expected him to be bitter and a bit mean. You think of people who write books like that one of his I read, and you imagine them as really nasty little people, all spiteful and supercilious. Before our date I braced myself for a racist and a homophobe and all sorts. A big misogynist. And certainly Jim is a tremendous snob, but he is also a generous man, very tolerant, not at all how Ola made him out. He says it amuses him how incapable people are of grasping that fiction is an act of the imagination, how much it seems to perplex them that perhaps not all the words and thoughts of his characters are his own.

Maybe in a way he is a bigot. Maybe I am too. I mean, I married and had a daughter with a Nigerian man. I have lived a life of personal and professional emancipation. But still I believe that there are differences between men and women, between black and white, and even if I see those differences as a beautiful, beautiful thing, these no longer seem like acceptable comments to be making.

I am from an older generation, a generation whose values naturally lag behind contemporary ones – naturally because things change. Even if I hated so much about the society I was born into, even if I spent my life fighting its more abhorrent failings, never could I have fully belonged in this one either. I would always have remained with a foot in each, ill at ease in both.

And it hurts, you know, because Ola and her age group, some of them go around as if just because there are flaws in the world we are leaving them, just because people are still not equal, just because life is still not perfect and the planet is in peril, well we have zero credibility as a result. We have absolutely nothing to teach them. If racism exists, if homophobia or misogyny exist and the climate is buggered, then it must be because all this time we were sitting on our backsides doing nothing. Which seems so grossly unfair to me. I guess if I had a message for them all it would be this. We are your parents and we are proud of you, but please stop blaming us for being human.

Maybe I should say that to Ola when she arrives. If she arrives. The last time I saw her was nearly a week ago, when I was chasing her down the street in my bloody bathrobe. Do I wish she could unsee her mother making love on the sofa? Of course I do. Can she unsee her mother making love on the sofa? No. I invited her for a pizza to smooth things over, because we cannot go on like this, permanently at war with one another, bearing grudges. I just wish she would stop being so stubborn. I just wish she could understand me better. To be honest I just wish I could understand her.

I struggle to pin down when and where it all started going so wrong between us. Maybe when she went off to America. It was her nineteenth birthday, I bought her a plane ticket, and she went with a group of friends from Oxford, all of whom had been accepted onto the Obama campaign team. She talks of those months as a time of delirium, working round the clock and sleeping on sofas, giving absolutely everything for somebody and something that finally and for once she could believe in.

Four years later she went again. The United Kingdom, in the meantime, she never missed an occasion to belittle. We were rubbish, we were boring, we were intolerant. And even if we did somehow produce an Obama, we would be far too backwards to ever elect him. Which, you know, is a right laugh, because you can keep your Obamas if it means getting a Trump. But she adored him, you know. Adored him the way my brother once adored Kenny Dalglish, blindly and with an almost violent devotion. Him coming to the end of his two terms, the amazing gracelessness of this other buffoon, seems to have broken the poor girl in half. I think she and so many of her peers are living these profound identity crises because of Trump; Jim thinks Trump has come about precisely because they insist on going through them so loudly.

I do worry about her. And whenever I get her to try and talk about her thoughts or her feelings, she always gets so angry. You know what I mean though, as if she needs to prove something to someone, or convince herself. If only her father was still around. Ola was eleven when he died. He suffered for a long time and that kind of thing is hell on a child. He was such a wonderful man, Ikenna, and I feel profoundly sad that Ola had to grow up without him around. Instead she had to go looking for him, and in places where he was never going to be found.

As soon as she graduated she decided she was done with England. She got on a plane to Lagos and spent six months there, working for an NGO. What hurt the most, when she came back, was that she was too proud to confess she had hated it. I know my own daughter, knew immediately that if she had gone to Nigeria to find herself, she was coming back still very much lost. It cannot have been easy, because probably she was pinning her hopes on arriving there and feeling some mythical sense of kinship, some connection with the soil, only to realise that she was far more of an outsider there than she ever had been in London. And I wanted to be there for her, but she never let me.

Still now, Ola seems intent on spending her life trying to find out who she really is and where she really belongs, instead of bloody living it. I wonder what I could have done differently to persuade her that she really is Ola, that she really belongs here. I think maybe her father would have helped her, you know? Much more than I could. Much more than I did. He could have made her feel more comfortable with herself and the world. He had the strength of mind to love both the place he was from and the place he had chosen as home. Which Ola never has, you see. Which still she refuses to do.

I do love this country, as much as I moan about it. But obviously I have failed to make her love it too. The sad truth is that she would sooner go to Burkina Faso and build a well, or teach in the Philippines, than she would board a train to Liverpool, ring a doorbell, and converse with a random Scouser. Which, you know, is painful. Because that there, this here, all of it comes from me. What I mean is, when she snubs that part of herself, what she is rejecting is me. Besides, I think you have to love your own country. You might disapprove of it at times, you might spend your time constantly raging against it, but if you try and ignore the realities that shaped you it will drive you bloody mad.

My phone buzzes with a text message and of course it is Ola, cancelling. She says something important has come up, that we will talk some other time. I check her Instagram and surprise surprise she has just posted. The picture is of her, with her arm around a beautiful Asian girl. The caption says cocktails with this one, all sorts of emojis and hashtags. I just… Really it hurts, you know.

Of all the different things I would like before I die, I think none would give me more pleasure than my daughter looking me in the eye and telling me she loves me. That she appreciates everything I did for her. That would be nice. Not that I did any of it to be thanked, just because.

Anyway, what else? The problem is, you wish for such impossible things. I have spent my whole life, wishing for impossible things. I remember that poem by Adrian Henri – another great Liverpudlian. *Tonight at Noon.* The one where he imagines everything happening but the other way round. Girls in bikinis moonbathing. Folk songs being sung by real folk. Politicians elected to insane asylums. Jobs for everyone and nobody wants them. The dead, quietly burying the living.

Then there are little things, like for one reason or another I have never actually eaten an oyster. So yes, I am curious to try an oyster. I would love to walk along Formby beach again. Other places I fancy visiting too. Here behind me on the wall, for example, is a picture of Naples. Jim says it truly is magnificent. And I think being from Liverpool, from a port city, maybe there is a certain affinity. All the ships and the destinations, the people coming and going. All of it gives you something to reflect on. It takes you out of yourself, you know. And maybe also those kinds of places make you realise: nothing is ever meant to stay the same.

chapter:twenty

Mount Vesuvius, what a thing. Julie spent the whole bank holiday weekend wondering where it stood in relation to them, like an infant anxiously seeking its mother. This unrepenting serial killer, this steadfast death machine, proved to be the perfect antidote to Luke and his sapping positivity. Whenever he began ruminating over the workability of some mad supranational scheme to neutralise mosquitoes or harness the power of tornadoes, Julie would gaze towards the volcano and comfort herself by remembering Pompeii. Civilisation, reduced to a layer of dust. She enjoyed knowing that even when future generations of Lukes set themselves the task of plugging its orifice, Vesuvius would remain.

Which nicely illustrated the extent of her depression. She would never be published, therefore existence was pointless and death the only relevant fact. Naples was charming her not in spite of this desolating nihilism, but precisely because of it. No other place she had seen seemed to laugh so hard at death, rather than cower in the corner until it could conceive of a way around or through it. This city had skipped through history suffering misery after misery, such that Neapolitans now awaited their next degradation with the same bored certainty that a Londoner anticipated new iPhones. In the meantime, they lived.

When Luke had asked Julie where she wanted to spend her birthday weekend, the choice was obvious. Julie had just completed The *Story of the Lost Child*, the fourth and final Neapolitan novel by Elena Ferrante. She needed to see this city that by now she felt so familiar with. Luke booked the tickets in late March, and Julie spent the next month reading everything of any importance that had ever been written about Naples.

She gleaned that somebody who was one hundred years old, who had lived there all her life, would have seen some mega, mega shit. Italian Fascism, German Nazism, Late Capitalism. This old woman would have seen invasions of various kinds, occupations of various kinds, liberations of various kinds. She would have seen war. Bombs falling from planes and blowing up buildings, bombs blowing apart cars. A volcanic eruption. Plague. Probably she had starved half to death, hunted for rats and boiled them in her pot. Maybe she had sold her body to American soldiers, for a measly can of rations. She would have witnessed corruption on an unimaginable scale, toxic waste ferried in from all corners of Europe to be buried in her backyard, murder and murder and more murder, mothers and babies murdered. And at the end of it all no doubt, she made a tomato sauce that would leave you spasming on the floor in orgasm.

Julie compiled an itinerary, suspecting that Luke would consent to whatever she proposed as long as it involved pizza and blowjobs. They arrived early on a Friday morning and went straight to the Airbnb to drop off their luggage. On the bus journey into the centre, Luke was visibly concerned by the state of the roads and the pavements. The walls, everything. The rubbish, the graffiti. Julie craned her neck in all directions, taking in the old and the new, the tramlines overhead running against the deep blue sky. She closed her eyes and listened to the horns and the whinnying engines. She let the bus rattle her body over cobbles.

The apartment was up great stone steps, on the top floor of a rust red building. Luke asked the host about wifi while Julie climbed a ladder, at the top of which was a tiled terrace with views over the city and across the bay. Everything was colour and confusion or sea. Sunlight beat back off domes and dishes. Already the day was warm. Luke suggested a shower, but Julie knew precisely what that meant, so she harried him out of the apartment and downstairs for breakfast.

They took a table outside at Gambrinus, a bar on the edge of a large square not far from the seafront. Luke engaged in a confusing discussion with one of the waiters about smoothies, while Julie commandeered his smartphone to read about the Bourbon Palace opposite. They drank coffee and ate sweet, perfumed pastries. Julie went inside to admire the Art Nouveau interior, because Elena had come here in *The Story of the Lost Child.* From there they walked up the via Chiaia, under the bridge and down towards the elegant Piazza dei Martiri, with its famous four lions in the middle. Here too was the bookshop where Elena had given her reading. Julie stood in front of the window, remembered that she might now never get to attend her own book launch, and wept.

She had not even been able to find an agent to represent *Wench,* let alone a publisher, and she had not taken the rejection well. Three years work, except it was more than work, because she knew people who worked, and most of them spent their days picking their noses, shopping online and reading about celebrities. Three years giving everything she could possibly give. Three years slaving away on her own. Three years of early mornings and late nights. Three years coming home pooped from shifts at the pub and still sitting down to write. Three years spent wandering through forests of the mind, forests so notoriously spooky that most people refused to even admit they existed. Three years alongside her protagonist, coming to terms with her, exploring her very darkest places, and the fact that she and her protagonist were one and the same did not alter the intensity of this companionship. If anything it made it more terrifying. Three years, and nothing to show for it.

Julie liked to tell herself that the money could not have bothered her less. To have worked so hard and for so long on something and for the material reward to be zero. Far less than zero in fact, if you took into account all the costs incurred during the time it had taken for her to write the book. Which was three years. Of course it bothered her though. Of course it did. It bothered her so much that it stopped her sleeping at night. She would lie awake and run through some of the bonkers sums she was confronted by on a daily basis, on the internet and on the television and on the radio. In life. The eighty billion pounds and more gone on improbable Brexit contingencies. The billion dollars wiped off the value of Snapchat just because Kylie Jenner said it was lame. All that cash, all of it swilling around, existing somewhere, and nobody could find even twenty quid to toss Julie for her toil.

But truly the money was incidental. It was irrelevant when compared with the other thing. Not merely a lack of validation, but more accurately the failure of anybody to so much as notice she had written a novel. Of the many dozens of agents that she had submitted it to, none had asked to see more than the first fifty pages or ten thousand words. She might as well have gone up to each and every one of them, stabbed herself in the chest with a biro, ripped herself open, carved the left ventricle away from her heart – still using the biro – yanked it out and plopped it on their desks. Only for them to grimace at the ventricle and say wowzers, those look like splendid vital organs, just not the kind we feel passionate enough about to sell.

Only Ola had read or at least pretended to read the whole novel, and even she only did it because she had been asked by their mutual friend, or because she thought it might help her scissor Lucy. The bitch. The absolute fucking lesbian bitch. She had sent it to friends, who had either not even bothered to read it, or shiftily told her it was not their sort of thing. And in an almost Boudican act of courageous folly, she had printed out her four hundred pages, with its sucking and licking and fucking and coming, and she had given it to her parents. Her mother abandoned it after the first chapter and asked how she was going to have a baby without Chris, when she was going to get a normal job, like a normal person. Her father suggested having a crack at a good thriller.

When he finished rereapplying his sun cream, Luke realised that Julie was crying. He took her in his arms. Of all the humans beings in this galaxy, he was the only one who had looked her in the eyes and told her that by writing this book she had done an extraordinary thing. Repeatedly he did it. Which, Julie assumed, was because his sex life depended on it. But he really had read *Wench*, and more and more he began to surprise her by looking up from his wok and congratulating her on a sentence that had just come back to him. Sometimes just a word. More and more she allowed herself to believe that he might have actually enjoyed the book.

For the very first time, he said, he had got a glimpse of what it must be like to be a woman, i.e. an absolute nightmare. He wondered how they summoned up the courage to even step outside their own houses. How they found it in them to go on dates. He wondered why he never loaded up *The Guardian* to find stories about mad women massacring five or ten or fifty men. Why that had never even happened once, literally not once anywhere ever. And periods, he barraged Julie with questions about periods. Tampons and mooncups. The pill. All of it was fucked, absolutely every single bit of it, fucked. He apologised on behalf of men everywhere and for all time. Which depressed Julie even more, because it confirmed her theory that if they would just read *Wench*, the world would be a better place.

Luke also praised Julie for her decision to set the book in London and the present day. That was the difference between *Wench* and the boring stories he had been forced to read at school, stories to which it was impossible to relate. Shakespeare for example, without wanting to name names. By this point, Julie was feeling like a conscientious Brexiteer, looking around and worrying that all the lunatics were on her side. But Luke had some criticisms too. The first had to do with the seven pages of vitriol, somewhere around the middle, directed at Sheryl Sandberg. He found it bewildering in terms of the plot, and argued that it was very probably slander. Julie could disagree all she liked with corporate feminism, but Sheryl Sandberg had played an essential role in building two of the greatest companies in the history of the world. And she was a widow. Her husband was dead. Yet again she was showing no respect for the dead.

His second issue was not with the book but with its author, with Julie, for stubbornly refusing to publish it herself online. For Luke, to have an unpublished book on your hands in 2019 was the equivalent of owning a second flat and not marketing it on Airbnb. It was to be a jobless person with a car who refused to make money on Uber. It was a miniature kind of suicide. Bang it on Amazon, he said.

Julie explained that to her, Amazon was the equivalent of Ebola and the Rwandan Genocide all rolled into one. She tried to explain that by flogging ebooks for free, by selling them at such dramatically low prices, Jeff Bezos had allowed people to believe that the value of a book resided in the paper it was printed on and the glue that bound it together, rather than the effort or ideas that had gone into writing it. For that, as far as she was concerned, he could take his undertaxed billions, build himself his rocket, and fuck off into outer space forever.

Luke looked hurt. He told her about the letter Bezos had sent shareholders in 1997. The visionary letter. He accused her of following old rules that had already been broken and served no purpose. But Julie told him Amazon was not even the point. The point was that there existed a stigma, and the stigma was basically correct: published books were better. Even in an era as brazenly individualistic as this one, it was still a type of insanity to believe that your own unfiltered bollocks was worth anything whatsoever.

Not true, said Luke.

True, said Julie.

Not true, said Luke.

True, said Julie. A good book needed a good editor.

Luke now ran rings around her, pointing out all the times Julie had complained about editors being out of touch, about having thoroughly abdicated any artistic role they may have once had. Which forced Julie to confront her actual issue, which was with the fact that she would have to go out there and sell herself.

Even a traditional publisher would have asked her to do promotion, but without one behind her she would need to hike up her fishnets, put on her heels and flog the fucking shit out of herself, whenever and wherever possible. Except this would be far worse than being a prostitute, because prostitutes elicit sympathy, and there would be none of that for Julie. She would just be another person on Twitter, another person on Instagram, another loser selling something nobody really wanted to buy. She would have to put all her actual opinions to one side and fake niceness with the world, even the men who responded to her sales pleas by asking if she liked to suck dick. Never would she be able to wade in, to tell them to suck their own dicks, or the dicks of their dads and dead grandads. Never would she be able to be honest, because she would be For Sale.

She would no longer be a person but a product, in a perpetual state of fear about losing market share. Her goal would be likes and retweets, and she would mould herself into whatever was most liable to garner those things, whether or not it was actually her. She would say nothing uncomfortable, nothing unpopular, nothing hard to reduce. She would become a part of the lowest common denominator circus that was sending the world disappearing up its own arsehole. In short, she would become Lucy.

Luke took Julie by the arm and navigated them towards Piazza Dante. He might have resembled one of those compelling leading men, the kind that littered old Italian cinema, but he was by now sweating so much that factor fifty was trickling down his forehead and into his eyes. His bumcrack had stencilled itself onto the outside of his beige cargo shorts. His Havaianas were chafing against the bridges of his feet and he cursed them every few metres.

By the time they walked into a bar called Mexico, he looked like a man who had just staggered across the entirety of the Chihuahuan desert. He went straight up to the counter and asked the barista for one very large and extremely cold frappuccino. After much confusion and some pointing, Julie deciphered that they were first supposed to pay at the till, where it became apparent that nobody in the establishment had ever even heard of a frappuccino. Which Luke refused to believe, because the word was Italian after all. Then he noticed there was nowhere to sit, so he told Julie just to get whatever she wanted and fill up their water bottles.

Julie had read that this was where one came for the best espresso in the city and she was eager to try it. At the counter, she closed her eyes and listened to the clinking of the cups, the tinkling of the spoons, the whirring of the machine. She lifted the porcelain rim to her lips and felt it singe. Luke stood underneath the air conditioning unit, watching with a mystified expression, as if the coffee was a shot of leaded petrol.

They walked through the arch on the opposite side of the square, along the street where Elena so often came to rummage for books. This was the old city now, the old old city, less elegant and more rundown, draped with laundry long dry and drumming with life. Tight and hidden alleys, running across Naples like lines in the skin.

Julie picked languidly through the rows and rows of used books in the stalls. She found a copy of the *Canti*, by Leopardi, took it and flicked preciously from page to page. Not that she spoke Italian. It was just words, all just gloriously senseless words, none of which had yet been debased by her knowing what they meant, by her hearing them misused. Luke eased the volume out of her hands and went inside to buy it for her. She smiled, turning back to the box and continuing with her browsing. She heard Luke in the background, asking whether he could pay using no contacto.

Now she came across a thoroughly battered paperback. *Tutti a Hiroshima*, by Jim Timmons. The cover was faded, the spine devastated. This book looked like it had been flattened by the biggest bomb of all time, then carted over potholed roads on a filthy wagon of jagged relics to another shop in another city, where it arrived just in time to feel the full force of another even bigger bomb, so big it made the first one, which up until then had been the biggest of all time remember, resemble a cartoon stick of dynamite. Thus it served as the perfect metaphor for the recent misfortunes of its author, because Jim Timmons and his career were now well and truly finished, blown right back to the stone age.

How? Why? After taking some time to reflect on what had happened, Ola asked her newest client Lucy to write an article about a black girl whose mother, race unspecified, had been the victim of inappropriate advances by white Jim Timmons. The Booker longlisted author had taken advantage of her, while she was battling a cancerous brain tumour. Ola sold the article to *Babe.net* and then, two days after it went online, her mother died. Which was threefold shitty news for Timmons:

1. He lost the first woman – he later told Julie – who he had shared a connection with in decades;

2. Ola was left motherless, and as the feeble bitterness of her feud became clearer, as she realised she could never now apologise, the desire to lash out at someone, anyone, became even greater; and

3. Timmons was left without his witness, without his lone alibi. Not only was she no longer around to refute the lies, but it was beginning to look uncomfortably as if the leery advances of Timmons were precisely what killed her.

The whole affair was reduced to a case of his word against theirs, to the protestations of one old, white, reactionary against the progressive and multiracial myrmidons of the internet. In other words, the bastard was broken on the wheel.

More than one tweet circulated alleging that he had actually raped a dead black woman. Twice he was interviewed, twice he lost his temper, after which he decided it was better to just lay low, wait for the storm to blow over. Mistake. The storm did not blow over. The storm swelled to the kind of proportions at which storms are christened with old white names. It became Hurricane Jim.

With no way for criminal charges to be pressed, the craving for mob justice intensified. Timmons exploded into the consciences of a generation that had never even heard whispered his name. Misogynistic lines were taken out of the mouths and minds of his characters and stuffed into his own. Former students testified that while he had never actually done anything to them, he had always had that look about him. The Norman Mailer footage surfaced, just the punching without the buildup, and it was rumoured that it had come about because Mailer – Norman Mailer, the man who got through six wives, one of whom he stabbed in the chest with a penknife – had been standing up for women.

Nor was there even the minuscule consolation of an upturn in sales, because books were not like movies. If Liam Neeson came out saying he wanted to run around looking for a black bastard to kill, he could always rely on a hardened clique of choleric white men going out and buying another copy of *Taken*, just to piss off those lefty liberal snowflakes. But no choleric white men read novels. Barely any white men full stop. Barely any men. They had to pick their battles these days, and one for the already tarnished reputation of a moribund scribbler was quickly deemed not worth fighting.

But as one dying star finally imploded, another rose. Lucy became a literary sensation overnight. She was interviewed by *The New York Times* and *The New Yorker* and *Vice* and *The Atlantic*. Her article was credited with capturing something essential that women everywhere were feeling about the sexual experience. Unwanted encounters that came about not necessarily through the use of physical force, but because of a complex cocktail of emotions and cultural expectations. Pride, embarrassment, anxiety, fear. She spoke openly about her own relationship, which had just ended in what she chose to describe as similar circumstances. She was given an advance of two hundred thousand pounds to write a book of short stories.

At this point, knowing none of the back story, Julie might still have been able to remain friends with Lucy. It would have been an almost bodily struggle for her to set aside her feelings about all this wildly unmerited success, but between that and living with the notion that she had dropped her friend because of basic jealousy there was no competition. She knew that Lucy had cheated on Ram, she judged her for it, but still loyalty to their friendship felt like a question of honour. It might therefore have survived, were it not for the fact of her continued correspondence with Timmons.

He had come back to her reply about *Dead Souls*, and done so humourously. Julie relished this kind of mock antagonism, and the two of them settled into a jocular rally about the novel, about what constituted a good one. As it became clearer that her own might never be published, she sought his guidance. After all, he had been honest, which nobody else had managed to be, and certainly nobody who knew the first thing about writing. She found his frankness a comfort.

Then came the article. She asked for his side of the story and he simply never replied. Already she had her suspicions, and when the furore increased, she went looking for his address on internet hate forums. It took him ten minutes just to agree to open the door, to accept that this was Julie his pen pal, not some Jacobin witch hunter or Stalinist agent of purge.

He was a broken man. From the moment Julie saw his face, she made up her mind to believe his version of events, before she even knew what it was. And that was the end of her friendship with Lucy. The bitch. The absolute fucking heartless lying mercenary bitch.

For lunch, in Naples, she and Luke ate pizza. They sat behind a red domed oven, burning away at a casual four hundred degrees. Poor Luke looked like he had spent the morning swimming over from Capri. Julie too was feeling the heat. She realised she had read her way through the Neapolitan Novels with a gentle breeze permeating her imagination. Light, flowing dresses. Cool shadows. Mediterranean bliss, even in poverty. But now her upper lip felt like a cattle trough. The backs of her knees were reservoirs for a good half pint of water.

After lunch they rode the funicular up to Vomero. Here too Elena came to wander around the Charterhouse of San Martino, where Julie and Luke found momentary shade. Timmons, who had a fascination with the Baroque, had told her to come here. Before she left for Naples, he had explained his theory, that the world needed a new Baroque. Colour, contrast, movement, detail. Exuberance, grandeur. Surprise. A sense of awe, to counter the bleak puritanism that was everywhere taking root. Which, he said, was ironic, because now even the Inquisition was on their side, flaming its faggots on a daily basis, not that you could say faggots anymore. Karl Ove Knausgård and other, similar purveyors of tedious autofiction he labelled Cultural Lutherans. He said that soon there would rise another Bernini, another Gentileschi to eclipse them all.

Julie gaped at the vaults, the moldings, the cornices, the stucco. Occasionally Luke would ask what he was looking at and she enjoyed telling him. He meanwhile rejoiced in the temperatures, resting his cheek against a cool marble column while Julie stared up at a gigantic fresco by Luca Giordano. *The Triumph of Judith.* Around and around twirled the celestial masses, while out at the edges and in bright, warm colours dwelled terrestrial life in its countless forms. Too many figures. Too many figures to even begin to comprehend, but all of them there.

chapter:twentyone

Why did he agree to this? They could have gone anywhere. If sun was what she fancied, they could have gone to Bodrum. When Julie first said Naples, Luke assumed she meant Capri or the Amalfi Coast. He started looking for affordable places to stay. But no, she wanted the city. Well if urban was what she was after they could have done Copenhagen or Berlin. Somewhere cooler, somewhere more normal.

This is madness. Temperatures hovering around thirty and everywhere you turn, the only option is carbs. Pizza, pasta, pastries. To be fair there is also dairy. There are also fat fistfuls of milky cheese. Vats of ice cream. No wonder their economy is flagging. Very probably it is gluten and lactose intolerant, holed up in some toilet blowing chunks, scratching its eczema screaming take me to a nutritionist. Holed up in Naples, like Luke.

But Julie is one of those snobs who cannot accept being a tourist. They refuse to go where everybody else goes, so they end up elsewhere, in exactly the same destinations as each other. Guidebooks are for sheep so they scour websites instead, which direct them to the same hidden places. They comb hundreds of restaurant reviews until they find where the locals eat, only to arrive at a veritable dining safari park, where the binoculars are all trained on one poor pair of locals sharing a bream.

Never ever ever must you refer to these people as tourists though. If Julie could have just accepted that there was no more travel, no more adventure, only different forms of mass tourism, Luke might have woken up to an infinity pool overlooking the Aegean.

Instead he wakes up drenched in his own sweat. The white sheets are now tainted with a mascarpone tinge. There is no air conditioning in the apartment, and for this he will be rating his host Amedeo no more than two stars. If by sunset tomorrow he has not provided at least a fan, Luke will publicly be denouncing him as a thief and mafioso.

He gets up and pads out of the bedroom. Outside a sunrisey vibe appears to be materialising so he approaches the ladder. The fucking ladder. Amedeo failed to specify that he would be needing his hard hat and dungarees. Julie says the apartment is authentic, but of course she does. Everything has to be authentic. The crumbly little streets, authentic. The used bookshops, authentic. The shirtless children playing football, the underpants hung out to dry. The pizza and the espresso and the granita, the mozzarella, the clams in the big blue buckets, so bloody authentic. Those vespas though. Luke draws the line at the vespas. Riding around three or sometimes four to a moped, helmetless with two toddlers in the footwell. That is authentic, to be fair. Authentic fucking lunacy.

He clambers up to the terrace and takes eleven pictures. Then back downstairs for coffee. But he can find no Nespresso machine.

Another thumbs down for Amedeo, who has instead provided one of those primitive stovetop contraptions. Luke unscrews the components, only to find coffee grinds still in the middle receptacle. Old, used coffee grinds. He turns around to the bin, where to his horror he sees zero potential for rubbish differentiation. Just one bin, for everything. Paper, plastics, organic waste. *Glass*.

This is supposed to be a G8 country. The native land of visionaries like Da Vinci, and here stands Luke before what is basically a bucket with a bag in. In all seriousness, there is going to have to be a cleansing, a good and proper purifying of all the places and populations that refuse to get their shit together on the environment front. For their own good.

Luke empties out the coffee grinds and turns back to the counter. Now he sees that the bottom vessel is literally brimming with mould. Whitey bluey greeny blossoms of mould. That is reprehensible, absolutely reprehensible. He leans in with his phone to document it, retches. He sends the picture to Amedeo and writes Amedeo, mate, this is really not on. As if that would ever, ever happen with a Nespresso machine. As if double Academy Award Winner George Clooney, whose wife is a leading Human Rights lawyer, would contemplate endorsing something even capable of spawning mould.

Which is what Julie just does not seem to get. The mere fact of something being old or authentic or traditional does not make it worthwhile. The whole point about Nespresso is that they looked at coffee and said we can do this better. The whole point about Amazon is that they have looked at everything, they continue to look at everything, and they say we can do this better.

No coffee then. Luke sits down on the sofa and begins reading emails. Tom has sent through his wireframes. Luke is not yet happy with the layout; some of the buttons need shifting around, and one or two of the other visual elements are a tad squiffy. But Tom has been a real addition to the team. Luke managed to bring him on board as user interface designer, selling him with the scope of the idea. In too came Tim, on the user experience side. He has written to say he wants to push for a full beta trail somewhere towards the end of summer. The functionality is getting there, but even the very limited tests are picking up bugs galore. Tim has no real gauge on stress and performance, simply because Luke is unwilling to roll out testing more widely. Which is because almost all of his users are dead.

He has therefore been busying himself with the marketing side, trying to find some actual sentient human beings. Which is never easy. He has been building a seductive landing page, building buzz, but he is fast running out of money, and he needs that positive beta trial if he is to attract any Series A funding. With all the uncertainty, any ordinary person would be drowning in daily returning tides of anxiety. But Luke refuses to focus on problems. Luke likes solutions.

Julie is up. Luke hears her close the toilet door. Now he hears her wee stream. This is his moment, not right now while she is sitting on the loo, but now more generally, before the heat ramps up, before the carbs are shoveled down. He slips out of his boxer shorts and hurries back to the bed. By the time Julie emerges he is casually reclining on it, like a

Pompeiian lover frozen in time. Rough as tits she looks, absolutely rough as tits.

'Morning gorgeous,' he says.

Julie yawns. 'Morning.'

'Sleep well?'

'Yeah, not too bad. Still quite bloated though. I mean do you think they literally eat pizza every day here?'

'No. They can't. Impossible.'

'I suppose. There's really not that much of it in Elena Ferrante. I might just be about to get my period though,' says Julie, rubbing her stomach.

'Yikes,' says Luke. 'About to, you say… '

'Luke sorry I can see you're all horny but I just can't face it. Sorry. If you like I can toss you off. Or you can toss yourself off. I'll just lie here.'

'No,' says Luke. 'That's okay, no thanks.'

They shower, dress, and go downstairs to find breakfast. Luke has long abandoned hope of baked eggs or granola, something with avocado, but would just a fruit salad be asking too much? Even while his Grandad was fighting the Wehrmacht at the battle of Monte Cassino, even while his comrades were dying around him in the mud, surely it would not have been impossible to procure just a cup of fruit salad. An apple, an orange, some pineapple. Three grapes.

Instead Luke has the choice between seven varieties of croissant. Plain croissants, croissants stuffed with custards, croissants stuffed with jams. Three different kinds of brioche. Oh, yes please waiter, already I am sweating uncontrollably so if I could just get one of those yeasty, buttery baps, that would be divine. No, why would you do a frappuccino, this is only Italy after all, in which case let me wash that down with half a pint of scalding hot milk. He orders a freshly squeezed orange juice, which is brought to him with four packets of sugar on the plate, as if it would be unthinkable to swallow something unambiguously healthy.

Julie wants to spend the morning meandering around the district behind the train station, because apparently it is central to her beloved books. Luke would almost rather visit the teeming, murderous ganglands where they filmed the Sky Atlantic series *Gomorrah*. Stations are in notoriously shit parts of even the nicest towns, as he remembers from his youth, when his mother used to put him on the train with instructions not to linger once he got to Kings Cross. Even that took north of three billion to turn into a vaguely respectable part of London, about four billion more than he assumes Naples currently has. And Julie can spaff over this Elena Ferrante all she likes, but the fact is that Luke has never heard of her, nor her equivalent of Platform 9¾.

The neighbourhood is precisely as he imagined it, worse in fact. He emerges from the metro barely alive, as if from the scorching belly of Vesuvius. They then have to traverse what he refers to as the AIDS Underpass of Death. This, claims Julie, is where Elena and Lila embark on their first adventure together. Condoms, syringes, soiled knickers: adventure indeed. Luke holds his breath as he walks through the tunnel, for fear of inhaling actual particles of human urine.

He comes out the other side to find himself in what looks like suburban Fallujah. Three petrol stations and a few squat, beige buildings, otherwise just dust and heat. One lone bush of brilliant Bougainvillea that

Luke has half a mind to uproot and repatriate to Kew Gardens. He who saves a plant saves the world entire. The graffiti is not street art; there are no uplifting or progressive slogans, only nonsensical tags and infantile squiggles. Posters pasted over posters pasted over posters pasted over posters. Announcements of deaths. Then there is the rubbish, but mentioning the rubbish is like mentioning the ground or the air, or the fact that Luke is alive. Just always be picturing rubbish, until advised otherwise. Julie says this is the real, authentic Naples.

They now turn onto the high street – high street in inverted commas the size of cranes. There is a salami shop and a cheese shop and a pastry shop. There is a pizza place, obv. A mechanic, a funeral parlour. Some monstrosity calling itself Naples Pub. Even if Luke pictures the worst, the absolute worst, the very grimmest Green Man in the very grimmest part of Grimsby, one of those hideous pebbledash bungalows, still that conjuring looks like a starred Fulham gastro joint in comparison with Naples Pub.

And that is the end of the high street. Now there is just nothing. More nothing then lurking in the distance some concrete skyscrapers straight out of *Blade Runner*. He imagines Harrison Ford and Ryan Gosling being asked to come here for filming and lols. Julie tells him the area is known as Little Manhattan and he lols again. He refuses to continue, not down this road. To do so would be genuinely irresponsible. He suggests an Uber back to the centre, but of course Uber have not yet made it to Naples, just as they have not yet made it to remote Papua New Guinea, so instead he has to retraverse the AIDS Underpass of Death then ride the metro down into the fires of Mount Doom.

Their next stop is at least more classically touristic, but still far from how Luke dreamed of spending his dirty weekend away. Mmm, the National Archaeological Museum of Naples. Mmmm baby, those extensive collections of Greek and Roman antiquities. Oh yeah baby, yeah, show me that Ptolemaic bowl made of sardonyx agate. For the sake of his grandchildren, for the sake of their grandchildren, Luke vows to help create more and more entertainment, such that none of them need travel to the town of Knebworth to see the plates and bowls and spoons he used to eat with. The glass cabinets filled with Panini sticker albums and Game Boy games. The airport terminals made of Lego and the posters of Carmen Electra. They will have better things to do with their time.

In one of the first rooms is a towering sculpture of the Greek god Atlas. He has long hair and a beard, looks in fantastic shape, like a slightly older version of celebrity nutritionist Joe Wicks. Luke initially assumes he carries the world on his shoulders, until he reads the information panel and understands that those are in fact the celestial spheres, aka the whole of the known universe. Which is logical, because back then they had no idea the world was round. Back then they probably thought it ended off the Algarve, the poor brutes. The panel explains that Atlas has been sentenced by Zeus to hold up the sky, and Luke remembers his own great mission.

There is at least, to his amazement, a room in this museum crammed with antique porn. It is called the secret cabinet, and as they enter it Luke looks around him like the male lead in an adventure movie, marvelling at the cave nobody ever actually believed existed. On the walls are faded murals and mosaics of Roman women, riding cowgirl and getting boffed from behind. Giving all the handjobs. There are orgies in both low and high relief.

As for all the cocks. There are cocks as candlesticks, cocks as wind chimes, cocks as neck pendants, cocks as amulets. Cocks in bronze and in marble. Terracotta cocks, basically a bargain box of terracotta cocks, so many that the curators have not even attempted to arrange them by theme, which in any event could only be Cocks. There are paintings and statuettes of men with erections bigger than themselves. Best of all, there is a sculpture of a nanny goat lying on her back, getting piledriven by a creature that has the horns and legs of a goat, but the body and the pubes and the cock of a man. This is apparently Pan. With his right hand, Pan grabs the nanny goat by her little tuft of beard, yanking her head forward so he can stare into her eyes. Luke leans in really very close, and he can see the marble phallus literally splicing what are presumably the minge flaps but could equally be the arsehole, for all he knows about goat anatomy.

For lunch, pizza. They scout five, six, seven streets around the museum looking for a restaurant that serves anything else but find niente. And the establishment that Julie finally chooses is so authentic that they serve only two variations: with or without cheese. No salami, no pepperoni. No rocket or peppers or onions or mushrooms or artichokes. Just bread and cheese, and a layer of tomato sauce so thin it would barely seal an envelope. Luke imagines that if he was to ask one of these authentic cavemen for some pineapple, Vesuvius would erupt in his face. All of it, all the ash and the molten lava, all of it right in his face.

Julie is speaking. She says she better understands Elena Ferrante now. She thinks there is an enormous amount of humanity in this city. Luke concurs: an enormous amount of the very, very worst of humanity. It surrounds him on all sides. The men have tattoos on their necks and fat spilling out the sides of their shellsuits. The women wear cheap, sequined dresses that compress their pizza bellies like tubigrips. They appear to have applied their makeup in their cars or on their scooters while travelling at Mach Ten. Everyone shouts at each other, shouting things that Luke cannot understand but assumes are Neapolitan translations of shut it Ricky you fat bastard, shut it Wayne you fat cunt, shut it Sharon you fat slag, shut it Grandma you fat old bitch.

Julie is still speaking. Now she is having a debate with herself about Greece versus Rome. Luke pictures the pool in his Bodrum idyll. Girls in white wielding mini mist aerosols. A mezze platter with cucumber, cherry tomatoes and olives. Hoummous. Instead the carbs and this heat and *ya, well, you see the thing about Rome is, culturally speaking it was only ever a pastiche of what the Greeks had already accomplished, although also the Etruscans blah blah blah*. That secret cabinet is yet more proof of what annoys him most about pretentious history gimps. Oh very authentic, very old, very good. Except for the fact that these people were essentially goat fuckers who kept slaves and enjoyed watching gladiators twat each other to death.

After the AIDS Underpass of Death, the museum visit, and yet another pizza, only one thing is missing before Luke can properly claim to have lived out his personal travel nightmare: the potter around a graveyard. But luckily Julie now wants to do a guided tour of some catacombs, further proving that she is only interested in things from eons and eons ago. Things that are figuratively or metaphorically or in this case literally dead.

They enter the Fontanelle cemetery and it is at least cooler underground. But imagine a cavernous necropolis with high walls of volcanic stone, and the heavily accented English of a rotund old Neapolitan. Now imagine that infinity pool in Bodrum, the sound of its little waves dribbling over the edge, and the gulf between those scenes goes someway to explaining how underwhelmed Luke is by Ciro, as well as everything he shows them and says.

They follow him around and Julie is gawping, literally she has her mouth open while this man talks about, amongst other things: the Emperors Nero and Tiberius, Saint Gennaro, Ostrogoths, the Duchy of Naples, Saracens, Lombards, Normans, Angevins, Aragons, the Spanish Hapsburgs, the Neapolitan Republic, the Bubonic Plague of 1656, the French Bourbons, the Parthenopean Republic, various boner parts (?!?), Horatio Nelson, the Kingdom of Two Sicilies, the Cholera outbreak of 1827, the Italian Unification, the German occupation, the Camorra. All those things. Ciro is incapable even for a moment of shutting up, and his every extra vowel clangs around the mausoleum in echo.

Now they enter – shitting hell, what even is this space? It feels like a depraved ritual cellar, as if Ciro might dive into a grotto and emerge wearing a hooded cloak, while a perfect circle of other hooded figures appear, all of them chanting as they slowly close in on Luke and Julie. Julie gets gashed across the palm and Luke has to drink her blood, but the real spectacle is still to come, because now the bleating nanny goat is dragged in, with Luke left under no illusions about what is expected.

Human skulls are everywhere, literally littering the gaff, stacked on top of each other in piles, filling little boxes on the floors and mounted on the walls. Luke asks how many dead and Ciro says forty thousand with more below the surface, many many more, certainly fifty thousand but probably a hundred and possibly even millions. Ciro falls silent and Julie is silent and Luke is silent, and suddenly all he can think about is data. The tragic waste of millennia and millennia of inexcusably unmonetized data. The leveraging potential of whole worlds of dead souls.

edward:gooderham

chapter:twentytwo

Vince crouches behind a distressed leather sofa. He discards his spent magazine, reaches into his ammo belt, taps a new one against his kiteboarding helmet. He clips it into his blaster and moves the slide backwards then forwards. This is the Nerf Elite Delta Trooper, suitable for ages eight and over, capable of firing twelve sponge darts almost thirty metres.

He rises and swivels and aims. Chris is on the other side of the room, hunched under the recessed woodwork of the bar, reloading his Alphastrike Series Alphahawk. Better accuracy but nowhere near the same rapidity of firepower. Beside him is Luke, wielding the Elite Infinus, aka the face annihilator. The trio have just won a firefight that left one of their enemies down and forced the others into retreat. Tom Owens was grounded by a dart to the chest. Vince executed him with another to the forehead at point blank range, before slinging the Thunderhawk over his shoulder to have in reserve.

Vince waves to Chris, points to himself, then to Luke, then to Chris, then to the corridor leading towards Meeting Hub B. What he means is: you lead, we follow. Chris accepts without much enthusiasm. He gets to his feet and starts off down the corridor, Vince and Luke at his rear. They are wearing bibs with POLICE emblazoned across the back, which Vince bought from an apparel company in Pimlico. Their enemies – the Tims and the one remaining Tom – are dressed in those bright yellow vests worn by protestors in his native France.

As Chris heads around the corner, to within sight of Meeting Hub B, Vince expects him to come under fire. But the door is closed, the blinds behind the glass partitioning drawn.

'Chris,' whispers Vince. 'Chris. Chris. Chris, Chris. *Chris.*'

Finally Chris turns round, mere metres from the door.

'Chris, they're dug in,' breathes Vince. 'You're going to have to… '

'Vince sorry I can't hear you,' says Chris. 'I can't hear.'

Vince is furious. He grabs Chris by the bib and pulls him close.

'Storm it. Luke and I will provide covering fire.'

Luke nods, inspecting the underside of his Elite Infinus.

'But they'll bumfuck me the minute… Fine, okay, fine.'

'Wait,' says Vince. 'Give me a sec to set up the Thunderhawk.'

Vince drops to the floor and mounts the gigantic machine gun. Luke stands behind, sights trained on the door. Vince gives Chris the thumbs up and watches him tiptoe towards the door. He pauses, pushes it open and is immediately felled, not by the enemy but by volleys of friendly fire into his back and neck and skull. The tactic is vindicated though, because a Yellow Vest takes the bait and crawls forward to seize his weapon, straight into the line of fire. Vince lets rip and Tim Bateman dies five times over, taking perhaps a dozen darts in the eyes and mouth and throat. Vince keeps hooning foam into his prostrate cadaver, until Luke shakes his investor by the shoulder and says:

'Vince mate he's down. He's down.'

Vince abandons the spent Thunderhawk, getting to his feet and ghosting towards the open door with Luke.

'Stop moving you cunts, you're dead.'

'Yeah but Vince his elbow is literally in my scrot,' says Chris.

'Shut up. Shut the fuck up.'

The corpses fidget into a more bearable choreography while Vince and Luke stand flat against the glass partitioning. They exchange nonsensical mimes before bursting into Meeting Hub B. Vince yells:

'Suck my fucking cock bitches.'

But the hub is empty; Bateman was a decoy.

Luke picks up his foam darts and reloads the Elite Infinus. Vince meanwhile kicks Bateman aside and exchanges his Delta Trooper for the Modulus. This is the weapon he wanted from the start, but he preferred the idea of prizing it from dead hands. It is both rocket launcher and assault rifle, with an adjustable shoulder stock and sniper sight. The two POLICE move down the corridor in formation, training their blasters left and right then back again. A human figure rounds the corner and receives a missile, straight in the belly.

'What the fuck?' says Vince.

'Sorry Amy,' says Luke. 'Did you not see the notice?'

'Jesus,' says Amy, stroking her belly. 'What notice? That actually hurt. It could have taken my eye out.'

'We put a notice up, saying there was a Nerf game in progress.'

'No,' says Amy. 'I obviously didn't see it, no.'

'Too bad babe,' says Vince, stooping to retrieve his wasted missile. 'Tell me where those two *Gilets Jaunes* are and I won't have to smash another up your skirt.'

'No, Vince, mate,' says Luke. 'That's not on.'

'Gross. Creep. Fuck off.'

Vince blows Amy a kiss and presses on towards the lift area. Luke is still back there apologising as he rounds the final corner. Nobody. Taped to the wall is a piece of paper: SEE YOU IN THE GARAGE, BENDERS. Vince rips it away and summons the lift.

By the time it dings its arrival, both men have their weapons aimed at the doors. Gloria turns out to be in there, one of the cleaners, but she barely even flinches, as if she has had actual real life machine guns waved in her face before, and therefore learned to spot the difference between genuine danger and dickheads being dickheads.

'Hi Gloria,' says Luke.

'Hello.'

'Going down?'

'Yes. Basement.'

'Okay, we're coming with.'

The doors close and for a few floors nobody says anything. Then Luke decides to warn her:

'Gloria, when we reach the basement it's possible some guys will start shooting at us. But they're only foam darts. Look, see?'

Gloria refuses to acknowledge the dart, as if Luke wants to show her a handful of dog shit. The lift arrives and the doors open.

'Ceasefire!' shouts Luke. 'Civilian, hold your fire!'

Gloria pushes her trolley out, providing momentary cover. Tim Price is lurking at the entrance to the garage, but seeing Gloria he turns and disappears into it. Vince leans out from behind her, shoots and misses.

'Fucking motherfucker,' he says.

Gloria will not be hurried. The disdain on her face is total. Now she peels off to the right and through double doors, towards whatever it is that happens down there.

'Bye Gloria,' says Luke.

'You ready for this son?' asks Vince.

'Ready.'

The two of them are crouched under window portals in the garage doors. Vince signals a count to three, and on four they push their way inside.

As a product of the French *Grandes Ecoles*, Vince was trained to think differently. Not to his classmates, but to ordinary people. Logically and critically and outside the box. He knows if he can make reason a weapon in this fight, his victory will be crushing. Foam darts are tracing in his direction as he advances, but Vince does not perceive things in an ordinary way, and they seem to move slower than regular bullets. Easily he dodges them, taking cover behind an electric BMW. The fools have given their positions away. Luke is cavalier, intellectually quite limited, and Vince watches him spray the garage with his Elite Infinus. Soon he will be hit, and as if to prove just how good Vince is at forecasting outcomes, that very instant he takes sponge projectiles in both knees and the hip.

'Those were hits. I hit you. I definitely hit you,' shouts Tim Price.

Prior to the game it was agreed that more than two direct hits equalled death, and Luke accepts his fate by sitting down and lying back. Vince is now alone. He stands and turns and pulls the trigger, firing seven darts that droop harmlessly to the floor before regaining his cover. Furiously he fires a rocket up and over his shoulder, which rebounds off the wing mirror and plops between his knees. Right then a foam projectile comes searing under the chassis of the BMW, slamming into his coccyx.

'Oof,' says Vince, scooching more neatly behind the wheel. Tim or Tom must have stealthed up to the car and lay down flat to get that off.

Vince jerks the Modulus to one side and lets it spit three, four, five bullets back under the car. Atkins is still lying there, hoping for another clear shot, and he wears each one of them, right in the face. He cries out in pain before accepting that he has been ended.

'Just you and me pal,' shouts Vince.

Price says nothing. Vince has no clue where he might be. He rolls onto his belly and crawls from one end of the BMW to the other, with his sights trained underneath it. He can see bicycles, a few scooters, and what looks like an Audi Q7 parked on the other side of the garage. How he would love to slay this final rebel across the bonnet of a diesel – the kind of diesel not one of those bastard yellow vests could ever afford.

Enough of these small town mongoloids. Going on television, using their chances to be heard to ask for a chance to be heard. A good whiff of grapeshot is what they need. Vince hardly even hates them. He pities them. He pities the fat ponytailed bastards, with their wizard hats and their cowbells. Their flags and their banners. Their processed meat at their roadside barbecues. Do they even understand their own resistance? Do they have the faintest idea what will happen if it all just stops? Go on, try and get off this train. Tax the rich, tax the businesses, see what happens when they fuck off and leave you there stranded. See what happens to your job, *smicard de merde*. See how you enjoy life without your shitty weekly shop for your trolley of shit at the local shitty hypermarket. You liked *les trentes glorieuses* so much, see how you like it when you end up back in them. No Facebook to share your shitty fake news, no Amazon to deliver your shitty kids their shitty toys.

Vince is about to round the boot of the BMW when he senses a presence standing over him. Luke is lying straight ahead and grimaces awkwardly at him, as if to say: mate, Price has creeped round the other side and is now right behind you, with his blaster pointed at the back of your head.

'Okay,' says Vince. 'Okay, okay, okay.'

He makes as if to surrender, but with lightning speed he flips over and lashes out with the extended butt of his Modulus. He hits Price flush in the chin, and Price, taken quite understandably by surprise, goes down. Vince leaps up, twirls round his gun and lets him have three darts in the temple.

'Woo,' yells Vince. 'Woooooo. Wooooo motherfucker. Wooo.'

He keeps bellowing his excitement, while Price lies groaning on the floor. He spits out one and then another tooth in globby mouthfuls of blood. Vince goes to give Luke a high five, and Luke accepts without really committing. His user experience designer looks to be in a significant amount pain.

Shit like that makes a man of you though. Price should be seeing it as a metaphor for what it takes to succeed. Vince puts him in a cab and sends him to the hospital to see if his jaw is broken. Chris and Luke meanwhile follow Vince back up to Meeting Hub B. Work hard play hard bitches.

Blank is ticking along. Simple concepts scale quickly, but the competition moves, so you have to move faster. Look at WeWork. Anybody can do what they do. You get some cash you buy a property you pimp it up you rent it out. Easy. Except try doing it quicker than them. Try prising $5 billion out of SoftBank, out of the hands of Masayoshi Son, the Mr. Fucking Miyagi of venture capital – try doing that in one financial quarter. Try boosting your operation from some pissy downtown loftspace for bearded wannabes to half a trillion dollars of real estate across every continent in the space of just six years. Try copying the best, then watch them outrun you.

The app is looking slick, but it needs some big second seed or a successful Series A round. But without more users, without a decent trial, no way is he gonna get the necessary level of cash. The kid is good, ballsy, but his operation now needs some adults in the room.

'Uh,' says Luke, staring at his phone as they enter the hub. 'Uh, Vince. I think there might be a problem.'

'Luke, stop being a pussy. It's a jaw. It breaks.'

'No, not Price,' says Luke. 'It's something else. Not good.'

'What?'

'So, apparently this article has been written about Blank.'

'Who? TechCrunch?'

'Yeah but no not that kind of article.'

'Well what?' asks Vince between vapes.

'So. Basically it's quite a long story but when I was struggling to get you to invest, I had this idea for how to onboard users. I ran it by my doctor mate who has clearly betrayed me, which is a shame. What I'm going to do is just link you both the article, because she's a backstabbing bitch but she actually explains the idea quite well.'

'Luke stop talking shit and tell me what's going on.'

'Okay, I'll read, dur dur dur, here: "The idea was simple: pass off dead people as users for his application. By taking the most basic personal information from the hospital database, Luke hoped to be able to return to Picpus with a long list of fictitious users that proved the appeal of his platform, thereby convincing Froissard to invest."'

'Motherfucker,' says Vince.

Chris in the corner, looking like all of the Nerf guns are suddenly real and pointed at his heart.

'But she goes on to stress,' says Luke, 'That there was absolutely nothing illegal about it. Nothing at all, because the data of dead people, and I really did specify this to Ram, is not covered by the Act. She's just saying that it represents the, uh, hold on, yes: "The moral trench that has been dug by this culture of bulldozing optimism, the *Yes We Can* of a decade ago turned in on itself. An aggressive positivity willing to break all codes, to crush everything and everyone in its path in the service of what it sees as the only relevant goal: that of building tomorrow." Which, you know, she can suck a dick.'

'Blank has no users?'

'No, yes, Blank now does have some users. And also, as she says, the strategy never even came off, because Ram was such a batty boy.'

'Ram?' says Chris. 'Not Ram Mitra?'

'Yeah. How do you know Ram?'

'Hang on,' says Chris. 'So where did you end up getting the users?'

'Well, to be fair, those original users were still dead. They were ancient university alumni that I managed to get from Queen Mary by pretending to be a journalist. But the woman who gave me them is also now dead, apparently. So there's no risk. I didn't kill her though.'

'Oh Jesus. Oh Jesus. You pretended to be a journalist to get the names of dead people who you could then pass off as users? You cretin. You fucking cretin.'

'Yeah, well,' says Luke. 'Since when does a lawyer understand what it takes to start a company?'

'Since when does... Since.... Maybe since he specialised in corporate law? You fucking dick? As in, the law of companies? As in, the understanding of what it takes to start a company? You fucking pillock. You fucking mug.'

Vince is now looking at the article.

'This is Lucy,' he finally says. 'This is Lucy, who's written this article.'

'Yes,' says Luke. 'You too have been betrayed.'

'Lucy as in Ram's Lucy?' asks Chris.

'Lucy as in little Asian slut Lucy,' says Vince, reading.

306

'But how do you know Ram and how do you know Lucy?' asks Luke.

'My ex, Julie,' says Chris. 'Lucy is her best friend.'

Luke nods silently. Vince now:

'Does this cunt have no remorse? What did I ever do to her?'

'Nothing Vince. It's a betrayal. Pure betrayal.'

'But wait Vince so how do you know Lucy?' asks Chris.

Luke provides the answer: 'He was shagging her for a while, back when Ram and Lucy were still together.'

'So Luke you were mates with her boyfriend?' asks Vince.

'Ram and Lucy are no longer together?' asks Chris.

'Yes. No. Look, anyway, we're getting… '

'"A culture that prides itself on disrupting,"' quotes Vince, '"Should not be surprised when we, the oppressed, turn our attentions to disrupting it in turn." Oppressed? *Oppressed?* I'll give her oppressed. I'm going to oppress her a new arsehole. Right, action stations.'

'Vince, look,' says Chris. 'I've got to call Nigel. This is it.'

'Do you though? Do you have to call Nigel?'

'Enough,' says Vince. 'Listen, I believe in this app. It is going to succeed, I know it is. Morons like this criticised Facebook at the beginning, and look at it now. This is what happens when you try to change things. First they call you crazy, then they fight you, then all of a sudden you've changed the world, whereas nobody even remembers their names. We're going to get revenge the only way we know how. I swear if it kills me I'm going to IPO this motherfucker, then stuff my money up her pissflaps.

'One hundred percent,' says Luke. 'Chris I don't even know what you're worried about. Nothing illegal has been done that anybody other than us three actually knows about. This is just a marketing issue. We'll swat it away, I promise you. She's… I mean, who even is she?'

Chris is pacing around the hub, shaking his head.

'Luke,' says Vince. 'Have you seen *Apocalypse Now*?'

'Yeah, why?'

'You know that scene, the surfing scene. Charlie don't surf.'

'Oh yeah, massively iconic.'

'Well you need to get out there and surf. You need to ride this wave. Show the enemy you know how to surf, show your troops you know how to surf. Beat this bitch and win this war.'

Vince walks over to the window, looks down to the street, at all the poor people riding up Bishopsgate in buses.

'"You smell that?"' he asks.

'Smell what?'

Chris sniffs the room.

'I'm quoting, shut up,' says Vince. '"Napalm, son. Nothing else in the world smells like that. I love the smell of napalm in the morning. You know, one time we had a hill bombed for twelve hours. When it was all over, I walked up. We didn't find one of them, not one stinking dink body. The smell, you know, that gasoline smell. The whole hill. Smelled like… victory."'

edward:gooderham

chapter:twentythree

Ram rode the red bus, reading:

Hinduism has a plurality of narratives because people are always asking different questions, looking for different answers, even within the same faith. Observe how the heroes of Indian epics are not single characters, rather tangled knots of character, the attempt being to portray a multiplicity of souls behind the veil of one or several stories. The Gods themselves are transcendant lords but also appear in the various traits of each and every person, and there is no distinction between the many and the one. Note how many retellings of the Ramayana have recast Ravana as the hero and Ramana as the villain. Are they not each perhaps hero? Are they not each perhaps villain?

Ram closed his booklet, dwelling on that passage. He was on the upper deck, in the very front row, on those seats that went some tiny fraction of the way towards recapturing that grand, panoramic thrill of the cockpit visit – a highlight of his and so many other middle class childhoods in the nineties. Too poor and you were not flying anywhere, not yet. Too rich and such experiences were banal. The stewardess beckoned you through, marched you down the aisle, and suddenly you were in there. Strangely small, it was. But the uniforms, the dashes, the dials, the sky, the sky. The captain let you handle the joystick. He looked at you and said there you go, son: you are now flying this aircraft. And you believed him.

Many were the reasons to pity somebody being born in the year 2019, none more tragic than the fact that he or she or they would probably never set foot in a cockpit. Especially if that child was brown. The terrorists had seen to that. To be fair, theirs was an extraordinary idea, and had Ram known just how much he would go on to hate the world, he might have had it first. If he had only foreseen the savage spectacle that was awaiting him in adulthood. The stabbings, the shootings, the boys under buses; the cheating girlfriends who then pretended to be lesbians, who became famous by peddling lies to the public. If he had only realised how completely his studies and his career would deaden the magic of being human, would expose its meaningless. If he had only known, back then, that he was just blood and bone and nerves and tissue. If he had only grasped that standing in the cockpit of a 747 was as good as things were ever going to get, he would have jammed his colouring pencils in the eyes of the crew, locked the door, and taken that baby down.

Ram sort of took his hat off to them. Terrorists. The problem, though, was that they never showed up at a time or in a place where they might actually have served a purpose. For example wherever Lucy was. For example wherever Ola was. For example wherever Vincent Froissard was. All impeccable venues for a knife attack or a vehicle ramming. Ram noticed the little red hammer, mounted beside the window. *Use in the event of an emergency.* What about in the event of rage? *Remove the hammer to break window glass.* What about to break the faces of the people on this bus, to break their fucking phones?

Perhaps he needed to get back into sport. At school, whenever somebody called him a paki, there had at least been that outlet. He had been able to channel his fury into the next dump tackle, the next bouncer, the next lofted six back down the ground. It felt good to imagine retribution being delivered via his shoulders, via his left arm, via the middle of a block of willow. None of which, sadly, was deemed acceptable street behaviour. How he would have loved to sit Vince down, explain the rules of cricket, and teach him how to catch by sending cuts and drives wanging towards his face and bollocks.

At the moment there was nowhere for all this frustration to go. It coursed through him, turning inwards and demanding answers. Which naturally leads us to the question of religion. Over and over again he had tried, still he was trying, but his atheism was proving unshakeable. It was more than just a faith. To have been born in Greater London in 1989, to have studied the sciences, to have owned Apple products and even be heard whispering the names of gods, would have taken no less courageous independence of mind than for a man born in Allahabad in 1889, the issue of Brahmin and a student of scripture, to voice his conviction that there were none. To find God or gods, in short, Ram would have needed to be no less of a monumental figure than Jawaharlal Nehru. But he was not. He was just Ram.

That said, he was perhaps not your routine atheist. Unlike most of the flock, he appreciated the difference between faith and belief. And there were aspects of his creed, aspects of its dogma that troubled him greatly. The notion, for instance, that Richard Dawkins might have been blessed with a subtler or more sensitive mind than Thomas Aquinas sat uneasily. He was skeptical about the prospect of a world based solely around reason, given the almost laughably consistent inability of humans to employ it. Not to mention the hundreds of millions of murders in its name, on the rare occasions when they had. The zealots troubled him, the basic zealotry. As did the fact that atheism only appeared able to define itself by waging war on religion, as if after millennia spent spying on the many different ones, it had decided to steal their very shadiest move.

Still he could not quite get there. His heart was empty, the world too full. Ram was certain it might have felt less like a cage of maniacs, had the deities not been so thoroughly despatched. He was sure he would have been more satisfied, if he could just have found some thread which bound the living to the dead. He yearned to be on some parallel planet which this, that or the other mythology had coaxed his species into not eviscerating.

If people only feared. If they only trembled. If they only felt karmically responsible for the rights and wrongs they wrought. Lucy and Ola, Vince: they were their own gods. They wrote their own rules, dispensed their own justice, knew for themselves who to kill and who to save. Ram they had killed. Eleven years of his life, gone. Or perhaps it was simply time. Among all kinds of killers, went the *Gita*, time was the ultimate. Because time killed all things.

Ram poked the bus bell and stood up out of his seat. He inched himself from rail to rail and down the stairs, like a man moving through a nosediving plane. He got off where Shoreditch became the City, where low brick buildings began rising into skyscrapers, where the High Street became Bishopsgate. His horizon was soaring towers of curved and mirrored glass. He walked towards it all, past the Department of Coffee and Social Affairs. This was where Lucy had come, that morning. On a pavement island in the middle of the road stood a City Police checkpoint, as if on the fringes of a conflict zone. Ram saw the Gherkin in the distance, and for the first time he thought it resembled a warhead.

He came to the door of WeWork. He had prepared a thousand excuses but none ended up being necessary. The receptionist simply smiled at him, perhaps confusing him with any one of the other Indian guys that rented space here. His Herschel backpack, his blue jeans and brown shoes and chequered shirt all made for flawless camouflage. He approached the turnstiles, scanned the badge that he had stolen from Luke, and headed towards the lifts. He checked his watch. Provided there had been no change to their schedule, the Nerf game would be over and the Monday morning strategy meeting would be underway. Sixth floor, Hub B.

As he began his ascent, Ram recognised the same fearful thrill that had preceded his debut surgical procedure, an emergency laporoscopy on a patient whose name he still remembered. Mr. Braithwaite had survived, only to die three weeks later in a car accident. Perhaps if Ram could have started over, he would have become something else. A secret agent or a hitman. But it was too late now.

Men

A Tragedy

Dramatis Personae

RAM, a Doctor

LUKE, an Entrepreneur. Founder and CEO of Blank, friend to Ram

CHRIS, a Solicitor

VINCE, a Venture Capitalist who cuckolded Ram. French

Amy, some Girl

Act One

Scene One

WeWork Bishopsgate, Sixth Floor, Meeting Hub B. Vince stands next to an aspidistra by the window. Chris and Luke sit at opposite ends of a light oak conference table, looking at their phones. Seven Nerf Guns are stacked in the corner of the room. On a whiteboard, in red, is written the word REVENGE. Ram enters.

LUKE

Ram? What are you doing here?

CHRIS

Ram. Long time.

RAM

Chris. What the hell are you doing here?

CHRIS

I'm his lawyer. Was his lawyer. It's being discussed. I didn't realise you two were friends.

LUKE

Ram mate what's going on? You can't be here.

RAM

Well, this is awkward. You know he's…

LUKE

Yes Ram I'm well aware, now if you could just please…

CHRIS

Who? Who am I?

RAM

Well it's just, what with Julie, I'd have thought it'd be difficult for the two of you to see eye to eye.

LUKE

Fucking hell Ram. Fucking hell. Is one betrayal not enough for a Monday morning?

VINCE

Any of you pussies mind telling me what's going on?

CHRIS

What about Julie? What about Julie?

LUKE

Fine. I date Julie. She's my girlfriend. I'm Julie's boyfriend. There.

RAM

My bad.

VINCE

(*stooping to pick up the Nerf Thunderhawk*)

Boring. This is boring. The next person who speaks and doesn't tell me what's going on gets a dart in the eye.

CHRIS

What? All this time we've been working together and you've been fucking my girlfriend behind my back?

LUKE

Err, first of all she's not your girlfriend. The two of you split up in like December. Second of all I only realised when you said you knew Ram. Which was about two minutes ago, so give me a break.

CHRIS

This is unbelievable. You sly piece of – *Arghh! (Chris receives a dart in*
the cheek.)

VINCE

(Pointing the gun at Luke now)
Okay Luke. Your turn. Who is this and why is he interrupting my meeting?

LUKE

This is madness Chris. I haven't done anything wrong. You've literally got
no right to be angry with – *Argghh! (Luke receives a dart in the ear)*
Vince, fuck off.

VINCE

(Aiming at Ram)
Who are you?

RAM

Get that thing out of my face arsehole. I'm Ram. I'm here to see you.

VINCE

About what?

LUKE

Look Ram, you shouldn't be here. You really shouldn't be here. Vince is
sorry he fucked your girlfriend but that's all in the past now, and from

what I hear she's actually a lesbian, so Vince has as much reason as you
to be chagrined or whatever.

VINCE

Eh bah voila! You're the ex.

CHRIS

Vince was fucking Lucy?

RAM

Yes I am. Yes he was.

LUKE

Plus you aren't going to find anyone in here defending Lucy. As it stands
this is the I hate Lucy club. She has betrayed every one of us Ram. We
are four men scorned.

RAM

What are you talking about?

LUKE

Her latest article. Today's article, the bones of which I'm assuming you
must have given her. You beautiful Bengali turncoat. I forgive you though,
so now go.

RAM

What article?

CHRIS

(*Showing his phone to Ram*)

This one.

LUKE

It's about Me. About Blank. About how I offered you the chance to
become a billionaire and you turned it down.

RAM

Oh, sorry mate. I told her the thing about dead people yeah, the idea
Julie gave you. But ages ago, when we were still together. I never
thought she'd…

CHRIS

Julie gave you the idea to steal the data of dead people?

VINCE

Bon, enough talking. What I suggest is a proper Nerf game. I'll pay for us
to get a floor cordoned off. No rules. You two versus me and Chris. Chris
hates Luke, this guy hates me, it's perfect. It can be like old times when
men went to war over bitches. Shotgun the Modulus, that's mine.

RAM

Put that thing down. I'm not playing any Nerf game. I came here to speak
to you.

VINCE

Oooooo. He came here to speak to me.

RAM

(*Taking off and opening his rucksack.*)
I've got something for you. Here.
(*Ram pulls out a pistol. It looks less like a Nerf Blaster than a real life
actual revolver. He raises it at Vince, who lowers his own plastic orange
Tommy gun.*)

LUKE

Ram what the fuck? Ram?

VINCE

Okay, easy tiger. Easy.

LUKE

Ram no. Ram this is mad. You've gone mad.

CHRIS

I'm not made for these situations. I'm just a solicitor. Please Ram, put
down the gun.

LUKE

Oh fucking hell. This cannot be happening. Ram where do you even get a handgun? This is London, not Baltimore.

RAM

Just relax. All of you. I'm not intending to shoot Vince. I just need him to take this rucksack and see what's inside. I have something for him and I need him to take it seriously. This is the only way.

(Ram kicks the rucksack towards Vince. Amy walks along the glass walls of the Meeting Hub now, but given that Vince is still holding his Nerf Blaster and wearing his POLICE bib, she assumes the terror on faces and hands in the air are all part of the earlier horseplay. In short, she will not be raising the alarm.)

VINCE

No way am I opening that rucksack. It's a bomb. It's going to explode in my face.

LUKE

Ram think about this. Think what you're doing for a second. If you go through with this you can kiss goodbye to the Cotswolds for a start. Never in a million years will they let you open your own practice, not if you do this.

RAM

I wanted you to be the first. So you wouldn't see it coming.

VINCE

Look dude, I'm sorry I fucked your girlfriend. But she was a bitch. You're well rid of her. If anything I did you a favour.

RAM

Just look in the bag.

CHRIS

(*All sorts of noises*)

LUKE

Ram, this is me. This is your friend. Know that it doesn't need to be this way. I read an article in *The Guardian* about these deradicalisation centres, and apparently they work absolute wonders, if you'd just…

RAM

Shut up Luke. Shut up, shut up, shut up. Just, mate, for once in your life, grasp that it is not your turn to talk.

LUKE

(*Luke mimes zipping his lips closed. Vince meanwhile slowly goes through the bag and removes a small plastic figurine.*)

VINCE

What the fuck is this?

RAM

Vishnu.

VINCE

And what am I supposed to do with Vishnu?

RAM

Nothing. You are supposed to accept him as a gift, as a token of my forgiveness. I forgive you for what you did. This is me, forgiving you.

CHRIS

This is bananas.

LUKE

Ram, look, sorry, but if you want to forgive Vince, are there not better ways to do it?

RAM

No. He would never have listened. It was important that this be proper, intentional action. Received and understood.

VINCE

Look pal, I don't know how they do things in Pakistan, but in France and as far as I'm aware in England, we do not forgive by pointing a gun at someone's head.

LUKE

Not Pakistan Vince. Never Pakistan.

VINCE

India. Whatever.

RAM

I just wanted you to listen. Besides, it's not a real gun.

LUKE

What do you mean it's not a real gun?

RAM

What do you think I am? Insane? To be honest I can't believe you all fell for it.

(*Ram now swivels towards the table and pulls the trigger of his remarkably realistic water pistol. Chris makes a noise of pure terror as he is sprayed in the face.*)

VINCE

You motherfucker. I'll have you behind bars for this.

RAM

For what crime? Bringing a water pistol into WeWork? There are seven other fake weapons in here.

CHRIS

I don't feel well.

LUKE

Ram I'm seriously worried about your mental health. This is not ordinary behaviour.

(*Vince now charges at Ram, who drops his shoulder and dump tackles him to the floor. Vince struggles but Ram easily pins him down.*)

RAM

It's over Vince. You're forgiven. I forgive you.

(*Ram gets off, backs away and Vince stands up. Luke keeps them separated but Vince now knows he is the weaker man, so he retreats towards the window.*)

VINCE

Chris, get into the office and find me a provable charge to press against
this cunt.

CHRIS

No.

VINCE

Do it. Do it now, or I'll call Nigel. I'll call Nigel, and tomorrow morning
you're fat bald ass will be picking up a P45 from Human Resources.

CHRIS

Good. Fine. I'm done. They can find a new resource. I'm going.

(Enter Amy)

Amy

Guys sorry to disturb but it's coming up to midday and I have the Hub
booked for a call, so if you…

VINCE

Well I make it three minutes to, so how about you go and fist yourself,
you bossy cow.

(Exit Amy)

LUKE

Vince you can't do that anymore.

VINCE

Fuck her, fuck you, and fuck you two too.

(Chris and Ram exeunt the Meeting Hub. Vince hurls Vishnu after them, misses, hits the door instead, and Vishnu falls to the floor. Very important that He lands upright.)

FINIS

edward:gooderham

chapter:twentyfour

The lift ride down from the sixth floor is silent and awkward. Ram has, after all, just discharged what Chris at that point still believed was a real revolver into his face. Even when it became apparent that his blood was just water, there was still a fraction of a moment in which Chris thought: this is death, I am dead.

They emerge onto the street and he turns to Ram.

'Mate, what the fuck was all that about?'

'The world is full of creators and destroyers,' says Ram. 'But I am neither. We all have a dharma to follow I think, and this is mine. See you around Chris.'

Ram sets off towards Shoreditch and Chris was in fact going to head the same way, but that was a searing goodbye, charged with cinematic enigma, so Chris respects it and lets Ram go. He leaves in the other direction, towards the Tesco Metro at Liverpool Street. The day is warm, the sky cloudless, and Chris walks with the sun on his face, getting about twenty metres before he realises he has effectively just quit his job. He is then hit by such a humdinger of a stomach cramp that he actually worries he might shit himself.

He has to sit on the steps leading up to a covered arcade of shops. The National Express coach to Stansted is parked but rumbling just in front of him, black smoke guffing from its exhaust. People are queuing to board. Chris closes his eyes, hears bags being wheeled along the pavement. He hears French and Spanish and Italian being spoken. German, Dutch, Portuguese. Scandinavian languages, Eastern European languages, noise.

He opens his eyes, looks above the bus and across the street. Men are staring down from high windows. These are famous windows; Chris remembers them from the news. About a decade ago, RBS employees leaned out of them, waving fifties at the protestors below. How much simpler everything seemed, back when bankers were the arch nemesis. Straightforward to spot, straightforward to loathe. But this new villain, the tech bro, had learned from their mistakes and mastered the art of subterfuge. He dressed casually, he pretended to be nice, and then he fucked your girlfriend. He tricked you out of a job. He was your worst enemy, hiding behind a smile. He had power, money and the masses on his side, and Chris pitied anyone brave enough or stupid enough to take him on. She would die resisting. She would be piled on top of her reactionary comrades, in the bottomless mass grave that is history according to its losers.

Chris climbs the steps up to the arcade. He passes Eat. He passes Pret A Manger. He passes Itsu. He passes Costa Coffee. He passes Starbucks. He passes another Pret A Manger, passes another Starbucks, as if he is spiralling downwards in a maelstrom of ever smaller circles. He always expected that spontaneously quitting his job would fill him with an awesome sense of liberation. Instead he feels very trapped, very afraid. He has no idea what he will do. Right now he is convinced that he cannot ever work again, simple as that, yet the money in his account is unlikely to see him through to the end of British Summer Time.

These past few years he should have been saving mountainous sums, stupendous sums. No though, all gone, spaffed on gadgets and rucksacks and shoes. He bought a Canada Goose parka for eleven hundred pounds and has worn it once because London is too mild. He has boxes and boxes of unused kitchen equipment. There are his lamps from Italy. Special American pens that float. And these are the objects – or at least a few of the countless objects – that exist, that he can go home and touch and say yes, I own this.

What of the thousands of invisible pounds, gone on sporting encounters he can no longer remember and barely even cared about at the time? The five figures he must have drunk in juices and smoothies and coffees since graduating. All that wine, all the pulled pork. Bottles of extremely expensive whiskey. Chris hates whiskey. Chris cannot even spell whisky. He should have been scrimping, adding to the pile that would have allowed him to board that bus to Stansted, to escape to some Greek island and live off twenty pence a day until dying of the syphilis given to him by a shepherd girl.

But leaving is not an option. He cannot leave, not without telling Julie he loves her, and when he tells her he loves her she will take him back, which will therefore be his reason to stay. It works perfectly. Everything will go fine as long as he speaks honestly and courageously, which he realises he has done just now for perhaps the very first time, up on the sixth floor of WeWork. Today must be the day for it then.

Chris enters Tesco Metro. Annie Lennox is singing *Walking on Broken Glass*. Not live in store but on the radio. The lunchtime sandwich and salad rush has begun; the store is mayhem. Chris has formulated a plan, and the first stage is to buy Julie a bar of her favourite dark chocolate, the Lindt Excellence variety seasoned with sea salt. All grand gestures she finds abhorrent, but this is just confectionery. Sweet, very thoughtful, without detracting from what matters, which is what he has to tell her.

He goes up and down the aisles looking for chocolate. In the time he takes to scour the whole supermarket, he is barged aside by four different people. Finally he finds what would not be an exaggeration to call the Lindt zone, a whole Switzerland of shelf not far from the checkouts. The queue snakes way back behind here, so Chris has to squeeze his way through. While he is searching for the Touch of Sea Salt, yet more shoulders and baskets bump into him. He crouches down.

Mint Intense. Orange Intense. Poire Intense. Cherry Intense. Raspberry Intense. Lime Intense. Cherry Intense. In the Crunch range, Chris spies Toffee and Hazlenut and Pistachio. Caramel. The Chilli one is there. The 50% Dark, the 60% Dark, the 70% Dark, the 78% Dark, the 85% Dark, the 90% Dark, the 99% Dark – they are all there, obviously. The White with a Touch of Vanilla, the Extra Creamy milk bar.

But the Touch of Sea Salt is nowhere to be seen, and Annie Lennox is wailing loudly over staccato violin strokes and checkout beeps, and somebody is shouting Buy on the phone, somebody is shouting Sell on the phone, and here, have another basket in the spine pal, and somebody reckons Trevor will go apeshit if he finds out, somebody asks whether Alison wanted crisps and if so what flavour, and the lights are so bright, his neck is quite hot, and now he sees the deep deep hole where Touch of Sea Salt is supposed to be, the categorical lack of any chocolate for sale there, now he sees nothing because his vision has spaced, the legs he is crouching on feel as if deboned, and the packaging of a bar of Tesco Cooking Chocolate seems to contain within it an abstract but very aggressive message of impending doom.

Then suddenly Chris is down. He is on his arse, on the floor.

'Are you alright mate?'

Could have been anyone asking. Could have been Nigel. Could have been his dead uncle.

'Me? Yeah no I'm fine. I'm looking for the salt. I'm fine.'

Fine but still down, still staring blankly at the swarming kaleidoscope that just seven seconds ago was a shelf of chocolate. The queue shapes itself around Chris, as he outstretches the legs that he can no longer be sure are his own. He puts his head in his hands to see if they constitute a less terrifying milieu. They do not, and the clamminess of his palms against his cheeks makes him feel as if his head is melting. Annie Lennox is still singing over deranged violins.

Vision of a kind now returns. Buy one get one free, he sees. Finally Chris recognises his brain slowing down just enough to flit between motley but at least identifiable thoughts. Metal. Trousers. Prison. Somebody in the queue asks somebody on the phone if they can make themselves free at half past four. Chris laughs and this earns him a few looks. Free is the word that is tickling him. Here he sits, on the floor of this Tesco Metro, a totally free man. As was he always, free. Free to live in this city. Free to dump or be dumped. Free to study law. Free to work until falling asleep on the toilet. Free to work until burnout became just a fond memory of cosy warmth. Free to quit too. Free to come in here at midday on a Monday, free to choose between forty different types of chocolate. Free to be taken captive. Free to be anything other than free.

He can once again sort of breathe.

'Okay, up we get,' he says.

He steadies himself with one hand, climbs to his feet but loses balance and tumbles straight into a woman holding a shoulder of lamb and a packet of hobnobs.

'Whoopsy daisies.'

'You're alright,' says the woman.

Is he? Chris walks between the shelf and the queue as if down the aisles of a speeding train. Lurching, swaying. He turns a corner into space, and that feels like the combined weight of the FTSE 100 being lifted off his chest. Trillions and trillions of tonnes of the heaviest nothingness, gone. He fixes on the door and then he is through it, never going back in that Tesco Metro, not even if his life depends on it. Sky and skyscrapers come smashing into his mind as he stumbles to a bus shelter, sits down on its bench, and begins coming to terms with the pantherlike panic attack that just slunk into Tesco and mauled him, before vanishing into the jungles of London.

Twenty minutes go by as Chris practises breathing. Nothing glamorous, no pulmonary theatrics, just sucking in and expelling little pockets of air. Which is a start. He comforts himself with the idea that after mornings like this one, even the most stoical of men would be mentally under the cosh. Not every day do you find out the love of your life is sleeping with a grinning sociopath, only to then get shot in the face with what you think is a real gun, only to then voluntarily get yourself fired.

Now he tries standing up, and being on his feet has a strange, novel feel. His walk to the curb might as well be across the surface of Pluto. He hails an approaching taxi. It is yellow with advertising, for a company or a product or a service called *Joie*. There is a picture of a delighted infant and slogans all over the side of the cab, slogans like honk honk and beep beep and share the joy. Chris stands there for a while, trying to establish what is being sold – childbirth? happiness? – before realising that the taxi is holding up traffic and he is supposed to get in.

'Where we goin mate?'

'To Julie,' says Chris. He is not his best remember.

'Oh yeah. And where's she Romero?'

'Oh, yeah, sorry,' says Chris. 'I think probably we need to go to the Chesham Arms in Hackney, which is on a road I can't remember the name of.'

'Yeah I know the one you mean.'

Chris collapses into the back seats. What magnificence. A driver who puns on Shakespeare. Who knows where random pubs are without using Waze. He senses that he will be safe in this carriage. In this Hackney Carriage.

'Why do they call them Hackney Carriages?' he asks.

'Inrestin question mate,' says the driver. 'You've gotta go back as early as the twelf century really. Back then Ackney was rural, wannit? It was where you put yer orses to pasture. And the orses were so good that when the French come over they leafed the word, Frenchified it. Ackney becomes *haquenée* which becomes *haque* which is basically the old frog word for nag. Naaa, there is anovver school of fought that says the French actually took it from the Dutch or the Spanish, but I fink the majority of lexicogwoffers are still saying it originates in Landan.

'Anyway. Long story short, we the English then took the word back again from the French, and araaand abaaat the fourteenf century you start to see the term Ackney Orse. Which is basically your avrage orse, zacly the kind of orse you find for ire. Which, you know, is why Ackneyed also wen on to mean knackered, worn aaat. In terms of cabs though, you're looking at 1654 when Parliament first referred to Ackney Coachmen, and you're looking at 1662 for the first proppa licensed carriages. Survived ever since mate. And then you know you've got your motorisation comin in, at which point Ackney Carriage is used to distinguish between black cabs, licensed to pick you up in the street, and your private hire, your minicabs. Your Ubers.'

'Fuck Uber,' says Chris.

Already he has decided – decided back when the driver said We the English – to die for this man if necessary.

'Yeah, fuck 'em. Anyway, nobody calls em Ackney carriages. Not anymore.'

'What do cockneys call cabs?'

'Well you've got all sorts. Flounder, for example.'

'Flounder?'

'Flounder and dab, cab. A smash and grab. Sandy McNab. All sorts.'

'Can we go around the back of Victoria Park? I'm enjoying myself.'

'You're in charge guvna.'

'Thanks. How long have you been a cabbie?'

'Forty free years and countin.'

'Are you gonna retire?'

'Na. You never retire.'

'What's it like?

'What, driving a cab?'

'Yeah.'

'A life, I suppose. Your hear some stories. Can get a little lonely. Like everythin else though. Every so often you gotta sit down with a mate and have a cup of tea, have a grumble. Aintcha? All in the same boat.'

'Would you recommend, for instance, that I become a cabbie?'

'Trade's dyin mate. Dyin on its arse. And the government ain't gonna save it.'

'Fuck the government.'

'Yeah, fuck 'em. Just noise mate, just talkin. Just gotta get yer head down and ignore 'em.'

'Nobody wants us. You and I, we're old economy. Jacob too. Jacob's old economy. Everyone I either like or care about is old economy.'

'Who's Jacob?'

'The cleaner. At the office where I work. At the office where I used to work.'

'Yeah, he's propa fucked. Give it a few years.'

'I need to find something to do with my life. I got shot in the face this morning.'

'Blimey.'

'It was a water pistol. But I thought it was a gun.'

'Not whatcha need on a Mundee mornin.'

'I think I've had a revelation. But I'm not sure what it is. Also though I might be going mad.'

'Bollocks to that mate. We're all goin mad. The world's gone mad.'

'Mm.'

'Who's Julie anyway?'

'My ex. I'm off to win her back. Without chocolate though, which was part of the plan.'

'Likes her chocolate does she?'

'Mm. What should I tell her do you think?'

'Blown if I know. Tell her you love her, all that claptrap.'

'She's got a new boyfriend.'

'Bugger.'

'He's a tosser.'

'Yeah, few of em hanging araaand.'

They continue circling Hackney. The driver is called Colin. Chris asks and answers questions, gradually rediscovering the basics of human interaction. Discussion becomes banal, and the banality feels

342

good. Reassuring. Colin supports Chelsea, Chris supports Leeds United, and they talk about football in the nineties and early noughties. Jimmy Floyd Hasselbaink. What went wrong for Jonathan Woodgate. What went wrong for Leeds United. That Dominic Matteo header. Lee Bowyer. The sale of Rio Ferdinand. Poor Gary Speed and that dreadful suicide business. Roman Abramovich.

All this nostalgia is bringing Chris back to life. Here he is, in a taxi, on his way to get the girl. He could be in *Love Actually*. This could be a scene in *Love Actually*. Everything smacks of a bygone era, of his youth. Back when life felt the way medieval Hackney sounded. Graspable, changeless, just horses put to pasture. Before the place became a word and the word became a carriage and the carriage became a car and the car replaced the horses that were in any event no longer there. Before everything raced out of control and in different directions, layering confusion on top of itself, birthing its own destruction. Before it was all buried under the ugly concrete of a rampant world.

Here they are, outside the Chesham Arms. Chris pays in cash and instructs Colin to keep the change. The eleven pounds of change. Colin tells Chris to look after himself, he drives away, and Chris realises that he forgot to get his take on Brexit. He could have asked to motor out to Hertford and back, happily he would have paid, and the journey would have given them ample time to discuss sovereignty, immigration, free trade. The Customs Union. Norway Plus. Now he will never know.

Chris has no idea whether Julie still even works at this pub, let alone whether she happens to be on shift. He simply wills her to be here, but of course she is not. Now, cascading down, come names and visions of the myriad places she could feasibly be, which is to say anywhere other than here, at the Chesham Arms. She could be inside Buckingham Palace. She could have gone to Gabon. He has zero clue, no idea where she now lives, but from the moment of its genesis he has been reluctant to muddy this gesture by resorting to technology. Which is what Luke would do. Luke would track her position, send in the flowers via drone, beam his hologram onto her retinae. Chris needs this victory to be total, pure, and to resort to the techniques of the enemy would be like torturing the minions of a regime you were out to topple for its barbarism. Also if she sees who is calling she might refuse to pick up.

He walks along Morning Lane and comes across a phone box. It is a colossal wreck, not one of the venerated reds but a basic old BT booth. The metal sides are dented and graffitied. The glass in the door has been smashed. Cans and bottles, plastic bags and kebab boxes hide the floor. Someone has attempted to set the ensemble on fire. Pasted above the payphone are the contact details of an obedient Romanian schoolgirl. Also a notice from the Council, advising that they will soon be removing this phone box, as part of a drive to declutter the streets. Not yet Council, you fucking bastard.

Chris picks up the phone and it appears to be working. But he has no change. He turns around and there, across the street, is the great foe Tesco. Chris crosses the road, telling himself he will be in and out in a jiffy. No messing, no chocolate, no panic attacks. He readies a twenty pound note, strides inside, and approaches an idle cashier named Aisha.

'Hello. I'd like twenty pound coins please.'

'Twenty?'

'Yes twenty. For a payphone.'

Judging by the look on her face, never has Aisha received such a baffling request. She opens the till.

'I can't give you twenty. The best I can do is ten and two five pound notes. Or a ten pound note, whatever.'

'What about if I take the two five pound notes in fifty pence pieces? Or twenty pence pieces. Tens even, but no smaller than tens I don't think. Thanks a lot.'

Aisha counts out twenty pounds in assorted change. Chris stuffs it all into his trouser pockets, thanks her again, and leaves. He returns to the payphone and piles his shrapnel on top of it. This call can go seven hours if it needs to, unless she actually is in Gabon. He dials her number from memory, and he wonders what Luke would make of that little touch, the twat.

Ringing, ringing. Chris remembers that Maroon 5 song, the one he privately and unilaterally anointed Song of their First Summer, the Olympic summer of 2012. *Payphone*. Julie detested it, because of course she did. How dare it have a catchy chorus and a decent beat? How dare it achieve major mainstream popularity?

'Hello?'

'Julie, it's me. It's Chris. I'm at a payphone.'

'Chris? What is it? Has something happened?'

'Yes actually. This morning I was shot.'

'Wh.. Oh my god, Chris, are you okay?'

'Well no I mean I wasn't actually shot. But there was a gun. Ram had a gun, and… '

'Ram? Ram had a gun? Jesus Chris what the hell is going on? Where are you?'

'I'm in a phone box on Morning Lane. But, just, I mean I should specify that it turned out not to be a real gun. When he pointed it at Vince and shot me I thought it was a gun, but in fact it was just a water pistol.'

'Chris, if this is a joke it's an extremely unfunny one.'

'No, I see that it sounds strange but it's not a joke. Also I quit my job. Also I had a panic attack, a really bad one, in the Tesco at Liverpool Street. It's not been a good day.'

'Okay, Chris, look. Ram, Vince, people getting shot – would you please speak slowly, speak normally, and explain what's going on.'

'Right, okay, yes. So basically it has today transpired that I am your boyfriend's lawyer.'

'You're Luke's lawyer?'

'I mean, yes, my firm represents Picpus, who have invested in his company, and… anyway, yes. Basically I am his lawyer. I have been working with him for a few months now, and only today did this coincidence, uhm, emerge. He claims he had no idea either. The point is, I feel it's my duty to warn you that with Luke, what we are talking about is the very lowest of the low, an absolute fuckpig of a… '

'Chris… '

'No, Julie, I know what you think, I'm just bitter, but honestly I'm telling you this because I care about you. He's a cheating, conniving little slug. He literally has the morals of a slug, which is to say no morals Julie. Are you aware of some of the shit he's been pulling to try and get his joke of an app off the ground?'

'I've read the article,' says Julie. 'I don't... But why should I believe Lucy, when all she's ever done is lie?'

'That's as maybe. I have no idea about Lucy, but I have no reason to lie. I mean I do, but I'm not. Luke tried to persuade Ram to let him have the data of a load of dead patients, so he could pass them off as users.'

'So it's true then,' said Julie.

'What's more, Ram said you gave him the idea. Which surely cannot be true.'

'It's true, but it's not accurate. I told him about the plot of a book. *Dead Souls*. I told him about it on our very first date. It's obviously come from that.'

'You were used, see! He used you. Like he used me, like he used Vince, but I'm less bothered about Vince. Also after Ram turned him down, he tricked someone at Queen Mary University into giving him the names of a load of dead alumni. And she's now dead.'

'Not... '

'He claims he didn't kill her.'

'This is bonkers. I'm very confused. What was the gun, with Ram? Where does Ram come into it all?'

'So we were in a meeting. Vince and Luke and I. Suddenly Ram comes in and stages this whole scene, pulling what turns out to be a fake gun but we all think is a real gun, which he later shoots me in the face with. Hence, you know, my terror. Anyway so he points the gun at Vince and he gets him to look inside his rucksack, and out of the rucksack Vince pulls this little statue of, I can't remember, one of the Hindu gods, and then he reveals that the gun's a fake and starts saying how this is him officially forgiving Vince for what he did. Apparently he was shagging Lucy.'

'Yeah. He was. That's just weird though. It's so weird. Ram's gone mad.'

'Possibly. Colin thinks we've all gone mad. But forget Ram. I mean Julie these are bad people. Luke, Vince. Today he told some poor girl to go fist herself. Just like that. These are not nice people. These are not the kind of people you want to be trucking with. Having truck with?'

'I'm now realising that yes.'

'When I found out about the whole scam I quit immediately. That's when I had the panic attack. I went into Tesco to buy you one of those Lindt bars, with a touch of sea salt, and I completely spazzed out. Actually it was really quite ugly. But then I got in a taxi with Colin, who dropped me at the Chesham, but you weren't there so I found this payphone. I got some change.'

Chris feeds another pound into the phone.

'Chris why are you telling me all this? Why did you feel the need to go looking for me at the Chesham?'

'Because, well, two reasons mainly. Firstly I wanted you to hear about all this from me, not read about it in some article. Crazy how Lucy's this big success now as well by the way.'

'Yeah, moving on.'

'So I wanted to be the one to tell you, also because Luke had been lying to me as well. I just thought you deserved to know. I just felt all this rage that he could treat you like that, and I realised how much I cared about you. Secondly, I had what I can only describe as a near death experience, and… '

'Chris, don't be dramatic.'

'I know it sounds ridiculous, but I actually did think I'd been shot in the face. It puts things in perspective. Then I had the thing in Tesco and I wasn't sure but I thought I might be about to die there as well. I thought I was having a heart attack, except the whole body rather than just the heart.'

'I'm sorry you had a panic attack.'

'It's fine. There was probably a lot of pent up… I don't know. But so after I came out of the office I just started reflecting on what's important, and essentially the answer is you.'

'Chris.'

'Just hear me out Julie, please.' Another pound. 'These last six months have been horrific. I think, I mean I don't know but I'm pretty much certain I'm depressed. That time I saw you in Dalston I tried to pretend I'm fine but I'm not fine. I feel like I'm just living for the sake of it. There's no point. I'm not at all fine. I need you. You were literally the one good thing in my life. And I know I was a dick and things weren't that great at the end but I know that now. I know I was a terrible boyfriend, and now that I know I can change. See?'

'Chris, look… '

'Just, all I'm asking is for you to think about it. To think about us. I want us to give things another go. I think we can. I know we can. You make me happy Jules.'

'But what about me, Chris? What about me?'

'Well I want to make you happy too. I want to spend my life with you. Love is the only thing that might give any sort of meaning to my life. Being with you was like... being asleep or something. Time passed without me actually having to worry about it. There was no suffering or emptiness or boredom, you know? I'm explaining this really badly, but love is just very very necessary I feel.'

'Probably you're right. But you and I, we're not in love. I'm sorry Chris. I really am. But I just don't feel the same way. I don't regret the time we spent together. You'll always be special to me, but what we had is in the past now. It's gone. There's no bringing it back, and I don't want to try. I'm sorry.'

'But... You're not even going to think about it? Think it over?'

'Chris, I know what I want.'

'You can't want him. Surely you can't. You can do so much better. You can do so much better than me as well, but that's beside the point. You don't need him. You need me.'

'This is just so typical. What makes you think I need either of you? Look, I'm really sorry Chris. I think you should go and speak to someone, if only about the panic attack. And also well done for quitting the job. You were always better than that. And I know there's someone out there you'll be perfect for, it just isn't me. I'm not the old Julie. People change.'

Another pound.

'I've got to go Chris. I've got somewhere I need to be. I'm sorry. Take care.'

The line goes dead and Chris leans into the booth, receiver still to his ear. *All those fairytales, full of shit.*

edward:gooderham

chapter:twentyfive

Disquietude was the word of the day, according to his bedside calendar. A state of uneasiness or anxiety. First recorded use in the late 1680s, as in: English Roman Catholics watched the Glorious Revolution unfold with a growing sense of disquietude.

Fast forward to the year 2020. January was supposed to entail newness, but here in De Beauvoir it was a case of *plus ça change*. Timmons shuffled to the bathroom, scratching himself in various places. He squinted at the mirror as he slipped into his beige waffleknit robe. He noticed his penis, the straw man in his downfall, peeking out the fly of his navy pyjamas. It was clamouring to be pissed, and he could only cede to its tyrannical authority.

Timmons washed his hands, rinsed his mouth, splashed water on his face. He yawned, grabbed the sink, and yawned again before leaving the bathroom. Back in his bedroom, he dressed into plum corduroys, a clean crimson shirt, magenta cardigan and oxblood shoes. He looked like red and purple had just gone four rounds in the poshest fight of all time. Treading heavily down the stairs, he yearned for this to be the moment that his ever increasing heft plummeted straight through the carpet, straight through the floorboards, straight into the vacuum cleaner or that box of old notebooks.

Oh god, the notebooks. They would have to be destroyed. If the Jacobins somehow found them it would be off with his head. They made those posthumously published Larkin letters look like the recipe binder of Mary Berry. Which actresses he wanted to boff and how, which critics he wanted to die and how. Which system of rule he wanted reimposed, and how. Timmons had even once, and in great detail, sketched out who he would surround himself with, as *Führer* in a Nazi party of his literary heroes. Swift as his Goering, for example, Gogol as Goebbels, Nabokov his Albert Speer. James Joyce Heinrich Himmler. Rabelais von Ribbentrop. Flaubert, Martin Bormann. The ensuing pages, jokingly explaining his choices, were... well, they would go down like ten lead Hindenburgs.

No joy with the floorboard plunge. Timmons envied the efficacy with which his other Philip, not Larkin but Roth, had recently willed himself to death. He must have looked out the window of his Conneticut cabin, seen this cultural storm approaching and said no thank you, not for me. Good old Philip. He had it right: old age was no battle; it was a massacre.

The kitchen was clean. Weronika had come yesterday – wonderful, loyal, Weronika. Either she had never heard of Twitter, she had somehow missed all the hate mail and graffiti, or she knew about the accusations but decided there were worse crimes. For example the ones in her native Poland during the Second World War, which wiped out twenty percent of its civilian population, ninety percent of its Jewry, and one hundred percent of her grandparents.

Making tea was a pleasure in such conditions. The space to work with, the range of available utensils. Yesterday Timmons had even braved the shops, so there was fresh milk. He took his favourite mug, a white enamel one with blue trim, the kind favoured by cowboys, for Timmons was nothing if not an outlaw with a bounty on his head, riding solo through the open ranges of the mind. He piled in the sugar and pulverised the bags against the side with the back of a spoon. He bent his right knee to ease the passage of air through his buttocks.

The office was a mess of works in progress. He went in there simply to fetch his bag of cantuccini, bringing them back to the kitchen table. Correspondence and administration beckoned, and Timmons refused to sully the desk he wrote on with even one envelope of that merde. Such mornings had nonetheless become a treat, because whenever he was opening mail he allowed himself the luxury of two teeny weeny wafers of Diazepam. This he had been prescribed for his galloping disquietude, but he forbade it himself before visits to the muse. Or rather she forbade it him. She hated his medication, refused to sanction it, refused to even see him unless he could look her straight in the eye.

Timmons brooded over his kitchen table like Churchill, over his war room map of the world. Like Churchill in late 1940. Enemies encroaching on all sides, allies either dead or staying silent across the Atlantic. Worse though, because without even an Empire to bleed dry. Timmons sat down and took his pills, chasing each one with a dunked cantuccini. He turned to the pile of letters. The great mystery was why he bothered to open them, why he insisted on putting himself through it. He supposed that if he could just figure that out, he would have answered the immortal question, the question so many of his heroes had died wrestling with. Something like: what makes a man?

He had, however, imposed constraints on this morbid curiosity. Principally all of the internet. That was now off limits. He had made the mistake of googling himself once, last summer, and his prescription for Diazepam was how that ended. That place, that thing: it was like a virtual Stalingrad. Just an incomprehensible wasteland of shouting and shelling, close combat and everywhere death, humanity rising up yet going definitively down the drain at the same time.

One prominent journalist, tweeting in the name of a publication over a century old, had posted a picture of Timmons underneath the caption fuck this fucking maggot fuck. The worst part, though, was scrolling through the comments – why Jim, *why?* – and finding that same sentiment couched in ever more graphic terms. One suggested mummifying Timmons in latex, leaving just a small hole for his junk, then scoring the end of his penis with a box knife and tossing him into a pond of piranhas. He counted only two defences, which were worse than the most savage attacks, because one came from an M16 superimposed over the Stars and Stripes, and the other read Heil Timmons, smasher of liberals to their cancerous deaths.

The articles, the testimonials, the pure hatred. And others had to suffer, all because of him. The collateral damage was visible from space, as if to tear down one crooked beech it had been necessary to raze whole forests of healthier surrounding oaks. Like all the best purges, in that respect. Nabokov was being felled, since most of what Timmons had ever gone on record to say was in praise of him. A former student wrote a *mea culpa* for manhood in *The New Statesman*, citing all the crude jokes Timmons used to make, the advice to go home and give *Lolita* a good thumbing. But come come that was obviously in jest. He was being droll. Timmons had not been minimising child rape.

The problem was that these people were what Rabelais had termed *agélastes*. Without humour, incapable of laughter. To which they would say yes, but some things can never be funny, which is precisely what they would say, being incapable of laughter. Timmons was terrified of them; they terrified him. Blind to the comedy of life, blind to the comedy of God, inhabiting a world in which Truth was simple, if only the simpletons could just see it. Not a world for novelists, in short.

So Nabokov was a goner. Timmons worried that Vladimir might hold this shattered legacy against him, if they ever met in heaven. He had always enjoyed imagining the two of them, strolling around the lake in Montreux, making acerbic asides about Freud. And speaking of Freud, how he would have adored the chance to dissect these millennial minds. Oedipus no longer sufficed. A new hero or heroine was needed, one so angry and entitled that it tried to kill everybody, to have sex only with itself. The Grendel Complex? Timmons had always taken Nabokov at his word, shunning psychoanalysis in favour of art, shunning the doctor in favour of Shakespeare. And speaking of Shakespeare, possibly not even he was safe. Watch out old friend: *We have seen better days*.

He opened an envelope. Timmons that is, not William Shakespeare. The written word was still the written word, and he was determined to give it its due. In his total war against the internet, people who were prepared to actually pen him a letter were ostensibly allies. *Dear pig*, it read, *Have you not yet keeled over and died?*

No, which was of course the great pity. Here again was Timmons as Churchill, a later yet no less beleaguered one, dragging himself out of bed only to be confronted by more chilling threats from Stalin, more chauvinist vitriol from De Gaulle. So often he must have wondered whether Hitler was really worth it.

Now the doorbell rang. Ordinarily he ignored what tended to be nothing more than the bugle call of a dog merde through his letter box, or an egging or a fruiting of the windows. Something that left him wondering where all the real psychopaths had gone, the ones with enough mettle to storm your living room and make good on their violent threats. But this morning he was expecting someone. He was expecting Roosevelt, the younger and stronger ally to whom he could pass the torch of resistance. She was right on time.

'Hello, hello,' said Timmons, opening and standing to one side.

'Hi Timbo,' said Julie. 'I think you should have the door repainted. Perhaps it would draw less attention.'

'I've tried, I've tried. But a fresh coat is like catnip to these buggers. They seem to be able to smell it. Before it's even dry they've come and defaced it again.'

'Eurgh,' said Julie, taking off her coat. 'It's the bad grammar I can't stand. *Death Rapist.* I mean what does that even mean? Death is a noun, not an imperative. They are literally accusing you of raping death.'

'Raping the greatest rapist of all. A public service if anything. Anyhow, what news from Dorset? Hardy still alive and well? Or is he in the stockade at Casterbridge, being pelted with pippin apples?'

'No he's fine. It was fine.'

'Come in, come in. Would you like tea?'

'Uhm, yes. Do you have green tea?'

'Afraid not, no. I can brew ordinary tea until it turns a shade of green, but I suppose that's not what you're after.'

'No, okay, just ordinary then.'

'Milk? Sugar?'

'Neither.'

Timmons walked towards the kitchen shaking his head, as if right there in those tea preferences was the answer to his question, namely: what the hell was wrong with the youth of today?

Special mug for Julie: Queen Elizabeth II, her silver jubilee in 1977. A recurring nightmare for Timmons was the one in which his monarch expired before him, and he had to watch the throne pass not to the regal Charles, nor the palatable William, nor any of his harmless infant children, but to Harry because of the brand strength of his American bride and biracial baby. He was by now adamant that if and when Her Majesty did die, he would just bite the bullet, or rather bite the barrel of a gun, because probably it would be hard to bite the bullet in the 0.00001 seconds it would take to leave his mouth via the dome of his skull.

'Here you go,' he said, delivering the mug to Julie. 'Have some cantuccini.'

'Thanks. What tea is it?'

'It's from the Piji plantations.'

'Ooo. Where are they?'

'Julie, it's PG Tips. Just drink it.'

Julie sat down at the kitchen table, picked up the opened hate mail.

'Do you not get angry?' she asked. 'Why do you not get more angry?'

'Drugs,' said Timmons. 'Diazepam. Valium essentially. A roaring success.'

'Seriously, though.'

'I am angry. I've spent seventy years being angry. But I'm no more angry about this than I am about everything else.'

'What do you mean, everything else?'

'All of it, everything, life. The world.'

'I just can't believe how much hatred people have. How eager they are to hate.'

'It's very Karamozovian,' said Timmons. 'Take God away, and suddenly everyone feels the need to step in and dispense His justice. All the fury, all the confusion, all of it needing to masquerade as righteousness. Probably those who would most like to see me buried are those who have never really suffered at all.'

'Speaking of which, have you seen *Granta* has named Lucy among their twenty best British novelists under forty? Despite the fact that she hasn't actually written a novel.'

'I wouldn't worry. As I said to Julian Barnes when they picked us for that in the Eighties: they chose the best forty from four.'

Julie smiled, put down the hate mail.

'What is amusing,' said Timmons, 'Is watching these buffoons unwittingly reinvent the Christian worldview. Sin, hell, orthodoxy. Blasphemy, apostates, heretics. They're leaving out all the good bits though.'

'Like what?'

'Like redemption. Like forgiveness. Yes, perhaps it would be nice to see a little forgiveness. Then again I would say that, because I'm in the dock rather than behind the bench.'

'But you're not guilty!'

'That's neither here nor there. Revolutions have no need of justice or measure. Revolutions need Robespierres, Saint Justs. Bakunins, Lenins. They need people both mad enough and stupid enough to believe that a better world might actually be born, once the last moderate woman and bourgeois child have been strangled in the entrails of the last straight white male. They need people who realise that when something isn't working it needs launching out the window, not repairing. Everyone thrown out the window together, the silent along with the guilty. These things are violent. Nothing can change without violence, and what greater violence than lies?'

'Erm. Actual rape. Actual murder. Actual widescale physical violence.'

'Yes, okay, fine. I was being lyrical, but you see my point. Let's move on. Tell me about Dorset. You've been gone a long time.'

'Yeah. My parents wanted to keep an eye on me. They think I'm depressed.'

'And what do you think?'

'That I'm depressed. They want me to see someone.'

'And what do you want?'

'To write, I think. What about you? Have you been writing?'

'Oh yes, lots and lots. Stories. I always wondered whether the absence of a woman was what was blocking me. But absence through loss is proving extremely fecund. All that tremendous pain.'

'That's not funny,' said Julie.

'It's not supposed to be,' said Timmons. 'Perhaps I should just confess to having killed her. Probably I was in love with the fact that she was dying. More time would have only lured us into some mediocre cohabitation. Some drawn out suicide pact of compromise. Silent dinners, long evenings on the sofa with our books. Instead things will always remain how they were for those dizzying few weeks.'

'You can be such terrifically bleak company.'

'Mm. Also I'm starting to wonder whether I might in fact *be* a misogynist. When you're as old as I am, you know, there's this little devil that lives in the back of the mind, preaching from its soapbox about what a woman should be, how she should behave, that sort of thing. You have to fight hard not to listen to the bugger. Difficult for you to understand maybe, as a woman.'

'No Timbo! This is precisely the point! This is a thing! This is what *Wench* was supposed to be about! Internalised misogyny! The inner misogynist! Every woman harbours one of these monsters too, far uglier and far more entrenched than yours. Ours looks like fucking Harvey Weinstein dressed as a construction worker, permanently telling us to get back in the kitchen, whistling from some citadel inside our brains. You obviously didn't read the bloody book.'

'Well... no, not all of it. But tell me what you're working on now.'

'There's nothing to tell.'

'What do you mean?'

'I mean, I'm convinced I need to write, if only for my own sanity, but I seem to have lost my subject.'

'How so? Have you stopped being a woman?'

'Very funny. It's just I used to identify with all these different causes and now I can't.'

'Why not?'

'Because they've become ridiculous to me. They make me laugh. I can no longer get angry about certain things because they literally make me laugh. And I think I needed that anger, to galvanise me.'

'Hmmm, yes. But what kind of things?'

'Okay, so,' said Julie. 'How to describe it? I think I've just... I've stopped understanding the progressive agenda that I used to champion. It's as if solidarity has atomised. It's no longer about the weak against the strong, but the weak all turning on each other, arguing about who's weaker and why. Meanwhile the strong keep getting stronger. Do you see what I mean?'

'I *hear* what you mean.'

'They all want to be equal yet they all want to be distinct. My issues are just that little bit more serious than your issues. So where do I fit in? How have I been specifically wronged? I listen to all these people on the telly and the radio, talking about their harrowing childhoods, their major traumas, and I think: nothing very bad has been done to me. There is nothing dramatic about the life I have lived.'

'Not true. All life is dramatic.'

'How though? What and how have I suffered?'

'It's not about suffering. It's about seeing and feeling. It doesn't matter what. It matters that you look *deeply*, that you feel *keenly*. And in that respect you will set yourself apart from the majority of your peers, simply by gazing beyond the depths of your own navel. Besides, you're a woman. Which they assure me is its own form of oppression.'

'Yeah but that's just it. Feminism has become a joke to me. It has thoroughly aligned itself with power. Precisely the kind of power it should have been resisting. It seems almost depraved to me that two of the most prominent feminists in the world are the advertising mastermind of Facebook, and the woman behind the most disastrous foreign intervention in recent history.'

'Cherie Blair?'

'Hilary Clinton. Sheryl Sandberg. Their brand of neoliberalism will always keep spewing up more and more monstrous injustices. My conception of feminism is not for women to try and beat men at their own game, to just become grasping egomaniacs who have found a way of outdoing them. Look at the human phlegm that approach has so far coughed up. Bloody Maggie Thatcher…'

'Margaret Thatcher, young lady, was the most…'

'Okay, fine, whatever. But to keep this ship afloat and just haul more women aboard is the stupidest idea I have ever heard. Who do we throw over the side instead? The fat? The poor?'

'I think I see. You want to sink the ship and build an arc.'

'No. Yes. Probably, ugh.'

'People have tried that. It didn't go so well.'

'I know,' said Julie, collapsing her head onto her folded arms.

'Would you like some Diazepam?'

Julie shook her head. Timmons continued:

'Why are you so obsessed with this idea that you have to write in the service of something? There's a word for people who do that that. They're called pamphleteers. They're ten a penny. You're a *writer*, you should be tackling things that are much more important than... I don't know, neoliberalism.'

'That is important.'

'No it's not.'

'Yes it is.'

'No it isn't. Not really.'

'Yes... fine, whatever. But we're living through a global bloody meltdown. To not write about that would be a titanic abdication of responsibility. Already I'm ashamed of the fact that I sit around essentially playing all day, when I could be, you know, stopping gay people from being murdered somewhere. Digging a well in Africa. Teaching a disabled child to spell.'

'Making art is the grandest of all political acts. Because if you're doing it properly, you're turning away from everything you currently think is broken about the world. You're in a room, on your own, saying no to greed, saying no to vanity, saying no to pride. Totally unsullied by power or influence or money. Free from the ugliness that helped birth this system that so exasperates you. Which, you know, is not the worst system, all things said and done.'

'That sounds a little fishy to me Timbo. That sounds like an artist trying to justify decades of disengagement.'

'*Touché.*'

'Plus, you know, I'm realising that even the best books can't make the world a better place.'

'Of course not. Why would they?'

'I just… that's what I always thought.'

'Look at us Julie. I'm a death rapist on anxiety medication, and you're a depressed traitor to your sex. Writers are awful people. Why would anything we have to say make the world a better place?'

'Fine, yes, fine.'

'But we can make the world *a* place. We can help ourselves and a few others momentarily find themselves within it.'

'In any event, I think maybe I have found my subject. I think I've decided what it is.'

'And what's that?'

'People. Lucy for example. Luke for example.'

'You hate him.'

'No, I don't think I do. He fascinates me. That culture fascinates me. All these people out grabbing whatever they can get, trying to pass it off as noble.'

'Mm.'

'I read this article about a delivery boy in Hackney who was hit and killed by a bus this summer. He was on his bike, distracted by his phone; the driver was behind the wheel, distracted by his phone. Nobody seems to get angry though. Nobody cares about the direction we're heading in. About the lies and fakery being spread without shame. The duplicity of the way these companies behave. Their bullshit about being out to make the world a better place, when all they really care about is money. And you know, what broke my heart was reading that second article by Lucy. The one about Luke. My first instinct was: oh my god, she gets it, she feels the same. Yet nobody even raised an eyebrow. They were only bothered by that stuff about you.'

'Maybe that was important too.'

'It was lies though. She ruined your life.'

'I'm fine with that. Live by the sword, die by the sword.'

'Is that a penis pun? Eww.'

'Actually I was talking about the pen.'

'Anyway, she tells that story and people literally don't flinch. Boring, next. They just want to get back to their sedated lives, with their phones and deliveries. Their bloody streaming. They don't want to hear anything that gets in the way of their comfort, unless of course it serves to justify the frustrations born out of the massive fucking holes those very same lives are excavating inside them.'

'Well, the rage is certainly still there. And I do think your generation is crying out to be defined by a novel.'

'But Timbo a generation would at least have to be conscious of novels to be defined by one. Ergo the problem. Nobody my age reads them. What would my generation do with a novel? Lie on it? Pour tea through it? Novels have nothing to say, nobody to speak to. We no longer even have the attention spans to get through one; our brains have been thoroughly zapped. They're irrelevant, and *that* is what depresses me. Not that I'm insane, but that society has relegated me to the leagues of the insane, for still being bothered about books.'

'Whether people care is irrelevant. The art is in the writing it all the same. It's in having the courage to sustain this quarrel of yours, with yourself and with society. With God. Tell me more about the idea.'

'It came to me in Naples. I was standing under this fresco by Luca Giordano, *the Triumph of Judith*.'

'At San Martino. Magnificent.'

'And I just saw… life.'

'The Baroque at its very finest.'

'I thought about the message, and I don't think I've ever seen revenge depicted so beautifully. The colour, the grandeur. I thought: wouldn't it be wonderful to write a novel like that, all these figures whirling round and round. To take that as a framework… '

'Oh stop it. Stop it Julie. You're at risk of giving me a reason to continue living. This is wonderful. Really wonderful.'

'But I just never had the story. I had no characters or plot.'

'Well that hasn't seemed to stop some of your contemporaries. Anyway, perhaps now would be an opportune moment for me to give you your present.'

'My present? You shouldn't have.'

Timmons rose to his feet with a demonic groan, hobbling arthritically to his office. He closed the door behind him, tightening and loosening his sphincter in an attempt to roll with the flow of his flatulence and thereby silence it – an attempt which failed. He took the present from his desk and squeezed out another, quieter fart before returning to the kitchen.

'It's really very kind of you. I didn't bring you anything from Dorset.'

'No, it's a trifle. But it's something I want you to have.'

Julie took the gift and contemplated its newspaper wrapping.

'You're a talented writer Julie. You are. And you must keep on. You must. Don't ever let the bastards grind you down. I did, and I regret it.'

Julie leaned over and kissed Timmons on the cheek. The fart had not followed him back to the table, *per fortuna*.

'Thank you. It means a lot.'

'But from the little I did read of *Wench*, I do think it promised to be doggerel. Really very bad.'

Julie laughed.

'More and more so do I.'

She tore off the wrapping and looked at the cover of a book: *Nikolai Gogol*, by Vladimir Nabokov.

'This has been an extremely important text for me,' said Timmons. 'In there, I think, is everything that is great about two very unique geniuses. And this version is signed by Nabokov, dedicated to me. It was a gift from the publisher of *Quadruped*.'

Julie opened to the inside cover.

December 1976, Montreux.
Dear Mr. Timmons,
To you, and the exalted struggle.
VN

'This is so generous of you,' she said. 'I'm really very touched.'

'Remember: forget the social critique. Focus on the characters, on what it is that makes them human. Do you recall that passage somewhere towards the end of the first part of *Dead Souls*, when Gogol presents us Chichikov? When he asks who he is, with respect to moral qualities?'

'I think so. Vaguely.'

'He argues that the fact of Chichikov not being a hero does not suffice to make him a total rogue. He is simply acquisitive, and to say that acquisitiveness is to blame for our ills has only become truer in the intervening centuries. What is it that makes him who he is? "It may be that in this very same Chichikov the passion that draws him on is no longer of his choosing, and that lodged in his cold existence is that which will later cast man on to his knees and into the dust before the wisdom of the heavens."'

'How do you remember all this stuff? I don't even think I could quote from my own two novels.'

'I taught *Dead Souls* for twenty years, and have loved it for thirty more. But I'm forever forgetting my internet passwords, if that's of any consolation.'

'There's an image: Gogol logging on, to go on Google and google Gogol.'

'Quite. Gogol was a complex soul in a simpler world. We, I fear, have been rendered simple by a world grown too complex.'

'It's just so hard,' said Julie. 'Trying to get a handle on it all. Trying to make sense of it.'

'That's what makes it worthwhile. If it wasn't hard, everybody would be doing it.'

'I suppose.'

'You know, there are two other memorable representations of Judith and Holofernes that perhaps you're familiar with. One by Caravaggio, another by Gentileschi.'

'Yes.'

'Look at the effort on her face each time. The help she needs, the fortitude. Of course the work is hard. It requires faith. You know, I've been thinking a lot about Philip lately.'

'Larkin?'

'Roth. I've been wondering what he would have made of all this. In his fiction he always managed to inhabit that moral nomansland – the one that is currently being shelled to kingdom come. I've been rereading his Zuckerman books. And somewhere along the line he quotes Henry James. It goes like this, and I think it's true. "We work in the dark, we do what we can, we give what we have. Our doubt is our passion, and our passion is our task. The rest is the madness of art."'

chapter:twentysix

Emily Ratajkowski is inbound, and this is not a dream. Luke is awake and lucid. He is sitting in the restaurant of the Hotel G, in downtown San Francisco, and this is Emily Ratajkowski, about to pass his table. She is shorter than expected, really incredibly petite. Stylewise she is rocking a grey tweed blazer over a tangerine jumpsuit, desert boots on her feet.

'Good evening,' says Luke, Britishly.

She turns and smiles and says hi without slowing down. Shit the bed shit the bed shit the bed. Breathtaking she is. Literally Luke would give his right arm. Even if the deal meant never getting a bionic replacement, still he would give his right arm. However big he goes on to become, probably he will always retain a soft spot for Emily.

He takes three pictures of her back before she disappears into the toilet, not that women of her calibre actually go to the toilet. The waiter arrives. His face is accessorised with half a dozen piercings and a perfectly trimmed beard.

'Hey welcome to Alaya how you doin tonight?'

'Amazing. How are you?'

'I'm great my name's Rory and I'm gonna be your waiter, so any problems any questions whatever just holler, okay?'

'You bet,' says Luke.

'Can I interest you in anything to drink for starters?'

'Absolutely. What do you recommend with regard to cocktails?'

'Okay, so are you more like a bitter or sweet kinda guy?'

'On the whole I'm tempted to say probably somewhere in between.'

'Maybe you could try our Diving Bell. Mezcal, yuzu, lime, falernum, gin, pineapple gomme and cayenne. Really nice.'

'Meh. Mezcal though.'

'Or another super option is our Officer and a Gentian. There you're looking at gentian obviously, scotch, italicus rosolio and lemongrass air. Also Meyer lemon.'

'Right, I'll have one of those.'

'And you already know what you wanna eat maybe?'

'Yes I'll get the red snapper in the lobster pho broth, then a side order of brussels sprouts.'

'Great choice,' says Rory, scribbling.

'Thanks. It's strange because in England, where I come from, brussels sprouts have always had this terrible reputation. We eat them at Christmas.'

'No way?'

'Yeah but nobody really wants them. And yet from a nutrients perspective they're insane.'

'Well you're gonna love these. That harissa is just, like, bam. Okay great well I'll get that order put through and you enjoy your evening with us. Like I said, any problems just shout.'

Rory leaves, and Luke reflects that Emily has been in the toilet for quite some time. He messages the Tims, the Toms, and six more people, inviting them to guess who he just saw, before sending the least obscure picture and narrowing down the possibilities by about seven billion. What time is it even, back home? Luke opens his world clock and sees that London is eight hours ahead. Everyone will be in bed. He checks what weather he has left behind. Five degrees, one hundred percent chance of rain. Ha, fucking losers. Fourteen degrees and sunny here tomorrow.

He opens Instagram and straight away sees Emily, wearing exactly what she was wearing just a few minutes ago, leaning into a bathroom mirror and spritzing her brioche of cleavage with Paco Rabane Pure XS. Posted this instant and with the restaurant tagged. Now something curious happens: Luke sees her there on his screen, sees also the actual real life Emily Ratajkowski, walking back towards his table. He remains, for a moment, dazed by the quantum insanity of her being here and there, then and now, all in this one spatial instant.

Then he pulls himself together and snaps seven decent pictures. Only when she has gone, around the corner and out of sight, can he process what has happened. She was in there working. Luke does some maths, reckons that with her twenty million plus followers, Paco Rabane should be paying about thirty grand for that one post. The restaurant will be chucking a few extra thousand her way, covering her airfare, sorting her a suite for the night. A few other sponsored partnerships perhaps, the makeup and the jewellery and the tangerine jumpsuit. All in all, she has earned what Ram makes in a year, simply by disappearing into the toilet for as long as it takes more ordinary humans like him to poo. Luke lols, at the awesome power of social media.

His cocktail arrives, and it is grammable as fuck. An inky flower, presumably the gentian, floats on a sudsy white foam in a straightforward tumbler. The solitary ice cuboid resembles a bar of soap, and the slight yellowy tinge evokes a pissed bath. Luke sips and says oh yes out loud. Definitely tasting the scotch there, definitely breathing the lemongrass air. He toasts himself, because this trip is cause for celebration. Which the past six months have not always given cause for.

Vince was fired for inappropriate conduct. He had no idea that Amy was the editor of a successful digital magazine called *Mind the Gap*. Given that its focus was on gender equality in the workplace, Amy was right up there with Queen Elizabeth II and Greta Thunberg on the long list of females it was probably unwise to tell to go fist themselves. Her ensuing article made quite the splash, without even having to mention the basic toxicity of an environment in which grown men run around pretending to shoot each other. Vince was out and Luke, once reassured about the ongoing validity of his seed capital, considered it a case of justice done. Feigning friendliness with him had been no picnic, particularly not after it turned out he had been screwing the girlfriend of his best friend, but Luke had done it for the sake of his baby.

His poor baby, who at the time had been showing symptoms of meningitis, the bad type. The Lucy article looked set to go viral. It should have killed him, but then it simply had no impact. Nobody shared it, nobody pinned it, nobody cared. And when Amy published her story about Vince, more or less breaking the internet, it relegated Luke and his harmless scheming even further down the news. When he met Gary, his new VC operator, the issue was not even raised.

Picpus remained committed to the initial investment, but that was the next problem, because there was only about thirty thousand of that left. Which was not a lot – not with developers to keep paying. Not with Luke out there snapping necks and cashing cheques, heavily pursuing new users. Yet again, he knew that if he could just get his hands on some more money, he would be able to grow and grow and grow.

The beta test came next, and it was only okay. Feedback was generally underwhelming: a slow and restricted platform, without a large enough network to make it interesting. But Luke did succeed in reloading Gary for another hundred grand, and he was confident that Tim and Tom could keep shipping better and better product, while Luke hit the marketing hard. Then, in December, Facebook reached out.

They wanted to speak to Luke. They asked him to fly out to California, meaning the interest was serious. Obviously they had seen the potential, and Luke contemplated his best play. He consulted Tim and Tom and Gary. Did they agree to sell Blank, allow Facebook to take things forward, maybe be kept onboard? If so, at what price? Picpus were now two hundred in for a total of nineteen percent, but no way would Luke have sold for less than a million bucks. Not even five, not even ten. Potentially twenty.

The other option was to turn them down. Thanks but no thanks, *à la* Snapchat. Which was not a decision Luke thought Evan Spiegel was now regretting, with his two billion dollar net worth and supermodel wife. Plus Blank had the potential to be far, far bigger. The consensus was to wait and see what kind of offer was put on the table.

Whatever it turned out to be, the initial trappings were rich. By the way, the red snapper and the brussels sprouts have arrived. The fish actually looks like a fish – eyes, fins, tail – which causes Luke no end of mirth. Anyway: the initial trappings of that offer were rich. Facebook were clearly courting them, because Luke was flown out Business Class. Once, when he was thirteen years old and on the way back from Orlando, the whole family had been upgraded to Economy Plus. But this was something else.

He checked in three hours early to extract maximum benefit from the lounge, where there was nothing and nobody stopping him from drinking ten pints of straight gin, apart from social norms. He ate five mini bacon baps, simply because they kept being offered to him. As for the plane itself, Luke was welcomed aboard with champagne. The complimentary toiletry bag was trimmed with leather. Just two booths away from him was sat the former London Mayoral candidate Zac Goldsmith. The seats extended into proper beds, and after lunch had been cleared away, Luke reclined with a Glenfiddich to watch *Bad Boys For Life*. This was the kind of luxury he could get used to.

And now this, the cool hotel, Emily Ratajkowski. Have Facebook sent her as part of the package? Luke finishes his fish and pushes the plate to one side. He gestures to Rory for one more Officer and a Gentian. He loads Tinder, edits his bio to include British, and absently swipes right while popping brussels sprouts into his mouth. Annie 27

Madge 23 Dongmei 22 Briana 24 Nancy 28 Hillary 24 Taylor 25 Lorrie 32 Darcy 30 Eliza 31 Jenny 40 Mary 26 Vicky 27 Holly 19. This is not everyone. These are just the matches.

Rory returns with his cocktail. He removes the sprouts plate and proposes dessert. Luke chooses the coconut panna cotta with mango tapioca, grapefruit, and almonds. He returns to Tinder and snares Clarissa 27 Flossie 18 Ehuang 24 Leanne 28 Jeannine 28 Tish 21 Mavis 22 Cleo 22 Rowena 20 Cecile 22 Kelsey 23 Vixen 44 Noelle 21 Felecia 23 Brittany 20 Hazel 21 Amber 27 Julie 25 Donna 26 Shuang 26 and Alejandra 33.

Dessert arrives and Luke gives his swiping finger a rest. He takes a picture of the panna cotta, tastes it, and returns to Tinder. Two schools of thought at this point. Tim advises accumulating matches before sending them all a blunt offer of dick, tonight. Tom favours the more gentlemanly approach, doing the same then saying he is only in town for one night, he never usually does this, but he is game if they are. Tomato tomato, potato potato.

Tim gets more action but he is also better looking, and Luke has no desire to blot his copybook in a city where he might one day be a prominent figure, so he follows Tom. He copies, pastes and sends the same message to all his matches, puts down his phone and concentrates on dessert.

Three minutes later only one grapefruit segment remains, and still no notification. Luke worries he has come across as too much of a pussy. Just as he is scraping up the last of his mango tapioca, he pings. Flossie 18 is keen to meet up. Eighteen is very young though. Luke googles the age of consent in America, sees that it can be basically anything *depending on the circumstances*, which then entail a lot of reading. In any event she would not legally be able to join him for a cocktail beforehand. Also she looks a bit goth.

His restraint is rewarded eleven seconds later, when Julie 25 asks if he really is British. Luke says he went to the same prep school as Draco Malfoy. No, not Hogwarts. The same prep school as the actor who played Draco Malfoy. All this in consecutive messages, followed by a cricket team photo featuring Luke and Tom Felton, which has been used as a prop before. In the meantime another potential piste has emerged with Shuang 26, but Luke prefers Julie 25 – not at all in a racist way, just because he does. He suggests a cocktail in the bar at the Hotel G and she accepts. Luke signals to Rory, tells him he will be needing a double espresso.

In the next half an hour, five other matches declare themselves eager, including Vixen 44, who would surely have performed unspeakable acts. Luke can therefore barely hide his frustration when Julie 25 arrives. She is sneaky big. Not obese by any means, but her photos have concealed an undeniable podge in the thighs and around the shoulders. She is pretty enough – brown hair, blue eyes, dimples – but no Felecia 23, for example.

Julie 25 opts for a Diving Bell and Luke orders himself another Officer and a Gentian. He explains the differences between cricket and quidditch. They spend fifteen minutes lamenting the endemic sexism that denied Hillary Clinton the White House, before Luke proposes taking this party upstairs. Julie 25 loves that he calls it a lift rather than an elevator. Everything moves quite quickly from here.

They are inside his room, they are kissing, they are undressing. Luke does that routine where his fingers are the plunger and her vagina is the toilet. Julie 25 pushes him onto the bed, takes him unconvincingly in her mouth for about forty seconds, before rolling on a condom and riding him for two, maybe three minutes max. Luke flips her over and runs through his repertoire of assorted pyrotechnics. She asks if he wants to choke her. Not really, he says, but now he is getting there, and seeing as her face is so nice he asks if he can come on it. She says fine so he springs to his feet, yanks off the condom, and bleurgh.

Julie 25 disappears into the bathroom for a few minutes, comes out and says she probably ought to be getting home. Luke offers to sort her an Uber and she accepts. It will be eight minutes, but Julie 25 reckons they always end up arriving sooner, so Luke sees her to the door and says maybe see you around.

He considers giving his willy a wash and messaging Felecia 23. It is nearly eleven though, he has been awake for thirty hours, and tomorrow he has his big meeting. He gets back into bed, takes a sleeping pill, turns on the television and watches fifteen minutes of *Big Bang Theory* before switching off because he can feel himself drifting. There are no dreams. He is living the dream.

At breakfast he thinks about Julie 25. If Tinder offered the option to rate, he would probably give her three stars. She is his eleventh conquest since technically being dumped by the other Julie, the real Julie, but some of those shags have been way hotter than her. Plus he was about to end it anyway. She was so bloody depressed, so bloody depressing. Luke pities her more than anything, pities anyone so boring, not to mention deluded about their own abilities. That awful fucking book of hers. When he becomes stratospherically important, perhaps he will throw her a bone. Get her published, give her a million quid. Anything that saves her from having to carry on being so bitter about everyone and everything.

Speaking of Julie, how to set eyes on this spread and not recall Naples, with its derisory breakfasts. Croissants, essentially. Continental in the same way Antarctica is continental, which is to say not even legitimately continental, devoid of any interest or importance, a total joke. Here there are muffins and bagels and waffles, pancakes both thick and thin. Five kinds of bread for toasting. Seven different juices. Silos of cereal stacked side by side like organ pipes. The omelette station, the smoothie station, the sushi station. If breakfast is the most important meal of the day and San Francisco is the most important city in the world, this right here is the very motherboard of civilisation.

For Luke, this morning marks the beginning of the end of his long long journey to Palo Alto. He looks at his life in the manner of a story. The chapters, his various achievements, have always allowed him to gauge his success against others. At fifteen months he could talk, at eleven he was moderately pubic, and both these things rendered him exceptional. To lose his virginity at only eighteen was a blow, but lotharios like Richard Branson never went to boarding school, where the ratios and curfews made it almost impossible to get any quim. Luke did at least design his first website before Steve Jobs, even if yes, the internet had not yet been invented when Steve Jobs was twenty. Overall, thirty is not an embarrassing age to be becoming a billionaire. Zuckerberg was younger, but Bezos and others were older. He is doing okay.

He climbs into an Uber and rides through Union Square, past the towering glass facade of the Apple store. Its sliding doors are open wide, people streaming in and out. Everything is beautifully engineered and on display. Nothing is ugly, nothing hidden, and this is what the whole world could look like, if only idiots would shut the fuck up and stop moaning about privacy. Luke gazes up in veneration. Here is a holy site in the holy land, bestowed with a double reverence, like a church in Bethlehem, not that he would ever condone Israeli oppression by visiting the West Bank, not that he is in any way whatsoever antisemitic.

They advance block by block. Luke is amazed by this city. Here, finally, progress appears to have solved the eternal question of how people live together. There do appear to be quite a few homeless though. Also his driver Kumar keeps whingeing about the traffic, so Luke puts his headphones on, isolates himself, and listens to the Steve Jobs biography.

Ten lanes of freeway skirt the bay, past the airport and south, towards the names that stilled his juvenile surfing. Mountain View, Cupertino, Sunnyvale. Palo Alto. To be honest everything looks a little more humdrum than what he imagined, which is perhaps to be expected, given that he imagined a shining Eden of driverless vehicles and money trees. This is more like Hatfield Business Park, just with bigger skies and wider roads.

Then suddenly he is arriving at the Facebook campus in Menlo Park, passing the famous Like sign, turning into Hacker Way. Steve Jobs is giving him a piece of advice: one way to remember who you are, he says, is to remember who your heroes are. Luke does, Luke will. But he knows he must do this alone, so he pauses Jobs and stores away his headphones. Each of his next movements are performed deliberately, richly, as if the cameras of the global press are pointed at him. Stepping out of the car. Walking towards the entrance. Calling himself by his name.

The assistant passes Luke an iPad and asks him to complete the asterisked fields while she announces his arrival. Luke is then given a security pass attached to a lanyard. Printed on the back are some basic rules, as well as a reminder to have fun. Luke is told to wait for his host, so he looks around at the murals and the signs on the walls. *Our work is only 1% finished*, says one. Luke opens his calculator and deduces that if this awesome promise is true, Facebook will one day be worth fifty trillion dollars.

'Hey, Luke is it?'

Luke turns around to see a thin guy in a sleeveless fleece. His whole face seems to be squished into a very small area in the middle of his head.

'Hello, yes, hi. Dan you must be.'

'Yeah hey I'm Dan.'

'A real pleasure Dan. Can I just say how happy I am to be here today.'

'Well we're glad to have you Luke. Really glad. So I'm gonna be taking you through to your meeting.'

'Oh. It's not with you?'

'No, I'm just your chaperone.'

384

Which means the hours spent stalking him have been wasted. Dan leads Luke outside and onto a long esplanade flanked with low, colourful buildings. A central stretch of naked trees and greenery runs between the pavements. Employees pedal up and down on Facebook bicycles. There are bars and restaurants, with neatly arranged chairs and tables outside. It smacks to Luke of what European cafe culture could potentially be, without the filth and tramps and pigeons and cigarette smoke and dog dirt. Without Europe, basically.

'We have about sixty acres of land here, and nearly a million square feet of office space between our nine buildings. Across the highway about the same again.'

'Question for you actually Dan: What is the difference between a highway and a freeway?'

'Gee, gosh. I think it has to do with lanes. A freeway has more lanes.'

'I see.'

Luke is thinking how quintessentially American this all is. Which is fair, given that the only other America he has experienced is Disneyworld, Florida. The pristine filmset surroundings, the buoyant atmosphere, his own euphoria – everything jives with his memories of that holiday. And now here he is, two decades later and nearly three thousand miles away, on another ocean, yet everything looks exactly the same, only with more geeks and boffins.

These look like the characters who were bullied at school, but really really bullied, bullied by the bullied, bullied even by those right at the bottom of the bullying food chain. All grown up and having the last laugh. Actually, Luke wonders whether there might be worse things than bullying, if it galvanises the bullied to go out there and build Facebooks, thereby revolutionising before hopefully eventually putting an end to all bullying. Should schools in fact be actively encouraging it?

Dan proposes a coffee and they enter the Epic Cafe. He is on a fasting protocol, but Luke orders a flat white and takes out his wallet. Dan explains that everything is free on campus. The food, the drinks, the electronics in the vending machines. Opposite there is even an arcade, where employees can come and relax. Where they can take five from refining the human soul, and challenge each other to a game of *Mortal Kombat*.

When Luke has finished his coffee they board an electric shuttle bus and cross the highway. Here the structures are more modern, all glass and uneven roofs. Dan leads Luke into a large common area where there are bike racks on the walls, where everything is either wood framing or exposed ceiling. Ducts, wires, mess. People are coming and going with their heads down and two or even three devices in their hands. Luke is shown into a glass cube in the middle of the open space. Dan sits him down and leaves, saying:

'Have a great meeting.'

But Luke is alone: a great meeting with who?

'Welcome to Facebook, Luke.'

The voice is familiar. Luke turns around and he is standing there, wearing his trademark grey roundneck and android smile. His hair is combed forward in neat caligulan curls.

'What do you think of the place?'

'Amazing,' manages Luke. Breathing is a difficulty.

'We're super psyched to have you here.'

'Me too. I mean, I'm psyched to be here.'

'Cool. Hey, so how about I take you for a walk around the site?'

'I… Yeah. Yes please.'

'So where we are right now is the newest part of the development. Frank Gehry came in and helped us with it. What an inspiring guy.'

Luke nods. He has literally nothing to say about Frank Gehry.

'I really wanted this kind of messy vibe that you're probably getting. It feels like a building site, right?'

'Yeah.'

'Well, that's because this whole thing *is* a building site. What we're doing is building, and I want our employees to remember that. Our work is never finished.'

They walk under crisscrossing wooden beams and arrive at a blackboard.

'Hey, why don't you step up and write what's on your mind. It's kind of a little fun thing we have here.'

Luke knows thousands of words. The combinations that he could therefore write on this board number well into the gazillions. But suddenly he can think of not one. He approaches the board slowly, stoops to pick up a stick of chalk, and after another moment of hesitation, he writes:

The best way to predict the future is to invent it – Steve Jobs

'I miss him every day.'

'What was he like?' asks Luke.

'He was a pretty difficult dude. A really difficult dude in fact. But Moses probably thought God was a difficult dude. Always pushing us further, always making our lives more challenging. But you could only acknowledge the greatness of what he was doing and the truth of what he was saying.'

They walk on, emerging into a sunken courtyard, with seating areas shaded under soaring redwoods.

'We call this the town square. Because it's the focal point of our community. We're always looking to remind our employees what the mission is: to connect people, to bring them together in the digital equivalent of those formerly real world spaces.'

'Yes,' says Luke. 'Exactly. And this is where I think there are so many similarities between our visions. With Blank, what I… '

'Luke, I'm gonna be very honest with you here: your company doesn't interest me.'

'But… What?'

'Look, I think you've not quite seen where social is going. Either that or you're seeing almost too far ahead.'

'Maybe,' concedes Luke. 'But why though?'

'See, people aren't always super intelligent. We've experienced a bit of a backlash over the past few years, and I'm starting to understand why. Folks can't seem to get over this hurdle of wanting to preserve their privacy. They should be out in the town square, but they're still stuck in their living rooms. They don't realise that privacy is a thing of the past, or should be at any rate. Privacy means you're hiding something. If we're going to build a better world, a more honest world, there's no place for

privacy. And that's why, until now, we've always been advocating radical transparency. All this glass you can see is supposed to illustrate that.'

'Mm.'

'What I mean is: gone are the days of there being different Lukes. Luke having a beer, hacker Luke, family Luke, boyfriend Luke. That is division, and division is bad. Imagine if I know everything about you and you know everything about me. With that kind of transparency, where is the potential for conflict? It disappears as we become more open, more tolerant.'

'Yes.'

'The fact is, people have one identity. Anything else is an example of a lack of integrity. Do you follow?'

'Absolutely, and my app… '

'Your app advocates a really super transparency. But it's going about things the wrong way. If I use your platform, I still have control over what I share. You're now obliged to give me the option to say don't scan my emails, don't check my web history, just sort through one or two of my social feeds. More and more of which will have to be end-to-end encrypted. Regs are seeing to that, because governments don't seem to get how important this all is. Now, we're hiring some super lobbyists who can open the right doors and get the message across, but it takes time. Nick Clegg, your old deputy prime minister, is working hard on that front. He's someone who's greatly respected in all the important places.'

'That's interesting,' says Luke. 'I always assumed everyone thought Nick Clegg was a twat. No offence.'

'In Britain perhaps, but we don't really care about Britain. It's kind of irrelevant. I mean within the European Union. He's greatly respected within the European Union, and they seem to have a particular issue with us. Probably because they're jealous that between nearly thirty member states they can't produce one tech company that's even a tenth as successful as the very cruddiest Valley outfit.'

'Is it true he speaks five languages fluently?'

'Nick? Yeah, he's super talented. But even he's having difficulty getting through to Brussels. Gone are the days of just being able to cajole the public, to trick them into giving up their data.'

'But so how do you lead them there, if not by building platforms that get everything out in the open?'

'You do build them, but that comes later. You start by seducing them into actively wanting to share more of themselves, and we do that by establishing as large and comprehensive a community as possible. When I think about the future of the internet, that is what I see. Already we're integrating our own four platforms. Connecting people with businesses via WhatsApp. Direct purchasing on Instagram. Then, you know, video calls on Messenger. More payments, commerce. And the greater our reach, the more total we become, the more people will feel the need to be a part of the community. We make them think it's all inevitable anyway, that if they want to take part in society they don't have any choice. And then we'll be sitting on a goddamn Arabia of data and revenue, which means sufficient political clout to start forcing things in the direction of transparency. But the community has to come first. The community has to grow. Maybe in ten years, maybe in twenty years, when we have three or four billion users all living their lives on Facebook, maybe then we can integrate your idea.'

Luke winces up into the Californian sun.

'I don't understand why you flew me all the way out here, why you yourself have personally taken the time to come and tell me all this. That my app won't work, or that it will but only twenty years from now.'

'I hear your frustration. Walk with me, I'd like to show you the roof.'

Luke briefly wonders whether he is about to be murdered. Whether this is where all threatening rivals are brought, before being thrown down into moving freeway traffic. Moving highway traffic, whatever.

They reach a graded terrace, with more greenery and sofa booths. From here they ascend, up to a verdant roof garden.

'Frank and I decided it was very important to bring things back to nature. We have a reclaimed water system, we have solar panels. Over two hundred trees. I like to come walking up here. The whole trail comes to just shy of half a mile, which is a neat workout if you can squeeze it in a few times a day. Listen to those birds.'

Luke listens. They sound like birds.

'I asked you to come, Luke, because I wanted to meet you. Not because of your company, but because of you. I'd like you to come and work for us. I think you have what it takes to make a difference.'

'Well... I'm honoured.'

'To make things easier, I'm going to make an offer to buy your company, simply so you can repay your investors. But I want you and only you.'

'That sounds… I'll have to see the offer, of course.'

'You don't understand. I want you to name your price.'

'Are you buying me off just to sideline my idea?'

'I'm buying off because I'm not interested in your idea. Or rather, I'm interested in you pursuing another one of your ideas. But here, for us.'

'Which idea?'

Luke wonders how he knows about all the other aborted business ventures. The pet marketplace. The bicycle seat lock. Matching socks and pants, labelled according to the weekday. The roundabout game app, dozens of others besides.

'About six months ago you came to my attention in an article.'

'Oh,' says Luke. 'That. No, that was just… '

'Tell me what happened. Tell me about it.'

'Well… okay. Basically I knew I couldn't get any funding unless I onboarded some users, but I was never going to be able to without a proper marketing budget, which would have had to come from funding. So I figured out a way round it. Dead people have never been covered by any of the data regs, so I decided to try and pass some off as users to attract investment, thereby allowing me to generate a proper user base of my own.'

'You see, that is genius. It shows me that you have the hacker spirit Luke. Which is precisely what we want around here.'

392

'Thanks.'

'No, thank you. Did you know that about five hundred Facebook users die every single hour?'

'Really?'

'About ten thousand a day. Three million a year. Overall there are fifty million dead users whose accounts have remained active. Possibly in thirty or forty years we will have as many dead users as live ones, numbering in the billions. The only idea we have so far had to keep them in the community is to turn their pages into memorials, but I want you to come here and work on something super, super exciting.'

'I think I see where you're going,' says Luke.

'You do?'

'Actually I had this idea. In Naples.'

'Florida?'

'Italy.'

'Go on.'

'What if it was possible to harness the dead,' said Luke. 'Package them up as data. It came to me again just before, back on your other site, when I saw your sign about being 1% percent finished. Which would mean your community might one day be as large as two hundred billion people, most of whom would have to be dead. Just imagine what you could do with those numbers.'

'Exactly. And what I'm imagining is this: online legacies. Users choose the kinds of sectors to which they would like to be marketed in death, thereby keeping their personalities alive. Perhaps we can even incentivise them in life – I don't know, maybe free access to certain tiered services, discounts for commerce, that sort of thing. Then, when they die, we acquire the right to use their online persona. If they like music, we sell their Like or Follow to a new musician. If they like pizza, we sell their Like or Follow to the new Italian restaurant in town. You come along as that musician or restaurant owner, and you're looking to make an immediate impact. You set up a Facebook page, you set up an Instagram account, you create your presence, but you need to make an impact. So you pay us a fee, say one thousand dollars for five thousand likes or followers, whatever. If you, as a business, could budget twenty thousand dollars for marketing, that's then one hundred thousand Likes or Followers.'

'You hit the ground running.'

'You do. And these are not bots. Regulation has caught up with buying and selling fake users. But these aren't fake. These are real people. They're just dead, that's all. So you have all these Likes or Followers, and in just a few days or weeks they're going to create the buzz that then leads to a more organic, interactive following. Once people have seen something is popular they won't ask too many questions. They'll just Like or Follow it themselves to go along with the crowd.'

'Yeah,' says Luke. 'The ultimate engagement driver.'

'What it would do for our revenue is potentially astonishing. And if our revenue grows, so too can the community. All the while, we are making it a more pervasive and cohesive ecosystem. Not just a bond between the living, but also between the living and the dead.'

'Absolutely,' says Luke. 'Absolutely.'

'With that kind of totality comes not only transparency, but even the ability to drive behaviour ourselves. Imagine: you land in a new city and know exactly what bar to go to, because we tell you. You turn up, and your favourite cocktail is brought straight to you. You look around, and who do you see?'

Emily Ratajkowski, Luke thinks.

'You see yourself. You see other people just like you, with the same interests and outlook. And you don't even need Blank to help you find them.'

'Right.'

'So how do you feel about this challenge Luke? How do you feel about the opportunity to build and deliver this service? Do you want to come and be a part of Facebook?'

'I do,' says Luke. 'I do.'

'That's fantastic. The paperwork is downstairs, all ready. You just have to fill in the numbers and sign.'

'Yeah. Just… No, nothing.'

'Go on. Tell me what you're thinking.'

'I mean, it's nothing. I know it's legal and everything. But… I just wonder… I mean, is it totally ethical?'

Luke is guided to the very edge of the roof garden. Silicon Valley is spread out beneath him.

'You know Luke, one of my favourite sayings is that there are two types of people in this world: optimists and pessimists. And the saying goes that optimists tend to be successful, whereas pessimists tend to be right. What do you wanna be?'

chapter:twentyseven

Masquerade was the word of the day, according to her online dictionary notification. Used as a noun: party, dance, or other festive gathering of persons wearing masks or disguises. A false outward show, as in masquerade of virtue. Used as a verb: to disguise oneself, to go about under false pretences, to assume a role. For instance, here you are still masquerading as an artist. Derived from the Spanish *masquerada*, reaching England in 1580, just before its Armada failed to. Back when Queen Elizabeth was going round masquerading as a virgin.

Julie closed the notification box. Others remained, but the rest of her laptop screen was filled with a maximised Microsoft Word window. A Microsoft Word window without any words, just a white nothing in the shape of a page, set under useless tools and toolbars. Literally useless, none of them of any use, because of the many thousands of functions available, not one could actually finish this novel for her. Not yet anyway. Another notification reminded her that updates needed installing – perhaps that was one of them.

The worst part was that staring at the empty screen also meant staring at herself. Late summer sunlight was streaming through her bedroom window in Dorset, splashing her face across the screen in shadows and glare. There was the cursor, right between her eyes, blinking. How many more pages than the three hundred she had already written would it take to properly describe the person behind those eyes? How many more characters, how many more books?

Just this one would suffice, for now. But she was lacking an ending. The general consensus was that a book needed one, although it was true that the very novel on which she was modelling her own had none. *Dead Souls* simply trailed off, while the Prince was making his appeal to people in whose breasts a heart still beat, begging them to swim against the current. Right in the middle of a sentence. But Nikolai Gogol had a) the kind of dazzling genius that permitted such eccentricity, and b) only done it because he very suddenly dropped dead.

Julie was convinced she had none of the former, and was not quite depressed enough to engineer the latter. There were moments when she really quite wanted to, when she looked at her reflection in that screen and saw a mess, masquerading as a woman. She was broke, she was alone, she was getting old. She would never amount to anything that pleased anybody, least of all herself. She was living with her parents, struggling to finish a novel that would never ever ever be published.

When she read back over what she had already written, she despaired. Fucking hell Julie, this is not what you set out to do. Do you not recall sitting down, evaluating the literary offering of the moment, taking note of what was garnering praise? You read both Sally Rooney novels, you said to yourself okay: you can do this. Short sentences, simple prose, stay in control. What went wrong? Your manuscript looks like Brexit in comparison, like something that started out as one thing then became ten different, irreconcilable things. Your dialogue looks like dialogue in the way those House of Commons debates were supposed to be dialogue. Well, you wanted it to be Baroque.

Julie was about to go downstairs for a third pot of green tea that morning when her phone rang. It was a London number.

'Hello,' she answered.

'Hi, yes, Julie?'

'Speaking.'

'Hi Julie. It's Ola Akerele, I'm not sure if you remember me?'

'Ola. Yeah, I remember you. What do you want?'

'I wanted to speak to you.'

'About what?'

'Well… look, I know you probably hate me. I know you… that you probably don't think I'm a very good person.'

'No. Not really.'

There was silence on the line.

'I owe you an apology,' said Ola finally. 'I owe Jim an apology.'

'I think if we're being honest you owe the world an apology.'

'I know. I know. I'll get there. I just… you know, it was a very difficult time for me. I'm ashamed of the person I was. I'm ashamed of the things I did. I'm ashamed of the way I treated my mother. I'm… so ashamed.'

Her voice began to break.

'Why are you telling me this?'

'I guess I just wanted to explain. I didn't understand myself and I know it's too late now, but it's so hard, when I think how I'm never going to be able to say sorry. To my mum. Probably she died hating me, and I have to live with that.'

'Yes,' said Julie. 'You do.'

She heard Ola sob.

'Look, Ola, I'm sure she didn't hate you. She was your mother. She loved you.'

'She'd have been right to hate me. I was selfish. I was ungrateful.'

'You made a mistake. Everyone makes mistakes. You can still do the right thing. What does Lucy say?'

'I don't know,' said Ola. 'I haven't spoken to Lucy in almost a year.'

'What do you mean?'

'I mean I haven't spoken to her. I don't speak to her. She doesn't speak to me. You didn't know?'

'No. Why?'

'She broke up with me. Personally and professionally. Ages ago now. Last summer. I was negotiating her an advance for a collection of short stories, I brought her an offer, but she said other agents had been soliciting her with better ones. She said the whole thing wasn't working out for her. You know we were together.'

'I'd heard something, yeah.'

'Briefly. Only very briefly. But obviously… '

'Obviously she lied to you too.'

'Maybe.'

'No, not maybe. Not maybe Ola. She used you. I'm sorry.'

'How could I have been so stupid?'

'You weren't to know. She was my friend; if anything I'm the stupid one. Why don't you come clean about what you did? Get your own back?'

'I suppose because I'm a coward. Because I'd have to face up to my own actions. Come clean about what *I* did. Probably I'd lose my job. And I don't think I could face it. The shame, the ridicule.'

'Maybe it's important. So you can move on. I don't know. You at least owe an apology to Jim.'

'I know. I've been writing and rewriting it for months. But I just... '

'Come and see him with me. We're friends. I'll take you.'

'I don't know. Are you sure it's a good idea?'

'I think he'd appreciate it.'

'Okay. Yeah, okay. Anyway, I wanted to get all that off my chest first, but there's another reason I'm calling.

'Go on.'

'You might not believe me, but I think about your book a lot.'

'Oh yeah.'

'No, I do,' said Ola. 'Really I do. I know you probably think my job is a joke, that all the excuses I gave for not representing you were rubbish, but they weren't. Certainly I always thought you were a talented writer. The amount of stuff I read, and honestly you stood out. Plus I did think *Wench* was a great book. And I guess with what's happened to me over the last year, some of it has started to ring even truer.'

'Mmm.'

'The fact is though, my job is selling books to publishers. And I didn't see any way I could have sold yours. Sadly the industry is the way it is, and a lot of great voices aren't being heard because... well, the market's not interested. And the market is everything.'

'Well,' said Julie. 'I'm not even sure *Wench* is a very good book. The more I think about it, the more I think it's a terrible book.'

'Obviously a lot of people out there beg to differ.'

'What do you mean?'

'Your account. Your Instagram.'

'Sorry?'

'I couldn't believe it at first. I remember when we met, everything you said about social media, about Instagram in particular. It must have taken an immense amount of maturity for you to take that step, feeling the way you do.'

'Ola, I don't... '

'To see how people have reacted to the excerpts you've been posting from *Wench* is just amazing. Really amazing. I guess I owe you two apologies: one for behaving the way I did, and another for totally underestimating the way audiences would connect with your work. I didn't see it coming at all.'

Julie sat back down and opened the internet. She typed *Julie Stanhope Instagram* into Google and waited 0.38 seconds to see the 480,000 search results. She clicked on the first: Julie Stanhope (@juliestanhope) · Instagram photos and videos.

'I think obviously it's speaking to the moment,' continued Ola.

Julie looked at the page in disbelief. This was her. She was this. The picture was of her, on Chesil Beach. Underneath her name, she was credited as being the author of two novels.

'What made you decide to do it? I mean ultimately we can think what we like about the medium, but the most important thing is to get the work out there, right?'

'Mm,' said Julie.

She was apparently the author of 132 posts. She was following 0 people. And she herself had 111,678 followers.

'Julie?'

'Hmm?'

'What made you decide to do it?'

'Erm, well... I don't really know. I suppose I thought it was time to... I don't know.'

She scrolled down through dozens and dozens of thumbnails, all just paragraphs of text that had been isolated, centred and recast in typewriter font. Paragraphs of her text.

'Well, it only came to my attention about a month ago. At that point you already had about fifty thousand followers. And it's grown to more than a hundred in just that time, which is... I don't think I've ever seen anything like it.'

'No. Me neither.'

'Was it a shock?' asked Ola.

'Yes, a shock. A big shock.'

'A good shock though.'

'Mm.'

'Anyway, as soon as I saw the reaction it was having. I took the liberty of approaching a few of my contacts. I told them I'd seen the whole novel, that I thought it was great. And Julie, guess what? I have nine houses who are interested in publishing you. They are literally fighting over you, and they haven't even seen the full manuscript yet. I wanted to ask you before sending it to them. Can you believe it?'

'This is… it's crazy. This is absolutely crazy.'

'I know. I know. I'm so happy for you. Really I am.'

'Ola.'

'Yeah?'

'The thing is… '

'What?'

'Well… '

'Well what?'

There was a long pause.

'My intention was never to get *Wench* published. I was doing this as an experiment. Simply to see what would happen.'

'But there are people climbing all over each other here for a novel from Julie Stanhope.'

'Well I've got one for them. Just not that one. I've got a new one. It's much better, I think.'

'I'd love to read it. I'd be honoured if you'd give me the chance. Honoured and grateful. I suppose getting you sold would be my way of making things up to you.'

'Okay, yeah. Sure. Give me a few weeks and I'll send you the manuscript. It's nearly finished. The ending's all clear in my mind now.'

'Whatever it is, I'm sure people will go crazy for it. I'll explain the *Wench* project and what you were trying to do with that. I think they'll appreciate it. Possibly it will give you an even bigger caché.'

'Yeah, cool. Thanks Ola.'

'So tell me about it then.'

'About what?'

'The new novel.'

'Oh,' said Julie. 'You know *Dead Souls*?'

'Again! You're obsessed with that book. I remember you mentioning it in your cover letter for *Wench*.'

'Yeah, well this is sort of modelled on it.'

Julie looked at the postcard on her desk. *The Triumph of Judith*.

'But what's it about?' Ola insisted. 'Who's it about?'

Her mind drew a blank. In addressing those two very basic questions, Julie had accumulated a pile of polished pages, as well as reams and reams of rubbish. She had started out with a vague notion of the answers. She had started out with a plan, with a vision, yet here she was now, somehow, without even the slightest idea what those were or had ever been. Here she was now, incredibly, bereft of even just one more sentence beyond the thousands she had already written, seemingly incapable of summarising them in even just a single word less. Suddenly she grasped what Timmons had tried to tell her, that her novel could be about anything, that if it was any good it would be about everything and nothing at the same time, and it counted little whether it was even published, because the only thing of any genuine importance was that she had written it. Here she was now, speechless, her mind drawing blank after blank after blank.

Printed in Great Britain
by Amazon

35779856R00233